# A STORM OF LIGHT AND DARKNESS

## ALSO BY MARION BLACKWOOD

Marion Blackwood has written lots of books across multiple series, and new books are constantly added to her catalogue. To see the most recently updated list of books, please visit: www.marionblackwood.com

## CONTENT WARNINGS

*The Oncoming Storm* series contains quite a lot of violence and morally questionable actions. If you have specific triggers, you can find the full list of content warnings at: www.marionblackwood.com/content-warnings

# A STORM OF
# LIGHT AND DARKNESS

## THE ONCOMING STORM: BOOK SEVEN

### MARION BLACKWOOD

*For everyone with darkness in their soul*

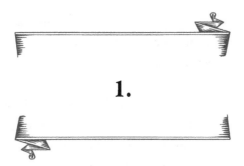

# 1.

Darkness blanketed the city. Heavy clouds blotted out the silver light of the moon and cast the normally so colorful city in shades of black and gray. I turned in a slow circle as I felt someone appear from the shadows behind me. My cloak billowed in the strong night wind that swept across the rooftops while I watched a tall man with dark brown hair tied back in a bun stride towards me.

*Man-bun*, was about to roll off my tongue before I caught myself. I wasn't sure how Shade's second-in-command in the Assassins' Guild would respond to my rather ridiculous nickname for him so I decided to keep my mouth shut. At some point, I had to ask what his actual name was. Though, that would certainly feel a bit silly after having known him for years. The corner of my mouth tugged upwards at the thought of that awkward conversation but the smile was quickly wiped off my lips as Man-bun stopped a few strides away. His face was grave as he locked eyes with me.

"Shade sent me." Even the tone of his voice was grim. "It's time."

My stomach dropped. "It's been confirmed?"

"Yes. Without a doubt."

I worked my tongue around my suddenly parched mouth and swallowed. Closing my eyes for a second, I blew out a deep breath before meeting Man-bun's gaze again. "Alright, lead the way."

We jogged in silence across the rooftops of Pernula until the obsidian walls of Blackspire rose before us. Instead of using my hidden entry point, I followed Man-bun towards the front gates. The guards took one look at us and opened the gates for us without question. Metal squeaked slightly behind me as they closed it again while we made our way along the path through the gardens inside.

When the immaculate garden had been replaced by smooth hallways decorated in black and red, my heart was beating so loudly that I almost expected to hear it echoing off the obsidian walls. I tried to force my heart rate to slow. We had prepared for this. It was all going to be alright.

Man-bun opened the door to Shade's study and motioned for me to enter. Wiping all traces of emotion off my face, I strode across the threshold.

The room was filled with people. King Edward and Lord Raymond, who was one of the senior members of his Council of Lords, were discussing something in hushed voices by the bookshelves on my left, while Queen Faye and Elaran stood straight-backed on the other side, their faces serious. Behind the large round table were two more figures. Malor in his sleeveless tunic of black and red waited patiently with his hands resting behind his back while the final person in the room was staring out the window.

A soft click sounded behind me as Man-bun closed the door and took up position by the wall next to it. At the sound, Shade finally tore his gaze from the night outside and turned towards us. His eyes lingered on me for an extra second before continuing around the room.

"We've just gotten confirmation." Shade's voice was steady but there was a tenseness to his shoulders that suggested that he perhaps wasn't as calm as he tried to appear. "Queen Nimlithil has made her move. The armies of Sker are marching on Pernula at first light."

King Edward tipped his head back and let out a heavy sigh. Next to him, Lord Raymond only nodded gravely.

"Well, we knew it was only a matter of time." Faye shrugged, her silver hair gleaming in the candlelight. "Otherwise, we wouldn't have come last week."

"You're right," Edward said. "But it's still terrible news."

The Queen of Tkeideru gave the young human king a sympathetic smile in reply. Paper rustled faintly as Shade smoothened the large map that covered most of the circular table between us, and bent over it.

"They're not trying for a surprise attack because they're moving along the most direct route." He drew his finger along the costal road connecting Sker and Pernula. "So they want us to see them coming. Probably to spread fear."

Elaran stepped closer to the table and nodded. "Which is one of the reasons we don't want a siege. The other being that with them controlling the rest of the continent, we wouldn't be able to outlast them anyway. So that kind of tactic would only be a slow death trap for us." Crossing his arms, he met each of our gazes. "We don't want a slow siege that we are doomed to lose in the end. We want a battle we can win."

"Which means that we need to go out and meet them," Shade finished.

Lord Raymond nodded while stroking his mustache. "Do you have a particular location in mind?"

Moving his hand, Shade traced his finger around a spot by the coast that was about halfway between our two cities, fairly close to Travelers' Rest. "Here. The terrain here gives us a strategic advantage because they'd have to charge uphill to get to us."

"If we can get there first," I said, my first words since this war council started.

The High King of Pernula shifted his gaze to me. "Correct."

Plans swirled in Faye's yellow eyes as she looked to Elaran. "How soon can you have the armies ready to march?"

"I've been getting them ready to leave on a moment's notice since you arrived last week," he replied. "They're ready to march tomorrow."

Silence fell over the room as we all nodded in acknowledgement. Even though the air was still fairly warm, as it usually was in Pernula, strong fall winds raged outside and beat against the windows of the palace. I resisted the urge to glance at the night outside the window where farther south, our enemies were getting ready.

Lord Raymond motioned between the map and the rest of the room. "And if we get there before the Sker soldiers–"

"*When* we get there before the Sker soldiers," Faye interrupted.

He cleared his throat and amended, "*When* we get there before them, what do we do then? What is the plan?"

He was here mostly as a representative of the Keutunian Council of Lords, it would seem, since he didn't appear all that informed about our plans. Good. It was always best to share the plan with as few people as possible in order to avoid leaks.

Several people opened their mouths to reply but Malor beat them all to it.

"What you need to do is draw out Aldeor the White." He crossed his powerful arms over his broad chest. "Kill the white dragon and Nimlithil, and then the spell shatters. When that happens, everyone who did the ritual will come back and realize what the spell actually did to them. They won't fight you after that."

"Wait," Lord Raymond spluttered. "We're talking about *killing a dragon*. How are we even supposed to accomplish that?"

"Leave that to me," Malor said.

We all turned to stare at him. Well, this was news to me as well. Did Malor have some kind of secret weapon that he hadn't told the rest of us about?

When he noticed our stares, the muscled advisor waved a large hand in front of his face. "It's best if as few people as possible know the specifics for now."

If it hadn't been for the fact that I had literally just decided the exact same thing about Lord Raymond's ignorance earlier, I would have protested. But I had, so I didn't. Instead, I gave him a nod in agreement. Whatever it was, we would find out sooner or later.

"I know I don't need to tell you this," Shade began, "but we are the leaders of the only free cities left. If we fail, it's over. For everyone. We will be forced to live our lives the way Queen Nimlithil wants."

"And given that she's an elf, that might be for quite some time," Edward added quietly.

Faye squared her shoulders and flashed us a grin. "So, we don't lose then."

Snorts and soft chuckling bubbled through the room at the queen's cocky statement. When the burst of merriment had died down, oppressive silence hung over the room as we all looked at one another with grim expressions. Shade drew himself up to his full height and met each of our gazes in turn.

"If you have any secret allies to reach out to, now is the time. Storm's rather impressive stash of stolen magical messenger doves is at your disposal." The others chuckled at that while a weary smile drifted across Shade's lips. He nodded at us. "Alright, get some sleep. We march tomorrow."

My heart thumped in my chest as our war council broke up and everyone filed out of the room. I stared at the dark line on the map marking the road between Sker and Pernula. In a few hours, it would be filled with soldiers. Two armies marching towards each other until they clashed. Glancing up from the beautifully drawn map, I found Shade watching me. When his perceptive eyes searched my face, I threw him a quick grin to hide the anxiousness building in my chest.

Two forces would meet on that battlefield but only one would walk away victorious. And I would make sure that it was us. No matter what it cost me, I would make damn sure that it was us. Whirling around, I stalked out of the room. War had come.

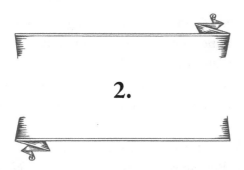

# 2.

The area around the main gate was in complete chaos. Soldiers and stable hands and horses hurried back and forth while wagons filled with supplies that would follow the army were being readied as well. Before I left the Black Emerald, I had instructed Vania and Yngvild to keep an eye on the Underworld while I was gone. Though, I had no doubt that Red Demon Rowan would keep all the underworlders in line regardless. Still, better to be sure.

"What do you think you're doing?"

I turned around to find Liam scowling at me. Raising my eyebrows, I tipped my hand towards the young man and gray mare a few strides away. "Waiting for that stable hand to finish getting Silver ready."

"You can't be serious about this," Liam said while shaking his head, his sparkling blue eyes pleading.

A slight smile spread across my lips even as I frowned at him. "What did you think I was planning to do when I asked you to meet me at the main gate?"

"Well, I don't know... but riding into battle never seemed like your style."

I huffed a laugh. "Ain't that the truth."

"But seriously, Storm." That pleading look was back in his eyes. "You're a thief, not a soldier. Do you really–"

"I'm also skilled with blades," I interrupted. "Not to mention a Storm Caster. And if you think for one second that I'm gonna let our friends go into battle alone, then you don't know me very well."

Liam blew out a resigned sigh and shot me a wry smile. "Alright, fine. But can you blame me for trying?" Narrowing his eyes, he raised a finger in the air. "And for the record, *I* was the one who knew you cared about people before even *you* knew you cared about people."

Not being able to stop it, I tipped my head back and let out a loud chuckle. Two horses snorted as they were led past by soldiers in dark blue armor, as if they too found Liam's statement funny. Their hooves clopped against the stones until the sound was swallowed up by a broad-chested man shouting orders close to the open gate.

After tilting my head back down, I returned Liam's smile. "True." Shifting on my feet, I peered behind him. "Where's Norah?"

"She's home. Resting."

I furrowed my brows. "Is she okay?"

"Yeah, yeah, she's fine." Liam smiled sheepishly before his expression turned serious again. "So you're really going?"

"Yeah."

He closed the distance between us and drew himself up next to me. For a moment, we just stood there in silence, watching the young man get Silver ready for the ride.

"Just..." Liam finally began. "Just don't do anything stupidly dangerous and heroic. I need you to come back. To Pernula." He glanced down at me. "To me. Us."

Twisting my head slightly, I arched an eyebrow at him. "Do something heroic? Me?" A wicked grin flashed across my lips. "Sounds like you really don't know me after all."

He gave my arm a soft shove and shook his head. "You know what I mean."

"Yeah, I know." I bumped his shoulder with mine. "And don't worry. No risk of me doing anything heroic for the greater good because when push comes to shove, I'm still a selfish bastard."

Liam huffed and shook his head again but then turned to face me head on. "Just... promise me you'll come back. Okay?" He nodded towards the gate. "And our friends too."

"I promise, I'll make sure our friends come back."

When he drew me into a tight hug, my heart cracked a little. I wasn't sure if he'd picked up on how I'd twisted the words of my reply, and I didn't like doing that to him, but it was the best I could do at the moment. *Promise me you'll come back.* I couldn't promise him that because I had also made a vow to make sure our friends survived no matter what. *That* was a promise I intended to keep. If I survived as well, it would just be an added bonus. Not something I could promise. Shoving my guilt down, I wrapped my arms around my friend and hugged him back fiercely. When we broke apart again, I forced a light smile onto my face.

"Take care of Norah. I'll take care of the others."

There was a faint sheen to his eyes as he stepped back and looked at me but then he ran his hands through his curly brown hair, exhaled deeply, and shot me a wide grin instead. "Go kick some ass."

"You know I will." If I drew out this goodbye further, I would never be able to leave so I lifted a hand to my brow in a mock salute and then strode towards Silver.

The young man who'd been holding her reins nodded at me when I reached him before he slipped back to the stables. After patting Silver on the neck, I swung myself up into the saddle. Liam was still watching me from across the stones teeming with people, wagons, and horses. I shot him a smile and then urged my trusted mare on. She started out and without a second look back, I rode out the gate and towards the army waiting outside.

IT WAS A DELICATE BALANCE, making sure the army marched fast enough to reach that strategic hilltop before our enemies did but not so quickly that we arrived exhausted and unable to fight at full capacity. Fortunately for me, I wasn't the one who had to make that decision. Elaran was.

I flicked my gaze to the grumpy auburn-haired elf riding at the front. He projected only strength and calm. And that's when I realized, Elaran had actually been in a war before. Against Keutunan. In fact, all the elves had. From across the grass, I met Haela's gaze. She fired off a beaming smile but stayed in formation.

My eyes swept across the wood elves in green and brown before scanning the human soldiers clad in the black and red of Shade's Pernula. Given what this continent was like, they had probably seen battle too. That meant the only ones who had never been in a war were the ones from Keutunan. Me included, of course. But if two thirds of our army actually knew what to expect, then we might win this yet.

Silver snorted and I leaned down to pat her neck as we continued trudging down the coast. To my left, the blue water sparkled in the bright fall sun while vast grasslands spread out on all other sides. Dust swirled around our horses' hooves as we marched along the wide dirt road. Straightening in the saddle, I buried my crippling fear that I wouldn't be enough to protect my friends deep inside me, and focused on the open horizon.

The grassy landscape was only rarely broken up by clusters of stone that looked to have been blown apart in some earlier war. I didn't know much about warfare but I noted them anyway as we hurried past. My heart beat in tune with the stomping of the army the closer we got to our target. Any minute now, we could round a bend in the road and find an army right in front of us. The logical part of my brain told me we had scouts for that but the inexperienced soldier in me still worried, so when the large hill we had aimed for finally appeared before us, I loosed a long shaky breath. We had made it.

Urging Silver on, I trotted across the wide flat top of it until I reached the far side. Behind me, soldiers were already busy setting up camp, no doubt under orders from the leaders of our three cities, so for a while I was alone there at the edge. I stared down the slope and towards the fields beyond it.

Undisturbed grass lay like a swaying green sea before me, cut through only by the dirt road on my left. That pristine greenery would be stained red before all this was over. I swallowed against the dryness in my throat. This peaceful swath of grass was where our fates would be decided. Where we would either win or lose.

Where I would fight and kill and wade through rivers of blood to make sure my friends survived. I sucked in a deep breath and turned my horse back to camp. This. This was where the greatest battle of our time would be decided.

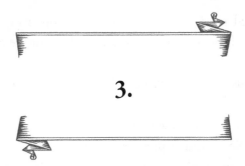

# 3.

The drums shook the landscape. Before we ever saw the first enemy soldier, their war drums boomed through the air, making my bones vibrate. Our scouts had returned with the news earlier so our entire army was already waiting in formation atop the hill but I still had to fight the urge to disappear into the shadows.

Whatever else Liam had said, he'd been right about one thing. I *was* a thief, not a soldier. My every instinct was screaming at me not to stand here on the front lines. Facing an army head on wasn't my style. Sneaking through the night and slitting their throats while they slept would've been so much more comfortable.

"You okay?"

Lost in thought, I jerked back at the sudden sound. Shade frowned down at me as if he also found it surprising that I hadn't noticed him until he was standing right next to me.

"I startled you."

Crossing my arms, I cut him a glare. "You're an assassin. All you've ever done since the day I met you is sneak up on me and try to startle me."

"Yeah, but you've never let me get this close before. And I wasn't even trying this time..." Shade trailed off. His intelligent eyes scanned my face and before I could open my mouth to retort, something dawned on his face and he cut me off. "You're nervous."

"Nervous? Me?" I snorted. "I've been in a fight before, you know."

The light tone of my voice rang false even to my own ears but thankfully, Shade didn't press the matter. He just took a casual step sideways until his arm was so close it brushed against mine. Side by side, we continued watching the horizon.

Leather creaked around us as soldiers shifted on their feet, and from somewhere to our right, Elaran was barking orders. The drums continued beating.

Then they appeared. Rank upon rank of soldiers clad in the brown and gold armor of Sker welled onto the vast field below. Afternoon light spilled across the grass and reflected off their gleaming armor. My heart slammed against my ribs. I had been included in most of the meetings we'd had both before we left and during our march here but I still didn't really know how war worked. Were we going to start fighting right away?

As if he had heard my thoughts, Shade spoke quietly to me while still not taking his eyes off the approaching army. "They won't attack today. They've also marched here and want to rest before starting the fight. This is just a show of strength."

"So they're gonna make camp down there on the field?"

"Yeah. And we are going to remain standing here ready to strike until the sun sets so that they will have to set up camp while worrying about whether we will attack before nightfall or not."

"Smart."

He nodded, still staring at the rows of soldiers flooding the plains. After the Sker army came a small section of silver and white. Star elves. There were so few of them compared to the humans. Apparently, the Queen of Tkeister didn't want to waste too many of her own elven soldiers but she still wanted to be here to supervise the battle. A strong sea breeze whipped through our hair as we continued watching the unfolding army in silence.

When golden light from the slanting sun filled the area, we were still standing there atop the hill. And the drums below were still beating. Only when the sunset had pulled its final red rays beyond the horizon and darkness crept across the world did Elaran order our forces back to camp. Leaving the sentries in place, Shade and I followed them. At long last, the drums quieted.

Eating dinner was about as much as I could manage before that anxious restlessness snuck up on me again. Mumbling some half-hearted excuse to my friends, I slunk back through camp. Since I didn't bother hiding my movements, the sentries saw me coming but they also knew who I was so they let me take up position by the edge of the hill unchallenged.

I chewed my lip as I watched the army on the other side of the field. What if they decided to attack at night? Should we really be sleeping? Just because it was dark didn't mean that it was impossible to fight. What if they tried something?

Grass crunched softly behind me. Turning, I found King Edward approaching me with Lord Raymond in tow. The young king gave me a small smile as they came to a halt next to me. In the dark space before us, insects of the night sang into the tense silence that separated the two camps. Lord Raymond shifted nervously on his feet as he scanned the area. Apparently, I wasn't the only one who didn't quite know what to do with myself. This waiting before the fight was a lot worse than I had expected it to be.

"Staring at them won't make them go away," King Edward finally said and shot another small smile in my direction. "Trust me. I've already tried."

"Well, you've clearly never seen me glare at someone."

He chuckled. "Good point. That is a rather terrifying sight."

I released a soft laugh as well. "Your brother tell you that?"

"Everyone who's ever met you knows that," a voice said from behind.

The three of us twisted to find the twins striding towards us. Haemir rolled his eyes at his sister's quip while the teasing elf in question just grinned at us. After coming to a halt on my other side, Haela threw her arm over my shoulder and leaned against me in a casual gesture.

"So you're nervous, huh?" she said.

"I'm not nervous," I protested.

"Really?" She arched a dark eyebrow at me. "That why you barely said a word during dinner and then skulked off before everyone was even finished?"

"I didn't skulk."

"I thought all you ever did was skulk."

"Can we please stop saying skulk?" And despite the looming battle, I laughed.

It was a desperate and exhausted sound but that laugh somehow made all the tension that had kept my chest as taut as a bowstring melt away and disappear into the soil beneath my feet. Bleak thoughts and despair were impossible when Haela was nearby. I was suddenly overwhelmed by a deep sense of gratitude for having her as a friend.

With that tightness in my chest gone, I drew in a deep breath. Cool night air smelling of damp soil, leather, and wood smoke filled my lungs.

Feeling lighter and more confident than I had since before that war council at Blackspire, I bumped my shoulder into Haela's side and shook my head. "Moron."

She grinned down at me but kept her arm draped over my shoulder. Her steady warmth helped chase away the last of my uncharacteristically skittish nerves. What would I ever do without her?

"Aren't you worried, though?" I asked, shifting my gaze between the four people around me. "About what's gonna happen tomorrow?"

"Yes," Haemir and King Edward said in unison while Lord Raymond nodded with quick jerky motions on Edward's other side.

Haela just shrugged. "No. Worrying about tomorrow doesn't change what's gonna happen. It just ruins all the fun things you could do today."

By Nemanan, if that wasn't the smartest thing I'd heard in weeks, I didn't know what was. I think a lot of people underestimate Haela when it comes to deeper matters because she's always joking and laughing. But I had a distinct feeling that she had been through a lot. Maybe that was why she had decided to always seek out and enjoy all the good things life had to offer.

With a teasing glint in my eye, I peered up at her. "Since when did you become the philosopher of the group? I thought Keya filled that role."

She put a hand to her chest in mock affront. "I'll have you know..." Trailing off, she squinted at something across the dark grass.

Haemir swore softly. Right as I was about to ask what they were looking at, it became visible to my human eyes as well. In front of the camp, figures moved. Silvery white hair peeked out from under deep hoods as they left something in the grass before hurrying back. Haela took her arm from my shoulders and made to turn around but before she had even opened her mouth to call out, the attack had already happened.

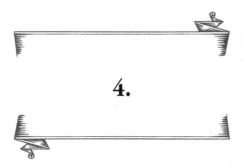

# 4.

White mist bloomed from the ground. It expanded with every second as it billowed towards our camp. Alarms were being called out by every sentry on the ridge. Behind us, clamoring rang out as soldiers shot to their feet to prepare for an enemy attack, but the twins were already moving.

"Stay calm! Don't lose your heads!" Haela snapped to everyone within earshot as she hurried away.

"What is going on?" Lord Raymond stammered while backing away.

Dread spread through my veins at the sight of the wave of thick white mist that was rolling towards us. I wasn't sure I would ever recover completely from what that mist had done to me in the City of Glass.

"It's a chemical weapon. A hallucinogenic mist that's been created to drive people mad." Shaking my head violently, I snapped out of the stupor. "Come with me."

We ran along the edge of the hill while the pale wave rose higher. People screamed behind me. As soldiers, they didn't fear a battle but they were trained to fight enemies who had actual bodies. There was no way for them to attack or defend against a chemical weapon that filled the air. The steady voices of Elaran, the twins, Shade, Malor, and some of Shade's assassins cut through the night and halted the spreading panic.

Throwing a quick glance over my shoulder, I gauged the distance to the wall of mist as I ran. My heart slammed against my ribs. It would reach us soon. Too soon. Another bout of cries rang out as the wave crested. Lord Raymond threw up his arms over his head, as if that would stop the mist's advance, and stumbled a step just as we reached the middle of the rim.

Green smoke shot towards the starlit sky. The dense pillar spread rapidly and fanned out along the edge of the hill and almost all the way to the dark sea on one side and far into the grasslands on the other. The white wave crashed against the green smoke wall and silence fell as everyone in camp held their breath.

Where the hallucinogenic mist met it, the green barrier turned purple but no white tendrils made it through. The seconds dragged on. Still, no one dared move or breathe. Then the haze cleared across the field and the white, green, and purple colors bled into the dark night until they dissipated completely. Every person atop the hill sucked in a collective gasp of relief.

"It worked," King Edward said, relief and surprise in equal measures on his face.

A small laugh bubbled from my throat. "Yeah."

Lord Raymond, who had always been so calm and collected every time I saw him back in Keutunan, seemed to be far outside his comfort zone here on a battlefield with an army and chemical warfare. Eyes still wide, he whipped his head from side to side.

"It's gone," he breathed. "Thank the gods."

"It's not the gods you have to thank." I jerked my head towards a tent a short distance away, just behind the line of sentries. "I have someone you should meet."

I almost felt a bit bad that we hadn't told Lord Raymond and all the soldiers about this but since we hadn't been entirely sure that it would work, and we also didn't want to risk any leaks, we'd decided to keep it quiet.

Brown fabric rustled as I shoved open the tent flap and strode inside. From behind a workbench, a man with glasses and a short moustache looked up at the intrusion.

"It worked," I stated.

"Did you doubt me?"

"Not for a second." Lifting a hand, I motioned between the bespectacled man and Lord Raymond who had followed me and King Edward into the tent. "Lord Raymond, meet Apothecary Haber, the genius behind that green smoke."

The surprised lord was just about to open his mouth to respond when the tent flap was thrown open again and two more people prowled inside. Elaran stared straight at the apothecary.

"It worked," he stated, just as I had.

Haber's eyes gleamed in amusement at the repetitive and rather superfluous statement but simply inclined his head. Coming to a halt next to the satisfied elf, Shade flashed Edward a quick smile before turning to Haber as well.

"Well done," the High King of Pernula said. "A bit too close for comfort, but well done."

"Ah, yes, apologies. The first time is always the trickiest," Apothecary Haber explained. "But now that I've tried it out once, I can get it up much quicker next time."

"Good," Shade said.

"I still can't believe you managed to create all that from a leaf." King Edward chuckled and shook his head. "*A leaf.*"

"Two leaves, to be precise." A smile tugged at his lips as Haber rolled out two large blobs on the table before him.

It was the unused green leaf that Vilya had given Elaran in that warehouse and the now purple one that I had used to survive the gas in the Rat King's basement. I wondered if that strange wood elf had known we would be using them for this. If it was, perhaps, why she had given them to us in the first place.

"Since I was able to study both an unused one and a used one," Haber continued, pointing between the two leaves, "I was able to create a synthetic replica of its effect. It's actually rather fascinating how..."

Before I could get stuck in one of Haber's lectures on the chemical properties of magical leaves, I put a hand to Edward and Lord Raymond's backs and pushed them forwards. Haber's focus instantly fixed on them as he continued his explanation about how he had created the wall of smoke. Twisting slightly, Edward cut me an amused glare. I grinned sheepishly before slipping away. Elaran and Shade appeared to see the opening I had created as well and followed me into the night before Haber's gaze could trap them too.

Elaran crossed his arms and glanced down at me as we weaved our way back towards camp. "You certainly keep strange company."

"Given that you're included in that particular group of people, I'd be inclined to agree."

Shade chuckled on my other side.

"Shut up," Elaran huffed at me before scowling at the snickering assassin. "And what are you laughing about? You're included in that group too."

The Master Assassin raised his hands in surrender but a lopsided smile still lingered on his lips. I shook my head. Idiots.

Once we reached the maze of tents that made up most of our camp, the atmosphere was a lot lighter. Gone were the panicked cries and instead the soldiers of our three armies sat around fires, sharpening weapons or trading stories with each other. Now that they knew we had protection against chemical attacks, they seemed a lot more confident in our ability to win the battle ahead. Good. We would need that.

When we reached the large tents that had been erected at the center of camp, we slowed down until we finally trailed to a halt between two of them.

"Get some sleep," Elaran said and nodded at the tent behind us. "We'll need every bit of strength we have from now on."

While Shade and Elaran clasped forearms, I just nodded in agreement. After they broke apart, the auburn-haired archer stalked towards his own tent. Right as we were about to return to our own temporary home, he twisted his head.

Still moving, he grumbled over his shoulder, "And remember that elves have great hearing."

"What?" I blinked at him but he had already disappeared behind the walls of green cloth.

Then understanding hit me. Heat flashed into my cheeks and burned so hot I had half a mind to follow that grumpy elf into his tent and stab him. Repeatedly.

Shade just chuckled and jerked his chin towards our tent. "Shall we?"

"Great hearing," I muttered but followed the smirking assassin. "Hmmph."

Lit candles cast the space in warm hues. It wasn't huge but it was enough to fit a temporary room fit for a King of Pernula. And a Queen of the Underworld, I suppose. Chests filled with weapons, clothes, and other supplies were scattered throughout, along with a small seating area. The double bed someone had taken the time to assemble was a far cry from the luxurious one in Blackspire but it was also a lot better than sleeping on the ground. Flipping open the lid of a chest, I started stripping off my knives.

A surprised chuckle drifted through the warm air.

I glanced from the amused assassin to the trunk filled to the brim with sheathed knives, and then back again. "What?"

"Planning on killing their whole army yourself?"

"Maybe." I shrugged and started putting in the ones I'd had strapped to my body. Then, for some reason, I found myself saying, "I had replacements made. I know I'll lose a lot of blades when the fighting starts and, I don't know... I didn't want it to be my original knives. But these," I motioned at the packed chest and the blades I'd just piled on top of it, "I don't care if I never find them again. I can just grab yet another set from here."

When I saw the range of emotions far too serious for my liking that drifted over his handsome face, I vehemently wished I had kept my stupid mouth shut. I knew that it was ridiculous. It was just weapons. But a lot of those knives had seen me through some of my darkest, most desperate and dangerous experiences. And I'd become... attached to them. They were as much a part of me as my Ashaana powers. Silly, I know. And I really wished I hadn't admitted it to that damn assassin.

Relief fluttered through me when those serious emotions disappeared from Shade's face and were replaced by a teasing smirk. "If you had better aim, you wouldn't need to worry about losing so many."

"Bastard," I muttered, more out of force of habit than actual annoyance.

He pulled off his shirt and folded it in his hands before setting it down. Raking his fingers through his hair, he heaved a sigh. "I'll be with my assassins tomorrow."

"You're not gonna lead the Pernulans?"

"No. Elaran is the commander so he's the one leading all three armies." A wicked smile flashed across his lips. "They're lethal. Elaran's a natural at this. All three of them are so synchronized under his leadership." He shrugged. "Better to not confuse them about who's calling the shots. And besides, my guild and I have a... slightly different method for sending people to the God of Death than normal soldiers have. We work best as an independent unit."

I chuckled. "True."

"And you?" He pulled off a boot and placed it neatly on the ground. "Which unit will you be fighting with?"

A strong fall wind swept through camp and beat at the tent walls. Fabric flapped and candles spluttered. Studying the flickering light that danced across the dark cloth, I considered.

"I think I'll join you," I said at last. Yanking off my boots, I chucked them next to the trunk and got to work on my vest. "My fighting style is much more similar to yours than to normal soldiers."

"I was hoping you'd say that."

After dumping the vest on top of the now closed chest, I pulled my shirt over my head. "Oh?"

"Yes." The smirk on his face deepened as he unbuckled his belt. "Because that means *I* will be your commander."

"You'll what now?"

Amusement played over his lips as he studied the murderous expression on my face. While Shade stripped down to his underwear and placed his neatly folded pants next to his shirt, I dropped the rest of my clothes atop my own pile and then stalked across the room in nothing but my undergarments.

"I'll be your superior," he said, the words laced with wicked satisfaction. "And you'll be following my command."

My eyes narrowed further at the smug tone of his voice while I kept advancing on him. He let me back him towards the bed before coming to a halt. With each step, I calculated distances, techniques, and weight distribution. Tilting my head up, I met his eyes while an equally evil smile spread across my own lips.

"When will you learn? I don't specialize in doing as I'm told." And then I shoved.

A yelp escaped my throat as he twisted and used my own momentum to throw me onto the bed instead. The mattress groaned in distress as his knees slammed into it on either side of me. With a firm grip on my wrists, he pinned them above my head. His eyes glittered as he tilted his head to the right and ran his gaze over my body.

"And when will *you* learn? You can never pull off moves like that unless I let you."

I glared at him. "We'll see about that."

He let out a dark laugh and stole a kiss from my mouth. When his lips worked their way down my throat and towards that sensitive spot between my neck and shoulder, a pleasant shudder coursed through me. I pulled against the strong hands still keeping my arms trapped against the mattress. Smiling against my skin, he released my wrists. I drew my fingers through his hair before locking them behind his neck and pulling him towards me. Our lips met in a greedy kiss.

Still straddling me, he pulled back slightly and traced soft fingers over my collarbones. His touch made my skin prickle with pleasure. When another shudder spread through my body and a soft moan followed it, he smiled in victory and then swung his leg back over on the other side, freeing me. The bed creaked as he dropped down next to me and pulled the covers over us. For a while, we just lay there next to each other, the heat from our bodies mingling under the sheets. Outside, the wind howled.

"Thank you," I said at last.

Shade propped himself up on an elbow to study my face. "For what?"

"For not asking me to sit out the fight tomorrow."

He furrowed his brows. "I would never do that. I mean, yeah, the thought of someone hurting you makes me want to paint the world with blood but..." Lifting a hand, he tucked a strand of hair behind my ear. His fingers lingered on my jaw while a knowing smile spread across his lips. "But you're more than capable of taking care of yourself. And you have as much right as anyone to fight for this. Maybe more."

My heart suddenly felt too large for my chest. This was one of the many reasons why I'd come to love this damn assassin. He understood me, understood who I was and what I needed to do, in a way few people did. Leaning over, I put a hand behind his neck and brushed another kiss against his lips.

"And besides," he breathed against my mouth, "I don't *ask* people to do things. I give orders. And people obey."

I gave his muscled chest a shove. It barely pushed him back and only made him smirk even more.

"Bastard," I mumbled and pulled him towards me again.

He chuckled. Shifting my position, I raked my hands through his silky black hair and down his back. His warm hands traced the curves of my body while his lips ravaged mine. I arched my back and pressed him tighter against me. Flickering candlelight danced over our lean muscles as we ignored the rest of the world and pretended, for one night, that tomorrow didn't exist.

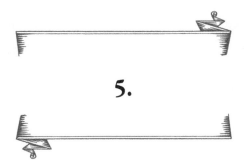

# 5.

Dawn arrived faster than I would have liked. Pale gray light filtered down from an overcast sky and leeched all color from the world. My heart thumped in my chest as I made my way towards the front of the army along with my friends. Elaran and the twins all carried both their bows and their swords. The Master Assassin striding across the grass next to me had his usual twin swords strapped across his back and no doubt a number of hidden blades as well. And I... well, I was more or less a walking armory. Let's just leave it at that.

"Remember," Elaran said to Shade as we neared the foremost ranks of soldiers, "everyone here has been informed of your unit so you won't cause any confusion. All our soldiers will stay in formation regardless of what you do." A slight smile, with a hint of wickedness, tugged at his lips. "So go create chaos. Be a wildcard that completely throws our enemies off their game because you're not following any logical tactics for a normal army."

Shade's mouth twitched into a smirk. "They won't know what hit them."

On my other side, Haela gave her arms a quick stretch. "Oh, I can't wait to see this."

I chuckled while Haemir shook his head and shot his sister an exasperated look. Even in the face of war, nothing could dim Haela's spirit.

When the ranks of soldiers started thinning out and we could almost see the white sky beyond the edge of the hill, the five of us slowed down.

Shade clasped forearms with Elaran and shifted his gaze between the twins before returning it to the elven commander. "Give them hell."

Elaran and Haemir gave him grim nods in return while Haela fired off a beaming smile. After one final exchanged glance between the five of us, the twins trotted off to where Queen Faye led the rest of the elven archers.

"Be careful," Haemir called over his shoulder.

"Always am," I shot back, which drew a burst of laughter from Haela.

When both of their black ponytails had disappeared into throng, Elaran turned to me.

"Don't die," he muttered.

I couldn't stop the chuckle that escaped my throat at the grumpy command. "Likewise."

He gave me a satisfied nod and then started forwards. Shade and I did the same, but set course for the mob of black-clad assassins farther down the field. Leather creaked as the soldiers around us shifted slightly.

"And Storm," Elaran's voice cut through the temperate morning air.

Stopping, I turned back towards him. "Yeah?"

"Remember how I always say 'don't burn anything down'?" Grim amusement danced in his yellow eyes. "Now would be the time to burn shit down."

A wicked laugh slipped my lips and filled the distance between us. Lifting a hand to my brow, I gave him a salute in promise and reply before turning back around and trotting away to catch up with Shade. We weaved through our army in silence until we reached the stone-faced Assassins' Guild. Taking up position by the edge of the ridge, we stared out across the plains.

The Sker army had also left their camp behind and moved closer across the grass but the rows upon rows of soldiers in brown and gold still waited a good distance away from us for the order to attack. I suppressed the urge to fidget as my pulse started thrumming in my ears again.

"You see that army down there?" Elaran's steady voice thundered through our forces. "Take a good look. And then look at your brothers and sisters beside you." A pause followed. "That's only one army. We have three, and we outnumber them two to one. As long as we fight smart, we will win this." Another small pause, then he raised his voice even further. "So fight smart. And then you can share war stories with your brothers and sisters by the fire."

Some of the tension that had clung to the armed people around us evaporated. Metal clanked and leather creaked when they shifted as if loosening the tightness in their shoulders. I drew a deep breath and let Elaran's confident words fill me as well. Fight smart. Then we would win this.

Drums boomed across the field. The very air seemed to quiver with each rhythmic pounding until I could almost feel the vibrations in my bones.

"What are they waiting for?" I whispered.

Shade glanced down at me before returning his gaze to the unmoving army in front of us. "I don't know."

Another couple of minutes passed. Elaran had explained earlier that we wanted them to charge uphill, so we wouldn't move until they did. They must have known that they'd be forced to attack us from that position, so what were they waiting for?

A ripple went through the elven part of our army. I flicked my gaze across the field in search of whatever had caused it, but found nothing. The drums continued booming.

Then I saw them. And my heart sank. In the distance, a wall of white and pale blue was approaching. Soldiers bearing the colors of Frustaz. A second army. A nervous murmur went through our forces and I could almost feel Elaran about to open his mouth but then an unsettlingly swift silence spread through our side of the field. Ice seeped into my veins as I beheld the reason for it.

Cresting a small slope next to the advancing wall of Frustaz soldiers was another force. The black and yellow of Beccus blotted out the green grass as a third army marched towards us. The two occupied human nations on the other side of the continent, by the White Mountains, had apparently been drafted into this war as well. And now *we* were outnumbered. I worked my tongue around my suddenly parched mouth. Dread swept through our ranks like icy rain. How were we supposed to win this now?

Armor rustled as the soldiers around me shifted their weight. Some of them glanced around as if unsure whether we should really just wait for the other two armies to arrive instead of attacking straight away. Elaran could probably sense it too because his steady voice rang out across the grassy hilltop once more.

"Hold the lines! We have the high ground. Charging now won't stop those two armies approaching, it will only waste our tactical advantage. Hold the lines."

The anxious shifting stopped. We continued watching the approaching forces in silence, the pounding war drums the only sound as they drew nearer with every passing minute. I briefly thought about Merina, Hestor, Meera, and Livia, the family who owned the Sleeping Horse tavern in Travelers' Rest. The battlefield was unnervingly close to their town, and based on the direction those two armies had come from, they must have passed right through it. They had been kind to me when my loss of identity had sent me spiraling into despair. I sincerely hoped the soldiers had left them alone.

My eyes flicked in the direction of the town. I might have to check on them after this battle was over. And if they weren't alright... Lightning crackled through my veins as I slid my gaze back to the advancing armies. Then I would drag the ones responsible back from hell and make them pay before I killed them again.

The pale gray light of dawn had grown brighter behind the thick cover of white clouds when the two armies at last took up positions next to their Sker partners. Nervous dread rippled through our ranks again at the number of enemies now staring up at us from across the vast expanse of grass.

"Remember," Elaran's voice once more cut through the air, "the men facing you are from occupied countries. And they have been robbed of their ability to feel pain. A soldier who cannot feel the pain of a friend, a brother, a lover, dying will never fight as fiercely to prevent that from happening as one who can. We can all feel that pain. And we want to keep our loved ones safe. That is why we fight! Remember that."

A boom rang out as the soldiers around us slammed their swords into their shields.

"They are not fighting for something they believe in. They are not fighting for someone they love. We are."

Another boom of swords on shields.

"Remember what we have to lose."

The pounding of weapons was speeding up now, each blow a defiant cry to drown out the war drums from the other side.

"Remember that!" Elaran bellowed across the field. "And fight like hell to protect it!"

A battle cry to shatter the heavens tore from the throats of every soldier in our army while weapons were hoisted in the wind. And just like that, the nervous dread that had spread like a disease the moment those two armies had arrived was gone. Replaced by courage and heart and stubborn iron will. I couldn't stop the slight smile playing over my lips. Shade had been right. Elaran *was* a natural at this.

Then a horn blared through the air. And all hell broke loose.

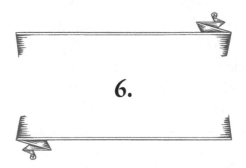

# 6.

My muscles burned. I ducked and threw out an arm. A wet sliding sound rose as the knife in my hand disappeared into the exposed skin under the soldier's armpit. He sucked in a gasp between his teeth but I was already moving. Yanking it out, I whirled around and slashed my other blade across his throat. Before his body had even crumpled to the ground, I had already engaged my next victim.

The first hour had almost killed me. Not the actual battle, but the worrying. I had never in my life been in a fight where I had this many people to worry about. King Edward had wisely been persuaded to sit this one out since he hadn't been trained as a warrior, but everyone else I cared about in this camp was fighting. Up on the grassy hill above me, where he could see everything from a vantage point, Elaran was directing the flow of the battle. The twins, Faye, and the rest of the elven forces were spread out along the ridge, raining death down upon the attackers with their swift arrows. And then, of course, there was the Master Assassin fighting next to me.

The thought of something happening to any of them had almost paralyzed me. During that first hour, I had looked more at them than my opponents. To make sure that they were still alive. Unhurt. Until I had come half a second from having a sword take my head clean off my shoulders because I had been too distracted to notice the soldier sneaking up behind me. Only Man-bun's quick blade blocking the strike at the last second had saved me from getting decapitated. After that, I had taken all that worry and fear for my friends and locked it so deep inside my soul that not a single emotion made it past the black ice and metal spikes covering my heart. Every hour since then, only a focused killer with a blackened soul and bloodied blades had looked out through my eyes.

A roar split the air. I twisted to the side right as a sword cleaved the space I had just vacated. My breath exploded from my lungs as an armored fist slammed into the side of my ribs. Crashing to the ground, I had to throw out my arm to stop my body from rolling down the hill we were fighting on. Pain shot through my forearm as I shoved it down on a sharp rock but it at least halted the downward tumbling. I slashed at the closest pair of boots I could see, aiming for the ankle tendon, while steel whizzed above me.

The blow coming for my neck fell short. Barely. While my opponent was busy screaming from the severed tendon, I shot to my feet. He wobbled off balance when one of his feet no longer supported him, and with the sloping ground, he simply tipped over. I danced out of the way and quickly jabbed a knife in and out of his neck as he crashed into the ranks of his own men below.

That maneuver bought me a few precious seconds of respite. With my chest heaving, I crouched down and stuck my hunting knives into the now flattened grass. My hands were slick with blood and it was getting increasingly difficult to keep a steady grip on my blades, so I used my hard-won break to wipe my red hands on the tunic of a dead Sker soldier at my feet. Dark smudges appeared on the brown fabric as I managed to get most of the blood off before ripping my blades from the ground and straightening again.

On the slopes around me, soldiers from Keutunan and Pernula battled waves of enemies. The three armies facing us were split up in separate units with Frustaz closest to the sea, Sker in the middle, and Beccus farther out on the grassy plains. Where their sections met, the fighting was chaotic. Apparently, they weren't entirely sure how to fight alongside another army. Our forces, on the other hand, worked seamlessly. The elves keeping the bulk at bay with well-aimed arrows, the men from Keutunan holding the lines steady with tight formation and their one-shot pistols, and the Pernulan soldiers with their curved swords dancing in and out of the ranks. It was a truly impressive sight.

Salt-tasting winds rolled in from the sea and whipped through my hair. I sucked in a deep breath and surveyed the rows of brown and gold in front of me. They were getting too comfortable. Falling into a rhythm again that could lead to a unified push upwards. Time to break that up.

Reaching into the deep pits of my soul, I yanked out the burning rage. My eyes turned black as death. The assassins around me didn't even blink as I sent a wave of black clouds crashing right into the unbroken Sker lines. Before it had fully reached them, I launched after it.

Startled cries rang out as the dark haze barreled into them and blocked out their vision. With my Ashaana powers, I could see through the mist and was aware of every terrified face around me as I slipped between them. Blood sprayed into the darkened air as I darted and whirled through their ranks like a wraith, slitting throats as I went. The death strokes became a dance, the dying screams a song, as I dispatched their souls to the God of Death.

The shrieks of horror and thudding of bodies hitting the ground sent a ripple of panic through the Sker lines, and the soldiers closest to the edge of the black clouds broke formation and scrambled away. Their unexpected retreat sent them crashing into other parts of their section which spread the chaos even further. Through the dark haze, I watched black-clad assassins sweep in from the sides and cut down the tangled-up soldiers.

If Shade's unit was our wildcard, then I was the wildcard of our wildcard. During the long hours of this fight, the Assassins' Guild had flashed back and forth across the battlefield, sweeping in and slaughtering, only to withdraw again. And then show up in a different place and cut through enemy ranks before disappearing once more. It made our opponents jumpy because there was no discernable pattern to where the black swarm of death would appear next. I moved with them and added another variable to the unsolvable equation. Whenever I felt like it, I sent a blast of wind, or a cloud of black smoke, or crackling lightning bolts into their ranks. More than one line of soldiers had broken formation and fled when that happened. A wicked smile flashed across my lips as I rammed my hunting knife into the throat of the last man standing inside my dark mist. They should've known better than to pick a fight with underworlders.

While the dead Sker soldier collapsed on the ground, I darted back up the slope and out of reach of the arrows now being fired into the black clouds. I pulled the darkness back into my soul as I reached Shade and a group of his assassins. He threw me a satisfied smile as we retreated behind our own lines again.

A horn blared into the afternoon air in a prearranged pattern. I snapped my gaze towards the east. There, on the road by the sea, a squad of soldiers were attempting to breach our lines and sneak up on the ridge to where our archers were positioned. Shade and I exchanged a look before we sprinted through our army towards the enemies advancing along the road. Good thing Elaran had devised that communications system that he could use from his vantage point to give new orders to our troops. Otherwise, we might have missed this threat.

We became black streaks shooting through the ranks as the Assassins' Guild and I closed the distance to the road. My muscles throbbed but I shoved the tiredness asides as we finally reached the top of the road. Clusters of our own soldiers were trying to beat them back while the elves concentrated their fire on the threat as well, but they still plowed ahead. When we stopped, I realized why.

They were moving in formation with their shields locked around and above them. The elven arrows got stuck in those metal shields and none of our soldiers could breach their defensive walls enough to stab them before being cut down themselves.

Gulping down a few desperate breaths, I stuck my hunting knives back in their sheaths and strode to the front of our lethal group.

"Get ready," I panted to Shade as I passed.

The Master Assassin's chest was heaving as well but he nodded at me and then signaled to the rest of his guild. On my left, waves crashed against the shore and on my right, the might of six armies clashed. The very air was coated with the metallic smell of blood, and my ears were constantly ringing with the clanging of steel against steel and booming of pistols. Planting my feet firmly on the dusty road, I drew another deep breath.

"Stand aside!" I bellowed down the slope.

Bows stopped firing and our forces close to the road scrambled farther inland, leaving the fast-moving shell made of metal shields to jog up the road unchallenged. I reached into the burning pits of my blackened soul again and called up the darkness. With eyes once again black, I raised my arms to my sides before slamming them forward.

Hurricane winds barreled towards the advancing soldiers.

"Now!" I screamed.

At the sound of my order, Shade and his assassins darted after it. The blast of wind collided with their metal-encased formation and sent them flying as if a great hand had smacked them away. Cries and thuds echoed over the road as they crashed down again farther back. While they were still bouncing to a halt, the black swarm of death reached them. Steel glinted in the gray light as the Assassins' Guild sent more souls down to their dark god.

Sinking down on one knee, I braced my hand on the ground and tried to refill my ever depleting well of strength. I had used my powers sparsely throughout the day in order to make them last until nightfall, so I still had energy left for my magic, but it was taking its toll. That and all the regular fighting that had gone on for hours.

"Finally kneeling before me, are we?"

I lifted my head to find Shade smirking down at me. His eyes glittered with mischief as he reached a hand towards me but I could see the weariness lingering on his handsome face.

"Bastard," I muttered but took his offered hand.

He scanned my body while helping me to my feet. "You okay?"

I didn't even bother dusting myself off because I was covered in blood and gore and dirty anyway so I just ran a hand through my messy hair and nodded. "I'll live."

Apparently deeming that acceptable enough, Shade jerked his chin towards the ridge behind us. "Come on. We all need a short breather and some water."

Not wanting to waste strength on a verbal reply, I just nodded again and followed him up the hill. The soldiers who had scattered at my command resumed their positions by the road as the rest of the assassins left with us as well.

We had only made it up the ridge and gulped down a few mouthfuls of water when Elaran's signal horn echoed across the plains again. Unknown threat. West. I dropped the ladle back in the water bucket and sprinted back towards the front lines.

The skies were still covered by thick white clouds but I raised a hand over my brow anyway as I squinted at the horizon. A large wooden structure was being pushed through the middle of the Sker army. We were too far away to see what it was.

"What the hell is that?" I murmured as soldiers in brown and gold continued moving it closer.

"I don't know," Shade replied.

We left the seaside road behind and hurried along the ridge towards where Elaran was located in the middle. The clashing of swords and booming of pistols still covered the slopes below us.

I cast quick glances over my shoulder while slinking through the fresh ranks of soldiers waiting to relieve the ones fighting on the front lines.

We had almost reached Elaran when a ripple of curses spread through our army. The contraption was finally close enough to reveal what it was. Well, not to me, but the Pernulan soldiers especially seemed to understand its purpose. I frowned at it. It looked kind of like a triangle with one long pole jutting out from one side of it.

I was just about to ask the closest Pernulan what it was when the long pole moved. It had been lying almost horizontal before but now it flashed upwards. A dark shape was hurled from it.

Shouts of warning and alarm rang out all around us as what looked like a small boulder flew over the Sker ranks and barreled straight for our own soldiers atop the hill. *Shit*. After sprinting the short distance that put me directly in its path, I skidded to a halt. Grass and soil were pushed aside as my boots left ruts on the field. The boulder had crested, its upward arc complete, and was now plummeting straight towards us.

Soldiers scrambled out of its path while I ripped the darkness from my soul and shoved my arms forwards and upwards. Our fleeing soldiers had created a gap which the Sker army had slipped through, and chaos was slowly spreading below me but I blocked it out. I was vaguely aware of someone bellowing orders to re-form the lines and streaks of black shooting through the crowd to kill the enemies who had gotten through, but my eyes were fixed on the projectile above. It continued barreling towards us.

Then, my blast of wind slammed into it. The boulder abruptly halted in its path and instead flew backwards. More shrieks of alarm rose, but this time from the Sker soldiers as the stone landed among their own ranks instead.

Relief shuddered through me, followed by a wave of tiredness. Shade and his unit had killed the enemies who'd gotten through and our soldiers were once again back in formation. I was about to start out towards Elaran again when a hand gripped my shoulder.

"Storm!"

I whirled around to find Queen Faye behind me. The three braids that held her long silver hair back from her face were messy as if she had dragged her fingers through them, and sweat trickled down her temple. She looked as if she had sprinted here.

"They're repositioning it." There was a hurried sort of panic that pulsed in those normally so confident yellow eyes. "West."

"Shit," I swore, but I understood what she wanted me to do so I took off in a mad dash without another word.

She joined me, her long legs easily keeping up with me even though I ran as fast as I could. Auburn hair fluttered in the wind before me but I didn't dare slow down. I just flashed past where Elaran was standing and continued west. Faye veered off back towards her archers while Elaran barked a command to someone somewhere behind me.

"Follow her!"

The rest of his orders were lost to the wind screaming in my ears. My lungs burned but I kept sprinting. And then the long wooden pole sprang upwards again and another boulder shot into the sky. I was still too far away. A desperate cry tore from my throat as I pushed myself to the breaking point and flew through our ranks, who refused to break and let enemies through this time. If the projectile landed, it would hit them.

The stone crested. It felt as though I was breathing shards of glass but I threw myself the final distance.

My body had barely stopped sliding across the grass when I raised my arms and shoved them forwards. The blast of wind smacked into the stone and sent it tumbling back into their own army again. I collapsed to my knees.

Bracing my forehead and arms on the ground, I heaved in one desperate breath after another. The smell of grass and soil filled my nose as I kept my forehead pressed against the ground. My limbs shook.

"Storm," a gentle voice said. "They're moving it again."

Haemir. So he was the one who Elaran had ordered to follow me. Then his words sank in. *They're moving it again.* Every muscle in my body was screaming. I wasn't sure I would survive another sprint like that but I nodded against the grass and then pushed myself up. Ignoring my trembling legs, I struggled to my feet.

"Where?" I rasped.

Concern was written all over Haemir's face. "East."

I swallowed but my parched throat was barely able to execute the command so instead of replying, I just nodded again. Right as I was about to run back in the other direction, the rows of soldiers farther back on the hill let out startled yelps and jumped out of the way.

Two horses crashed into the open space and skidded to a halt before us. Haela threw me the reins of the riderless silver mare before jumping down and shoving the others into the hands of her brother.

"Hurry!" she called and practically shoved me up in the saddle. "East. Now."

Not even having enough strength to thank her for this genius solution, I simply dug my heels into Silver's sides and galloped back along the ridge. Haemir followed me on the chestnut-colored horse that Haela had arrived on.

We sped back towards the sea while I willed my heart to stop slamming so hard into my ribcage that I thought it might crack. When the next projectile flew, we were almost in position. Still seated atop Silver, I focused my gust of wind into a smaller concentrated blast in order to save strength. The boulder went crashing back into the enemy army again.

Tiredness rolled over me while I waited for Haemir's superior elven eyesight to spot which direction they were aiming in next. West. Not being able to muster enough strength to confirm that I had heard him, I just urged Silver on and galloped back across the hill again.

My life narrowed down into three things. Moving back and forth across the ridge, staying in the saddle, and sending concentrated blasts of wind into flying boulders. Everything else became background noise as I fought to stay conscious.

When evening fell and the vast plains grew too dark for fighting, our enemies finally stopped firing. The wooden contraption was hauled back towards their camp along with their retreating armies. As soon as Haemir had confirmed that there would be no more stones to defend against tonight, I simply let go of the thin thread of consciousness I had clung to towards the end. I tipped over in the saddle and was gone before I hit the ground.

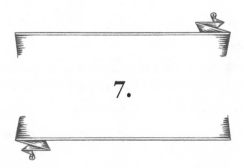

# 7.

Flames flickered over grave faces. Shade, Edward, Elaran, and Faye were standing around a large round table. Figures had been placed across the open map that took up most of the tabletop, and lit candles cast dancing shadows over their metal forms. Outside, the wind beat at the cloth walls of our war council tent. I leaned forward in the chair I was currently slumped in and braced my elbows on my knees.

"We can't keep doing this," Faye said, her voice laced with both exhaustion and steel. "We have to take out that trebuchet."

"I agree, but how?" Shade said.

King Edward traced a finger across the map. "Short of leading a force all the way through enemy lines and hacking it to pieces, I don't really see any other solution." He motioned at me. "Storm's power is not enough to break it with wind from this distance so we need to get closer."

I winced. My powers were not enough. I knew already that, of course, but that failure on my part still made me want to stab something. Preferable the damn trebuchet.

After I collapsed yesterday evening, I had slept through both dinner and breakfast but after gobbling down some food under the fast-rising sun, I had joined them on the front lines again. The contraption that flung boulders, which I had since learned was called a trebuchet, had been fired throughout the day so I had been pulled from Shade's unit and was now on falling stones duty. All day today, I had ridden back and forth across the ridge with Haemir and shoved back the projectiles with concentrated blasts of wind. Since I didn't have to run and fight as well, I managed to ration my energy throughout the day so that I was still conscious when night fell. I was exhausted, though, which was why I was slumped in a chair instead of standing around the table.

Edward noticed my wince at his words and embarrassment flashed over his face. "I didn't mean it like that. Without your powers, we would have been overrun already. You're doing great."

I just waved a hand in front of my face to show that I understood. And he was right, without my powers to block the stones, our soldiers would either have to break formation, which would leave a spot open for our enemies to pass through, or get hit by the boulder, which would ultimately produce the same result.

Elaran crossed his arms and scowled down at the map. "If you have any bright ideas, now would be the time. Because right now our only option seems to be sending a unit on a suicide mission to try to break through their ranks and reach the trebuchet."

"We could also try sending a unit to their camp while they sleep, and disable it," Shade offered.

Silence fell as the rest of them pondered this. Only rustling fabric sounded for a while as the tent walls flapped in the strong fall winds. I massaged my brow but couldn't muster enough energy to voice my thoughts.

"Wouldn't that also be a suicide mission?" Edward said, echoing my own thoughts. "Infiltrating an enemy camp isn't exactly easy."

Faye arched a silver-colored eyebrow in Shade's direction. "What about your assassins? Could they actually succeed doing that?"

The Master of the Assassins' Guild lifted his toned shoulder in a shrug. "Honestly? They could probably get in, maybe disable the trebuchet, but get out too? Probably not."

"Would you be prepared to sacrifice some of them to try?" she asked in a voice that was much softer than usual.

"To win this war? Yes."

My cold black heart cracked a little at his words. His guild was his family. And he would still be willing to send some of them to their deaths for a chance to win this battle. No. I wouldn't allow it. Wood groaned as I pushed myself off the chair at last.

"We're not that desperate yet," I said. "I mean, yeah, it's exhausting but I can still keep the stones away from our soldiers."

Shade's gaze locked on me. "But for how long?"

"Long enough for us to figure out another solution." I lifted my chin. "So enough with the suicide plans."

Relief, pain, and gratitude mingled in his dark eyes as he gave me a slow nod. When the four of them moved on to other topics and I deemed the matter settled, I excused myself and slipped back to our tent. I was asleep, fully clothed, atop the covers before Shade even got back.

MOONLIGHT BATHED OUR camp in pale light. I murmured softly to Silver as I snuck towards the edge of our encampment after a few hours of sleep. The sentries we had posted all knew who I was so they let me out without challenge. I cast a glance at the glittering midnight stars before climbing into the saddle and riding west, straight out of camp.

A twinge of guilt coiled in my gut when I thought about the assassin still sleeping in our bed, completely oblivious to the fact that I was galloping away. But Shade would never have agreed to this. None of them would. However, I knew that I was the only one who could pull it off. And to spare Shade from having to sacrifice his family, I would risk it all. To spare him from that, I would sneak into our enemies' camp and disable the trebuchet on my own.

Only the crunch of grass beneath Silver's hooves disturbed the silent night as I galloped towards Travelers' Rest. I couldn't very well approach their camp from across the battlefield. They would spot me straight away. Instead, I had to sneak up from the side.

When I could see the quiet town in the distance, I steered Silver back east. The dark blue sky covered in glittering stardust was infinite out here on the plains. Even in the face of what I was about to do, I found myself staring up at the glimmering sky. It really was beautiful.

As I reached the small hill that the Beccus army had crested when they arrived, I slowed my horse to a trot until finally coming to a halt beside a cluster of tall bushes. There was a tiny mountain called the Stone Maze here on the east side of the plains. Well, it was tiny compared to the White Mountains at least. That tangle of rocks would have been a better hiding place for my horse but it was too far away. If I was to have any chance at making it into camp and then back out again before the sun rose, I had to risk riding as close as possible. Which was to this spot.

After tying Silver's reins to the brittle bush and telling her that I would be back soon, I slunk through the darkness and towards the top of the small hill. Out here there were no sentries so I was able to move unhindered down the slope and across another expanse of grass before guards in armor of various color became visible in the night. I drew a soft breath and called up the darkness.

Black tendrils snaked around my body. I pushed them outwards until a thin mist, only slightly darker than the rest of the landscape, spread across the grass in all directions. Staying in the middle of it, I let the black clouds swallow me completely.

The sentries would be less likely to see the figure of black smoke that I had become if I also coated it in a wider but thinner layer of mist. Hoping that I had calculated correctly, I snuck forward.

Their eyes kept scanning the grasslands as I simply walked straight towards them. No alarms rose. Yet. Good thing they were human and not elves at least. I barely dared breathe as I crossed the invisible line that the guards protected. Since having fires out here would only ruin their own night vision, they didn't notice that the night snuck right past them.

As soon as I reached the first wall of tents, I pulled the darkness back until it was only snaking around my body and fading out the area a few strides around me. Against the tent cloths, a larger cloud would be spotted. I used every lesson

Elaran and the twins had drilled into me about moving quietly through grass as I slunk through the sleeping camp.

Armor clanked faintly up ahead. I jerked back and pressed myself into the deep shadows of a tent. A second passed. Then, a guard strode right towards me. My heart hammered in my chest as he drew near. His eyes swept across the erected tents. I held my breath as he passed by my hiding place and, as luck would have it, gazed towards the other side of area at that moment and missed the swath of black smoke hiding in the shadows. And then he continued on.

Sending heartfelt prayers of thanks to Cadentia, Goddess of Luck, I stepped out of the shadows and continued forwards. The trebuchet was located at the north side of camp, which was good for me because that meant I didn't have to sneak into the heart of it at least.

My pulse continued smattering in my ears as I slunk towards it, but there were only a few guards moving through the camp proper since most were stationed in a ring around it, so I managed to arrive at my target undetected.

The wooden construction was much larger up close. I craned my neck and stared up at it while reconsidering how in Nemanan's name I was going to disable it. If I just cut a rope or pulled out a nail or something, they could just repair it. I needed to wreck it completely, which I had planned to do by setting it on fire, but there was a lot that needed to burn before it was destroyed. Tapping a finger against my lips, I ran through options in my head.

I had planned to do it stealthily by just setting it on fire and sneaking away. Since I had thought it was much smaller, I had estimated that it would've burned down before the alarm could be raised. But that plan wouldn't work with this monstrosity. I tipped my head from side to side. Oh well, if stealth wasn't an option, I might as well go for a really loud bang.

Taking four items from my belt pouches, I calculated trajectories and moved into position. Then, I threw four glass orbs onto different parts of the trebuchet.

The night exploded.

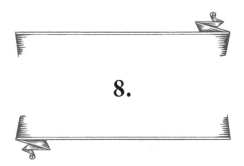

# 8.

Alarms blared into the silent night. Skidding to a halt, I stared at my handiwork. I had darted around the structure and thrown one of Haber's exploding orbs at each of the legs and then one onto the long pole that flung the stones. Flames now licked the wooden surface. I grinned.

The stamping feet of bellowing men rushed towards me. While backing away from the burning trebuchet, I called up the darkness and sent a few strategic gusts of wind to hasten the destruction. A whoosh sounded as the fire spread. Blood pounded in my ears. The rushing boots were getting closer but I had to make sure that the whole thing was beyond saving, otherwise it would all have been for nothing. Raising my arm, I squeezed my hand into a fist and then yanked it down. Lightning split the sky and struck the center of the trebuchet.

All around me, men were closing in, their shouts booming across the dark grass. I ignored my smattering pulse and fed the flames with more wind. Wood popped and fire crackled as orange sparks sailed up towards the silver-speckled heavens. *Just a little more*. I threw a hurried glance over my shoulder. *Come on*.

A loud crack echoed through the night. I whipped my head back towards the trebuchet in time to see one of its legs snap. Wood groaned and the whole structure tilted. And then it slammed into the ground with a deafening boom, cleaving the long pole in two as well. Victory sang in my heart.

And then the first group of bellowing soldiers cleared the mass of tents behind me. Time to go. I threw my arms out. Black clouds and hurricane winds barreled towards them. Cries of terror rang out as the force crashed into them and sent both men and tents flying through the cool air. Slowly raising my arms, I gathered more force. The dark smoke around me grew with each second until it blanketed a good portion of the camp. Earsplitting thunder boomed around me. While still making the clouds billow further out, I raised one arm again, squeezed my hand into a fist, and yanked down. Once. Twice. Three times. Four times. With each jerk of my arm, lightning bolts cleaved the darkness and zapped four different tents. Bright yellow and orange flames leaped up to devour the cloth.

The world around me had turned into a living nightmare for anyone unlucky enough to come near me. Screams of the dying mingled with shrieks of terror. A blanket of darkness blinded them to everything except the flames now leaping from tent to tent, and thunderclaps loud enough to deafen filled the blackness around them. I let an evil grin slash across my lips. And then I ran.

Soldiers blundered through the black haze with their swords out, trying to find their hidden enemy, but they could do nothing as I sprinted right past their unseeing eyes. Broken tents and supplies lay in rubble before me. Not daring to even slow down, I hurtled right through it, leaping and ducking as I made for the western edge of camp.

When I was getting close to the edge of my storm clouds, I threw out my arms and extended them further. My already depleted strength was draining rapidly now but I had to keep the darkness spread wide so that it wouldn't be so obvious which direction I was fleeing in. Wood snapped and fabric rustled as I continued my mad dash.

A squad of soldiers crashed through the tents on my right. Air exploded out of my lungs as I slammed straight into one of the men. He released a yelp and stumbled to the side but then gathered his wits quickly and whipped his head in my direction. Even though he couldn't see me, he knew where I was because I had yet to detach myself from his armored body so his hand shot out with alarming speed.

I threw myself backwards to escape it but his fingers closed around my throat before I could get out of range.

"Who's there?" he snapped.

"There's someone here?" another man said from a few strides away while turning in our direction.

"Yeah, and they're too small to be one of ours." His fist tightened around my throat. "Who. Are. You?"

He held me at an arm's length so I was too far away to stab his neck or any other vital area directly. While he shook me brusquely for emphasis, I shot a stiletto blade from my sleeve and rammed it through his forearm.

A roar split the darkness. While his grip slackened, I ripped the blade back out and jerked my throat from his hand. Ducking under his still raised arm, I slipped up in front of him and slashed the stiletto across his throat.

"I am death," I whispered as his blood splattered my face.

And then I was running again. That short delay had cost me precious time and I had to make it out of their camp before my powers were completely drained. Dark clouds still billowed around me but I pulled them back a bit from the east side of camp so that I could extend them in this direction instead. They would figure that out soon but I hoped it would be too late for them to do anything about it.

Plumes of smoke from the burned trebuchet and raging tent fires rose towards the sky, and ash coated the air. I sucked in deep breaths anyway. Soon. I would soon be in the clear. Blood rushed in my ears and black spots started dancing in the corner of my eyes. Damn. I couldn't hold on to my powers for much longer. The edge of camp was so close. My boots thudded against the ground as I sprinted towards it.

At last, I cleared the mass of tents and the ring of sentries appeared before me. I didn't have enough strength for both, so I pulled the black haze from the camp and slammed it in front of me instead.

The sentries cried out in alarm but were blind to me as I dashed between them and out into the grasslands. Just a little longer. And then I would be out of sight. Darkness that wasn't mine pressed into my vision. I gauged the distance I had to clear before I would be out of range. That unwelcome blackness threatened to drown me any second. My heart sank. I would never make it.

With no other choice than to risk it, I snapped the darkness back into my soul.

Shouts rose behind me. And then boots smattered against the grass as they began their pursuit. *Fuck*.

If I used my power even a little right now, I would pass out. Which meant that I had to outrun them. Their feet thundered behind me. I kept sprinting.

My heart slammed against my ribs and my lungs were burning as I finally reached the hill. If I could just get to Silver on the other side, I would be alright. Soil and loose bits of grass rolled down the hill as I pushed my body towards the top. *Almost there. Almost there.*

The soldiers bellowed orders behind me as I crested the small hill and sped down it so fast I almost lost my footing. Throwing out my arms, I managed to stabilize myself. The cluster of bushes where I had tied Silver was so close now.

Twigs tore at my clothes as I crashed through the vegetation and skidded to a halt in front of Silver. Only, my horse wasn't there. Panic pulsed through my body in searing waves as I whipped my head around to find the area empty.

Silver was gone.

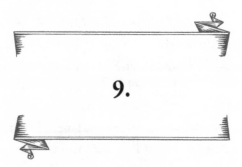

# 9.

My brain threatened to shut down as I tried to get that thought through my head. The only chance I had of outrunning my pursuers was gone.

Men shouted behind me. I almost cried with exhaustion and hopelessness as I stared across the empty plains. There were too many soldiers to fight, especially when I was this exhausted. But the chances of outrunning them were incredibly slim too. Again, especially when I was this exhausted. This would not end well. For a few seconds, I just stood there, frozen on the grass.

But then those deep-rooted survival instincts bellowed at me to keep moving and I took off at a run again. Straight north, towards our camp. That short stop had allowed me to catch my breath a little but it had also made the soldiers close in further. I wanted to scream at the heavens about the unfairness of it all. I had managed to destroy their godsdamn trebuchet. All on my own. And now I was going to die out here on the plains because my damn horse had run off.

The logical part of me told me that it had most likely happened because I'd sent deafening thunder roaring across the landscape but the desperate and furious part of me didn't want to hear it. So I kept sprinting.

Every breath was like inhaling glass and my head pounded so loudly that it drowned out the sound of my pursuers. But I knew they were close. I could almost feel them snapping at my heels. This was the end. In less than a minute, they would catch me. Disappointment coursed through my body like a frozen sea.

Then a shrill voice cut through the bleak hopelessness. Before I could piece together where it had come from, it sounded again.

"Storm!"

Down to the last dregs of strength, I barely managed to twist my head to look at the source.

Two horses were galloping across the plains. Pale moonlight gleamed in the wild brown hair of a young girl as she barreled straight for me on a black stallion while keeping a tight grip on the reins of a silver-colored mare.

The horses plowed into the ranks of my pursuers, sending them scattering across the dark grass. Barely slowing down, the rider tugged on the reins and sped towards me. I stared in absolute disbelief as she threw me Silver's reins while steering her own horse in a circle around me.

"Get on!" she called. "Hurry!"

Behind us, the soldiers had recovered and were scrambling towards us again so I launched myself into the saddle and dug my heels into Silver's sides without question. My savior did the same. Shouts of outrage echoed into the night as the two of us disappeared across the dark plains. When we were at last a safe distance away, I twisted my head and stared at the most unlikely rescuer I could've imagined. Livia.

"How?" I asked.

The horse-loving daughter of Merina and Hestor shot me a beaming grin. "I couldn't sleep. After the army passed through, I've been too worried to sleep through the night so I was out in the stable, because that always calms me down, and then I heard this noise and I looked out and Silver galloped straight towards me and I knew she was your horse and she was saddled so I thought something was wrong so I saddled my own horse and let Silver lead me and she led me here and then here I am."

I stared at her. Then the shock and relief caught up with me and a mad laugh ripped from my throat. When it had calmed into a somewhat normal-sounding chuckle, I threw her a knowing smile.

"Did you even breathe once while saying all that?"

Livia looked like she was pondering it carefully for a few seconds. Then she shook her head, making her wild curls swing around her face. "No."

We exchanged a glance that told me she also remembered that it was one of the first things we'd said to each other. And then we both burst out laughing again. Hers was a rippling joyous sound while mine still bordered more on insanity, but the relief singing through my soul didn't care. I tilted my head up towards the glittering stars and laughed until my already burning throat couldn't produce any more sound.

Riding like she had been born doing it, Livia didn't even need to look at the landscape ahead as we moved. She continued watching me. I turned my head to look at her as well. Silvery light from the moon was reflected in her brown eyes as I met them.

"Thank you," I said.

Those two words were so inadequate for what I really felt but she seemed to understand the depth of my gratitude regardless because lines of silver sprang up in her eyes.

"You're welcome," she said and reached up to wipe her cheek. "I'm glad you're alive."

"Me too." I smiled at her. "Me too."

Livia continued studying me for another few seconds. Then, she flashed me a mischievous grin and waved a hand towards my horse. "I missed Silver, though. That's probably why she ran back to Travelers' Rest. Because she missed me too, I mean. Did you know that after you came to get her..."

While the lively young girl who had saved my life tonight launched into a very long tale about what she had been up to since we last saw each other, we continued galloping across the vast expanse of grass.

When the camp finally rose before us, I dared a deep sigh of relief. And exhaustion. I barely managed to stay in the saddle as we cleared the ring of sentries and trotted the final distance to the first line of tents. The sentries must have spotted us from afar because Shade, Elaran, and the twins were waiting for us.

The Master Assassin was dressed in full battle gear and looked to have barely been persuaded not to gallop straight into enemy territory to find me as he paced back and forth across the grass. A lightning storm danced in his eyes as he looked at me. I had no energy left to argue so I just broke his gaze and turned to the twins.

"This is Livia," I said as our two horses came to a halt. "She saved my life tonight. She lives at the Sleeping Horse in Travelers' Rest. Can you find somewhere for her to sleep tonight before we escort her back tomorrow?"

Silence fell as Haemir and Haela glanced at each other and then at Elaran and Shade. The assassin still had murder in his eyes and the ranger was no better.

"Please," I said.

"Of course," Haemir replied and motioned for Livia to join him.

While Livia nimbly jumped off her horse, Haemir pulled at his sister's sleeve as if to say that it was better to stay out of the fight that was bound to break out any second now. Mustering a scrap of strength, I half slid, half fell off Silver. I wobbled as I hit the ground and had to brace a hand on my horse's side to keep from toppling to the ground. Once I was sure my legs would support me, I strode towards the fierce-eyed girl. Livia let out a surprised noise as I pulled her into a tight hug.

"Thank you," I whispered against the top of her head before releasing her again.

"Promise you'll come visit sometime." She waved a hand at the sleeping army around us. "When it's all over."

I didn't have the heart to tell her that I wasn't sure I would still be alive when it was all over so I just nodded. She shot me another wide grin in reply before following the twins into the maze of tents. While a couple of Pernulans led away our horses to the stabling area, I turned to the two fuming warriors across the grass.

"Trebuchet's gone," I said before either of them could start.

Elaran raised his eyebrows. "So that fire...?"

"Yep." I shrugged and flashed him a smirk. "You did say that now was the time to burn shit down."

"That fire looked a lot bigger than one trebuchet," Elaran observed.

"I may or may not have set fire to part of their camp too."

Drawing his eyebrows down, he crossed his arms and leveled a hard stare at me. "That was bloody reckless."

"Yes, it was."

The elven commander continued glaring at me as if not sure what to do with me, but then he just gave me a slow nod. "Good job."

Shade whipped his head towards him while lightning flashed in his eyes again but Elaran just held up a hand.

"I already said it was reckless," he cut off before the assassin could say anything. "But we also needed that trebuchet gone." Shade opened his mouth again but Elaran just turned to me and huffed a short laugh. "I was right. Every time you go somewhere, *something* blows up."

"One of my finer qualities." I gave him a theatrical bow that set my head spinning and almost had me falling face down into the grass. Gods, I was tired.

Elaran just shook his head and spun on his heel. "I'm going back to bed," he grumbled over his shoulder while striding away. "Try not to destroy anything when you fight."

I watched his auburn hair disappear between the tent walls before finally dragging my eyes to the furious assassin.

"Why didn't you tell me?" he demanded.

"Because you would've tried to stop me."

"Damn right I would!" His eyes bored into me. "What the hell were you thinking?"

"I was thinking that we needed the trebuchet gone, so I made that happen."

Shade stalked towards me. "I know we needed that! But why the hell did you decide that *you* would be the one to take on that suicide mission?"

"Because I was the best person for the job!" I snapped back. "I can shroud myself in darkness and I specialize in hurting, destroying, and burning things to the ground." I threw out an arm towards where Elaran had disappeared, and had to take a step to the side to avoid falling over as my knees wobbled. "You heard him, things always blow up when I'm around."

"This isn't funny," Shade growled down in my face as he came to a halt before me. He took my chin in a firm grip and forced my head up so that I would look him in the eye. "You could've been killed."

He was now standing so close that I could feel his breath on my skin and see the devastating worry that swirled in his eyes. But I was too pissed off and tired to deal with the feelings that stirred in my heart at the sight, so I slapped his hand away and then shoved him backwards. When he actually retreated a short distance, I knew he had willingly yielded those steps because I could barely muster the strength to lift my arms, so I would never have been able to push him away unless he let me.

"Don't you think I know that?" I snapped. A tidal wave of exhaustion swept through me and I had to blink repeatedly to get my eyes back in focus. "But if I didn't go, you were going to send your assassins."

Confusion mingled with the fury on his face. "So?"

"So they would've died if you sent them. And they're your family." My voice grew softer as the last of my failing strength left me. "I couldn't let you send your family in there to die."

Every spark of anger disappeared from Shade's beautiful face as shock and incredulity slammed into his sharp cheekbones instead. Then my legs gave out, and before I could see the rest of the emotions flashing across his face, I dropped to my knees on the ground.

Grass crunched softly, telling me that Shade was closing the distance between us. He stopped in front of me but I was too tired to lift my head so I just remained there on my knees before him, staring at his boots.

Leather creaked as he crouched down in front of me. He gripped my chin gently and raised it until I met his gaze. The softness in those black eyes as he looked at me made something in my chest crack.

"You are my family too," he said.

My eyes burned and I swallowed against the tightness in my throat.

"My reckless stubborn little thief." Shade let out a long sigh and shook his head before repeating, "You're my family too. Do you hear me?"

Before I could respond, he let go of my chin and reached down. His strong arms wrapped around my body and lifted me from the ground. Having no strength left to protest, let alone actually walk on my own, I simply rested my cheek against his muscled chest as he carried me towards our tent.

"Elaran was right too, though," Shade said. I heard the smile in his voice more than saw it. "You did a damn good job." He huffed a laugh as we passed through the silent tents. "And you do excel at blowing things up."

"Told you," I mumbled into his shirt.

His rippling laugh was the last thing I heard before exhaustion claimed me. And despite everything that I'd gone through that day, a smile lingered on my lips when I at last tumbled into sleep's waiting embrace.

# 10.

Clashing steel filled the afternoon air. I snatched two throwing knives from my shoulders and hurled them at the gigantic soldier from Beccus who barreled straight for me with his sword raised. Wet cracks sounded as the knives embedded themselves in his skull. Pulling the darkness from my soul, I sent black clouds billowing around me and drew my hunting knives. Blood sprayed into the dark haze as I twisted and twirled through enemy lines, slashing throats as I passed.

It had been close to noon when I finally woke up after my little adventure last night. Our forces had been fighting for hours but my friends hadn't wanted to, or perhaps not been able to, wake me. Livia was, of course, also long gone when I at last strode towards the front lines, having inhaled some food and loaded up on weapons.

With the trebuchet out of play, I could once again join Shade's unit and spread some chaos through our enemies' ranks. We continued with the same strategy as before: suddenly appearing in a place where the soldiers were getting too comfortable, wreaking havoc, and then disappearing again. I much preferred that way of fighting. After all, why fight honorably when you could fight to win?

I pulled the darkness back into my soul. In a wide circle around me, dead bodies lay like sheared stalks of wheat. The Beccus soldiers at the edge of the ring of death stared at me with true terror on their faces. They might no longer be able to feel pain in their hearts but that primal fear that drives our survival instincts was apparently impossible to stamp out. Good. I let a grin tinted with insanity flash over my lips.

They flinched. And then a smattering of elven arrows rained down on them from above. I darted back up the slope towards where Shade and the rest of the Assassins' Guild had retreated behind our own lines again.

A hand clamped around my ankle and yanked my leg back. I released a startled yelp as I lost my footing and slammed face first into the grass. One of my hunting knives went flying on impact but I managed to keep hold of the other one as I scrambled for purchase. Kicking my free foot backwards, I tried to hit the person holding me but since I was aiming blind, the attack missed its mark. I swung myself around but had just barely managed to flip over on my back when I was yanked downwards.

Earth and stone scraped against my back as I was hauled down the slope by a Beccus soldier who had somehow survived whatever slaughter had taken place this far up on the hill. Now that I could see my enemy, I aimed my boot at his face and kicked again. He jerked his head to the side and snaked his other hand around my ankle. Panic shot through me when I realized that both my legs were trapped. I slammed my palm forward.

The blast of wind went harmlessly over his head since he was already lying flat against the ground. Swearing viciously, I reached for a throwing knife right as he tugged hard. My arm was jerked off target by the motion. Grass and pebbles burrowed into my clothes as I slid straight at him, and before I had time to stab him with my remaining hunting knife or blast him with wind, he launched himself on top of me.

Air exploded from my lungs as the full weight of his body mass and armor crashed into me. I slashed blindly with my knife while trying to suck in a desperate breath but he slammed my arm into the ground and pinned it under his knee. The movement made him ease off my chest a fraction and I gasped in air to refill my lungs while also aiming my other palm towards him. Hurricane winds screamed into the sky as they missed him and shot over his shoulder instead.

"The Death Storm," he hissed in my face.

He reeked of sweat and blood. The long gash on the side of his neck sent a small stream of crimson running below his black and yellow armor but his grip was strong as his fingers encircled my free wrist and forced it down on the ground. I yanked against it and the knee keeping my other hand trapped, but the sheer bulk of him couldn't be moved. Thrashing against his weight, I tried to think past the blaring panic in my head.

"You've killed too many of my brothers," he growled in my face. "But no more."

He reached up with his free hand and pulled one of my own throwing knives from my shoulder. I bucked my hips to try to throw him off but he remained firmly straddling my chest. Afternoon sunlight glinted off the blade as it passed over my head and towards my throat. My heart slammed against my ribs. *No, no, no.* I fought against his grip with every smidgen of strength I had as he placed the edge of the knife against my throat.

A grin slashed across his lips. "The Death Storm no more."

Blood rained down over me. I closed my eyes as the curtain of red poured over my face and chest. Then, the weight pinning me to the ground disappeared. Lifting a hand, I scrubbed my eyes with the back of my hand and then blinked repeatedly. A black-clad assassin stood over me, one hand curled around a blood-dripping sword and the other held out to me. I drew two fingers down my face, over my throat and towards my chest. They came back soaking wet and red. Motioning at the pool of blood now covering me, I glared up at Shade.

"Really?" I huffed.

A wicked smile spread across his own blood-splattered face. "Would you rather I'd let him slit your throat?"

Throwing him another glare, I took his outstretched hand and let him help me to my feet. After gathering up my missing weapons, I turned to my now dead attacker. A gaping hole was visible across his throat and his unseeing gray eyes stared into the blue sky above. I scowled at him.

"And it's *the Oncoming Storm*. Not the Death Storm." Bending down, I picked up a fallen sword and drove it through his already unmoving chest for good measure. "Idiot."

Shade huffed a laugh behind me. Ignoring him, I swept my gaze over the enemy ranks farther down the slope. Our own lines were holding steady in front of them. Thanks to Elaran's carefully constructed strategy we were still standing strong, despite being outnumbered. I wondered how long it would remain that way.

"Our eastern flank is taking a beating," Shade said as if he had read my thoughts.

I glanced towards the sea on my left before shifting my gaze back to the assassin.

He jerked his chin. "Let's go."

Since he had technically saved my life a minute ago, I let his presumptuous command slide. Just this once. So instead, I just nodded and followed him higher up the hill. The metallic smell of blood still assaulted me every time I drew breath so I scrubbed my face a couple of times and wiped some of the blood on my pants. I had a feeling I was only smearing it out more and also adding black streaks of dirt to my red mask, but it was worth a shot.

"Thanks," I said at last, glancing at Shade from the corner of my eye.

"Oh don't thank me yet. This just means you owe me." A smirk played over his lips as he flicked his gaze over my body. "But don't worry, I'll find a way for you to repay me."

Narrowing my eyes, I gave his upper arm a shove. "Bastard."

He stumbled a step to the side but continued jogging while a wicked chuckle slipped his lips. I shook my head. Damn assassin.

But the bantering had helped pull me back from the white-hot panic that had still been pulsing through me after I'd almost had my throat slit with one of my own knives. Which was probably why Shade had baited me. Gods, I just wanted this war to end. Before it started, I had assumed that the physical act of succeeding in killing trained soldiers before they managed to kill me and my friends would be the most difficult part. Not the... feelings.

The survival instincts that were screaming at me nonstop, the sheer bone-deep terror that I would have to watch my friends die, the fear that I wasn't enough to protect them, the uncertainty that haunted me every minute of every single hour – that was by far the hardest part. I didn't have much of a heart but that cold black thing in my chest was now raw all the time because of all these emotions. By Nemanan, I really hated feeling.

A swarm of black-clad assassins had fallen in around us as we made our way towards where Elaran was overseeing the battle. The auburn-haired archer stood straight-backed, sweeping his gaze across the battlefield with a grim expression on his face when we arrived.

"I heard our eastern flank is getting hammered," Shade said by way of greeting. "Do you want us to reinforce?"

"No," Elaran replied. "I've already sent units to back it up. The Sker army is finding their stride in the center, though." He nodded at the soldiers in brown and gold down the hill. "Break them up."

Shade just inclined his head. "Consider it done."

If we hadn't been in the middle of a battle, I would've laughed. Those two had been at each other's throats since the day they met about who should be giving orders, and now Shade–*Shade*–was just obeying Elaran's orders without question. But out here, he was the commander. And we all knew it.

The Master Assassin jerked his chin at his guild and started down the slope. I took a step forward to follow them when a ripple went through the elven archers behind us. As one, our black-clad unit stopped and whirled back around right as Haela shouldered past the closest ranks.

"Elaran," she said, a sharp note in her voice.

The commander just kept staring at the horizon. "I see it."

"What?" I demanded, whipping my head between the two of them and the far end of the battlefield.

Elaran remained silent and I could almost see the strategies and schemes swirling in his yellow eyes, demanding all his attention, so it was Haela who answered.

"Trebuchets." She nodded towards what to me was only dark smudges in the distance. "Six of them."

Dread slithered down my spine like a cold snake. "*Six?*"

Haela nodded before shouting over her shoulder, "Get a horse ready!"

The low-hanging afternoon sun painted the scene below the hill in orange and gold. I could hold my own against one trebuchet flinging boulders at us. Maybe two, if I was really lucky and calculated everything just right. But six of them? Not a chance.

Ringing steel mixed with gunshots and screams of the dying and wounded while the six new siege mechanisms that would decimate our defenses moved closer. If they launched them all at the same time, creating holes in our ranks at six different locations simultaneously, then we were done for. There was no way we would be able to patch up all those gaps before enemies slipped past our ranks. I swallowed against the bile rising in my throat.

"Elaran," Haela said again with that sharp edge to her tone.

"We can't pull our flanks to create another layer behind our ranks," Elaran said at last, more to himself than anyone else. "Then they could easily surround us."

"What if all the archers concentrate their fire on the holes?" I offered. "Killing them before they can get in? Until our ranks have closed the gap?"

Elaran didn't take his eyes off the advancing trebuchets as he shook his head. "We're outnumbered. Our archers are the only thing keeping them from rushing all at once and overwhelming us."

Cold dread sank into my stomach. "So what do we do?"

Silence hung heavy over the grassy hill for another minute. Then Elaran turned to Haela.

"Have them pull some soldiers from every unit and form smaller mobile units." He jerked his chin towards the front lines. "They're to move back and forth, behind our lines, providing cover until the ranks can close again." While Haela took off to carry out his orders, his gaze slid to Shade. "Your unit will do the same."

The assassin nodded once before signaling to his guild to get moving. Before he disappeared down the slope, his eyes lingered on me and it looked like he was about to say something but then he shook his head and trotted down the hill.

Elaran's gaze was calm and steady as it shifted to me. "Keep riding along the ridge so that we shield our ranks evenly."

"If I block one boulder, five will still land in other places," I said quietly.

"I know." His face was an impassive mask. "Once you've blocked one, move to another location. We can't have one part of our army getting hit harder than the others."

My chest tightened but I nodded at him. We both went back to studying the approaching trebuchets while I waited for my horse to arrive. Bowstrings continued twanging across the ridge.

"Will this work?" I asked at last.

Elaran didn't reply. I guessed that was answer enough. Blood pounded in my ears. There was a good chance that this was the beginning of the end for us.

Silver snorted as she was led forward. I patted her neck before climbing into the saddle and drawing a deep breath. Without another word, I urged her on and began moving along the ridge.

When the trebuchets came to a halt on the other side of the field, my heart was slamming so hard against my ribs I feared they might crack. I had stopped close to the eastern edge of our troops and would then work my way west. Brisk winds from the sea behind me pulled at my clothes. My eyes went black as death as I yanked out the darkness. Tendrils of dark smoke snaked around my arms as I waited. Time dragged on. My pulse smattered in my ears. Any minute now. I reached up to push back a few strands of hair that the wind had torn loose from my braid.

And then the arms of all the trebuchets launched into the air and six boulders flew towards our unprotected ranks.

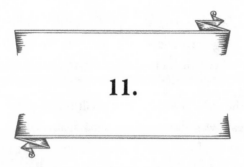

# 11.

Fear rippled through our ranks at the approaching death. Farther inland, Elaran was bellowing orders that were echoed by Faye and Haela down the line. I dug my heels into Silver's sides and moved us directly into the path of the easternmost boulder. Hopelessness flooded my chest as I raised my arms and got ready while five more projectiles barreled unchallenged for other parts of our army. This was never going to work.

Deafening booms echoed across the battlefield.

Silver startled and I had to snatch up the reins to keep her from bolting. Panic and desperation blared in my mind as I tried to keep my horse from fleeing while also trying to get my blast of wind off before the boulder slammed into our ranks. Jerking the reins with one hand, I whipped my head back to the incoming death and threw up the other arm.

My mouth dropped open. All six boulders were blasted backwards simultaneously and the easternmost trebuchet had been reduced to a pile of rubble.

Another earsplitting boom reverberated through the air.

Throwing one arm over my head to guard against the unknown threat, I kept the other one on the reins to keep Silver from taking off once more. She snorted and threw her head while stamping her hooves but remained in place.

And then the next trebuchet exploded.

I whipped my head around and stared at the sea behind me and my heart almost stopped. There on the gold-glittering waves, just off the coast, were three pirate ships. I recognized one of them because I had sailed on it more than once. Zaina had come.

The ship next to Zaina's fired and another cannonball tore through the air and crashed into the next trebuchet in line. However, the three westernmost ones had managed to load more boulders and flung them towards our ranks. I spurred Silver on and galloped towards them. Dread welled up inside me. I was too far away. I would never make it in time.

All three boulders were blasted backwards again. I blinked at the sight just as another cannon was fired from the sea. The next trebuchet was too far inland so the cannonball missed its mark but screams of terror still rose from our enemies.

And then I reached Elaran and realization clicked in place.

"Hey, Storm," Marcus called up at me with a wide smile on his face. "I got your letter."

Incredulous laughter bubbled from my throat as I swept my gaze along the ridge behind and in front of me and took in what I had missed while I hurtled along it. Storm Casters. Spread throughout our ranks of elven archers was a mass of Ashaana with their arms raised, ready to blast back any more boulders.

Zaina and her pirates continued firing from the water while I slid down from the saddle and handed the reins back to the stable hand who had brought Silver. Then I took two quick strides and wrapped my arms around the muscled Storm Caster.

"You came," I said into his chest before drawing back again.

"Sorry we're late. We left as soon as I got your letter but it took a bit longer for us to get down from the mountains than it did for you to get here, I suppose." He glanced from the red smudges I'd left on his clothes after our hug to my still blood-drenched body and frowned. "You look like someone spilled half their blood volume on you. What happened?"

A wicked glint crept into my eye as I gave him a casual shrug. "Someone spilled half their blood volume on me."

He chuckled and shook his head.

Another series of deafening booms echoed across the water as Zaina and her pirates fired upon our enemies once more. The shots tore into their ranks close to a destroyed trebuchet but didn't touch the other three. A surge went through the frontlines and they rushed for our own soldiers with renewed aggression.

"Break the wave!" Elaran bellowed over the ridge.

Twangs filled the air as the elven archers loosed arrow upon arrow on the charging men.

"Incoming," our commander said.

Marcus relayed the information to the other Ashaana with a shout that traveled over the entire hill. A second later, three more boulders were launched into the air. While the elves continued firing down the slope to stop the advancing soldiers, the Storm Casters got ready to intercept the stones coming for our ranks. Wind barreled across the plains and screams rose as the projectiles landed among our enemies instead.

"Push!" Elaran ordered.

Bows started firing faster around us, and down the hill, our soldiers locked together and started taking synchronized steps forward. Cannons boomed from the water.

Then, a horn sounded. I almost sagged to the ground in relief when the armies of Sker, Frustaz, and Beccus began retreating. Arrows chased them on their way. When at last the late afternoon sun fell over empty grass beneath our hill, I dared a deep sigh.

Blond hair flowed in the corner of my eye. "Elaran."

I turned to find Faelar striding out of the throng. The light that sparkled in Elaran's eyes when he took in his longtime friend and brother-in-arms warmed my soul.

"I'm glad you're here," Elaran said, a rare smile on his lips.

Faelar smiled back but whatever he had been about to say was drowned out as another blond head appeared from the ranks of elven archers.

"Is that a smile on your face, brother?" Faldir said and pulled his little brother into a bone-crushing hug.

A chuckle escaped my lips as the taciturn elf snapped his mouth shut and glowered at his older brother. Faldir, the cheerful elf who owned the War Dancer tavern in Tkeideru, just grinned back.

Hiding his own amusement, Elaran turned back to the army spread out across the grass and started calling orders to pull back as well. Metal clanked as they trudged back up the slope while the elves atop it lowered their bows and retreated as well. I kept my eyes fixed on the swarm of black making its way up the blood-splattered hill.

"I hear you've gone and fallen in love," Faldir continued teasing Faelar somewhere to my right. "Where are you hiding her?"

Boisterous laughter rang through the air as Queen Faye approached as well. "I wanna know that too."

Embarrassed grumbling came from the blond elf in reply. I shifted my gaze towards them long enough to see Cileya, her red-golden hair gleaming like fire in the setting sun, make her way towards them. The love beaming from Faelar's face as he introduced her to his friends and family gave my heart some much needed hope. My eyes flitted between Marcus, who had joined them, and the pirate ships out on the glittering sea before returning to the blood-drenched battlefield before me.

A lot of bodies remained on the trampled grass even after our armies had retreated, and they weren't all enemies. Soldiers of Pernula and Keutunan who would never see their home again lay staring unblinking into the red-streaked sky. Our lines were holding. But barely. Our position and Elaran's leadership kept us from being overrun but it wouldn't last. Even with three pirate ships and the whole Ashaana camp to back us up, our enemy still outnumbered us two to one, which meant that they could keep sending in fresh troops while our own only grew more exhausted.

Elaran seemed to be thinking the same thing because he remained staring at the emptying battlefield as well. We had to finish this fight quickly. Otherwise, we were doomed.

FABRIC RUSTLED AS TWO more people shouldered through the tent flap and into what had become our war room. Faye and Elaran nodded at the rest of us before taking up position in front of the map-covered table. No one talked. Emotions from today's battle were still running high so we all seemed content to just gather our thoughts in silence until everyone had arrived.

A gust of wind blew into the warm tent and sent a stack of papers scattering as the tent flap was thrown open once again. I slammed my forearms down over the reports to keep them from falling off the table, which instead made the candles on the table rattle. Marcus winced and sent an apologetic smile through the room as he lowered the thick fabric behind him again to keep the wind out and then approached the rest of us.

I never thought I would live to see the day when I became the common denominator between people but as I looked at the ones gathered here, I realized that not all of them knew each other but *I* knew all of them. Suppressing the incredulous chuckle rising in my throat, I threw out an arm to encompass the room.

"Alright, not all of you know each other so here's a crash course." I moved my hand from person to person. "Faye, Queen of Tkeideru. Elaran, Head Ranger of Tkeideru and Commander of the Joint Forces. Edward, King of Keutunan. Malor, Senior Advisor of Pernula. Zaina, Captain of the Mistcleaver. Marcus, leader of the Ashaana force you just watched blow boulders out of the sky." Scattered laughter at that. "Shade, High King of Pernula and Master of the Assassins' Guild." When I'd pointed to everyone in the room, I shrugged. "And me you already know." I grinned at them. "A thief."

Shade cut me a glance. "And Queen of the Underworld."

Leather groaned as Marcus whirled towards me and raised his eyebrows. After an exasperated glare at the Master Assassin next to me, I waved a hand in front of my face to tell Marcus that I would explain later. He gave me a wide smile before turning back to the others. But then his gaze snagged on Zaina.

Furrowing his brows slightly, he studied her. "Have we met before?"

She cocked her head as well. "I don't know. Have we?"

"You've met her sister," I supplied. "Norah. When you visited Pernula last year."

"That was your sister?" Marcus raised his eyebrows but the confusion lingered on his face. When Zaina nodded in confirmation, he nodded back and then shrugged. "That must be it then."

In the silence that followed, King Edward cleared his throat and shifted his gaze between Zaina and Marcus. "Thank you for coming to our aid today."

"Of course." Zaina flashed me a wicked grin. "When Storm sends magic doves after someone, I figured it's best to show up. Sorry it took a while. Had to drop off some wares and get a couple of crews ready first."

"Well, as far as dramatic arrivals go," I grinned back at her, "I'd say you nailed it."

Another bout of soft laughter rippled through the room. Outside, clanking metal from pots of food mixed with the sounds of soldiers trudging past the tent. I rolled my shoulders to try to get the lingering tension out of my body. It didn't work.

"Your arrivals were indeed well-timed and we won today because of it," Elaran said. He was silent for a moment before continuing. "But it won't be enough to tip the scales."

A collective sigh went through the room.

I lifted my eyes from the map I'd been staring at to peer at Marcus. "Morgora?"

He shook his head. "No. She said she'd come when the time was right."

"What the hell does that mean?"

"No idea."

Shifting my weight, I turned to Malor and raised my eyebrows expectantly. The tall senior advisor just crossed his arms over the black and red tunic covering his broad chest and stared back at me with those strange reddish-brown eyes of his. When he didn't reply, I blew out a frustrated breath. Whatever secrets those two were harboring had better be worth it.

"We won't win if we keep fighting like this," Elaran said. If I hadn't known him so well, I would've missed the slight hint of dread in his voice as he said, "She hasn't even sent in her own soldiers yet."

"The star elf army," King Edward said.

Elaran nodded. "One of our biggest advantages so far is our ranged attacks. Since they're human, and they don't use pistols, *and* they need to fire uphill, we've basically neutralized any ranged attacks." He huffed out a forceful breath. "Except the trebuchets."

"But we've got those covered now," Marcus filled in.

"Yes. But if they send in a host of elven archers, we're screwed."

Shade nodded on my other side. "Because then they could start picking off our own archers from a distance."

"Correct."

Faye drummed her fingers on the table while she surveyed the map. Running her other hand over her hair, she looked up at Marcus and scrunched up her silver brows. "Can't you just blow all their forces away with your powers?"

"Not without hitting our own forces," Elaran interrupted before he could answer. He lifted his toned shoulders in an apologetic shrug directed towards his queen. "It's downhill."

"He's right. We can blast boulders out of the sky because we're aiming upwards but we can't make the wind jump over our own ranks and then fall back down to shove away our enemies." Marcus crossed his muscled arms and tapped a finger to his left bicep while considering. "If you pulled all our forces back behind the ridge, we could do it."

"Will that kill them?" Zaina asked, a dubious expression decorating her sharp cheekbones.

"A few maybe. But it'll mostly just keep them back."

"What's the point then?"

Silence descended over the tent as we were all forced to acknowledge that the pirate was right. Just blowing the soldiers backwards over and over again would do nothing except drain our Ashaana. We needed to defeat them, kill them, not just hold the hill.

"How long can we hold them off?" Edward asked from across the table. "Before..." He didn't finish the sentence.

"Longer now that we can deal with the trebuchets." Elaran nodded to Marcus before shifting his gaze to Zaina. "And with you raining hell down on them from the coast. But..." He didn't finish the sentence either.

"We need to fight differently," Shade said. "Smarter. We won't win if we keep doing what we're doing now."

"That's what I just said," Elaran muttered while glowering at the map before him. "But how?"

"Remember the objective," Malor said, his strong voice cutting through the tent for the first time since the meeting started. "The only ones we need to kill are Nimlithil and Aldeor. Not leagues of soldiers. So don't waste your energy on them. Find a way to kill those two, and the armies will break apart."

"Aldeor?" Zaina said.

"The white dragon," I supplied. "The one that takes all the magic and directs it at the spell."

"Exactly," Malor rumbled. "And when they're both dead, the spell will shatter, along with the reason all those soldiers are here fighting. So don't get distracted by unimportant matters. Remember the real objective."

Elaran crossed his arms and drew his eyebrows down. "I wouldn't exactly call an attacking army *unimportant*."

"So how do we kill those two then?" Faye cut in before Elaran and Malor could get into a glaring contest. "Isn't that dragon back in the City of Glass?"

"Yeah," I said.

Wind ripped at the tent walls. I shielded the candle closest to me with my hand when it spluttered precariously after a sneaky draft had somehow made it inside. White wax ran down the edge but it remained burning. Removing my hand again, I looked back up at my friends right as Shade spoke up.

"We need to draw out the dragon. And Queen Nimlithil." Shade's dark eyebrows creased as he tilted his head to the right. "We need to do something that forces her to call out her pet dragon to the battlefield."

"What?" Edward asked.

"What she wants is magic wielders who will then give their powers to the dragon." I met Marcus' golden-brown eyes from across the table. "Let's bait her with that."

Marcus tapped his finger against his muscled bicep again. "We take a group of Storm Casters to a different location. While the rest of her army is busy fighting ours, the star elves will have to come for us. And will walk right into our trap." He tipped his head from side to side. "Could work."

Shade shifted his calculating gaze between the two of us. "How can we know for certain that Queen Nimlithil will go herself? Or that simply the possibility of getting her hands on a group of Ashaana will make her send for her dragon?"

"We can't." I shrugged. "But we won't know until we try."

The Master Assassin pressed his lips together but nodded.

"Sounds risky," Queen Faye said. "What if you do get caught?"

"Get caught? Have you met me?" I flicked my braid over my shoulder and flashed her a grin. "When have I ever gotten caught doing anything?"

Several pairs of eyebrows rose. When I noticed the amusement dancing on their faces, I realized that an alarming number of people in this room had been present when I'd gotten caught doing one thing or another over the years. Before they could remind me of all those times, I raised a hand.

"You know what, don't answer that."

Marcus, a smile still on his lips, met Faye's gaze. "We'll be careful."

The Queen of Tkeideru nodded back. We all shifted our focus to Elaran, who ultimately called the shots in this fight. The grumpy elf continued glaring at the map before him as if he could make it reveal its secrets while we waited in silence. Then, he blew out a forceful breath.

"Alright. Zaina, you'll continue bombarding them from the coast. We'll continue holding the lines and fighting them on the slopes of the hill." He turned to Marcus. "And you'll leave enough Storm Casters to deal with the trebuchets and then take the rest to draw out Queen Nimlithil." He pointed to a spot on the map. "Here."

His long graceful finger rested on the black markings that depicted the Stone Maze on the western edge of the battlefield. I'd ridden past it when I went to sneak inside their camp.

"The Stone Maze?" Edward said, a frown on his face. "Are you sure that's the best location? Isn't it just a jumble of rocks?"

"Yes. They need to be close enough to camp to make it back in case they need to escape, but also far enough away that Queen Nimlithil needs to send her own soldiers instead of just grabbing a couple from the western ranks." Elaran nodded to himself. "And the jumble of rocks will be a good place to set up an ambush."

"The Stone Maze it is," I concluded while Marcus backed me up with a nod.

"Alright." Our elven commander met each of our gazes in turn. "Go eat something. Get some sleep. And then tomorrow, if we're lucky, we might be one step closer to ending this war."

We all nodded back at him. After replicating the gesture, he strode out into the dark evening. Faye followed, along with Malor and Zaina. Edward raised his eyebrows at Shade, who joined him a few seconds later, running a hand over my arm before leaving. When there were only two of us left, I raised my eyes from the map. Marcus smiled while striding closer.

"And now we just need to plan an ambush, right?" he said.

"Right."

"Any ideas on how to do it?"

An evil grin spread across my lips in reply.

This wasn't exactly my first ambush. I had planned and gotten trapped in enough of them to have several different versions of how to do it. It was my first time trying to ambush star elves, though, and I wouldn't pretend that it was without risk. On the contrary, this was probably going to be more dangerous than fighting on the front lines. But if it gave us a shot at victory, it was worth it. I lifted my head to stare at the tent walls, as if I could see through them to all the friends that I was constantly worrying about. By Nemanan, it was so damn worth the risk.

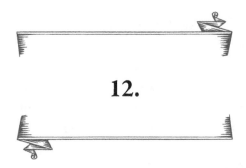

# 12.

A jumble of large gray rocks lay like a dark stain on the otherwise bright green grasslands. I squinted at it as we crept closer. It looked like a mountain that some giant had smashed apart and then just thrown the broken bits back haphazardly. Not exactly pretty. But a great place for an ambush.

"Remember," I said, keeping my voice low, even though the area around the Stone Maze was completely deserted. But it somehow felt wrong to talk too loudly when setting up an ambush. "Don't use your powers before the trap is set. We can't risk luring them here until everything is ready."

The others nodded in acknowledgement.

Farther east, the battle raged once more. I cast a glance at it over my shoulder, hoping that my other friends were safe, before turning back to the group of Ashaana following me. Lifting a hand, I pointed at the northern entrance to the Stone Maze, where we would sneak in to set everything up before putting on a rather impressive display of our powers to lure the star elves here.

Grass crunched next to me as Marcus fell into step beside me. The others split into pairs as well until we formed one long line. Nervous anticipation hung over our group when we left the grasslands behind and finally reached the Stone Maze. Drawing a soft breath, I took the first step into the narrow opening in the mountain of rocks.

Nothing moved in here. All the animals might have left the plains as well to avoid the war but at least out there, nature was still alive. Grass shifted and bushes swayed in the breeze. The few trees that dotted the landscape rustled when strong fall winds swept through them. But in here, nature didn't appear to be breathing at all.

Long shadows fell across the passageways as the tall stones blocked out the light from the morning sun. I studied the rough walls. No moss. No vines. Nothing. Only dark, jagged, uncompromising rock.

Up ahead, the path we followed twisted. Marcus and I exchanged a glance before creeping forward and peering around the corner. A slab of stone had fallen over the passage at some point and was still there so we would have to duck under it to get through, but at least it was still possible to use the path we had found marked on one of the maps Shade had brought from Pernula.

Marcus made to test the way first but I stopped him with a hand on his arm. When he turned back to me with raised eyebrows, I flashed him a grin.

"Ladies first," I said.

He huffed a laugh and shook his head but then bowed theatrically and motioned for me to proceed. I kept the grin on my face as I slid past him and approached the fallen stone. The rough surface was cool against my palms as I prodded it to make sure it wouldn't collapse on top of me when I snuck under it. A few bits of gravel clattered as they tumbled down the side but the road block appeared to be in an otherwise fairly unmovable state.

Bracing my hands on the stone, I edged under the dark slab. It remained wedged firmly between the walls when I straightened on the other side.

"It's clear," I whispered.

The words, though soft, seemed to echo through the maze. I suppressed the sudden urge to cringe at the noise I had produced and instead moved further in to let Marcus, Cileya, and the other Storm Casters clear the passage too.

When we were all on the other side, I waved a hand to indicate that we should get moving again. Pebbles clinked faintly somewhere, but other than that, everything remained silent as we moved deeper into the Stone Maze.

A fork in the road appeared before us.

"Which way?" Cileya asked quietly as we trailed to a halt.

The map hadn't indicated that the path would be splitting in two this soon. Tilting my head, I glanced up at the stretch of pale blue sky visible above the high stone walls. I couldn't see the sun, or any landmarks to gauge distance, but we hadn't walked that far yet. I returned my gaze to the branching passage and pursed my lips. The one leading to the right looked to widen out into some kind of circular area while the one continuing straight ahead stayed narrow.

"This one." I nodded at the smaller path that continued forwards. The other one was probably a dead end that hadn't been marked because it didn't lead anywhere. "We keep going straight."

Cileya nodded, as did Marcus, so I started out again. I didn't get far before panic crackled through me like a lightning bolt.

"Back!" I hissed.

Dark red mist curled along the rough stone floor. I slammed into Marcus as I backpedaled to get away from it.

"What–" he began.

"Hurry!" Twisting slightly, I put my hands on his broad chest and practically shoved him backwards.

Startled yelps rang out as he stumbled into the Storm Casters behind him but when he saw the dark red tendrils clawing their way towards us, his eyes widened and he started pushing the others back as well. My heart hammered in my chest as I kept my eye on the growing mist while backing away.

Cries of alarm rose from the back of our procession. I whipped my head around but before I could open my mouth to ask about it, I saw what had caused it. A curtain of dark red smoke filled the other end of the narrow passageway as well.

The star elves were here. They were already here. We had somehow been betrayed and they had gotten here before us so that they could trap us here in this claustrophobically narrow passageway with whatever chemical weapon was currently blocking off our escape routes. My pulse smattered in my ears.

Reason sliced through the numbing panic that threatened to turn me stupid.

"Into the side path!" I called above the rising dread that my companions were succumbing to as well. "Get into the side passage there and cluster at the back."

We already had a plan in case something like this happened. Only, I hadn't expected it to happen right now. The shock of realizing that the star elves were already here had thrown me but I was slowly wresting back control of the situation.

Boots scuffed against stone as our group hurried into the other opening. On both sides, the red mist had risen high between the walls and rolled towards us at a steady pace. I forced myself to continue taking steady steps back and not start shoving my way past my fellow Ashaana. Blowing it away with wind wouldn't work. Not here. Not in this narrow passageway. The force needed to get all traces of mist out would also make the stone corridor collapse on top of us. No. We had to do something else.

The two curtains of smoke had almost reached each other when everyone had finally made it into the wider space. Marcus and I backed into it as well with quick steps. It was indeed a circular stone room, for lack of a better word, with a dead end at the back. But it would actually work in our favor because we needed somewhere that would keep our backs protected while we dealt with the mist.

"Ready?" I asked.

Throwing a glance over my shoulder, I found all my companions standing in the shallow pool of water that had formed by the back wall. They nodded in confirmation. My boots produced wet splashes as I backed towards my friends while keeping one eye on the red mist that had started leaking into the room and the other on the item I drew out of my belt pouch.

"Now," I said, and hurled a small glass vial forward.

Glass shards skittered across the dry stones as it shattered against the ground a few strides before me. Still staring at the red mist, I came to a halt with my back against Cileya's chest while a fizzling sound rose.

Green mist shot into the air before sweeping out to form a barrier straight across the middle of the room. The waves of red rolled towards it. I forced myself to keep breathing as it crashed into our only protection. When the green haze turned purple, our group drew a collective sigh of relief.

"Thank the gods," Marcus whispered next to me.

A smile tugged at my lips. "Thank Haber."

"That too."

While Apothecary Haber's portable mist screen continued neutralizing the red threat before us, Marcus spread the word to get ready. We might have evaded their chemical weapon but the star elves were still here which meant that we would still have to fight our way out of here. I rolled my shoulders. With this many Ashaana, and in this wider room, we could use our wind to slam them against the stone walls and render them unconscious before they could attack. We had to time it right, though.

At last, the purple and red mist dissipated and where the red fog had been, a mass of elves now stood. The streaks of sunshine that made it down over the edges of the giant bowl we now occupied glinted off white and silver armor. I narrowed my eyes at them. Damn. They were wearing helmets, which would make knocking them unconscious a bit more difficult.

"Surrender," a steady voice said.

Irritation, mixed with disappointment, flowed through me at the sound of that voice, for it was a voice I knew very well by now. And though all the star elves' faces were half concealed by the white helmets, I found the source of the voice straight away. Hadraeth. Captain of the Queen's Guard. He had let us escape when we'd been captured by Queen Nimlithil, more than once, so I owed him. But more than that, I also kind of respected him. At least as much as one can respect someone who fights for one's enemy.

"It's been a while," I replied while nudging Marcus and Cileya, hoping they understood the order and relayed it to the others as well.

Hadraeth's dark violet eyes were hard and there was a long scar down his cheek that I hadn't seen before. "Surrender."

"Really?" I clicked my tongue. "I thought you would've figured it out by now. Surrendering isn't really my style." Right as he was about to open his mouth again, I yelled, "Now!"

Our entire group of Storm Casters, who had spread out into one long line, slammed their arms forward and blasted hurricane winds into the ranks of star elves.

Nothing happened.

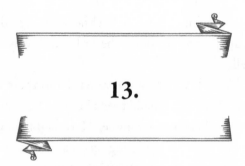

# 13.

Shock rippled through our line as we stared at our hands. And then towards the elves still standing in their gleaming armor on the other side of the room. Not a whisper of wind had blown across the dark stones. Nothing. I could feel the power inside me but I couldn't get it to do what I wanted.

Satisfied smiles stretched the lips of our enemies. I stared at Hadraeth.

"When we heard that a whole host of Ashaana had appeared, we had to find some way to counter your powers." Captain Hadraeth jerked his chin towards the sheet of water coating the stones we stood on. "What you see here is the result."

Marcus raised his powerful arms and slammed them forward again while Cileya squeezed her hand into a fist and jerked it down to summon lightning. Similar gestures were made by the rest of our group as well. Still nothing. I ignored the dread coiling in my stomach.

"You found a temporary way to block our powers," I said.

It wasn't a question and Hadraeth didn't bother confirming it but I knew it was the case. Then the only question was, how long would the block last. I glanced down at the water surrounding my boots. And was contact with the liquid required for it to work.

"This was your plan all along?" I continued while taking a small step forward. "The red mist was just a distraction to get us here. So that we would step into this little puddle of yours."

Another step forward. How in Nemanan's name had I not noticed it? Everywhere else was dry. Why would this specific spot be filled with water? Idiot. I edged another step forward.

"This will be used on all your friends soon," was all Hadraeth said.

My boots finally left the water. I slammed my arms forward. Snickering rose from some of the star elves before me but their captain just continued staring at me with hard eyes.

"As soon as you stepped in it, the effect started," he said. "There's no way out, so just come quietly."

Maybe I could stall them until it wore off. Cocking my head, I tried to think of something to say that would keep him distracted.

"If you really have a whole stash of this," I said, fixing the captain with a piercing stare, "why haven't you used it before now?" When he didn't respond, I continued. "This is all there is, isn't there?"

Hadraeth's eyes flicked to the side for a fraction of a second before he met my gaze again. Oh he was such a terrible liar. Man, he and Elaran were so similar in so many ways. I had even tried to teach Elaran to lie convincingly these past few months, though I couldn't say how much good it had done, but someone should've done the same for Hadraeth. That little tell had all but confirmed that this pool we were standing in was everything they had.

"Quit stalling," Captain Hadraeth snapped. "Now, surrender."

We couldn't. By all the gods, we couldn't surrender. If we did, they would take us straight to Queen Nimlithil and then they would torture us until we agreed to give up our magic. I risked a glance behind me to where Marcus and Cileya stood. The mountain elf remained silent but her shoulders were squared as if she was thinking the same thing. That determined expression was replicated by the other Storm Casters as well. Marcus gave me the shallowest of nods. A fight it was, then.

My hand shot up towards my shoulder holster but I didn't make it. Pain sliced through my face as an arrow fired from the left grazed my cheek. I froze. Blood ran down from the cut along my cheekbone. With my hand still hovering above my throwing knives, I stared at the ranks of star elves who now pointed drawn bows at us.

Groaning wood behind me told me that Cileya and some of the other elven Ashaana had drawn their bows as well, but the rest of our company didn't have ranged weapons. Here, trapped in this damn stone room, facing down a host of elven archers in full armor, we were at a severe disadvantage. Cold dread trailed its fingers down my spine. We were going to lose.

"Surrender," Captain Hadraeth pressed out between gritted teeth and pointed at the floor. "Now."

Bowstrings creaked as arrows were drawn back further and then several of them shifted to point straight at Marcus. I cast a panicked glance over my shoulder. Wood groaned again.

"Alright!" I called, and whipped my head back to Captain Hadraeth. "Alright. You've made your damn point." Slowly taking my hand from my throwing knives, I motioned for the others to stand down.

Holding my gaze, Hadraeth just stabbed a finger towards the ground again. I glared at him but kept my hands raised as I got down on my knees. The splashing sounds behind me informed me that the others were doing the same. My pulse smattered in my ears. I had to find some other way out of this. Maybe we could somehow slow them down on our way back to camp so that our powers returned before we became lost beyond all hope.

Shining armor glinted in the sunlight as the throng of star elves shifted. They let their bows slacken but kept the arrows nocked as a few of them pushed through the ranks to approach us. I swept my gaze over them.

Or was it a mistake to let them take us? Perhaps we should've just made our final stand right here. Worry gnawed at my chest as a couple of star elves broke from the group.

*This was a mistake.* The thought clanged through me. I should fight. I had to –

White and silver shapes flew through the air. My brain refused to process thoughts as I stared at what was unfolding before me. Heavy thuds and metallic clattering filled the whole space as the mass of star elves slammed into the stone wall on my right. At the far left stood a lone figure, also clad in white and silver.

"Don't just stand there!" she snapped. "Get your weapons. Attack!"

I blinked, dumbfounded, at the female star elf who sent another burst of wind into the crumpled ranks of elven soldiers in white armor.

"Maesia?" I blurted out.

The star elf Storm Caster who had helped me escape the City of Glass shot me a satisfied smile before slamming her arms forward again. By the wall on my right, Hadraeth and the others had been struggling to their feet but were now once again shoved down by barreling winds.

"Get ready to fight!" Maesia called again.

The order appeared to snap us all out of our stupor because steel rang and feet slapped against wet stone as the Ashaana behind me charged at the star elf soldiers.

Yanking out a throwing knife, I hurled it at the closest elf. It bounced off the piece of well-crafted armor guarding his throat and tumbled to the ground with a metallic pinging. Huh. Up close and personal it was, then.

Besides, they had more archers than us, so we had to turn this into a melee as fast as possible to make sure they couldn't use their ranged weapons. I pulled the hunting knives from the small of my back and ran straight into the commotion.

Steel glinted above me as the elven soldier before me got to his feet and swung his sword at my head. I ducked under it and swiped at his side. The blade left a deep rut but failed to pierce the hard material of his breastplate. His answering elbow to my back forced the breath from my lungs and sent me stumbling deeper into the fray.

Twisting and bending, I barely managed to escape the onslaught of swords around me. I swore as I parried a swift thrust. There were a lot more of them than there were of us and not all of us were close-range fighters. Not to mention that they all wore armor.

Marcus bellowed a battle cry and swung his heavy longsword into their ranks, forcing several of them to jump back to avoid being cleaved in two. I saw my chance to catch them unawares and stabbed towards an unprotected neck. The blow fell short as I was yanked backwards by a fist buried in the back of my shirt.

A small cry of pain escaped my lips as I slammed back first into the rough stone wall behind me, and only my highly developed instincts had me throwing up my knives to block the coming sword. Metal ground against metal as I stared at my attacker across our locked blades. Captain Hadraeth glared back at me.

"You should've surrendered," he ground out.

"And you shouldn't even be here!" I let his sword slide off my knives and stabbed at his neck again. "Do you think Princess Illeasia is proud of you? Do you think she will love you for rounding up her friends to be tortured, huh?"

When hurt and anger flashed in his dark violet eyes, I knew I'd struck deep and true.

"Shut your mouth." He blocked my blades and began an attack so swift that I could barely see his sword flash through the air, let alone block it. "You don't know anything about it."

"I know enough," I spat back and then hissed when his sword sliced through my shirt and the skin of my upper arm. "When are you gonna figure out that you're fighting for the wrong damn side?"

"Serving my queen is the right side," he snapped and swung so hard at my head that I was forced to duck completely.

Steel whizzed through the air above my head but my back slammed into the rough stones behind me again, cutting off my ability to evade further. If I could just use my powers, I could force him to fight in the dark and then he would stand no chance of winning. But without them, I couldn't. On the other side of the stone room, Maesia was sending lightning bolts zapping into the ranks of star elves but she kept the black clouds around herself because she knew as well as I did that the dark smoke would blind us too now. Damn.

Steel sang before me. I met his sword. Barely. My muscles shook as Captain Hadraeth pushed his blade towards me, forcing my knives backwards while I couldn't back away with the stone wall behind me. The sharp edge moved closer with every second. Letting out a frustrated shout, I rallied my strength and shoved it forwards again. He flicked his wrist. Sparks flew as my hunting knives slid off his blade and my arms tumbled downwards at the sudden lack of resistance. I sucked in a hiss as cold steel pressed into my exposed throat.

Captain Hadraeth leveled dark eyes dripping with command on me. "Surrender."

Behind his shoulder, the fight was still going but we were losing. Our more inexperienced close-range fighters were already on their knees and the ones still fighting were quickly being overwhelmed. I flicked my gaze from the sharp point resting at the base of my throat to the captain before me. His grip on the sword was firm, his posture confident. He knew they had already won.

"Now," he ordered.

A disappointed laugh ripped from my throat. Holding his commanding gaze, I bared my teeth but let my knives fall to the ground. They clanked against the stones next to me. He lifted the hilt of the sword slightly, angling the blade downwards. I understood the order straight away but still took a couple of seconds to glare at him before lowering myself to my knees. The point of his blade stayed at the base of my throat the whole way down.

"I hope you spend every second of every day for the rest of your life regretting this moment," I said quietly.

"You—"

A shout rang out. And then one of the star elves guarding the kneeling Storm Casters toppled backwards with a gray shaft sticking out of his chest. Whizzing projectiles filled the air and mingled with the cries of alarm that echoed between the stones.

Hadraeth whirled around to find the hidden threat and was forced to throw himself backwards to avoid another gray arrow. I seized the opportunity to roll out of reach of his sword. Jagged rocks dug into my back and gravel scraped against my skin but I managed to get away.

"Retreat!" Captain Hadraeth bellowed. "Retreat!"

Crouching, with one hand brandishing his sword to fend off the rain of arrows, he hauled his men back towards the mouth of the stone room. Every time someone tried to drag a Storm Caster with them, they found the torrent of arrows focused on them until they abandoned the effort and sprinted back into the Stone Maze. Captain Hadraeth met my gaze one last time before he disappeared down the passageway and I couldn't for the life of me decipher what swirled in his eyes.

"Ydras!" Cileya called, utter surprise on her face.

Then she tipped her head back and laughed, her red-golden hair cascading down her back and swinging with the movement. I tilted my head up as well and studied the rocks above us. All around the edge of the bowl we were stranded in, dark figures had appeared. They were all dressed in various shades of gray, making them almost impossible to spot until they stood up and became silhouetted against the bright sky beyond.

"Are you unharmed?" Ydras called back, his ice-blue eyes still fixed on Cileya.

"Yes," she answered, chipping for breath and shaking her head at the miracle that had saved us at the last second.

"Good. Then get going. We'll guard you from above until you're out."

"You heard the man," Marcus said. Flapping his powerful arms, he began herding our flock of Ashaana towards the exit. "Hurry before they come back."

After snatching up my hunting knives again, I did the same. Silver hair flowed in the corner of my eye. I reached out and grabbed Maesia's arm before she could slip past.

"Thank you," I said.

"You're welcome." Her dark violet eyes turned longing as she looked at the other star elf Storm Caster, the one I'd seen in the White Mountains, who had stopped to wait for her by the exit. "I figured if there was ever a time to blow my cover, it was now."

Following her gaze, I nodded. I wondered what the two of them were to each other, but I decided that it was none of my business, so I just released her arm and gave her a small smile. She nodded back before disappearing into the passageways with the silver-haired elf.

When everyone was at last out of the circular stone room and running down the path towards the northern exit again, I followed as well. As I weaved my way between the stone walls, I cast another glance up at Ydras.

"I thought you left the outside world alone," I called up at him.

The mountain elf elder continued sweeping his gaze around the area while nimbly leaping from rock to rock above me. "I also told you that we always back our own people." A slight smile tugged at the corner of his lips as he flicked his gaze from me to the redheaded mountain elf running ahead of me. "Cileya, the brave stubborn fool, decided to go to war. So we did too."

I chuckled. "Stubbornness is such a good quality."

Ydras barked a laugh. "You *would* say that, wouldn't you."

"How did you even find us?"

"We left after Cileya and the other Ashaana so we only arrived at camp this morning. They said you were here. So we went after you."

"I meant, how did you find us inside this impossible-to-navigate maze of rocks?"

He arched an eyebrow at me while still keeping his observant eyes moving across the stones. "We *are* mountain elves."

"Right." I huffed a laugh before turning back to him, my voice serious again. "Ydras?"

"Hmm?"

"Thank you."

A smile spread across his lips. "Stubborn fools."

Another chuckle bounced off the rough stone walls while I continued through the narrow passage and towards the grasslands outside. Stubborn fool I might be, but I was so glad I wasn't the only one. I made a mental note to buy Maesia, Cileya, and Ydras a drink when all this was over.

This mission had been a bust from the start, because Queen Nimlithil hadn't shown up herself to find us, but it had almost turned into a downright disaster. If Maesia and the mountain elves hadn't shown up when they did, we would've been heading towards certain doom by now. I was very grateful that we weren't but I was also annoyed that my plan hadn't worked. We couldn't try the same thing again because the element of surprise was gone.

A swath of pale blue sky appeared at the end of the passageway. I glared at the bright colors mocking my irritation. We had to find another way to kill both Nimlithil and Aldeor the White. Or our little miracle today wouldn't matter. Booming cannons and clashing steel echoed across the plains as we finally left the Stone Maze behind. I stared towards the battle. Because if we didn't, we would all be dead anyway.

# 14.

The throbbing from the cut on my cheek and arm was drowned out by the exhaustion coursing through my body when I at last stumbled into the war tent later that evening. Nodding a wordless greeting to King Edward and Malor, I slumped into the nearest chair. The magic blocking chemicals that the star elves had used hadn't worn off until well past midday but I had joined the fight as soon as we got back to camp anyway. Now, both my powers and my body were telling me that I couldn't keeping this up. I promptly ignored them.

"How are you holding up?" Marcus asked, glancing down at me.

"I'll be fine." I looked him over. "You?"

"Same."

Despite the wide smile on his face, I could tell that he was as tired as I was. He and the other Storm Casters were using their powers to the limit as well in order to stem the constant tide of enemies and rain of boulders. If we kept using this much, this frequently, we wouldn't be able to fully refill our energy reserves. But if we didn't, our lines could break.

Ydras had followed Marcus into the tent and now stood close to the wall with his hands behind his back. Zaina arrived a minute later. Then Shade, who ran scrutinizing eyes over me before taking up position on my other side. I didn't bother telling him that I was fine because he already knew that I was lying.

"Our western flank almost caved today," Elaran muttered by way of greeting as he stalked into the tent with Faye close behind.

The Queen of Tkeideru nodded to Ydras, who replicated the gesture. The mountain elf elder had met everyone in other parts of camp earlier so there was no need for introductions.

"We could pull some Storm Casters from the coast," Marcus waved a large hand in Zaina's direction, "since you can keep them busy with your cannons. We could use them to reinforce the western flank."

Elaran drew himself up in front of the map-covered table and crossed his arms. For a moment, he just stared at the light flickering across the paper. Everyone except me was standing around the table so it was more than a little embarrassing to remain seated alone, but with my special missions, I had been going at it harder than the others so I decided that conserving strength was more important than my pride. Even though it went against my instincts.

"Alright," Elaran said at last. "Do it."

King Edward cleared his throat and took a half step forward. "We're also running low on bullets."

The young king wasn't a fighter but he had a shrewd mind and had taken it upon himself to oversee our stores of arrows, bullets, food, and other supplies while the rest of us were out on the front lines.

Elaran gave him a grim nod. "I'll tell the soldiers to make them count." He shifted his gaze to Ydras. "But with your archers bolstering our own, we should be able to even out the impact of fewer bullets."

After the blue-eyed mountain elf had nodded in acknowledgement, Elaran turned to me and Marcus. The rest of the room did the same. We had only had time to inform them that the ambush had failed, but hadn't been able to go into any great detail on what exactly had occurred. It appeared as though it was now time for that.

"What happened?" was all Elaran said.

Drawing a deep breath, I got ready to explain but before I could start, Marcus beat me to it. I sent him a grateful smile as I slumped back in the chair again. The tent was silent while everyone listened to his story.

"Seems like we have more than archers to thank you for," Faye said to Ydras once Marcus was finished.

"We always back our own people," Ydras replied but inclined his head to the silver-haired queen.

Wood creaked as Elaran braced both palms on the table and leaned against it. His auburn hair slid over his shoulder and hung like a gleaming curtain in front of his face. A deep sigh sent the papers below him fluttering in distress.

"So we have a spy," he said, still not looking up from the table.

Shade's dark brows narrowed slightly. "It would appear so."

"A spy?" Zaina cut in. "Considering their pale glittering hair, I'd assume any star elves would stand out like beacons in this camp."

"It doesn't have to be a star elf." King Edward shrugged. "They could just send in some random human soldier from one of their armies. With the right clothes, we'd never know the difference."

"So what do we do?" Marcus asked.

Silence hung heavy over our war council. Zaina shifted on her feet, making the curved sword at her hip sway, while Faye kept her eyes fixed on Elaran's still bowed head. Towards the back, Ydras continued watching us in silence.

"I could have my assassins look into it," Shade offered. "Have them scout out the camp at night while our soldiers are sleeping to see who is behaving suspiciously."

"Do it." Elaran at last lifted his head. Running a hand through his hair, he pushed it back behind his pointed ear and met Shade's gaze. "But do it in shifts. The ones who are looking for the spy at night don't fight the next morning. They need to sleep and we can't afford mistakes because of exhaustion."

Shade nodded in acknowledgement. Faye was about to say something when Malor spoke for the first time during this meeting.

"Remember the objective," he said. Sweeping reddish eyes through the tent, he met each of our gazes. "Kill Nimlithil. Kill Aldeor."

"We know," Faye snapped. "But how? Our attempt today backfired. She didn't even go herself, let alone call for her dragon."

The muscled advisor only looked back at her with steady eyes, not in the least ruffled by her tone.

"We've gotta make Queen Nimlithil desperate," Zaina mused. "Make her think she's gonna lose the war if she doesn't call in that dragon."

"If we were capable of winning this war, we would be doing that already," Faye said, her words frank but not unkind.

Wood creaked as I straightened in the chair. "What if we give her what she wants?"

"And what's that?" Faye said.

"Magic-wielders." Before they could tell me that we'd already been down this road before, I barreled on. "If I let myself be captured by her, she might send for Aldeor so that I can give my magic to him when I complete the ritual."

"Absolutely not!" Shade and Elaran snapped in unison.

"That seems like an unnecessarily dangerous plan," Edward said before the assassin and the grumpy elf could scold me some more.

A scowl settled on my own face as I waved a hand around the room. "What other plan have you got for getting the dragon here then?"

Marcus opened his mouth but then frowned and closed it again. The sound of a blacksmith's hammer somewhere outside was the only thing breaking the silence that had once more settled over our tent.

"Do you..." I began, staring straight at the muscled senior advisor across the table.

Malor's gaze slid to me.

"You said earlier you and Queen Nimlithil have a complicated history," I began. "Do you know...? I mean, if we killed her, do you think Aldeor would come out on his own? You know, to get revenge."

He drummed his fingers on his arm for a few seconds. "Yes. Yes, he would. Nimlithil and Aldeor have been companions for a long time. He wouldn't let her death go unanswered."

"Alright, so then doing the first solves the second."

Faye raised her eyebrows at me. "No, doing the first gets the dragon out. It doesn't solve how we're supposed to kill him."

Fair point. I rubbed my temples. "Can we just worry about that after Her Star Glittering Majesty is dead?"

The Queen of Tkeideru barked a laugh and tipped her head from side to side as if considering. Leather creaked as Marcus turned and stared down at me with an incredulous look on his face.

"Oh, sure." He chuckled and shook his head. "Let's just bait an angry dragon to come and attack us without actually making a plan for how to kill it."

Before I could answer, Zaina shrugged and waved a lazy hand around the room. "Between my cannons, the wood elf and mountain elf archers, and your Storm Casters, I'm sure we'll figure it out."

Soft chuckling spread through the room at the pirate's confident proclamation. I met Marcus' baffled gaze and tipped my hand in Zaina's direction as if to say 'what she said.' After another few seconds of bewildered staring, Marcus let out an exasperated laugh as well.

His golden-brown eyes twinkled as he looked at me. "I forgot how normal stuff like this is to you."

I flashed him a mischievous grin in reply because I didn't want to admit that dealing with dragons was far outside my comfort zone and not something I considered normal. Clothes rustled faintly by the tent wall as Ydras uncrossed his arms and took a step closer to the table. Candlelight cast dancing shadows over his grim face as he swept those ice-blue eyes over everyone.

"What's your plan for killing Queen Nimlithil then?" he asked.

"She won't be anywhere near the front lines, and based on what happened today," Shade flicked his gaze between me and Marcus, "it seems unlikely that she'll leave the safety of her camp no matter what we bait her with."

"How do we even know she's here?" Edward added with a shrug in his brother's direction. "We know her guards are here but we haven't actually seen her at all. And like you said, she didn't take our bait today. What if she isn't even here? What if she's still back in her castle?"

He did have a point. I had kind of assumed that Nimlithil would be here to oversee everything, just like she had been when they conquered Sker, but there was no guarantee that she would do the same this time too. After all, the fall of Sker had involved politics and scheming. This, on the other hand, was an all-out war.

"She's here."

We all jerked up and turned to Elaran. The grumpy elf crossed his arms but refused to meet anyone's gaze. When he didn't offer any further explanation, Faye and I exchanged a glance.

"How do you know?" she asked.

For a long while, Elaran remained silent, his yellow eyes fixed on the flickering candle on the table. Just when I thought he wasn't going to answer, he lifted his gaze and heaved a sigh.

"Because I went to her camp."

"What?" Shade demanded. "When the hell did you do that?"

"The first night after we got here."

"No wonder you let Storm off the hook so easily after she snuck out on her own. You'd already done the same thing." Shade raised his eyebrows expectantly. "When were you planning on telling us about this?"

Elaran cut the assassin a glare. "When it became necessary."

"What were you trying to do?" King Edward interrupted before the argument could get out of hand.

Winds ripped at the tent walls and footsteps outside rose and fell while silence once again descended on our war council.

"I went there to see if I could... meet someone," Elaran said at last.

*Oh. Ohh.* Of course. He had gone there to see if Princess Illeasia was there and to talk to her if she was.

"I couldn't get close enough to... accomplish my mission. But I saw Queen Nimlithil. From a distance. She's here." He pointed to a spot on the map where a grove and a stream flanked a bit of open field. "The star elves' camp is separate from the other armies. She's staying there with her guards."

"Alright, so we know where she is," Zaina picked up smoothly. "How do we get her to come out?"

"We don't," Shade said. "We come to her."

Edward drew back a little. "You mean...?"

"Yeah. We assassinate her in her own camp."

"That's a risky move, boy," Malor cut in, his dark brows furrowed and his gaze fixed on Shade.

"Of course it is. But this is war. Everything is risky." With a firm set to his jaw, Shade drew himself up to his full height. "Which is why I will be the one to do it."

I shot to my feet. The chair wobbled precariously behind me but remained upright as I whirled on the assassin and leveled a hard stare on him. "Oh, I don't think so."

He grabbed my chin and stared down at me with steady eyes that glittered in the golden light from the flames. "I think you're forgetting the part where I don't take orders from you."

Glaring up at him, I said nothing. How many times had *I* told *him* that over the years? Damn him for throwing my own words back in my face. He winked at me as if he had read my thoughts before releasing his grip on my jaw.

"I agree with Storm," Edward said. "Send someone from your guild, but you can't go yourself. You're my brother. Not to mention the High King of Pernula. You're too important to risk."

"I'm also the Master of the Assassins' Guild." His eyes were soft as he turned to look at his little brother, but the voice that filled the tent was full of command. "Not just an assassin, the *Master* of the Assassins' Guild. There's a reason that I was the one who managed to claim that title. I'm better than everyone else in my guild." There was no bragging, no arrogance, in his words. "If this mission is to succeed, we can't afford to send anyone else."

The words clanged through my hollow chest. Deep down, I knew he was right. If anyone stood a chance of assassinating the Queen of Tkeister, it was him. But unfortunately, that didn't stop my cold black heart from screaming that this was a horrible idea. I was apparently not the only one who felt that way because the whole tent seemed to suck in a collective breath in order to protest.

"I have to plan," Shade cut off before that happened. He shifted his gaze to Elaran. "I'm going to need to know everything you saw when you were at their camp."

For a moment, the auburn-haired elf looked like he was about to start arguing with him about the stupidity of this mission but then he just drew his eyebrows down and gave him a grave nod.

"Are you sure–" Edward began.

"Yes," Shade interrupted and swept hard eyes through the room. "This is our shot at winning the war. At winning before every single soldier from Keutunan is dead." His gaze flicked between me and Marcus. "Before your people are hunted to extinction." A glance to Elaran, Faye, Zaina, and Ydras. "A shot to win before we have to watch our friends and family get turned into empty husks." Finally, his eyes settled on Malor. "Before the whole world is destroyed beyond repair."

No one said anything. Because we all knew he was right. When no more protests were voiced, he nodded and strode towards the exit.

"I have to go get ready," he said to no one in particular. Stopping with his hand on the tent flap, he cast a quick look back at us over his shoulder. "If I'm not back by morning... consider me a casualty of war."

And with that, he was gone. I stared at the swinging piece of cloth while cold dread coiled inside me like venomous snakes. Drawing deep breaths, I fought the nausea that threatened to have me throw up all over this pretty map.

He had to come back. I'd sworn it before the war started. I would wade through rivers of blood and sell my soul to every demon in hell to make sure he survived. But now he was about to walk right into mortal danger, and there was nothing I could do about it. Swallowing against the panic clawing its way up my throat, I stared at the empty spot where he'd been standing only minutes before. He had to come back. He had to.

# 15.

His chest rose and fell in a steady rhythm. I stared at the pale scars decorating his skin, my gaze tracing the curves and jagged edges all the way until they disappeared below the sheets. He had survived so much already. He had to survive this too.

After Shade had grilled Elaran for information about the star elves' camp and gotten everything else ready, he had set aside two hours to sleep before leaving. Much easier to kill someone when you weren't fighting exhaustion too, he had said. Which was true, of course. He had trusted me to wake him after two hours, and though I was very tempted not to wake him at all, I had promised him, and I would do it. Glancing at the small clock on the table, I drew in a shuddering breath. It was time.

The mattress creaked and shifted below me as I leaned over and placed a hand on his arm. His eyes shot open as soon as my fingers brushed his skin. Rolling over, he blinked at me.

"You've geared up for battle," he said.

It hadn't been a question but I nodded anyway.

While he had slept, I had gotten dressed in my most assassination-friendly clothes and strapped on a whole arsenal of weapons and tools. Because if he was going on that damn suicide mission, then I was too.

"I'm going with you," I said.

A hint of sadness, and something else, fluttered in his eyes. However, before I could identify it he sat up and swung his legs over the side of the bed, turning his back on me. His muscles shifted as he pushed himself up and strode towards the neat piles of clothes and weapons waiting for him.

"No, you're not," he said, picking up a pair of black pants and pulling them on.

"I thought you and I agreed long ago that both of us are capable of taking care of ourselves, so if this is you trying to protect me from–"

"It's not. I have to go alone." He paused after buckling his belt and threw me a quick glance but his face was an unreadable mask. "Because if you come, you'll just..."

When he trailed off and didn't reply, I connected the dots on my own. "I'll just get in your way," I finished.

"Yeah."

I swallowed my wounded pride and nodded because I knew he was right. Being a thief, I was skilled in the art of sneaking, and my more murderous side was perfect for assassinations but no matter how much I tried to deny it, I was nowhere near Shade's level. I drew my legs up until I sat cross-legged on the bed and continued watching him dress.

Flickering candlelight played over his lethal body. I studied the ridges of his abs while he strapped daggers to his skin using custom-made holsters.

"Do you want to know how the Assassins' Guild chooses its next Guild Master?" he asked as he slid home a couple of blades in the straps along his ribs.

That was something I had asked him about before. More than once. He had never answered. Had claimed it was guild secrets. What it meant that he was offering me the truth now, I didn't want to think too long about.

"Yeah," I answered.

Kneeling down, he got to work on securing knives inside his boots. "When the current Guild Master dies, we hold a competition. Everyone who wants to claim the title can sign up for it. The last man standing becomes the new Master."

"The one who wins the competition?"

Shade finished lacing up his boots and straightened. "No." Twisting slightly, he met my gaze and held it. "The one who is still alive at the end."

My mouth dropped open. I blinked at him but couldn't think of anything to say.

Breaking my gaze, he picked up the neatly folded shirt and pulled it over his head. "All the other assassins who wanted the title... I slaughtered my way through them until they were all dead and I was the only one left." He tugged the black fabric over his concealed blades and met my eyes again. "That is how I became Guild Master."

The sheer skill and endurance it must have taken to accomplish something like that was insane. No wonder all other assassins obeyed their Guild Master without question. After a display of power like that, even I would think twice about crossing someone with those kinds of skills.

"So you see," Shade went on, stopping before me in front of the bed. Placing a hand on my jaw, he tilted my head up and locked eyes with me. "I do know what I'm doing."

I reached up and grabbed a hold of the black fabric of his shirt. Still not breaking his gaze, I pulled him towards me until his lips met mine in a steady kiss. His warm breath caressed my skin when I drew back slightly.

"I know," I breathed against his mouth. "I know you do."

He gripped my wrists and pulled me to my feet before locking me in a tight embrace. My arms circled his muscled back. For a while, we just stood there, sharing each other's warmth. With my ear against his chest, I could hear his heart beating its steady rhythm.

Then, Shade ran a hand over my hair, kissed the top of my head, and stepped back. The cold that swept in when we broke apart was so palpable I almost shivered.

"I'll be back before the sun is up," Shade said, striding back towards the table. Steel sang as he pushed his twin swords into the sheaths across his back. "If I'm not, then I'm already dead, and it will be up to you to find another way to kill Nimlithil."

Crossing my arms, I arched an eyebrow in his direction. "As if you'd ever allow the God of Death to claim you when you could come back to camp and have people worship you for killing our greatest enemy." Shaking my head, I huffed a laugh. "I'll see you in the morning."

A lopsided smile tugged at his lips.

Searing panic and freezing dread threatened to shred my body into bloody pieces but I buried it far out of sight and shot him a confident smile. Some light returned to his grave eyes as he smiled back. Then he was striding across the room.

When he was almost at the tent flap, he paused and looked back at me.

"Thank you," he said. "For not doubting me. And for not saying goodbye."

And then he walked out, taking my scarred heart with him.

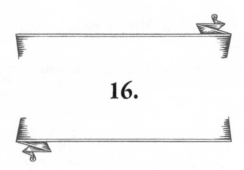

# 16.

I didn't sleep that night. After he walked out of our tent, I remained staring at the dark cloth wall for hours. Silent. Unmoving. There could have been a meteor strike in the middle of camp and I wouldn't have noticed. I didn't even remember sitting down on the bed, but I must have done it at some point because I was pulled out of my trance by pain throbbing through my fingers. Apparently, I'd been gripping the sheets so hard for so long that my muscles had started protesting. Relaxing my grip, I leaned my head back against the headboard and continued waiting for Shade to walk back inside.

Metal clanked. I jerked awake and whipped my head around. According to the clock ticking on the desk, I had dozed off for a couple of hours. Still in my fighting gear, I shoved away the tangle of blankets and shot out of bed. It was still empty. I stalked towards the exit and shouldered open the tent flap.

Brisk winds met me outside, along with the pale light of dawn chasing away the final strands of darkness. A shrill ringing started in my ears as I stared at the sun that was beginning to peek over the horizon, while my mind finally caught up with what I'd seen on the clock. It was morning.

My heart leaped into a furious beat but I shook my head. Shade had probably just gone to see Elaran first. To give a report on what had happened. Working my tongue around my parched mouth, I started towards Elaran's tent. I only made it three strides before green fabric rustled and an auburn-haired elf stalked outside.

"He's sleeping?" Elaran asked and nodded towards our tent.

Relief flooded through me. "You've seen him?"

He jerked to a halt. Frozen on the grass, he flicked his gaze between me and the dark tent behind me. "No. He's not with you?"

My voice refused to cooperate so I only managed to shake my head. Boots crunched in the grass to my right. I whipped my head towards the sound, hoping to find an assassin being unusually loud as he approached us. The disappointment must have been visible on my face because Marcus, who appeared to have jogged here from his own tent, trailed to a halt. Concerned eyes flicked between me and Elaran.

"He's not back?"

"No," Elaran answered for me.

"That doesn't mean anything," Marcus tried in a voice that I think was supposed to sound comforting. "It probably just took a bit longer to get it done. He's probably on his way back right now and–"

"Elaran."

Whirling around, I found Faelar standing a few strides away. I hadn't even heard him approach. But then again, it was hard to hear anything over the ringing in my ears.

"There's movement at the front," the blond elf continued.

"They're attacking?" Elaran demanded.

"No." Faelar's gaze passed over me before returning to Elaran. "Two star elves."

I didn't even bother looking at the rest of them before taking off towards the ridge. All around me, the camp was getting ready for another long day of fighting that would start about an hour after sunrise, as it always did. Metal clanked as armor was donned and steel sang as grim-faced soldiers sharpened their blades. I barely noticed any of it. Blue and black and green were a blur around me as I hurtled through the mass of tents.

When the edge of the hill finally became visible across the wide stretch of grass, my heart was beating so hard in my chest that I was sure it would break out of my ribcage. Our sentries were posted along it as usual but I set course for the two figures in the middle. The twins. Haela and Haemir had their bows drawn and pointed towards something down the hill.

My other friends had apparently also sprinted here with me because we all skidded to a halt together. Still keeping their eyes fixed on the grassy field below, the twins nodded towards elves in white armor.

"Down there," Haela said.

Two star elves were indeed approaching our camp. They had no weapons drawn but they each carried a long shield crafted of the same white material as their armor. The silver details cut into the design gleamed in the early morning light as they moved, keeping the shields in front of them.

When they reached the invisible line in the grass that our armies had held these past days, they stopped. That infernal ringing in my ears grew louder with each second. There was movement behind their shields. Then, they straightened and started walking backwards at a much quicker pace than they had approached at. The pale light of dawn glinted off the steel they left behind.

My head went silent. Utterly, devastatingly silent.

Down there in the grass were two swords. They had been driven into the dirt at an angle, so that they formed an X. I stared at them, and I wasn't sure I was breathing. Even from this distance, I recognized those blades. They were Shade's twin swords.

"Don't!" Elaran snapped.

"Why not?" Haela hissed back. "Let me kill them."

"They might take it out on him."

At that, I managed to tear my gaze from the swords buried in the grass and turn towards the rest of my companions. Haela was baring her teeth at the retreating star elves and appeared to be still debating whether to put arrows through their eyes regardless of what Elaran had said. Next to her, Haemir had lowered his bow but his eyes tracked the blond elf now descending the hill to retrieve the swords. I dragged my gaze to Elaran.

His face was cool and impassive as he watched Faelar pull the blades from the dirt but his eyes... There was enough fury and devastation crackling in his eyes to shatter the world. I spun on my heel and stalked towards camp.

A strong hand encircled my arm before I had taken two steps.

"Where are you going?" Marcus demanded.

"To get him back." I yanked my arm from his grip and started out again, but his other hand shot out and held me firmly in place.

"Stop! Think!" His eyes were pleading as they searched my face. Throwing out his free hand, he gestured towards where Faelar was climbing the hill with Shade's swords. "This is a trap. They did this because they want you to charge right in there."

There was nothing kind, nothing human, in my face as I stared back at him. "I don't care."

Blond hair flowed in the morning breeze as Faelar returned and came to a halt next to me. Wordlessly, he offered me the swords. I glared at Marcus until he released my arm. Swallowing, I reached for the blades. My fingers felt numb as they wrapped around the hilts. The material bit my palms like ice with its lack of Shade's touch. I turned the swords until the flat of them faced the sun. Dark stains splattered the gleaming steel. Blood.

*If I'm not back by morning, consider me a casualty of war.* That was what he had said. *If I'm not back before the sun is up, then I'm already dead.* My head was still silent. So silent that the lack of sound was smothering my mind.

"If they went to all this trouble to taunt us with the swords," Haemir said quietly, "it's possible that he is still alive."

Still alive. Still alive. The words clanged through the empty darkness in my head.

"Of course he's still alive," Haela snapped.

The sheer certainty in those words yanked me back from the edge of the abyss. My eyes came back into focus. I tightened my grip on Shade's swords and leveled hard eyes on my friends.

"I'm getting him back," I declared.

"You'll be walking straight into a trap," Haemir said.

"I know."

His yellow eyes were sad but he only nodded. As did Haela. On my other side, Marcus shook his head.

"Don't do this," he said. "Please. I know that saying this makes me a bastard, but don't do this. Shade is the Master of the Assassins' Guild and he had surprise on his side *and they still caught him.* This time, they'll know you're coming. They'll be waiting for you. All it will accomplish is get two people killed instead of one." He threw out a desperate hand towards Elaran. "Tell her!"

Elaran had been staring at the swords in my hands but now he lifted his gaze. I felt the weight of these decisions pressing down on him. Completely abandon a brother in the hands of our enemies or send another friend in there to most likely die with him.

The Commander of the Joint Forces locked eyes with me. "Go get him."

A grateful smile spread across my lips as I nodded. Of course Elaran would never leave any of us behind.

Haela opened her mouth to no doubt declare that she was coming with me but before she could get a single word out, Elaran cut her off.

"No." He swept eyes dripping with authority through our group. "No one else. They came so close to breaking our lines yesterday. We need everyone we can get to hold them off." When Haela tried to protest, he cut her off again. "Rescuing Shade won't matter if we lose this war."

She blew out a frustrated sigh. "Fine." After sticking the arrow she'd been holding back in her quiver, she clapped a hand on my shoulder. "Go bring him home."

When she just sauntered back towards camp without another word, I understood why Shade had been so glad that I hadn't said goodbye. Saying goodbye meant doubt that we would see each other again. But Haela didn't doubt it. She was certain that I would come back with Shade. And I needed that confidence.

"Be careful," Haemir said and squeezed my arm before hurrying to catch up with his sister.

Leather groaned softly as Marcus reached up and raked his fingers through his hair. "I won't apologize for wanting you to be safe." He blew out a deep sigh and then met my gaze. "But I'm sorry if I came across as cold. I do care about Shade." A small smile tugged at his lips. "And I would be doing the same stupid bullheaded thing that you're doing right now, if it had been one of my people."

"I know," I replied with a sad smile.

He drew me into a tight embrace. For a moment, we just stood there. Then, he pressed a quick kiss to the top of my head and stepped back.

"Go be a wildfire," he said, and then strode away.

Faelar had drifted further down the ridge to give Elaran privacy to say whatever it was he was about to tell me. I watched Marcus disappear across the grass before turning to the auburn-haired elf in front of me. With arms crossed and eyebrows drawn down, he studied me in silence.

I flipped Shade's swords in my hands and held them out to Elaran hilt first. "Take care of them until I return."

He knew I didn't just mean the swords.

Uncrossing his arms, Elaran reached out and wrapped strong hands around the hilts. "Always."

"I'll be back soon."

"Yes, you will." The words were both a promise and a threat.

I nodded and turned to leave, but then stopped when Elaran spoke again.

"If you can..." He trailed off. "If you see Illeasia... could you just... make sure she's safe?"

Twisting back around, I held his gaze. "Of course."

Elaran nodded once and then cleared his throat. "Alright. I'll see you soon."

Before I could reply, he stalked across the grass towards where Faelar waited. The blond elf gave me a slow nod as well.

Across the hill, our soldiers were getting ready to march onto the frontlines again. While I moved towards the bustling camp spread out before me, I wondered if I was ever going to see it again. Ever going to see my friends in it again. Wondered what Faye and the others I hadn't said goodbye to would think if I never returned. What Edward would think.

He still didn't know that Shade hadn't come back. That awful selfish part of me was glad that I didn't have to be the one to tell him that. I wasn't sure I could handle the heartbreak it would cause. The devastation in Elaran's eyes had almost fractured the tiny piece of me that still clung to sanity and I would need my wits if I was to succeed in bringing Shade back. Blowing out a slow breath, I tried to pull myself together.

A tall figure stepped out between the rows of tents. I trailed to a halt and studied the assassin blocking my path. Man-bun. Shade's second-in-command.

"You coming with me?" I said.

"No," he replied. "I'm here to prevent you from leaving."

"Excuse me?"

"The Master gave us explicit orders. No one is allowed to go after him." The tight set of his jaw spoke volumes about how he really felt about that command. "And when he gives an order, we obey."

I scoffed and started out again. "Yeah, well, you might take orders from him but I sure as hell don't."

Before I had taken two steps, more assassins appeared from behind the tents around me until they formed an entire circle around me. Man-bun's eyes were hard as he fixed me with a commanding stare.

"We were ordered to make sure you and Edward didn't go after him either."

Shaking my head, I stared back at him in disbelief. "Seriously?"

"Why do you think Edward wasn't with you? He had already found out that Shade wasn't back. We caught him by the horses trying to ride into Queen Nimlithil's camp and trade himself for Shade."

So that was why I hadn't seen him. I thought it was odd that he was still sleeping when we were all waiting anxiously for his brother to return, but he had apparently beaten us all to it. Regardless of how I felt about Shade's orders concerning me, I was glad that the Assassins' Guild had stopped King Edward from trying to trade himself to Nimlithil. That would only have ended with both brothers captured.

"Now he's under supervision in his tent until we're sure he won't try it again," Man-bun continued. "Which is what will happen to you as well, unless you back off."

"You know that's not gonna happen," I said, holding his gaze. "So just step aside."

"Can't."

I yanked out my hunting knives. "I said, get out of my way."

Steel rang through the busy morning as the assassins surrounding me drew their blades as well. Gripping my knives tighter, I crouched into an attack position and flicked my gaze around the area. The tents around us were deserted and the soldiers who occupied this part of camp were giving the weapon-wielding assassins a wide berth. I glared at the swords that were pointed at me from every direction but didn't back down.

Shade's second-in-command gave me an appraising look. "You're going to fight half the Assassins' Guild? That's your plan?"

I couldn't use the darkness because I needed to save my already depleted powers for the rescue attempt and I didn't want to hurt these people because they were Shade's family. But they didn't need to know that.

"If you try to stop me from getting Shade back, then yeah, I'm gonna kill you all." I pointed my blade straight at him. "Now get the hell out of my way."

Emotions that I was too annoyed to decipher passed over his face for a moment but then Man-bun drew his own swords as well. I sprang forward.

Fighting half the Assassins' Guild went about as well as you would expect. I managed one strike that Man-bun easily deflected, before the rest of them had swarmed me. While I tried to parry three different blades in front of me, the assassins had cut off my escape on all sides. And then I was suddenly standing on the grass with a ring of swords around my neck.

Hopelessness washed over me as I realized that they could keep me here by force if they wanted to and there was nothing I could do about it. I met Man-bun's brown eyes from the other side of the lethal barrier.

"Don't do this. Please." I hated this. Hated that I was essentially pleading. But for this, for Shade, there was nothing I wouldn't do. "I am begging you. Don't do this. Let me go after him."

Something flickered in Man-bun's eyes, as if he also knew how rare it was for me to beg for anything, but he only pressed his lips together without replying.

"You once told me that the guild always takes care of its own and that you wouldn't forget what I did for Shade when he was ambushed and paralyzed back in Pernula." Still gripping my hunting knives, I spread my arms wide. "If you ever considered that a debt, then I'm cashing it in now. Let me go after him."

His eyes softened and a sad expression blew across his features. "I do. But we can't. When the Master gives an order, the guild obeys."

Irritation crackled through me like lightning. I was going to kill Shade for trying to pull this bullshit on me. The wildfire rage that roared inside my soul burned away the last fuck I had to give and I let out a laugh tinged with insanity.

"You'd better kill me then." I stuck the hunting knives back in their sheaths and shrugged. "Because that's the only thing that will stop me from leaving. Now get the hell out of my way."

I took a step forward. Cold metal kissed my skin as I met Man-bun's blade. I continued forward. The sharp point dug into the base of my throat but I kept advancing even as blood startled trickling down as the tip punctured my skin. On the other side of the sword, Man-bun stared at me with wide eyes. Madness danced over my lips as I flashed him a smile and pressed forward again, forcing the sharp metal deeper in.

Steel whizzed through the air and the sword abruptly vanished from my throat. With a flick of his wrist, the rest of the blades surrounding me disappeared as well. Man-bun's bewildered gaze flicked between my face and the blood on my neck as if he wasn't quite sure whether to be impressed or terrified by the maniac who had been prepared to walk through a sword in order to leave on another suicide mission. Pulling himself together, he blinked and gave his head a quick shake. Then, the Assassins' Guild's second-in-command dropped his eyes and stepped aside.

Using the hole he had created, I strode out of the ring of assassins. I was very well aware that he could have just knocked me out and locked me up while I was unconscious, if he really wanted to, but I had gambled on his emotions. The tight set of his jaw and the expression in his eyes had told me that he wholeheartedly disagreed with these orders, so I figured that if I used extreme measures to force an opening, he would be able to justify letting me leave. After all, Shade would kill them all if they had actually let me walk through that sword. And apparently, I had gambled correctly.

Man-bun gave me a nod as I passed him. "Bring him back."

"I will."

*If he's even still alive*, a dark voice whispered in the back of my mind. No. He was still alive. I snuffed out the voice of doubt as I left the Assassins' Guild behind and continued down the row of tents. Shaking my head, I stalked towards the stabling area and the horse that would take me straight to the star elves camp and the trap that awaited me there. Shade was still alive. Because if he wasn't... then by all the demons in hell, I would burn down the fucking world and its cruel gods with it.

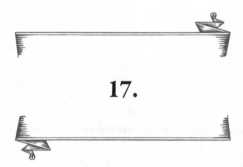

# 17.

Water gurgled below. Lying flat on my stomach, I peered over the top of a small rise and studied the stream before me. It was impossible to tell how deep it was but given how wide the slow-moving body of water was, I would probably be forced to swim. And even if I wasn't, I would have to wade across it. Right in the open. Making all kinds of splashy noises. In broad daylight. No. The stream would be a death trap.

The smell of warm grass and dirt followed me as I crawled back down on the other side. Since it was light outside, I couldn't approach their camp from the plains on the other side either. That only left the grove at the opposite end of camp. It was probably filled with all kinds of traps but at least it offered some concealment opportunities.

While I skirted around the star elves' camp and made my way towards the looming trees, I couldn't shake the feeling that this was exactly what they wanted me to do. They'd known that I wouldn't dare wait for nightfall and that my only viable route would be through the trees. But I couldn't see any other way in. Despite the annoyance at playing right into their hands, I shrugged as the grove rose before me. I had known that this was a trap before I even left camp, so it mattered little which route I used when walking into it, I supposed.

Stopping right before the tree line, I peered into the shadows. Only brown trunks and green foliage stared back at me. I took a step forward.

Nothing happened. Flicking my gaze around the area, I waited for some hidden trap to descend on me. When the trees remained silent and stationary, I snuck forward. The morning sun cast long shadows across the ground but thanks to the elves' tutelage, I was still able to avoid making noise as I stepped through the dark and light patches.

A soft hiss sounded. I whipped my head around in search of the source but no snakes shot out to devour me. Instead, something pale swirled in the corner of my eye. *Oh, shit.*

Light blue mist bloomed from the ground and rose in an ever-expanding barrier between the trees. It rolled towards me from all sides so there was no running away from it. My heartbeat quickened. Haber's portable mist wall was our most impenetrable shield against attacks like this, which was why we had used it that day in the Stone Maze, but the difference between then and now was that this time I didn't have a safe space to retreat to once I'd deployed it.

That left my own powers. Blowing away mist with wind was tricky because there was no guarantee that all the mist would be swept away. But it was all I had.

The pale blue wall billowed closer. I let it. If I was going to create a solid barrier of wind around me to counter it, I couldn't make it too large.

Once it was within a few strides of me, I reached for the burning rage inside my soul and called up the darkness. With eyes black as death, I raised my arms above my head and began moving them in a circle. Faster and faster I went. And then I released the wind.

Air spun violently around me. Still moving my arms above my head, I stared at the blue mist. One more step.

The pale cloud of chemicals around me crashed into the spinning winds.

Relief flooded through my chest. It held. I twisted my head and studied every part of the Storm Caster barrier around me. It worked. It–

Tendrils of blue fog leaked through my air shields. I sucked in a sharp breath between my teeth as alarm bells tolled in my head. Moving my arms faster, I poured more power into the wind, willing it to become stronger, faster, thicker. *Come on. Please.*

The snaking mist was swept away by the compact hurricane winds I now wielded but my energy was leaking away with it. Because I kept draining my powers to the dregs every day and barely slept enough to recharge them, I hadn't even been at full strength when I left the camp and keeping up this forceful shield used up too much too fast of my already dwindling reserves. I blinked against the tiredness that washed over me. Just a little more.

When the pale haze surrounding me on all sides finally dissipated, I sagged down on my knees. Bracing my palms on the warm grass, I heaved a few deep breaths. Whatever I had done to trigger that mist would probably reach the star elves' camp soon. I had to be long gone by then. After drawing in another lungful of sweet-smelling air, I pushed myself up. Brushing dirt and blades of grass off my hands, I took off between the trees again.

White tents became visible between the trunks up ahead. I slowed my approach. There had been no other traps waiting for me in the grove and no star elves either. My mind kept screaming that this was too easy. Pulling myself up against the rough bark, I peered around the tree. Guards were stationed on the open swath of grass beyond. Why weren't there any hiding in here? Too easy. This was too easy. I studied their spotless white armor as it gleamed in the sunlight. But then again, they were star elves. Not wood elves. They were probably about as uncomfortable in the woods as I was. Maybe that was the reason they weren't stationed inside the grove.

Leaves rustled above me as a gentle breeze caressed the thick canopy. I let my eyes travel over the pale tents beyond the tree line. Where were they keeping Shade? *In a shallow grave in the ground*, that dark voice whispered in my mind again. I crushed it beneath the weight of my own darkness. He was still alive.

The camp was far too large for me to see everything from here but there had to be some way of figuring out where I should be focusing my attention. My gaze again settled on the star elves monitoring the trees, and an idea formed in my mind. My survival instincts were screaming at me that it was a terrible idea but I ignored them and picked up a small rock from the ground. Aiming as best as I could, I hurled it.

A sharp thwack rang out as it hit a tree trunk closer to the edge. The elven guards straightened and whipped their heads around. I jerked back behind my bark-covered hiding place and peeked out only far enough that I could keep an eye on the soldiers. They were scanning the area but didn't move. Spitting out a silent curse, I picked up another rock.

Chips flew from the rough trunk as my next projectile struck close to the first one with another thwack. The elves were saying something that I was too far away to hear and then signaled with their hands to each other. I kept myself hidden but watched the unfolding events. At last, the guard closest to my tree target broke from the line and prowled towards it. Crouching, I kept my eyes on him while throwing a hand out in search of another rock.

He was almost at my used projectiles when my fingers closed around another stone. The rough surface was cold against my palm as I lifted it and threw it in another direction. It struck a tree further in and a bit to the side of me. The guard whipped his head around. Pulling out his sword, he moved towards it. I skirted around the tree trunk while he moved until he had passed me.

Since I hadn't wanted to risk him getting too close, I would now have to close the distance between us before he decided that this was nothing and went back to camp. Focusing on everything Elaran and the twins had taught me, I sprinted silently across the grass. Blood pounded in my ears. If I made one unintentional sound before I reached that guard, it would be over. Green and brown flashed past as I dodged and weaved my way through the trees.

The star elf had stopped and was now scanning the grove before him. *Please don't turn around.* His sword lowered slightly. Then he heaved a sigh and began turning. Screeching to a halt, I threw myself behind a tree. Bark scraped against my skin at the impact and I prayed that it hadn't made enough noise for him to come investigate. My heart slammed against my ribs. The seconds dragged on. Then steel sang as he sheathed his blade, followed by footsteps going back towards camp. It was now or never.

Once again skirting the tree in step with him, I waited for him to move past me. Then I shot forward. Yanking a hunting knife from the small of my back, I threw it up against his throat from behind.

He was a star elf. In full armor. He was a lot taller than me so I barely managed to position the blade and because of the armor, I couldn't grab on to his clothes to pull him back so that I could reach better, but I gambled on the element of surprise.

"Call out and tell them you're gonna go search further in," I hissed while I angled the knife along the side of his neck.

A slightly stiffer posture was the only thing that betrayed his shock.

I tightened my grip on the blade. "Do it n–"

Faster than I could react, his hands shot up and wrapped around my arm and then I was flying through the air over his crouched body as he flipped me over. My breath exploded from my lungs as I slammed back first into the grass in front of him. Still keeping a tight grip on my wrist, he yanked out his sword. Black stars danced before my eyes after the impact but I managed to throw up a hand.

Wind shot from my palm and hit him straight in the chest. He was flung backwards by the force, and the strong fingers keeping my other wrist trapped disappeared. I shot to my feet. The forest swayed around me, and my shoulder blades and the back of my ribcage pounded after the rough landing, but I blinked the black spots from my vision and pulled out a throwing knife.

A few strides away, the guard was struggling to his feet. I aimed and got ready to throw but then hesitated before the blade left my hand. He was wearing full armor. Elven armor. So my knives wouldn't be able to penetrate it. The only vulnerable places were his face and parts of his throat but I didn't want to kill him. I wanted him to tell me where Shade was. And if he was dead, he wouldn't be able to do that.

While I'd hesitated, the stunned soldier had managed to pull himself together and get to his feet. He drew in a deep breath and I realized too late what he was going to do.

"She's–"

His warning was abruptly cut off as my throwing knife buried itself in his throat. But the damage was already done. Whirling around, I found the other guards scrambling towards the tree line. *Shit.*

I sprinted away. The trees were a blur around me as I hurtled over rock and root. If I could just get out of sight before they saw me, then they would be left to search through the whole grove and I might be able to slip inside camp while they were distracted. They were star elves, not wood elves, so they might not know how to track me in here. My heart slammed against my aching ribcage. I had to get clear. Orders were called out somewhere behind me.

Grass and dirt sprayed into the air as I skidded to a halt and threw myself behind a thick tree. My chest heaved. Leaning my head against the rough bark, I concentrated on pushing air in and out of my lungs for a few seconds before peering back out from behind the tree.

In the distance, the star elves were searching the forest in one long line. Moving only in bursts of speed and screeching stops, I snuck from tree to tree until I had passed behind their line and had a clear shot at camp. When I got to the edge of the grove, I hid in the shadows of a mighty oak and swept my gaze through the open area ahead.

Guards still remained standing watchful between the white tents but there were a lot fewer of them. Other than the soldiers on the perimeter and the structures of pale fabric, I couldn't see much but every second I wasted here brought those guards in the forest closer to me. Sending a quick prayer to Nemanan and Cadentia, I dashed forward.

In my black and gray attire, I stood out like a smudge of dirt in the star elves' brilliant white camp. But the God of Thieves and Lady Luck seemed to have my back because I managed to clear the open stretch of grass and reach the first gleaming tent without being spotted. Pressing myself against the canvas at the back, I waited to make sure that no alarms had been raised.

Maybe it was my imagination but I could've sworn that the very fabric of the tent smelled like jasmine and roses, even though we were far from the City of Glass. It sent icy dread tumbling down my stomach. I hated that scent. Hated the memories connected to it. Shoving away the awful feelings that had started to resurface, I detached myself from the tent wall and snuck towards the next one.

Without knowing where they kept Shade, I would have to blindly search the whole camp and that wasn't a viable plan. I had to figure out some other way.

Rushing footsteps sounded up ahead. *Shit.* I whipped my head around in search of cover but only white tents shining in the morning sun surrounded me. In this bright landscape, there was nowhere for a dark-clad thief to hide. The hurrying figures drew closer. If they came charging down this path, they would see me.

Seeing no other alternative, I yanked open the closest tent flap and darted inside.

Pale violet eyes blinked at me in surprise.

# 18.

A female star elf in an unadorned white dress blinked at me in surprise. Before she could open her mouth and scream, I sprang across the tent filled with supply crates and tackled her to the ground. She went down in a tangle of long limbs. Straddling her chest, I slapped one hand over her mouth and used the other to rip out a hunting knife and press it against the delicate skin of her throat. Her eyes went wide.

On the other side of the cloth wall, boots thundered past. I kept my grip on the elf beneath me while the running figures outside passed by our tent and then continued in the direction I had come. Once the world outside was quiet again, I met her frightened gaze.

"Scream and I will slit your throat," I said. "Understand?"

She nodded against my palm.

"Good." I slowly removed my hand from her mouth but kept the blade against her throat. "What's your name?"

"Gaelasa," she breathed.

"Gaelasa," I repeated. "Queen Nimlithil is keeping a human man in this camp. Where?"

"He's chained up in a tent."

A sob of profound relief almost escaped my lips when she confirmed that Shade was indeed alive and I couldn't prevent the slight catch in my voice as I said again, "Where?"

She raised an elegant arm off the ground and pointed south. "Over there."

'Over there' wasn't exactly much in the way of directions so I climbed to my feet and hauled her with me. She was taller than me but unarmed, and based on her clothes and the fact that she was in this supply tent, she was probably some kind of servant, so I didn't expect much of a fight from her.

"You're gonna take me to him," I said. "And you're gonna make sure we're not spotted. Okay?"

"Okay," she breathed.

"Good." I grabbed her shoulder and turned her towards the exit before placing my knife against her back. "If you betray me, I will kill you."

A tremor went through her body but she said nothing as she led me back out into the sunlight. We followed a path between the tents that led straight south. The fresh green grass had long since been flattened by stomping boots and now looked more gray than green. But at least it stayed silent. As did Gaelasa. Her shoulders shook slightly from time to time, and from behind I couldn't quite tell if she was crying or not, but she kept her word and led me through the tents unseen.

Servants were much better than soldiers or ordinary workers at moving through crowded places without being spotted so I sent a quick prayer of thanks to the fickle Goddess of Luck that the elf in that supply tent had been a servant.

Soft chattering hung over most of the camp but the closer we got to the south side, the quieter it became. I bunched my fist into Gaelasa's dress and kept her close in front of me as the silence grew.

She gasped as we left the narrow row of tents behind and moved into a slightly more open patch.

"I didn't..." she stammered. "This wasn't me. Please. You have to believe me. I didn't know. I didn't..."

Still keeping my blade against her back, I leaned out and studied the area she had taken us to. Relief and dread and hope and rage exploded like black powder in my soul.

A whole squad of star elves in gleaming armor stood waiting before a large tent. Queen Nimlithil was seated in an ornate chair in the middle, with Captain Hadraeth on her right. Without his helmet, the scar down his cheek stood out in even starker contrast.

The silver headdress decorated with white gems that the elven queen wore glittered in the morning sun as she rose from the chair and cocked her head. Soft curls of silvery white hair spilled over the shoulder of her regal dress at the movement. My mind barely registered any of it because there to her left was the cause of that detonation of conflicting emotions. Shade.

He was kneeling on the ground between two star elves in sturdy armor, his hands shackled in front of him and a gag between his lips. Bruises covered his jaw, cheekbone, and temple on the right side of his face and his tight-fitting black clothes sported multiple slashes. Dried blood coated his skin in the places where his clothes had been torn. Next to him, the two guards each held a sword to his throat.

I met his gaze from across the grass and my heart almost broke. There was no relief or happiness in those black eyes when he saw me. Only devastation.

"Let him go," I growled at the star elf queen.

Queen Nimlithil smiled pleasantly as if I was an old friend. "Oh, there you are. I was wondering when you would arrive."

"Let. Him. Go."

"I have been waiting here all morning," she continued as if I hadn't said anything, and smoothened her dress. "I was beginning to think that you would not come." Another smile drifted over her lips. "But here you are. And you brought one of my subjects."

Keeping my grip on Gaelasa, I moved us both a bit closer. When we reached the middle of the open space, I kicked at the back of her knees. Gaelasa crashed to the ground. Positioning myself directly behind her, I pressed my blade to her throat.

"Let him go," I ground out. "Or I'll kill her."

A choked sob ripped from Gaelasa's lips and now that I stood above her, I could see the tears dripping down her cheeks. I didn't have much of a conscience on my best days but I might have felt bad for her if the circumstances had been different. She was an innocent, after all. But they had taken Shade. They had *hurt* Shade. All bets were off now and whatever scrap of humanity I sometimes pretended to possess was dead and buried.

I called up the darkness. Black smoke twisted around my limbs as I thrust out my free hand. Screams rang across the camp as a blast ripped the tents on my left from the ground and sent them flying through the bright morning.

"I'm not fucking kidding!" I bellowed and aimed my hand in another direction. "Let him go. Now."

When Queen Nimlithil didn't respond straight away, I slammed my palm forward again. Winds shot out and flattened another row of tents. Rage and insanity danced in my eyes as I watched those pretty little tents crumble beneath my power. However, producing that impenetrable air shield to survive the mist earlier had used up too much of my already depleted powers and I could already feel in my soul that if I used them one more time, I would pass out. But Queen Nimlithil didn't need to know that.

Pointing my arm in another direction, I let a mad smile dance over my lips. "If you want me to destroy your whole camp, I can keep going."

"No, you cannot." Queen Nimlithil gave me a small smile. "Because if you were capable of producing enough power right now to destroy my whole camp, you would have done so already."

Damn her for calling my bluff. If I couldn't use my Storm Caster powers as a threat then I would have to use something else. Malice replaced the madness on my lips.

"You know, my patience was already gone before I got here so if that's how you wanna play it, then fine." I reached up and grabbed Gaelasa's hair. Tipping her head back, I pushed the knife harder into her skin while still keeping my gaze fixed on Nimlithil. "You have three seconds to release him. Then I kill her."

Queen Nimlithil studied me as if I was some kind of curious animal. "Go ahead."

"What?" I blurted out.

"Go ahead and kill her, if that is what you wish. Why would I give up my leverage to save one simple servant?"

"I..." I trailed off.

Didn't she care about her own people? I mean, I had already known that she considered some people to be more important than others, but to blatantly tell me that she didn't care if I murdered one of her subjects... I hadn't expected that.

With panic clawing its way up my spine, I flicked my gaze across the area in a desperate attempt to formulate a new plan. Nimlithil *had* probably been sitting here all morning, waiting for me, because everyone was positioned in exactly the right spot. Or the wrong spot, for me.

If I tried to blast her or her guards away with my wind, I would also hit Shade. Blanketing the area with black clouds wouldn't be of much help because Shade was too far away and surrounded by too many hostiles, plus he was shackled, so freeing him in the initial seconds of panic would be impossible. I might be able to zap a couple of them with lightning, but the problem of being outnumbered still remained. Not to mention the fact that if I tried any of that, I would pass out.

"You really expect me to believe that you don't care if I kill your people?" I asked, trying to call her bluff.

"My people understand that sacrifices are necessary in war."

The weeping servant on the ground before me might beg to disagree but before I could point that out, Queen Nimlithil pressed on.

"Besides, I have what you want." She lifted a graceful hand to motion at Shade. "And if you do not do as I command, I will kill him."

I remained staring at her in silence. She was probably bluffing. Killing Shade was a bad move since she could use him for so many other things in this war. As if she had read my thoughts, Nimlithil gave me a smile that a teacher might give a particularly stupid child.

"You do not believe me." Gems clinked in her hair and around her neck as she shrugged. "What I needed him for was to lure you here. And since you have now arrived, he has outlived his usefulness." She waved a hand at the guards next to the kneeling assassin.

One of them grabbed a fistful of Shade's hair and pulled his head back to expose his throat while the other pressed his blade further in. A line of red appeared against Shade's pale skin.

"Stop," I snapped.

Nimlithil arched an eyebrow at me. "The only thing that will prevent me from killing him right here is if you surrender."

Even with a guard gripping his hair, Shade still managed to shake his head. I swallowed hard. If I surrendered, I might be dooming us both. But if I didn't, she might actually kill him. Was she bluffing or not?

"Fine," she said before I could reach a conclusion. "Suit yourself."

The guard on Shade's right pushed the blade again.

"No!" I cried out.

Blood slid down Shade's throat in a thin red band but the sword stopped moving. I took my own blade from Gaelasa's throat and held it out wide.

"Okay," I said. "Okay, you win." Grabbing the back of Gaelasa's dress, I hauled her to her feet and said under my breath before shoving her away, "Sorry."

She didn't acknowledge me at all as she stumbled away from me and then ran back the way we had come. Across the grass, Queen Nimlithil motioned expectantly at the ground before her.

"Remove your weapons and surrender."

Muffled grunts and the sounds of a struggle broke out between Shade and the guards but I didn't dare meet his eyes as I dropped the hunting knife in my hand. It landed point first in the trampled grass. One by one, I stripped off the rest of my blades and let them fall to the ground as well. Nimlithil smiled blandly at me until a rather impressive pile had formed next to me.

"Come," she said and waved a slender hand at me. "Kneel before me and surrender."

After letting the darkness slip back into the deep pits of my soul, I strode across the grass. Shade was still struggling to speak past the gag but I kept my gaze on the star elf queen before me. All I wanted was to kick her perfect teeth down her perfect throat but I suppressed the urge as I stopped a few strides from her. If there was even the slightest chance that I could save Shade, I would do anything. Give anything. So when Queen Nimlithil nodded, I swallowed my pride and smothered my survival instincts and got down on my knees before her.

Shade's muffled shouts tried to pull my attention away but I kept my chin raised and continued watching the satisfied queen in front of me. Captain Hadraeth moved towards me.

"Hands," he ordered.

I offered them, palms up, to him. It took all my self-control not to break the queen's stare as Hadraeth locked sturdy manacles around my wrists. Steel rang across the grass as he drew his sword and then hauled me up by my shirt before he placed his sword along my throat.

"If you do anything other than follow orders, Shade will die," Queen Nimlithil said simply before turning to the assassin on her left. "And you, I have already explained to you in quite some detail what will happen to the Oncoming Storm if you disobey a single command."

Shade stilled. Since Nimlithil had broken my stare first, I was now free to look away as well. My eyes slid to the Master Assassin who was also being pulled to his feet with a blade to his throat. An unrelenting lightning storm of fury crackled behind his eyes and he was clenching his jaw so tightly that the muscles in it twitched.

"Move them inside," the queen said.

The guards nodded. While they started shoving us towards the structure a bit farther away, Nimlithil simply glided away without a second look back.

With all those white tents shining in the morning sunlight it had been very bright outside, so it took my eyes a moment to adjust to the duskier conditions as we were hauled inside.

A large table with chains on it occupied the middle of the room. Along the pale cloth wall on my right stood several chairs as well as smaller tables overlain with papers, tools, and equipment. I flicked my gaze to the other side of the tent and panic fluttered briefly in my chest at the sight. There was a metal cage waiting there.

The star elf who was leading the procession opened the door made of close-set bars. Captain Hadraeth pulled us to a halt while Shade was shoved inside. I glared at the Guard Captain but he refused to meet my gaze. When the assassin had been deposited inside and the other star elves had moved aside, Hadraeth hauled me forward and pushed me into the cage as well. Metallic ringing filled the tent as he slammed the door shut and locked it behind him.

While Shade reached up and ripped off the gag, I studied the star elves. Most of them left but Captain Hadraeth and one with pale white hair remained. Both of them picked up a long white bow and a quiver, and then sat down in two of the chairs by the opposite wall.

Holding Hadraeth's gaze, I picked the lock on my manacles. When the mechanism clicked open, the guard next to him shot to his feet, nocked an arrow, and drew back. I shifted my stare to him as I moved towards the bars of the cell and stuck a hand outside it. Wood groaned as the white-haired elf drew the bow further. Hadraeth didn't move at all. Still leveling hard eyes on the aiming guard, I dared him to fire as I demonstratively dropped my now unlocked manacles on the ground outside.

If I tried to pick the lock on the cage, I knew he would shoot me, so removing my shackles didn't actually improve my odds of escape a whole lot. But that rebellious act at least gave me back some sense of control over the situation.

The handcuffs clanked as they landed on the ground. A wicked smile stretched my lips as I stared down the white-haired guard, still daring him to shoot me for my insubordination. He didn't.

A second later, metal clattered again as Shade threw his own manacles through the bars of the cage as well.

Only when Captain Hadraeth had motioned at the other guard to stand down did I turn to the Master Assassin next to me.

The fury blazing in his eyes had me retreating a step in surprise.

"What the hell do you think you're doing?" he growled at me.

"What do you think I'm doing?" I snapped back. "I came to get you out."

Shade advanced on me. "And now you're stuck in here with me."

I reached up to shove him back but he flashed to the side, grabbed my wrist, and whirled me around. A huff escaped me as my back slammed into the bars of the cell. His other hand shot out. With one hand pinning my wrist to the cold metal and the other keeping my chin in a firm grip, he held me immobile while he leaned down until I could almost see the lightning dancing in his eyes.

"I told you that if I wasn't back by morning, you were to consider me a casualty of war," he said in a voice dripping with authority and silent threats.

Letting him keep his grip on me, I glared up at him defiantly. "If you thought for one second that I would leave you here to die, then you don't know me at all."

"You weren't supposed to come!" he yelled desperately, his fingers digging into my jaw. "You weren't supposed to throw away your godsdamn life! Not for me."

"Tell me you wouldn't have done the same." I held his guilt-ridden stare. "Look me in the eye and tell me that if our situations had been reversed, you wouldn't have done the same for me." Letting out a humorless laugh, I flicked my free hand towards the floor. "Hell, do that, and I'll even get down on my knees and beg your forgiveness for disobeying your orders."

For a moment, we just continued staring at each other. Then he released me and let his arms fall down by his sides but didn't step back. Instead, he closed his eyes and rested his forehead against mine.

"You weren't supposed to come," he whispered against my lips again.

I ran my hand through his messy hair and down the uninjured side of his face. "I know. But it's who we are."

A slight tremor went through him as my fingers continued down his neck and then came to a halt against his muscled chest. He rested his own hand over mine and then placed the other one behind my neck before pulling me the final bit towards him. His lips were gentle as they traced mine in a soft kiss.

When he stopped, I smiled against his mouth. "Besides, you really should've learned by now... I don't exactly specialize in doing as I'm told."

His warm breath danced over my skin as he huffed a laugh. "Yeah, I really should've learned that by now."

Opening his eyes again, he took a step back and studied me. He opened his mouth to say something else but before he could, I slammed the heel of my palm into his stomach.

A strained gasp wheezed out of him as he doubled over and staggered backwards. I stalked after him.

"You ordered your guild to forcibly keep me from going after you." Grabbing a fistful of his shirt, I yanked him back up until his face was level with mine while he desperately tried to suck air back into his lungs. "If you ever pull that kind of bullshit on me again, I will kill you. Do you hear me?"

His face appeared to have gotten stuck somewhere between shock and amusement but he managed a strained chuckle and a half smirk. "Come try it."

"Careful now, or I might take you up on that." A smirk tugged at my own lips as I held his gaze for another few seconds before finally releasing my grip on his shirt and stalking over to the back wall. Sliding down the metal bars, I sat down on the ground and rested my arms on my knees. "But I'd really rather not, because going through all this trouble to save your stupid ass only to kill you myself would be a bloody waste of time."

Having recovered from my blow, Shade chuckled again and lowered himself to the ground next to me. For a moment, we both just sat there and stared across the tent. By the wall opposite us, Captain Hadraeth and the white-haired guard were still watching us from their chairs. I briefly wondered what they made of us, of all our fighting and kissing and threatening, but then I decided that I didn't particularly care. Shade appeared to have reached a similar conclusion because he threw them a disinterested stare before turning his head to me and arching an eyebrow.

"How did you even get my guild to let you leave?"

"I threatened to kill them all."

A surprised laugh ripped from his throat. "I imagine they took that well."

"Better than expected, actually." I shrugged. "But they still wouldn't let me leave so I pulled knives on them."

Shade's arm brushed against mine as he turned more fully towards me. "You took on my whole guild?"

"It was more like half, but yeah."

"How did that go?"

I shot a half-hearted glare at him. "How do you think it went? They had me surrounded and staring down a ring of swords in a matter of seconds."

A proud smirk tugged at his lips. "I trained them well."

Huffing, I jabbed an elbow in his ribs. "Shut up. But yeah, you did."

When Shade's smirk deepened, I debated hitting him again but managed to suppress the urge and settled for an eye roll instead. Then his eyes turned suspicious as he looked me up and down.

"But you're still here," he said. "So how did you get out of it?"

An evil grin stole across my lips as I lifted one shoulder in a nonchalant shrug. "I told them they'd have to kill me if they wanted to stop me." Reaching up, I pulled my shirt collar down a little to show him the small wound at the base of my throat. "And then I walked straight into the closest sword until they lowered them."

Shade's mouth dropped open as he looked from my face to the wound and then back again. "You...?" Leaning his head against the metal bar behind him, he looked up at the ceiling and raked a hand through his hair. "Wow. I didn't see that coming. Gods, I can't even punish them for disobeying my orders if you pulled that kind of crazy shit on them."

"You know, if–"

The tent flap fluttered open.

Captain Hadraeth and his companion shot to their feet as Queen Nimlithil swept into the room. Her delicate eyebrows bunched in a frown when she took in the discarded manacles outside the cell but then she just shook her head slightly and let her gaze drift to me.

"Tomorrow at dawn, a prisoner transport will arrive to take you back to the City of Glass where you will surrender your magic to Aldeor," she announced. "Do not worry. Your other Ashaana friends will follow shortly."

Dread and disappointment sank down my stomach like a block of ice. After getting captured, my one comforting thought had been that it might at least serve as bait for the white dragon. That Queen Nimlithil would call him here for the magic-stripping ritual, which would give the rest of our army a chance to kill him. But apparently, that was not the case. Because why would anything ever be easy?

"However, before that point, there is something else I would like you to do," the star elf queen continued. "You are plagued by pain, hurt, and sorrow, which is why you are acting out in this violent way. To ensure that your journey to the City of Glass and the destiny that awaits you there transpire smoothly, as well as to help you live a happier life, I would like you to complete the other ritual right now."

Shade and I shot to our feet while blaring alarm bells went off in my head all at once and panic ripped at my chest.

"What?" I blurted out.

Queen Nimlithil gave me a benevolent smile. "Yes. Today is a joyous day because today is the day that you finally get rid of all the pain you have been carrying your entire life."

A scholar in a crisp white suit strode into the tent. Stopping next to his queen, he clasped his hands behind his back and waited. The Queen of Tkeister smiled at me again.

"Your life in the light starts today."

Her words echoed through the blackened pits of my soul. This was not happening. This could not be happening. The white walls of the tent seemed to close in around me. There had to be a way out of this. There had to be. Because if not, then this would not be the day that my new life in the light started. It would be the day when everything that made me who I was would be wiped from the world. I swallowed. It would be the day I died.

# 19.

Silver skirts rustled as Queen Nimlithil turned back to Captain Hadraeth and his companion. Some form of silent communication passed between them because the white-haired guard bowed and left the tent for a brief moment before returning with six more soldiers. I tried swallowing past the dread rising in my throat but it didn't work. She couldn't make me do this.

"Proceed," the queen said.

Shade stepped in front of me and squared his shoulders as two of the guards approached the cage. The love behind that protective gesture stopped the panic from fracturing my soul further and helped center me again. I was going to be fine. Nimlithil couldn't perform the ritual unless I did it willingly so as long as I kept refusing, nothing would happen. I placed a hand on Shade's back in silent thanks.

Queen Nimlithil looked us over and blew out a sharp breath through her nose. "If he does not move, shoot the Oncoming Storm in the leg."

Underneath my palm, I felt Shade's posture stiffen but I just drew my fingers along his side and stepped out from behind him. Before I removed my hand, I gave his arm a quick squeeze.

"I'll be okay," I said.

Metal clanked as the guards unlocked the cage and drew open the door. I took a step towards them but Shade's fingers gripped mine for a second.

"Whatever happens, don't do it," he whispered, and then released me again.

Not wanting to show Queen Nimlithil any weakness, I gave him a shallow nod and strode forwards without turning to meet his gaze. The two star elves waited just outside the bars. As I took the final steps towards them, I buried my anxiety deep inside me and put on the rather formidable mental armor I had built over the years. Adopting a confident swagger, I schooled my features into a cocky grin and stepped out of the cell.

"It is a very simple ritual," Nimlithil said and tipped a slender hand in the direction of the scholar beside her. "You only have to repeat the ancient words of power of your own free will. After that, you will feel a slight pulse, and then it will be finished."

After closing the cell door again, the two guards flanked me as I came to a halt a few strides away. The other soldiers in the tent watched my every move carefully while nocked arrows waited in their long white bows. Everyone except Hadraeth. He only continued studying me with a face like carved marble. I shifted my gaze back to the silver-haired queen in front of me.

"Ah, but you know," I began, "the key part of that sentence is 'of your own free will' and there's not a chance in hell that I'll be doing that of my own free will so..." I shrugged.

The queen smiled in that annoyingly superior way of hers again. "Yes, but you see, the interesting part of ancient rules like these is that there is always room for interpretation. What makes you decide to say the words of your own free will is not regulated.

While threatening *you* might be too much rule-bending," she motioned at Shade, "threatening *him* is not."

Wood creaked as three of the guards by the wall drew their bows and aimed them straight at Shade. I had been expecting this. Outside, I hadn't had time to establish whether she was bluffing or not but now I'd had more time to think things through.

"The choice is simple," Queen Nimlithil continued. "Perform the ritual and start your new life in the light. Or my archers will kill Shade."

The Master Assassin in the cell tilted his head to the right. "She's bluffing."

"I beg your pardon?" She placed a hand over her chest in affront.

"She won't kill me. She can't." Shade's eyes slid to me. "Because as soon as I'm dead, she loses her leverage over you. If she kills me, she can never get you to complete the ritual."

A small smirk tugged at my lips. I had come to that exact same conclusion as well. The only thing that annoyed me was that I hadn't realized it before I surrendered. But when I saw that guard draw his sword across Shade's throat, I hadn't been able to think past the roaring in my head.

"Clever," Queen Nimlithil said with a poisonous smile on her lips.

As far as I knew, she didn't often lose her composure but she appeared to be quickly running out of patience now. A muscle flickered in her jaw and something incredibly dangerous flashed past in her pale violet eyes.

"I do not understand why you and everyone on this forsaken bit of land are making this so difficult," she spit out. "All I want for you is a world free of pain and suffering. Why are you resisting me?"

"Are you seriou–" I began but she cut me off.

"Why do you cling to your life in darkness and despair? Why do you refuse a better life in the light?" She scoffed. "Weraldi, *world of man* indeed. Our ancestors should never have come to this awful continent where humans have been allowed to roam unchecked and destroy nature and usher in an era of darkness." Incredulity filled her eyes as she looked at me and shook her head. "And even despite everything you have done, I still try to save you – and still you refuse."

Before I could figure out what in Nemanan's name I was supposed to reply to that, she flicked her wrist. Two of the guards by the white tent wall broke off from Hadraeth and the others and instead moved towards the cell door. The ones flanking me stepped closer to me and took a firm grip on my arms.

"You are correct," Queen Nimlithil said in a voice that suddenly sounded more tired than irritated. "I cannot kill Shade without losing my leverage. However, I can still have him tortured."

I whipped my head towards her. She just lifted her slender shoulders in a shrug and waved a casual hand at the table in the middle. Suddenly, I understood why there were chains on it. They weren't shackles that simply sat there waiting to be picked up and used on prisoners, they were restraints bolted to the wood. Frantic, I cast my gaze around the room. And the tools and equipment on the smaller tables by the pale tent walls... By all the gods.

Metallic ringing filled the room as the cell door banged open. I jerked back around. Shade glanced at the arrows that were now trained on me instead and just walked out of the cage and towards the waiting guards without putting up a fight. His black eyes met mine.

"No matter what," he said.

*No matter what happens, don't do it*. That was what he had said earlier, as if he had anticipated this. I shook my head at him but he just gave me a firm nod and let the soldiers grab him and lead him towards the table. The fingers around my arms tightened as I desperately jerked against their grip.

"You claim you want a world free of pain and suffering," I spat at the silver-haired queen. "And this is how you do it? *You* are the one inflicting the pain! Can't you see that?"

"The ends justify the means," she said calmly. "I want you to live a happier life but this is also bigger than you. I need you to give your powers to Aldeor so that he can make the spell stronger, which will help everyone live a happier life. Since you are so consumed by pain and darkness, you need to complete this ritual first in order to ensure that you will complete the other one later." White teeth flashed in a smile. "For the greater good."

The guard on Shade's right nodded at the assassin's shirt and then jerked his chin at the table. "Strip. Then get up."

Shade's face was an unreadable mask as he yanked off his tight-fitting black shirt. Dried blood smeared his skin in places and there were bruises on the right side of his ribs but he didn't even look at his injuries as he dropped his shirt on the ground and pulled himself up on the table. He held my gaze for one extra second before lying down on his back.

"Don't do this." The words were out before I could stop them.

"If you do not wish to see him hurt, then perform the ritual," Queen Nimlithil answered and motioned at the scholar in the crisp white suit.

Chains clanked as the two star elves by the table clamped shackles around Shade's ankles before striding towards the other side of the table. Gripping his wrists, they positioned them above his head and locked them there with another pair of manacles. My heart raced in my chest. I worked my tongue around my mouth while I tried to silence the roaring that had started up in my head again.

Shade just stared disinterestedly at the white cloth ceiling above. Struggling against the elves holding me, I whirled towards Captain Hadraeth.

"Don't let them do this," I said, my voice pleading. "You know this is wrong. Please. Stop this."

Something flickered in the Guard Captain's dark violet eyes but he made no move to intervene. I was just about to open my mouth and beg him again when Queen Nimlithil cut me off.

"Hadraeth cannot help you this time," she said sharply. "He knows where his loyalties lie."

One of the guards had left the table and returned with a wicked-looking knife in his hand. My heart slammed against my ribs and my breath was coming in fits and starts. I couldn't let this happen. *No matter what happens, don't do it.* The words were quickly being drowned out by the deafening roaring that pounded in my head.

"Please," I said, and I didn't care how pathetically my voice cracked.

The guard lifted the blade. Shade's chest rose and fell at a slow and steady pace as if he wasn't worried at all.

Not taking my eyes off him, I pressed out another string of half-broken words. "Please don't do this."

At the table, the soldier in his silver-decorated armor paused and looked back at Queen Nimlithil. She nodded. I thrashed against the guards holding me, kicking, yanking, and snarling, but they only wrenched my arms up behind my back and tightened their grip. The blade moved closer. A scream shattered from my throat. Grunts came from the elves holding me and I nearly dislocated my shoulder as I fought with everything I had to get free.

The star elf by the table placed the sharp edge against Shade's chest. One drop of blood appeared as a fraction of it made contact with his bare skin. And then something cracked inside me.

"Stop." I ceased struggling. My chest heaved and my words were little more than a sob. "I'll do it."

Chains rattled as Shade jerked his head back to look at me. "No."

I tore my gaze from him and turned to Queen Nimlithil. "I'll complete the ritual, if you swear you won't hurt him."

"Storm," Shade warned but I didn't look at him.

"You have my word," Queen Nimlithil said.

She flicked her wrist and the guard with the knife backed off. Wood groaned and metal clanked as Shade started struggling against his restraints.

"Don't do this, Storm!" he yelled. "You promised me. No matter what. Don't do this!"

Queen Nimlithil turned her back on him and motioned for the scholar to approach. Glittering bracelets clinked as she moved. *I'm sorry*, I mouthed at Shade before turning away as well. Behind me, the furious screaming and banging continued. I blocked it out as I fixed my gaze on the silver-haired scholar.

"Now, simply repeat after me," he said.

Shade's warnings and threats echoed between the silent white walls. Then, they were cut off abruptly. Muffled grunting took its place. I drew a deep breath and balled my hands into fists to keep them from shaking.

This was the day I would cease to exist. In a few moments, I would become an empty shell only capable of seeing the world through artificial bliss. I resisted looking at the assassin behind me. But if it saved Shade, then that was a price I was willing to pay. My life for the man who held my cold black heart. Yes. That was a trade I was happy to make.

The scholar gave me one final nod and then began speaking a series of words I did not understand but that made the very air thrum with power.

When he paused, I repeated the sounds. He gave me an encouraging nod and continued.

Furious banging and muffled screaming continued echoing behind me. I concentrated on the words of power vibrating in the air before me.

Another pause. I repeated the strange words. The scholar started up again but this sentence was much shorter and had a sense of finality to it.

I thought I would be frightened. I had been shaking when we started. But now, a steady sort of calm before my inescapable fate smothered everything else. Everything except my mind. In there, my desperate survival instincts were futilely pounding and screaming at me not to do this.

I drew one final breath as the person I used to be, and repeated the last words of power.

A force shot out from me and pulsed through the air.

And then everything went silent.

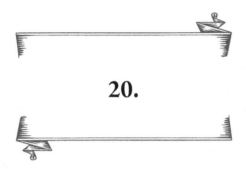

# 20.

It felt as though my soul had been ripped out by the roots. Everything was so silent. So hollow. Staggering back, I sank down on my knees and pressed a hand to my chest. When I held it out in front of me again, I half expected my palm to be slick with blood from the wound because surely there was nothing but severed tendons left where my core used to be attached. I stared at my palm. No blood. Only this vast nothingness echoing inside me. I hadn't felt this empty since...

"How curious." Queen Nimlithil placed a slender hand under my chin and tilted my head up.

Still on my knees, I just stared back at her.

She frowned slightly before letting go of my chin and waving a hand towards the table in the middle of the white tent. "Proceed."

It took great effort to turn my head and look at whatever was about to happen. A man in black pants was still chained to the sturdy stab of wood. I blinked. Right. Shade. At the queen's command, one of the guards in silver-decorated armor stepped forward again. There was a wicked-looking knife in his hand. I shook my head violently, trying to think past the deafening silence inside me. This was... This...

The events of the past few minutes flooded my mind as if someone had shattered a protective dam. Shade. Queen Nimlithil had been about to torture Shade. I had agreed to do the ritual in order to stop that. Metal glinted as the blade moved towards his skin again. And now she was going to torture him anyway.

I didn't have enough energy left to use my Storm Caster powers again without blacking out but I didn't care. If I blew this whole damn tent to hell then Shade might be able to escape. It didn't matter that I wouldn't be able to leave with him. As long as he got out.

Reaching into the deep pits of my soul, I slammed my arms forward. The feeling stunned me so much that I actually gasped. There was nothing.

Desperately, I whipped my head between Shade and Queen Nimlithil, but she had already motioned for the guard to back off again and was now studying me with curious eyes. I stared at my palms and once again tried to call up the darkness. Nothing.

When I'd been forced to drink Haber's magic blocking potion this summer, I hadn't been able to use my powers. I had reached into my soul but it had felt as though I was sticking my hand into an empty hole. But this time... This time I couldn't even reach into my soul. Even with the potion rendering me unable to use my powers, my soul had still felt the way it always did. Now, it felt as though the core of it was gone. Because it was. My Storm Caster powers were gone.

"Your Majesty," the scholar said somewhere above me. "I did warn you that performing this ritual on an Ashaana before they had surrendered their powers is unprecedented and that it might produce unintended consequences."

"I am not interested in your excuses, Raemsal," Queen Nimlithil said. "I want to know what happened."

The scholar, Raemsal, crouched down in front of me and peered into my face. There was a monstrous tidal wave of emotions crashing down on top of me so all I could manage was to sit there on the ground and stare back at him.

"Ashaana powers come from the wielder's emotions." Raemsal tilted my head slightly as if to look into my eyes. "It is usually brought on by an event of profound pain or sorrow. This ritual is designed to remove those emotions." He released me and stood back up again. "Since she reacted in such a frenzied way when you gave the order to start torturing the assassin again, she appears to still be able to feel the full spectrum of emotions, which means that the ritual ultimately failed its original purpose. However, nothing happened when she tried to attack. All this leads me to believe that the ritual... cancelled out her Ashanna powers."

My powers were gone. I could hear him talking but I barely registered what he was actually saying. Inside me, blood from my torn-out soul continued dripping into the gaping abyss that had been left behind.

"Are you saying that her magic is gone?"

My powers were gone. That repeated thought continued free-falling through the void inside me, echoing off every surface. Dripping blood accompanied it. My powers were gone.

Clothes rustled as the scholar shifted on his feet in front of me but before he could answer, Queen Nimlithil opened her mouth again.

"All I want to know is, does she still have value?" She flicked her hand towards me, making her gem-covered bracelets clink. "Is she still useful?"

"I believe so," he replied carefully. "What gave her the ability to use her powers is gone. However, the... spark of magic she was born with is still there inside her. She can no longer use it but we should still be able to extract it and give it to Aldeor the White."

"Good. Then we should–"

"It's still there?" I blurted out as parts of his statement finally caught up with me. A tiny seed of hope sprouted in my chest. "My magic is still there? But then why can't I feel it? Or use it?"

"Think of it like a body part that no longer functions," Raemsal said.

"What?" I frowned up at the two of them.

"Ah," Queen Nimlithil said as understanding lit her eyes. Her lips stretched into a condescending smile. "It is quite simple. If I sever your spine, you would still have your legs but you would not be able to feel them or use them. They would be there. But useless. I imagine the concept is the same. Your magic is there, but whatever connected you to it has been severed for good."

My anger connected me to my powers. And that fiery pit of rage had been burning inside my soul for so long that I could barely remember what it felt like without it. I hadn't felt like this since... Rain.

Panic crackled through me like lightning.

Rain. I still remembered her. Remembered what we had done together. Remembered that I was the one who had accidentally gotten her killed because I had wanted to help some random girls who were being attacked and because I had hesitated in killing one of the attackers. Remembered that she had bled out in a darkened back alley.

Those memories had always been infused with so much emotion. I had learned to live with that mistake but when I thought back on my time with Rain, a storm of emotions had always followed it.

Now I felt nothing. No guilt. No pain. No sorrow. No... love.

The intense panic flaring through me was enough to block out everything else that was happening in the star elves' prison tent at that moment.

Rain. I pictured her face in my mind. The girl who had been my sister in all but blood. Laughing. Sparkling brown eyes full of life.

Nothing.

I called up the scene of her death to my mind. Blood bubbles popping at her lips, me pressing my hands against her stomach to stop the life from bleeding out of her. The coppery tang that hung over the whole darkened alley. The moment her eyes glazed over and she went still.

Nothing.

Though I remembered every detail, I felt... nothing. Thinking of Rain was like thinking of a distant acquaintance. Someone I had met briefly, long ago, but hadn't formed any sort of connection to. I remembered who Rain was but everything I had felt for her was gone.

Desperately, I tried to love her again. Tried to start loving her like my sister again. Because I knew, I *knew*, that I was supposed to feel that way about her. But it was like staring at a painting of someone and trying to love the person who had modeled for it.

My love for Rain was what had caused me to feel such pain and sorrow when she died. So in order to solve the problem and remove my pain, the spell had taken away my love for her. And without the love and the pain and the sorrow, there was no cataclysmic rage that worked as the bridge between me and my Storm Caster powers.

There was nothing now.

I was nothing now.

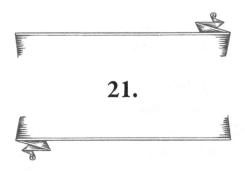

# 21.

My surroundings came back into focus. White fabric filled the background and then there were tables and two guards seated in chairs in front of the cloth wall. But between me and all of that were metal bars. The same cold material dug into my back as well where I sat on the ground. Beside me, a black-clad body leant me warmth. I blinked. How had I gotten back into the cage? I didn't remember them locking me up again.

"How long?" My voice came out sounding like a strained croak.

Shade started slightly at the sound of my voice and turned to look at me. "A few hours."

By Nemanan, I had been uncontactable for hours? When I had found out the extent of what had been done to me, I had fallen headlong into that gaping chasm inside me. I knew that it would take some time to process but I hadn't expected this. Swallowing against my parched throat, I tried to remember how to be a functional human being again. Strange emotions swirled inside me. I had managed to claw my way back out of that empty abyss but I couldn't really make sense of my feelings.

"Here." Shade held up something that looked like a plate. "You should eat this."

Nodding, I took it from him. I had no idea what it was but I shoveled it down anyway. Even though I couldn't bring myself to care what it tasted like, the food helped restore a scrap of energy and left me feeling a bit more clear-headed.

When the plate was empty, Shade passed me a wooden cup filled to the brim with water. I drank it all in a couple of gulps. Setting it down next to the plate, I let out a long sigh and pushed to my feet. Pacing back and forth, I raked my fingers through my hair. I had to do something. There were too many emotions inside me that I couldn't make sense of and then there was the nothingness that echoed where my powers had been. It was too much. I had to think of something else.

Stopping, I shifted my gaze to Shade. "Why didn't you fight?"

"What?"

Confusion blew across his face as he pushed to his feet as well. There was so much worry and devastation in his eyes when he looked at me that another wave of tangled emotions welled up inside me. I couldn't do it. Couldn't deal with this right now.

"When they took you out of this cage, why didn't you fight back?" I flung an arm out in the direction of the table outside the metal bars. "You just got up and lay down on that table like some obedient little slave. Why the hell would you do that?"

*Fight me. Please fight me. I need to feel something other than all the messed-up parts bleeding inside me.*

Shade had been walking towards me but now hesitated. Behind his eyes, I could almost see the wheels turning while he tried to figure out what was going on.

*Please fight me.*

I hated that I was doing this to him but if I didn't replace all the soul-shattering emotions inside me with something more manageable, I was going to fall into that gaping abyss again.

His eyes cleared in sudden understanding. The confusion melted from his face and a mask of fury took its place. And I loved him for it. Loved him for realizing what I needed, what I think we both needed, right now.

"You think I didn't want to fight back?" He stabbed a hand towards the two elven archers sitting by the opposite wall. "While we were outside waiting for you this morning, Queen Nimlithil took the liberty of explaining exactly what her people were going to do to you if I stepped out of line. If I'd fought back, they would've taken it out on you."

"Well guess what?" My voice rose to a scream. "They took it out on me anyway!"

"I told you not to do it!" Shade stalked towards me. "I told you not to do that damn ritual no matter what happened."

He continued plowing towards me, forcing me to retreat or to have him slam straight into me. Walking backwards, I shot him a furious glare. When my back abruptly hit the metal bars of the cage wall and he still didn't stop, I raised my arms to shove him back.

"In case you didn't hear, they were gonna–" I was cut off when his hands shot out and caught my mine before they made contact with his chest.

"No. Matter. What," he growled in my face as he forced my arms back against the bars above my head. "That's what I told you."

"They were gonna torture you!"

I jerked up a knee towards his groin, forcing him to release me and jump back to avoid it. Pressing the advantage, I sprang forward and hitched a foot behind his boot while throwing my whole weight behind a shoulder tackle. The element of surprise worked in my favor because my move had him toppling backwards. A thud rang out as he slammed into the ground with me on top of him.

"Do you really think I would let anyone torture you?" I demanded, rage roaring in my voice while I tried desperately to pin his arms below me before he could counter. "Ever?"

Shade snatched his hands from my grip and grabbed a hold of my shirt. With a jerk of his arms and thrust of his hips, he threw me to the side and rolled on top of me.

"I'm an assassin!" he snapped back at me. "I've been trained to withstand torture!"

Using my momentum, I twisted and jabbed a knee into the side of his ribs. "I don't care!"

He winced when my knee made contact but it wasn't enough to force him off me. Instead, he used the moment when my attention was focused on my kick to trap my wrists in an iron grip. Irritation flashed through me when I realized it too late but there was nothing I could do as his strong hands pinned my arms to the ground.

"You weren't supposed to come." He leaned forward until I could feel his breath on my skin. "You weren't supposed to throw away your life for me. But now you've done it again! Everything else—"

"To hell with everything else!" I jerked against his grip and bucked my hips to try to heave him off me but the mass of packed muscle above me kept me mercilessly trapped. "Don't you get it? There is nothing I wouldn't do for you. Nothing I wouldn't sacrifice. Before this war started, I swore to all the gods that I would wade through rivers of blood and sell my soul to every demon in hell if it meant you lived."

Blinking in surprise, he sat back and relaxed his grip on my wrists. "What?"

After freeing my hands from his fingers, I slid out from underneath him. Pushing myself up so that we were sitting knee to knee, I frowned at him. "How in the world is that news to you?"

"I just..." He sighed and drew his fingers through his hair that had gotten tousled after our fight. "My guild would die for me because I'm their Master but I've never had someone who... I'm not used to..." Shrugging, he trailed off self-consciously. "Even Edward. We love each other but I don't think even he would do something like this."

"Well, for your information, Edward was the first one to realize that you weren't back and apparently, he got all the way to the stabling area before he was caught by your guild." A small smile tugged at my lips. "He's now being kept prisoner in his own tent by your assassins because he refused to accept that he couldn't go after you."

Shade's dark eyebrows rose higher with every word. "Seriously?"

"Yeah." Chuckling softly, I shook my head. "What the hell did you think?"

"I don't know. I've never had people who..." He trailed off again.

Reaching up, I pushed back a few strands of silky black hair from his face. A shudder went through him when my fingers brushed his skin. I rested my hand against his uninjured cheek.

"Well, you do now." I held his gaze. "Edward, me, Elaran... we would all do anything to protect you."

Still keeping eye contact, he lifted his hand and placed it along my jaw. "And I for you." He drew it down my throat and then started tracing my collarbone with his fingers while a smile drifted over his mouth. "My black-hearted thief."

"My cold-hearted assassin." I pulled those smiling lips towards mine.

For a moment, everything else dropped away. There was no metal cage around us, no star elf guards watching our every move from two chairs by the white cloth wall, no clank of armor or sound of people hurrying past outside the tent. Just me and him. And a desperate kiss trying to keep the heartbreak away.

After we drew back and the events of the past few hours came crashing back again, I found Shade's dark eyes roaming my face.

"Are you okay?" he asked.

"I don't know."

While we returned to the back of the cell so that we could lean against the metal bars and have a full view of the tent, I explained to him what had happened to my feelings about Rain. He already knew that the failed spell had severed my connection to my Storm Caster powers since Nimlithil had said as much, but he didn't know what exactly that meant. When I was finished, he just reached out and rested his hand on my leg.

"I'm sorry," he said.

"Yeah. Me too." I tipped my head back against the cold metal bar behind me and heaved a deep sigh. "I mean, I always knew there would be casualties in this war. I just never expected it to be someone who's already been dead for over a decade."

Shade leaned his shoulder closer to mine but said nothing.

Raking my fingers through my hair, I shook my head. "It's such a strange feeling, grieving for someone who I feel absolutely nothing for anymore, even though I know I should. Or not grieving for them anymore, I guess... Grieving for the loss of love I know I should feel but don't. Ugh." I let my hands drop into my lap again. "Everything is so damn complicated now. I'm sad because I'm not sad anymore and there's this burning rage inside me because I'm furious that the rage is gone. That spell messed with my emotions on a fundamental level and now I can't make sense of my feelings anymore."

Cloth flapped faintly as the fall breeze outside pulled at the tent walls and carried the smell of warm grass into our cage. The white-haired star elf in the chair closest to the exit got up and walked over to the tent flap. After peering outside for a few seconds, he returned to his partner. Wood creaked beneath his armor-clad body as he sank into the chair again.

"I mean," I continued, "am I even the same person? If I don't love Rain anymore and don't feel sad about her death or guilty about how she died, doesn't that make me another person?"

Shade started tracing idle circles on my thigh. "Do you feel like a different person?"

Cocking my head, I considered the question. I didn't love Rain anymore but I did have a lot of other people that I loved, and I wasn't sad about her death but I had plenty of other things that had happened in my life that I was still sad about. And I no longer felt guilty about the role I'd played in Rain's death, but even before I came here, I had already found a way to live with that guilt.

A few years ago, the loss of my feelings towards Rain would have significantly altered who I was as a person but by now, I had already worked through those feelings. And besides, I had been through so much other shit these last few years, so I had experienced a rather broad range of feelings in other circumstances as well. What Queen Nimlithil had done to me today filled me with sorrow and rage but no, I didn't feel like a different person.

"No," I said at last.

"Good. I don't think you've become a different person either." A smirk played over Shade's lips as he looked at me. "You're still stubborn, arrogant, and violent. And you still can't beat me in a fight."

Narrowing my eyes, I rammed my elbow into his ribs. "Bastard."

He chuckled and massaged his side while I shook my head at him. The gaping abyss inside me had closed a little. Some part of it would probably always be there as a reminder of the strange vacuum that had been created when my feelings towards Rain had been artificially removed. But in war, there was always a price to pay. And I guess this was mine. In order to save my new family, the love for my first family had been ripped from my soul.

That, along with my Storm Caster powers. I hadn't felt this empty since before Rain died and I had become Ashaana. Back then, it was hard to separate all the emotions because of the sadness and rage that followed Rain's death, but now in hindsight I realized that awakening my powers had been like putting a missing piece into the puzzle that was my soul. I hadn't even realized that the piece was missing until it was there, and now gone again. But I had lived a decade without it before, so I could learn to live with the strange echoing hole in my soul again.

I had vowed to do anything to make sure that Shade survived. Apparently, the gods had taken me up on my offer. Glancing at the handsome assassin next to me, I placed my hand over his and gave it a squeeze. Now, I just needed to figure out how to keep him alive and get him out of here. Otherwise, it would all have been for nothing.

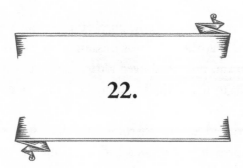

## 22.

Escaping from a simple metal cage would have been so much easier if there hadn't been two star elves with huge bows constantly monitoring every single move I made. I couldn't even twitch my fingers without them seeing it. Pacing back and forth in our cell, I tried for the hundredth time to figure out a way to get me and Shade out of this before we were shipped off to the City of Glass. Only immovable metal bars and watchful guards stared back.

Fabric rustled as the tent flap was thrown open, letting in both a fragrant night breeze and another pair of star elves. *Oh for Nemanan's sake!* I had been hoping that they would at least keep the same guards here the rest of the night so that there might be a chance of them falling asleep. But apparently not.

Captain Hadraeth flicked his gaze over me as he strode into the tent. After dumping a bundle of something on the table in the middle, he approached the two seated guards. The white-haired one who had trained an arrow on me when I picked the lock on my handcuffs followed him close behind.

"Captain," the two seated guards said and nodded as they got to their feet.

"Any trouble?" Hadraeth asked.

"They got into a fist fight around midday but since then it's been quiet."

Shade had joined me by the bars at the front of the cell to study the interaction between the guards, and presumably to see if there was some kind of weakness we could exploit. At the mention of the fight, he glanced down at me and shot me a smirk. I threw a mock scowl back at him before returning my attention to the conversation on the other side of the room.

"Good," Captain Hadraeth said and jerked his head in the direction of the exit. "Go get some food and rest before your next shift starts."

They nodded in acknowledgement before filing out through the slit in the white cloth wall. Wood groaned softly as Hadraeth and his white-haired companion lowered themselves into the chairs that the other two had vacated. I glared at the Captain of the Guard but he refused to meet my gaze. The other one, however, met my stare head on while taking out his bow. Still locking eyes with me, he pulled out an arrow with calculated slowness and nocked it.

"Babysitting two humans feels like a grand waste of time," he remarked to Hadraeth in an annoyed voice. After the words were out of his mouth, he seemed to remember who he was addressing and winced while adding, "Captain."

"Queen Nimlithil needs the girl's magic," Captain Hadraeth replied flatly.

"I wish we could at least kill the assassin."

"Agreed. But we need him in order to control her."

From behind the metal bars, I shot them a psychotic grin that made the white-haired one jerked back slightly and tighten his grip on his bow. A soft huff of laughter escaped Hadraeth's lips at that. Shaking his head, he handed his companion a waterskin that I wasn't sure actually contained water.

"Here," he said. "This is going to be a long night."

He accepted it gratefully and took a large swig. "That it is."

Captain Hadraeth still refused to meet my gaze but I continued glaring at him anyway. Now that he was here, our chances of escape had plummeted with rather impressive speed. There was no way that annoyingly honorable workaholic would ever doze off while on watch, and with him studying our every move, any attempt to pick the lock on the door was doomed from the start.

"Captain?" the second guard said.

"Yes?"

Metal and wood clattered through the tent. I blinked. Captain Hadraeth was standing in front of his chair, staring down at the white-haired guard who had just toppled forward and fallen face first on the ground. A grunt made it past the captain's lips as he heaved his companion up. When the guard's unconscious body was once more slouching in the chair, he turned around and finally met my eyes.

"What's going on?" I asked, suspicious creeping into my voice.

Captain Hadraeth stalked towards the cage. "You're getting out." Keys jangled as he unlocked the door and then yanked it open before stabbing a hand towards the white bundle on the table. "Put that on."

Shade and I exchanged a glance. Both of us were most likely trying to figure out if this was a trap but since no apparent threat appeared at the moment, we only nodded at each other and slipped out of the cell.

Placing a hand on the pale silken fabric, I pulled it upwards. Sharp objects tumbled out of it in a clattering of steel. Knives. My knives, to be specific, as well as some I assumed Shade had brought. Captain Hadraeth had stalked over to the tent flap and had been peering outside when I'd caused the cascade of weapons, but at the noise, he turned back and shot me an irritated glare. I rolled my eyes. If he had actually told me there were blades in there, I could've avoided making such a racket.

With practiced moves, I strapped on my knives while Shade did the same next to me. The bundle of white fabric turned out to be two cloaks. I handed one to Shade and swung the other one around my shoulders. Since it had no doubt been made for a star elf, it was far too long for me so the silken fabric pooled around me on the ground. By the entrance, Hadraeth was still watching the outside through a narrow slit.

Shade met my gaze for a brief second but before I could say anything, he had already moved. A soft hiss sounded. I tried to resist the urge to once again roll my eyes but failed. Instead, I just walked over to where Shade and Hadraeth were standing.

The assassin had pulled a knife and snuck up behind the elf. With a blade pressed against his throat from behind, Shade backed Hadraeth away from the exit.

"Give me one good reason why we should trust you," Shade growled in his ear.

"Apart from the fact that I just drugged one of my own men, released you, and gave you weapons?" he said in a voice brimming with barely restrained anger.

"You've been playing both sides for far too long now. How do we know this isn't just some trick to get us to lead you back to our friends?"

Captain Hadraeth barked a harsh laugh. "Distrusting much?"

"Yeah, it's one of our core traits," I interjected and lifted my shoulders in a light shrug. "But I think you already know that."

"Maybe we should just kill you and take our chances." Shade pressed the blade harder into the captain's throat. "I *should* kill you for everything you've let your queen do to Storm."

Still standing with a knife-wielding assassin behind him, Hadraeth spread his arms wide. "Go ahead, then."

Shade flicked his eyes to me. I studied the grim expression on the elf's face for a few seconds before shaking my head. After giving me the tiniest of shrugs, Shade removed the blade from Hadraeth's neck and stepped back. Running a hand over his throat, Captain Hadraeth turned around to face us both.

"Done threatening me?" he demanded.

After sticking the knife back in its sheath, Shade gave him a mocking smile and a nod.

"Good," Hadraeth said and stalked back towards the tent flap. "Now get ready to move as soon as I give the word."

While Captain Hadraeth went back to peering through the slit in the tent wall, I shot Shade an exasperated glare to inform him that threatening to kill the one person who might get us out had been a stupid move. Shade only replied with an innocent shrug and a smirk. He did have a point, though. Hadraeth had played both sides since the day I met him, mostly because of his feelings for Illeasia, so it was a bit hard to trust him completely.

Outside the tent, people were moving about and probably getting everything ready for the night. I wasn't sure what we were waiting for but just standing around doing nothing was making me nervous so I decided to ask the question that had been going through my mind ever since the still unconscious guard had toppled to the ground.

"Why?"

Captain Hadraeth didn't answer. Didn't even look back at me. He only continued watching the area outside the tent. Just when I thought he wasn't going to respond at all, he let out a long sigh.

"Because it's the right thing to do."

"Illeasia?" I asked, knowing that he would understand the full question embedded in that one word.

"No." Still not taking his eyes off the night outside, he ran a hand through his dark silver hair and shook his head. "I mean, yes, she's in on it. But it was my idea."

He was quiet for a long moment. Then, he cast a brief glance back at me. Emotions I recognized but still couldn't quite decipher swirled in his dark violet eyes.

"You were right," he said. "This is wrong. What Queen Nimlithil is doing is wrong." Breaking my gaze, he turned back to the hole in the tent wall. "I've known it for quite some time but I haven't done anything about it because... Well, I'm the Captain of the Queen's Guard. My honor is everything to me and when my queen gives me an order, it's my duty to obey."

He sounded so much like Elaran that my chest tightened. Here was another elf who valued honor and loyalty and who was caught between love and duty. Hadraeth might have been my enemy as often as my ally but I still couldn't stop my cold black heart from breaking a little at his words because all I could hear was Elaran's voice when he admitted that if it came down to a choice between Tkeideru and Illeasia, he didn't know what he would choose.

"Doing this, outright betraying my queen, is shredding my soul," Captain Hadraeth continued. "But I can't stand by and let things like this happen anymore." Twisting his head, he flicked his eyes from Shade to me before going back to studying the outside. "She wanted to torture and break you, all in the name of a world free of pain. It's not right." He let out another long sigh. "So yes, if Illeasia had asked me I would've done it for her but that's not why I went to her with this plan. I'm doing this because..." Trailing off, he let out a humorless laugh. "I'm doing this because I'm on the wrong side in this war."

Wow. Captain Hadraeth had indeed been playing both sides for a long time, but it appeared as though he had finally picked a side. And to my complete and utter surprise, it was ours. I opened my mouth to reply but before I could get any words out, he cut me off.

"Now!" he hissed and flicked his hand at us.

All three of us darted into the night outside.

# 23.

Cicadas sang into the darkened landscape somewhere outside camp. There also appeared to be some kind of gathering of people on the opposite side because the rows of white tents we snuck through were mostly deserted while chatter and laughter came from the other direction. No doubt thanks to Princess Illeasia. I pulled the hood of my cloak down deeper as we moved farther away from the prison tent.

"The forest is in the other direction," Shade breathed.

"It's booby-trapped with mist that knocks people out," Captain Hadraeth whispered back. "In this darkness, it's impossible to spot all the triggers so walking out the front is our best option."

The bright fall day had turned into an equally clear night. Cool winds tugged gently at my too long cloak as I walked, and overhead, countless stars glittered in the dark blue heavens. It was beautiful. But the glowing moon also bathed the entire area in silvery light, making it easier to see through the blackness. If someone looked too closely at me, they would notice that I was far too short to be an elf. Slinking between the shadows, I prayed to both Nemanan and the fickle Cadentia that no one would be suspicious enough of the Guard Captain to study his companions in too much detail.

"Captain!" a voice called.

I sent a silent string of curses at the cruel Goddess of Luck. *Really, Cadentia?*

An arm slammed into my chest as Hadraeth shoved me and Shade into the shadows of a tent. The assassin and I shrank back into the darkness but in our white cloaks, we were still far too visible for my liking.

"What?" Captain Hadraeth demanded as two other star elves appeared.

Both of them were dressed in the spotless armor that marked them as guards, but at least they didn't have any weapons out. They trailed to a halt a few steps from their captain. Violet eyes flicked from me and Shade to the impatient elf before them.

"I was just..." the one on the right began. "Well, we were just wondering if you were heading to the gathering?" He waved a hand towards the opposite side of camp. "Princess Illeasia said she had something exciting and important to tell us and we just thought... well, aren't you gonna be there?"

"I'll be there."

The two guards exchanged a look. When no other explanation was forthcoming, the bolder one gestured to me and Shade. I wanted to pull my hood further down but that would only look even more suspicious so I just remained standing there, trying to look nonthreatening. Shade rested his palm against the small of my back.

"Who's this?" the guard asked.

"They're... uhm... human defectors from the army." Hadraeth cleared his throat. "I have to get them set up first, then I'm joining you at the gathering."

It took great effort not to facepalm. By Nemanan, he really was as bad at lying as Elaran. The actual lie in itself was a good one but the execution was seriously lacking in credibility.

"Okay," the guard replied with another glance at his friend. Then they both dipped their chin. "See you at the gathering then, captain."

Hadraeth nodded brusquely before grabbing my shoulder and hauling me back out. I kept my eyes on the ground. Two pairs of white boots passed me while the captain steered Shade forward as well. With a small sigh of relief building in my chest, I listened to the grass crunch under their feet as the two guards moved past. Then it stopped.

"Hey, wait, isn't that the assassin we caught last night?" the star elf guard said. He sucked in a sharp breath between his teeth. "By the Stars, it is! Call for backup! Captain, they're impostors–"

I shot forward. Next to me, a streak of black and white flashed through the night as well. Steel sang as I yanked out a hunting knife and whipped it towards the closest guard's throat.

"Stop!" Captain Hadraeth hissed.

Nervous violet eyes stared down at me from the other side of the blade but I didn't push it any further into the guard's throat. From the corner of my eye, I could see another sharp knife hovering by the second guard's neck. A lethal Master Assassin was attached to the other end of it but he had also halted his attack at the same moment I had.

"Put those down," Hadraeth growled. "You do not kill my men."

Shade and I exchanged a quick glance.

"I said back off!" the captain snapped.

After lifting one shoulder in a lopsided shrug, I removed my knife from the anxious guard's throat and stepped back. Shade did the same but let out a frustrated sigh.

"This is a mistake," he said in a low voice.

"Shut it." Captain Hadraeth turned his dark stare on his men. "Queen Nimlithil has tasked me with a crucial mission but it's also highly secretive. You did not see me. Or them. Understood?"

"Of course, captain," they stammered in unison.

"Good. Now go back to the gathering. I'll join you shortly."

Armor clanked as they hurried away. I watched the moonlight reflect on their polished breastplates until the mass of white tents had swallowed them. A heavy weight settled in my stomach.

"This is a mistake," Shade repeated, echoing my own thoughts. "They'll betray you."

Captain Hadraeth flicked his wrist and stalked forward again. "No, they won't betray their captain. And I might be helping you, but these people are still *my* men, and I will not allow you to kill them."

Shade pressed his lips into a thin line but said nothing. I didn't either as I followed the two of them towards the front of camp. Being an underworlder, I of course agreed with Shade that it would have been better to kill them. But I also understood Hadraeth. We all had family. And these guards were his.

Cheering rose from somewhere behind us. I cast a quick look over my shoulder but the gathering was too far away to yield any clues as to what had caused it. Returning my gaze to the path ahead, I hiked up the too long cloak and hurried after my two long-legged companions.

The rest of the way to the front of the star elves' camp was mercifully uneventful. Wide plains spread out before us as we cleared the final row of tents. I flicked my gaze across the area and panic crackled through me when I took in the ring of guards blocking our way to freedom.

"Now what?" I asked as Hadraeth shoved us towards a small wagon strapped to a white horse.

"Wait here," he said.

Leaning against the back of the wooden cart, I crossed my arms and did as he said. Shade took up position next to me. Even through the cloak and my clothes, I could feel his body heat where his arm brushed mine.

The minutes dragged on.

Then, clothes rustled as a figure in white ran right for us. Shade and I straightened, hands going to our weapons, but Hadraeth appeared to visibly relax at the sight. When my human eyes understood what I was looking at, I let a smile drift over my lips.

"Sorry it took so long," Princess Illeasia panted. If there was such a thing as a joyous summer breeze whirling over the grass in a fluttering of white skirts, that was what she looked like as she skidded to a halt in front of us with a smile on her face. "They wouldn't stop congratulating me."

A hint of pain crept into Captain Hadraeth's expression but it was gone so fast that I wasn't sure I'd seen it.

"I'm glad it worked, Princess." He gave her a slight smile before motioning at the wagon. "We should go. Right now."

"Of course." Illeasia drew her fingers through her loose silver curls to smoothen them after her run while a broad smile spread across her lips. Sparkling life seemed to radiate from her beautiful face. "Storm. Shade. It's been a while. Sorry about my mother and all that." Shooing us towards the back of the cart, she let out a soft laugh. "We'll chat more once we're out."

My eyebrows shot up. "You're coming with us?"

Wood creaked as Shade jumped onto the wagon bed and leaned down with an arm outstretched. I considered ignoring it and climbing up on my own but decided that speed was more important than my ego so I took his offered hand. The slight smirk that ghosted across his lips when I allowed him to help me informed me that I should have listened to my initial instinct. Damn assassin.

"Yes," Princess Illeasia replied as she and Hadraeth pulled out something they had stashed next to a large white tent nearby. "In fact, we both are."

I shifted my gaze to the captain and raised my eyebrows.

Carrying a bundle of brown tarp, he gave me a self-conscious shrug. "There's no going back after this." He nodded at the flat part of the cart we were sitting on. "Lie down. No, not there. In the corner. We need to cover you."

After wiggling as far into the back corner as I could get, I lay down on my side with the short wooden wall against my back. Boots scraped as Shade scooted over as well. When he was close enough that he was almost sitting on top of me, he paused but didn't lie down. Instead, his eyes were fixed on Captain Hadraeth.

"Thank you," the Master Assassin said in a voice filled with sincerity. "Sorry I doubted you."

Hadraeth let out a soft chuckle and nodded in the direction of Shade's face. "Well, I did give you those bruises."

"That you did." A wicked smile that promised there would be a reckoning for that at some point flashed over his lips. "That you did."

Then, he lay back and curled up beside me. Illeasia and Hadraeth unfurled the tarp in a snap of cloth and draped it over us. At a prompt from the captain, Shade pulled his legs up further and pressed himself tighter against me. I folded one arm under my cheek to make the position more comfortable while I let the other one rest on his upper arm. His face was so close to mine that my lips almost brushed his.

Seemingly satisfied with our disguise, the captain and the princess climbed into the front seat, making the wagon rock slightly, and flicked the reins. The cart lurched into motion.

Though I still didn't quite understand how they were supposed to just ride out of here without being stopped, I kept silent and trusted that they had a plan. Alright, fine. The athletic assassin tracing circles over the side of my ribs while staring into my eyes from only a breath away was slightly distracting as well.

It was ridiculous. I was the Queen of the Underworld, not some lovesick schoolgirl, and we were in the middle of a daring escape, but Shade's graceful muscles shifting against my body were still taking up a disproportionate amount of my attention. Absolutely preposterous. I narrowed my eyes at him. His hot breath danced over my skin in a silent laugh at that but his fingers didn't stop caressing my side. Damn assassin.

"Princess Illeasia," a male voice said somewhere outside our dark hiding place. "Captain Hadraeth. Where are you going? Shouldn't you be back at the celebration?"

"So you have already heard? Even all the way out here?" the princess said and let out a rippling but slightly embarrassed laugh.

"Of course. It's not every day that our princess and our captain announce that they're getting married."

It took all my considerable self-control not to gasp. They were getting married? But what about Elaran? This was going to break him. Panic pounded through my veins with ever increasing strength until Illeasia spoke up again.

"I suppose not." She let out another light laugh. "But everyone is just making such a fuss and well... we wanted to celebrate on our own. Just for a little while. Out here in the open. Under the stars."

*Oh.* This was the ruse. Both for making sure everyone was gathered and preoccupied at the opposite end of camp and for getting out without raising any alarm. By all the gods. I wasn't sure for whom this lie was more painful. Illeasia, who was in love with someone else, or Hadraeth who actually was in love with the princess and probably dreamed about marrying her. And they had done this for us.

Shade gave my side a comforting squeeze as if he was also thinking the same thing.

Outside our cloth cocoon, our two rescuers were accepting congratulations from the guards around us. Based on the voices, there appeared to be an alarming amount of them. But at least no one had lifted the brown tarp bundled in the corner. So far so good.

I could barely believe it. We were getting out. Even though my chest was still filled with emotions that didn't quite add up and that I wasn't sure what to do with, a profound sense of relief filled me. When I left, I had feared that Shade was already dead. But here he was. His warm strong body pressed into mine. His intelligent black eyes holding my gaze. He was alive. I was alive. Illeasia and Hadraeth were joining our side. And we were all getting out. I smiled into the darkness. Maybe there was some kindness left in the world after all.

Shade's gaze turned suspicious. I frowned at him. Then I realized what it was that he was hearing. Or rather, not hearing. From one second to the next, all the voices around us had gone silent.

I screamed as a pair of hands wrapped around my ankles and yanked me out from our hiding place.

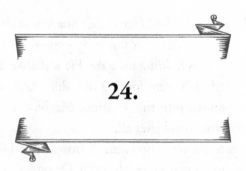

# 24.

Wooden splinters ripped at my cloak as I slid along the rough surface. Twisting, I tried to get to a weapon but my heart dropped into my stomach when the wagon bed underneath my back suddenly disappeared and I was plummeting downwards.

My breath exploded from my lungs as I crashed down on the grass. On instinct, I rolled to the side to escape my assailant but a foot on my cloak had me coming to an abrupt halt. The garment dug into my throat. Reaching up, I flicked open the clasp and continued my roll. Air rushed out of me again as the next boot took me straight in the stomach.

Black spots danced across my vision. I sucked in a strained gasp while trying desperately to hold on to consciousness as my body spasmed from the blow. Grass appeared under my cheek. The smell of damp soil enveloped me as I forced a breath into my starved lungs. Someone was twisting my arms behind my back but I could do nothing about it because my body was still trying to shut down on me. I was vaguely aware of someone dark-clad struggling a few strides away and of someone, or perhaps several people, screaming about something. Cold metal wrapped around my wrists.

Still failing to make my body obey me, I was helpless when someone hauled me up and dumped me over their shoulder like a sack of grain. The way back into the tents passed in a blur as my mind fought against the unconsciousness that the boot to my solar plexus had tried to produce, but the one thing I did see was the face of an anxious guard watching me with nervous violet eyes. The face of the guard I had almost killed before Hadraeth stopped me. The one who had betrayed us after all.

Pain shot through my hip as it slammed into the ground. I blinked. Something black flew in after me and then metallic ringing vibrated through my skull. Closing my eyes, I focused on making the world stop being so wobbly. Boots stomped around as if a number of people were entering and leaving the area and there were sounds of a scuffle from somewhere close by.

"I am truly disappointed in both of you."

Shards of ice scraped against my bones at the sound of that voice.

"You have defied me time and again. It will not happen again."

I opened my eyes. My vision still swam slightly at the edges but it was at last clear enough to take in my surroundings. A metal cage inside a white tent. An assassin handcuffed beside me. And there on the other side of the bars were five star elves. Two of them were aiming nocked arrows at the one kneeling in the middle of the tent. Hadraeth. Shackles gleamed around his wrists. Next to him, Princess Illeasia was staring between the captured captain and the final elf in the room.

Clad in a regal silver gown and a glittering headdress of white gems was the person I wanted to stab more than anyone on this entire continent. Queen Nimlithil.

When I went to push myself up, I realized that I was handcuffed. Or *still* handcuffed was probably more accurate. Rolling back onto my side, I drew my fingers along my belt in search of a couple of lockpicks I'd sewn in there but before I found them, a pair of gentle hands wrapped around my shoulders.

Shade lifted me until I was sitting up on the ground and then went to work on my manacles.

"You okay?" he breathed in my ear.

I nodded. When a soft click sounded, he removed my handcuffs and placed them on the ground next to his own discarded ones before helping me to my feet. The world swayed around me. I braced both hands on the metal bars before me to make sure I didn't topple over. Shade slid up next to me, his muscled body a steady weight against my side.

While the two of us had been busy getting out of our restraints, Queen Nimlithil had been lecturing her daughter and her Guard Captain like some kind of disappointed school teacher. I squinted at them. The cold metal underneath my palms helped ground me and push away the last of the fog in my vision.

Was that a...? By Nemanan, it was.

There was a long white shaft sticking out of Captain Hadraeth's right shoulder. It had gone clean through his armor and appeared to have severed something important because when he tried to lift his shackled hands, only his left arm moved.

"This is entirely my fault," Queen Nimlithil went on. "I should have been more strict with you from the beginning." Shaking her head, she flicked a slender hand in the direction of Hadraeth's face. "After you allowed them to escape the dungeons in Sker, I truly believed that giving you that scar would be enough to remind you. That every time you looked into a mirror and saw that scar it would remind you of your dishonor and where your loyalties should lie, and what the punishment for treachery is. But it appears as though I was wrong."

Anger crackled through my veins. The scar down his cheek was from Nimlithil? She had deliberately scarred his face as punishment for letting all of us escape after she captured us in the Red Fort? I curled my fingers around the metal bars and squeezed so tightly my knuckles turned white. She had hurt him for helping us. I was going to kill her. By all the gods, I was going to kill her.

Shade stepped closer to steady me as if he could feel the fury burning through me.

"However, it appears as though the reason you keep defying me is because of my daughter." Queen Nimlithil turned to Illeasia, her silver skirts rustling with the movement. "You, my dear, have been taking every opportunity to work against our goal of a better world. I truly believed it to be a phase, but your actions tonight prove that you are too lost in your own pain and sorrow to see clearly. I am sorry that I have let this go on for so long. Tonight, we will change that. Tonight, you will receive the help you need." She raised her voice. "Raemsal!"

The scholar from before lifted the tent flap and stepped inside. After smoothing his crisp white suit, he bowed to his queen and then took up position next to her. My thoughts were spinning out of control. She said she was going to help her daughter and then called in the scholar who had performed the pain ritual on me. Icy dread spread like a cloud of poison inside me. *Please don't tell me that she...*

"You will complete the ritual, Illeasia." The silver-haired queen gave her daughter a hopeful smile. "And then everything will be as it should once more."

"What?" Illeasia blurted out, speaking for the first time since we arrived in this tent. For the past few minutes, she had only been staring between her mother and Hadraeth as if in shock, but this piece of news appeared to have snapped her out of it. "No way!"

"My dear, you are clearly hurting, which is why you are acting out." She smiled sadly. "And to make it worse, your behavior is making other people act out as well. Only see what you have made Hadraeth do."

"She hasn't *made me* do anything!" Captain Hadraeth snapped. Chains clanked as he tried once more to lift his arms, but only the left one moved this time too. Still on his knees with two drawn bows pointed at him, he glared up at his queen. "This was all me. I'm the one who decided to free Storm and Shade because what you're doing is wrong. I've known it for a long time. A world free of pain would be great, but this isn't the way. Torturing and breaking people is not the way to a better world!" He snarled at her. "And there is nothing you can do to me to make me change my mind."

"I am sad to hear that, but it matters little. You have already been stripped of your position as Captain of the Guard and that is not why we are in this tent tonight."

Hadraeth looked like someone had struck him but Nimlithil only shot him a disdainful look before shifting her gaze to Illeaisa.

"You will perform the ritual." She motioned for Raemsal to step forward. "Right now."

Princess Illeasia backed up a step and shook her head. "No."

Blowing out a sharp sigh through her nose, the elven queen reached out and picked up Captain Hadraeth's discarded sword from the table next to her. Her gleaming silver bracelets clinked as she lifted the blade and stepped around the kneeling captain. The sword looked so out of place in her slender hands but she held it with surprising confidence.

"I did not want to do this, but you leave me no choice." Queen Nimlithil raised the sword and placed the tip of it at the base of Captain Hadraeth's throat. "Illeasia, you will do the ritual. Or Hadraeth dies."

My eyes widened. She couldn't be serious.

"What?" Illeasia jerked back. "Mother, are you out of your mind?"

"No." She gave her daughter another sad smile. "This is for your own good. As soon as you complete the ritual, you will understand. It is all for the best."

Releasing my grip on the metal bars, I retreated a step. I couldn't let her do this. If Illeasia performed the ritual, she would stop being who she was. All that made her into the loving person full of bubbling life would cease to exist. I had experienced only a part of it myself. To stop the pain, the spell removed the cause for it: love. Illeasia would turn into an empty shell. I couldn't let her.

Elaran's words echoed through my mind. *If you see Illeasia... could you just... make sure she's safe?* I had to make sure she was safe. For her own sake. And for his.

Spitting out a silent curse, I stalked towards the cell door. Shade hissed something behind me but I didn't care anymore.

I had to stop this. Pulling out a pair of lockpicks, I closed the distance to the door.

A twang rang out. I sucked in a sharp breath as I was yanked to the side by a strong fist gripping my shirt, but not before a spike of pain flared up my arm.

"The next one goes into his leg." The white-haired guard who Hadraeth had drugged, and who had been guarding his former captain for the past few minutes, nocked another arrow and shifted it towards Shade. "Back away from the door."

I glanced at the tear in my shirt and the blood trickling down from the wound in my upper arm that his first arrow had given me. If Shade hadn't pulled me back, it would've gone clean through my arm. The door was only one stride away. I flicked my gaze between the white arrow in front of us and the assassin it was aimed at. Wood groaned as the white-haired guard drew back further. Gods damn it.

Rage burned through me but I backed away until I had returned to my previous spot. If he shot Shade in the leg, our chances of ever escaping would go from incredibly slim to not a chance in hell.

"Do you see what violence your actions foster?" Queen Nimlithil said to Illeasia. "You have to do this, for your own good." She shifted her gaze to the scholar. "Raemsal. Now, please."

"Don't do it," Hadraeth said in a steady voice. "Let her kill me. I don't care. Just don't do this." His dark violet eyes turned pleading as he looked at the princess. "Please. If you care for me in any way, please don't do this."

Tears welled up in Illeasia's eyes as she gazed back at him. "I do care about you. I always have. Which is why I can't let anything happen to you."

"Please don't–"

Queen Nimlithil cut him off with a wave of her hand. "Illeasia, you have three seconds." With the point still against Hadraeth's throat, she lifted the hilt of the sword higher. "One. Two."

"Okay!" Princess Illeasia cried. Tears now streamed down her pale cheeks. "I'll do it, Mother."

"No!" Hadraeth and I snapped in unison.

Raemsal stepped in front of Illeasia. Shackles rattled as Captain Hadraeth tried desperately to get to his feet. Another twang sounded and then a scream pierced the tent as the second guard fired an arrow through the captain's thigh. Illeasia cried out in shock and pressed a hand over her mouth. I took a step towards the cell door. Wood creaked as the white-haired guard drew back further and shifted his aim to me while the other one nocked another arrow and aimed it at Hadraeth's other leg.

Another twang and another scream of pain echoed through the tent. I froze in place. For one heart-pounding second, I didn't dare turn around because I didn't want to see if the arrow that had been fired had been for Shade. Then Captain Hadraeth collapsed to the ground with a second arrow through his other leg.

"Stop!" Illeasia cried out, her voice breaking. "Stop it!"

The white-haired guard stared me down but his bow was still drawn, which meant that Shade was still unharmed. *For now,* the guard's hard stare seemed to say. Slowly lifting my hands, I retreated again.

Hadraeth was moaning softly on the ground. Blood welled out from the wounds in his legs and dripped down his white armor. Illeasia was on her knees with both hands pressed over her mouth and tears streaming down her face.

"Proceed," Queen Nimlithil said.

While the princess struggled to her feet again, Shade slid up next to me.

"We have to do something," he whispered.

"I know." I didn't dare take my eyes off the guard with the bow pointed at us. "But what? He can fire before we reach the door."

The scholar cleared his throat. "Repeat after me."

A choked sob escaped Illeasia's throat as she took her hands from her mouth. I desperately cast my gaze around for anything to use as a shield while we forced the door. There was absolutely nothing in the cell. Not even a plate.

Raemsal began reciting the first part of the spell. The power of those words seemed to vibrate through the air.

My heart pounded in my chest.

"Don't do this!" Hadraeth called out, his voice a broken rasp. "Please, Illeasia!"

The princess repeated the words spoken by the scholar. Her voice trembled.

"I'll draw his fire and you'll get the door open," Shade hissed under his breath.

Before he could take another step, my hand shot out and yanked him back. "No! He's an *elf*. From a few strides away, there's no way in hell he'll miss! And if you're hurt or... dead." My voice cracked slightly on the word. "I can't survive it."

Power thrummed through the tent as Raemsal recited the next part.

"Illeasia, please!" Hadraeth tried crawling towards her but with practically no working limbs, he didn't get far. "Please don't do this! I love you, Illeasia. I love you. Don't do this."

The pain in his voice was so heartbreaking it almost sent me to my knees. Princess Illeasia looked to her friend. Tears flooded her cheeks and her lips wobbled as she held his gaze. Then, she repeated the scholar's words.

Black flashed past me as Shade shot towards the door. The scream got stuck in my throat as the white-haired guard moved with him and fired. Faster than I could see, the assassin twisted and dove towards the locked gate in order to escape the arrow. A shocked gasp ripped from his lips. I darted forward.

Shade was on the ground, blood pouring from a slash in his side. I skidded to a halt next to him, my knees scraping against the ground with the speed, and pressed my hands against the wound. Warm blood welled over my fingers. Panic clawed its way up my spine as wood creaked again on the other side of the metal bars. I slid in front of Shade, shielding him with my own body, and spread my bloody hands wide.

"Don't," I croaked. "We get it. Okay? I'll make sure he doesn't move again. We'll stay right here."

For a moment, the white-haired archer looked like he was going to fire again, just for the hell of it, but he only continued staring us down. The scholar began the final part of the spell.

Behind me, Shade grunted as he pushed himself into a sitting position.

"How bad?" I asked, not daring to turn around to look.

"I'm fine. It's just a scratch."

It was probably worse than that but there was nothing I could do about it now. Everything was spinning out of control. Like a dropped ball of yarn bouncing down the stairs, unspooling its thread in a mad rush before it could be caught and rolled back up.

Hadraeth screamed and clawed at the ground as the scholar finished the final passage. Stains covered Illeasia's white dress from the tears that continued running down her face. I flicked desperate eyes between the door and the archer pointing a lethal arrow at the assassin who had struggled onto his knees next to me. The metallic smell of blood wafted into the air as Shade took his palm from his wound and pressed it to the ground to stabilize himself. My heart slammed against my ribs.

Illeasia started the final part of the spell.

There had to be something. I cast my gaze around. There had to be something I could do to stop this without getting Shade killed. Hard violet eyes monitored every move I made from behind the huge white bow. There had to be something!

The air in the whole tent vibrated with power as Illeasia neared the end of the final sentence.

Captain Hadraeth pounded his fist on the ground.

I reached towards the metal bars.

A pulse shot through the tent.

And then a scream shattered through the air.

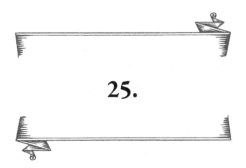

# 25.

Hadreath sucked in a ragged breath and released another earth-shattering howl. Shock and searing panic rang through my skull like deafening bells as I shifted my gaze to the silver-haired princess. Illeasia's facial expression smoothed out. The tears stopped. Cocking her head slightly, she blinked. Once.

"How do you feel, my dear?" Queen Nimlithil asked.

Princess Illeasia tore her gaze from the heartbroken Hadraeth choking back a broken sob on the ground and shifted it to her mother. A smile spread across her lips. It did not reach her eyes.

"Much better," she said. "Thank you, Mother."

"I am so glad to hear that. I knew you would understand that this was for the best."

The words clanged through me. I stared into Illeasia's pale violet eyes, trying to see the real her behind the bland mask that had descended on her face. Trying to see the joy of living that usually beamed from her like bright sunlight. There was nothing. Only a shell. The real Illeasia was gone.

This was going to kill Elaran.

"By your leave, Your Majesty?" Raemsal said, his tone clipped.

The queen leveled a commanding stare on her scholar. "Yes. However, before you are excused, answer me this. Why did we do this inside this tent tonight?"

Something flickered in Raemsal's eyes. "Because you did not want anyone to know that you had to force your daughter to complete this ritual because you could not control her."

An incredibly dangerous expression flashed over Queen Nimlithil's face. Raemsal jerked back slightly and cleared his throat.

"Because screams inside the prison tent would not cause alarm so it was the best location," he amended. "And you did not want anyone to know what happened here."

"Correct," she said. Her gaze was full of authority as she moved it between the scholar and the two guards. "Make sure it remains that way."

The unspoken 'or else' was loud and clear. Raemsal bowed at the waist before slipping back out into the night. With bows still drawn, the two archers nodded their acknowledgement as well.

I continued staring at Illeasia. The shock was wearing off now and replacing it was an unending torrent of fury. It helped clear my mind enough that I finally dared look at the wound in Shade's side.

Blood still dripped down his pale skin but it had slowed considerably. By the looks of it, it would need stitching. But Shade had been right. It wasn't life-threatening. Thank the gods for that at least.

Inside me, the pounding anger was building to a fiery hell. Throwing a glare at the archer still aiming a nocked arrow in our direction, I struggled to my feet.

"How could you?" My voice was a cold deadly caress of night air. "Your own daughter. How could you do this to her?"

Queen Nimlithil arched a delicate eyebrow at me as if she had forgotten that I was there. A sneer curled her lips when she looked at me. "I do not expect a murderous thief to understand. I know what is best for my daughter. And for the rest of the world."

Raging fury crackled through me like wildfire. If I'd had my powers, I could've blown this entire tent to smithereens with the force of my fury. A sharp pang echoed through the gaping hole inside me at the thought, but I pushed the devastation over my lost powers aside and slammed my hand into the metal bars. It produced a dull clang that vibrated through my very bones.

"How dare you–"

"Silence!" Queen Nimlithil cut me off.

Both guards shifted their arrows in my direction. Shade was still seated on the ground next to me with a palm pressed to his side, probably trying to disturb the wound as little as possible in order to allow the blood a chance to clot. Provoking them could make them take their anger out on Shade, and that wasn't worth it. So I narrowed my eyes at them but kept my mouth shut.

Queen Nimlithil pointed the sword she was still holding at Hadraeth. He had managed to push himself up on his side but the arrows through his legs and shoulder, along with the shackles, made it impossible for him to move further than that. When the blade appeared before him again, he barely registered it. His eyes were locked on Illeasia's expressionless face.

"You have betrayed your queen to our enemies and you have declared yourself an enemy of our mission," Nimlithil said. "Do you deny this?"

"Illeasia?" Hadraeth said, completely ignoring his queen.

"Yes?" she replied blandly.

He swallowed hard but before he could say anything else, Queen Nimlithil stepped more firmly in front of him and placed the sword against the base of his throat.

"I said, do you deny this?"

At last, he tore his gaze from the princess he loved and shifted it to his queen. The pain and devastation and sheer hatred that crackled in his dark eyes could have burned down the world. Gritting my teeth, I tried desperately to smother the raging wildfire of fury inside my own soul before I did something stupid, but it was growing increasingly difficult.

Captain Hadraeth raised his chin. "The only thing I regret is not doing it sooner."

Looking down on him, Queen Nimlithil gave him a pitying look and scoffed delicately. "I suspected as much."

And then she shoved the sword clean through Captain Hadraeth's throat.

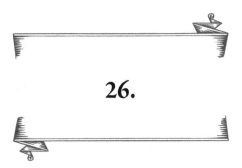

# 26.

A shocked gasp was abruptly interrupted as sharpened steel severed Captain Hadraeth's windpipe. It was replaced by wet gurgling. Blood welled out from the wound and slid down his throat while a squishy sound echoed into the dead silent tent as Queen Nimlithil pulled out the blade. The two guards slackened their bows and stared at their queen in open-mouthed horror as she rested the red-smeared tip on the ground.

Metal chains rustled as Hadraeth tried to raise his hands to his throat but since his right arm was still nonfunctional, he didn't make it. Instead, he collapsed onto his side. Blood bubbles popped as he struggled to breathe and terror flared behind his eyes. His body convulsed in tune with the wet gasps that burst out of him. Then it slowed. Limbs went limp and his head thumped down on the ground.

And then the last light that the world would ever see from the Captain of the Queen's Guard died in Hadraeth's dark violet eyes.

Captain Hadraeth was gone. Forever. Body and soul ripped from this world in one cruel act. Never again would he put on his white armor with pride and go out to protect the princess he had loved with his whole heart full of honor and loyalty.

"What a shame," Illeasia said, not even a flicker of emotion crossing her impassive face. "He was a good soldier."

Princess Illeasia, who had loved Hadraeth like family, had given up her own ability to feel in order to save his life. But Nimlithil had murdered him anyway. Had killed him in cold blood as he lay shackled and incapacitated on the ground, not even allowing a soldier to die on his feet. And the princess who had sacrificed everything for him couldn't even mourn him because she no longer loved him.

The screaming rage inside me had given way to a silence that boomed so loudly it was deafening.

"Yes, a shame. However, it was necessary." Queen Nimlithil flicked a hand at the corpse before her as if it was garbage. "Get him out of here."

In the span of a few minutes, three lives had been destroyed. The honorable and loyal Hadraeth who had saved my life more than once. The joyful Princess Illeasia who would never again laugh and beam and dance through the world like liquid sunlight. And the grumpy elf who loved her more than life itself. Elaran. Elaran, who was family to me and who I had vowed to protect from harm. All of them. Ruined beyond repair.

"Come, my dear, we must–"

Something snapped inside my soul.

A scream of raw fury shattered from my throat. Tipping my head back, I threw my arms out and bellowed my world-ending rage into the night. Fabric tore and metal creaked and snapped and clanged. Darkness to rival the blackest pits of hell wrapped around me like a silk cloak while lightning cleaved the air in earsplitting claps. Shrieks of terror vibrated through the roaring anger I unleashed upon the world.

Tilting my head back down, I found dark tendrils whipping around me like lethal snakes while lightning crackled over my skin. Shade was still seated on the ground beside me, but instead of pressing a hand to his wound, his arms were looped tightly around my leg. The rest of the camp around us was... not there anymore.

Tents had been ripped and flung away in a large circle around us. Even the cage we had been locked in had been cracked apart from the inside. Metal bars lay scattered on the grass along with tables and other furniture that had previously occupied the prison tent. White ribbons from torn tents flapped in the night breeze.

I studied the silver-haired elves who had been tossed aside like dolls but who were now struggling to their feet in the billowing black clouds that blanketed this part of their camp.

This was my doing. Sudden clarity pushed the shock away. I reached into my soul. Burning rage flickered in the blackened pits.

I was a Storm Caster again.

With the return of my senses came a blaring sense of urgency. We had to get out. I had to get Shade out. My hand shot out and I grabbed a fistful of the assassin's shirt.

"Come on!" I snapped.

When he let go of his crushing grip on my leg, I realized that it was probably the only thing that had saved him from being flung away by hurricane winds as well. That, and his proximity to me.

"Storm, I can't see." For someone who had just experienced what he had, his voice was surprisingly calm and steady.

While hauling him to his feet, I pulled the darkness back into the deep pits of my soul. Guards from farther away were shouting orders, and stomping boots were closing in on the flattened part of camp. Armor clanged as the star elves who had been stationed here tried to untangle themselves from whatever debris had trapped them.

"Mother?" Princess Illeasia's voice came from behind pile of tents a short distance away. It was followed by a series of coughs. "Where are you? Are you unharmed?"

Relief so intense I almost sagged washed over me. Illeasia was alive. I hadn't accidently killed her when I unleashed my fury.

From another spot across the grass, Queen Nimlithil answered in a voice like the crack of a whip. "Get them!"

Reality slammed back into me like a basher's bat. Right. The guards. With the black clouds gone, Shade could see the area around us. Unfortunately, so could the star elves.

"Forest," I said and shoved him in the direction of the grove.

He took off across the ruined camp without question. Shouts rose as soldiers closed in on all sides. I knew that Shade was still wounded and that the burst of power when my Ashaana bond had snapped back in place had used up a lot of my energy. But we couldn't stop to think about that right now.

I didn't even have time to stop and feel the relief that had coursed through me when I realized that I was a Storm Caster again. That the gaping chasm in my chest had disappeared, replaced by the blackened pits of burning wildfire rage. I didn't have time to think about that or the world-ending sorrow over Hadraeth's death and Illeasia and Elaran's shattered life. Or the guilt that coiled in my stomach because I knew that the only reason I had gotten my powers back was because Hadraeth had died. The emotions that his death had torn from me were so similar to what I'd felt after Rain died and it, along with the rage for Elaran and Illeasia's broken happiness, had been enough to tip the scales and form a new bridge to my powers. Their loss of life and happiness had made me Ashaana again. And inside my soul, relief, heartbreak, and guilt fought like wolves because of all those conflicting emotions.

However, this was neither the time nor the place to deal with them so I shoved the jumble of feelings aside and kept running. If I was to get Shade out alive, I had to stay focused.

"There they are!" someone shouted on my right.

Wind ripped at my hair as I leaped over broken wood and shredded fabric in an effort to keep up with Shade. His longer legs carried him over the field of debris like a streak of black lightning. My heart pounded in my chest. Everything hurt. Breathing hurt, moving hurt, thinking hurt. After what had gone down this evening, everything godsdamn hurt and my feelings were so tangled up that I didn't know how to make sense of any of it. That awful pain and confusion were clawing their way towards the surface again so I spit out a curse and forced them back onto the pile of shit I'd deal with when life was less crazy. Renewing my efforts, I once more focused on putting one foot in front of the other. If we could just make it to the woods.

"Down!" Shade snapped.

Not hesitating a second, I immediately dove for the grass. An arrow whizzed past in the spot I had just vacated, missing me by scant margins. Grass and dirt coated my clothes as I rolled to my feet again and continued sprinting. Shade flicked his hand a couple of times at the maze of still standing tents before us. I nodded. They wouldn't be able to shoot at us with all those tents in the way.

Grabbing a wooden pole sunk into the ground, I whirled around and darted after Shade as he sped into the sea of white cloth. Countless boots thundered behind us. The prison tent had been fairly close to the edge of the grove. If we could only make it there, we could lose them in the woods and maybe find our horses somewhere on the other side. Then we'd be okay.

The shouting around us was getting louder. I zigzagged between tents and deserted fire pits while my breathing grew increasingly labored. Clanking metal and stampeding feet sent spikes of panic shooting up my spine. They were practically snapping at our heels now.

Ahead, the white tents were thinning out and a wall of trees rose in the darkness. This was it. Only a few more strides. Blood pounded in my ears. The final ring of tents was coming up. Just a little further and then...

We broke through the last row of shining cloth walls and shot into the open stretch of grass between the camp and the forest.

Pain spiked through me. Shade had screeched to a halt so abruptly that I had slammed right into him from behind. Giving my head a quick shake to clear it of the ringing inside my skull, I detached myself from his muscled back and took a step to the side. The change in position provided me with a full view of what had caused him to stop.

"Shit," I panted, my chest still heaving.

Along the tree line stood the perimeter guards. All of them were facing away from the grove and towards camp. Towards us.

Huge white bows shone in the silvery moonlight that flooded the plains and all of them were drawn and pointed at us.

Steel rang through the warm night air as the soldiers hunting us from behind closed in as well. The weapons that Captain Hadraeth had given back to us had been confiscated again when we were caught, so both Shade and I were unarmed.

My powers were too depleted to take out every guard along the tree line because they were standing too far apart. I could probably manage a few concentrated bursts. But as soon as I hit the first section of them, the others would fire. Our best bet was most likely to allow the rest of the star elves to catch up and then somehow fight our way through them and disappear in the chaos. I cast a quick glance at the assassin next to me.

He met my gaze and nodded, confirming that we were thinking the same thing, before sinking into a fighting stance.

I turned and did the same. "And now we fight."

Back to back, we waited for the army of star elves to break through the tents while also knowing full well that the archers on the other side could shoot us at any moment. Only the knowledge that they needed us alive kept the dread from rising all the way up my throat. The noise of rushing elves continued echoing through the night.

The odds of pulling this off were next to none, I knew that. And this was probably the last chance we would ever have to escape. If this failed, we were doomed. I swallowed against the rising panic and instead concentrated on the warm muscled body behind my back. Even though I couldn't see his face, I could picture it. Could picture the way the silver light from the moon shone over his silky black hair. The way the stars glittered in his dark eyes. The way his muscles shifted under his clothes as he moved. He had to make it through this.

Behind the rows of fluttering tents, the soldiers were advancing. The sound of their pursuit was slower, more orderly, as if they already knew that we would be standing here. Unarmed. In the open. Staring down a line of archers. All while they took their time to spread out and make sure that we had no chance of fighting our way out of this.

By all the gods, Shade had to make it through this. But I was pretty sure that neither of us would.

Twangs rang out. Followed by projectiles whizzing through the air. I whipped around right as dull thuds and soft grunts rose from all along the tree line.

My mouth dropped open. The arrows hadn't been fired at us. Cries of terror ripped from the star elf archers as they collapsed one after the other. Shot by unknown attackers somewhere in the trees.

"Why aren't you running?" a female voice bellowed across the grass. "Get to it!"

That voice. I could have wept at the sound of that voice. But we didn't have time for that either so I gave Shade's shoulder a shove and sprang forward. The wall of archers was gone but the soldiers behind us were still closing in.

Grass crunched under my feet as I ran with everything I had towards the edge of the forest with Shade next to me. I pushed my legs to go faster because I knew he had slowed his pace so that I could keep up.

Shouts vibrated through the air behind us. Our pursuers had reached the open stretch of field. Metal clanged and bows groaned as orders were barked and weapons were drawn.

Arrows flew from the woods. Screams rose.

And then we broke the tree line.

Darkness enveloped us as Shade and I hurtled through the trees. I knew that our rescuers would find us so we kept running straight ahead without stopping. With the thick canopy above, the moonlight barely reached the ground. Stumbling half blind over roots and rocks, I prayed that I wouldn't run right into a tree trunk at least.

"Seriously, here we are, staging a daring rescue, and you hesitate," a cheerful voice suddenly said right next to me. "What's up with that?"

A laugh full of relief and desperation spilled over my lips. "I promise I'll have a much more dramatic response next time."

Haela fell in beside me and flashed me a grin. "Good. I'd hate for you to start behaving like a boring normal person."

"How about we focus on escaping first and then lecture them on being boring?" Haemir said from somewhere on Shade's other side.

The excited twin next to me let out a theatrical sigh. "Fine."

Looping her arm through mine, she steered me towards whatever exit point they had picked. I assumed Haemir did the same with Shade. With their superior night vision, I felt much more confident that I wouldn't accidentally run straight into a tree. But then again, with Haela, you never knew.

Far behind us, there were still sounds of pursuit echoing through the darkened grove. However, the star elves lived in bright cities full of white glass. The twins were wood elves. They'd spent their whole lives in a forest. It would be a cold day in hell when a city dweller managed to outfox the twins on their own home ground.

"How did you even get through the mist?" I pressed out between heavy breaths.

Man, I was so tired of running, and that kick to my solar plexus earlier laced every move I made with throbbing pain.

Haela lifted something in her free hand and held it up. I squinted against the gloom. It looked like round flat blob of some kind. Grinning, she shook her hand, making the dark blob flap in distress.

"Haemir and I got magic leaves too, remember?"

Oh, right. I had used mine to survive the poison in the Rat King's basement and Elaran had given his to Haber so he could develop our mist wall against chemical attacks. But the twins still had the leaves that Vilya had given them.

"We figured we could use them to get in and then you could just use your wind to get us out," Haela continued.

I wasn't sure which part of that made cold hands squeeze my heart harder. The reminder that if I hadn't gotten my powers back, we wouldn't have been able to make it out. Or the fact that if the twins had come here and I had already been gone, then they would have been trapped here as well. And that they had been willing to risk that. For me and Shade.

When I didn't respond immediately, Haela frowned down at me. "You do have energy left to use for that, right?"

"Yeah, but not a lot. We're gonna have to run like hell."

As if on command, the pale mist that was somehow deployed when people moved through the edge of the grove appeared on our left. Tendrils of it crawled along the ground and reached for us like clawed fingers. From the corner of my eye, I could see it blooming on our right as well.

"Fall in behind me," I said as the smoke walls rose on all sides. "As tight as you can."

Shade and the twins pressed in so close that it was a miracle we didn't trip over each other as we continued running.

The light blue mist was a compact shield between us and the tree line. I sucked in a deep breath.

"As soon as I blow it away, run like hell and don't stop," I said. "I'll keep doing it until we're out."

*Or until I run out of power and pass out.* I forced the thought out of my mind and raised my arms as we reached the smoke wall before us. Bracing myself, I slammed my palms forward.

A gust of wind hurtled through the trees and shoved the mist back. We sprinted into the temporary pocket of clear air. Once the walls began closing in again, I threw another blast of wind at it.

I hadn't been able to do this before because I'd come from the other direction. The purpose of the mist was to keep people out. Not in. So it had enveloped me from all sides right at the edge of the grove. But this far in, it had only been swirling in sporadic clusters. Well, until this solid wall of it that I'd been trapped in last time. And besides, last time I hadn't known how thick the wall would be. Now, I did. So I could shoot blasts on it because I knew we'd be out soon.

Right as the thought passed through my head, the mist and the dark trees gave way to an open stretch of plain. Moonlight danced over the grass and countless stars glittered like silver dust above me. We were out.

Tiredness crashed over me like an ocean wave. Blinking, I stumbled a step. A strong hand shot out and kept me from falling over. Shade.

This time, I could actually see the silver light play in his silky black hair and the stars that were reflected in his dark eyes. He drew me into his arms and rested his chin on top of my head. For a moment, I just closed my eyes and breathed him in. Blood and dirt coated us both but he still smelled like himself. Like the night. Dark and alluring. I rested my cheek against his chest and let his strong arms hold me tightly.

He was alive. I was alive. And we were both out. By some miracle, Shade and I had survived all of that. My heart sank. But the same could not be said for everyone. Illeasia's impassive face and Hadraeth's lifeless eyes drifted through my mind. Now all that remained was telling Elaran that the love of his life no longer existed. That he would never get his happy ending. Tears welled up in my eyes. By all the gods, this was going to break him.

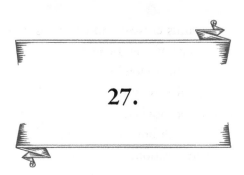

# 27.

Shouts rose. Up ahead, there was a group of people gathered at the edge of our camp. One was standing with his arms crossed over his chest while a short figure was pacing back and forth across the grass. I pulled on the reins, urging Silver to slow as we neared them.

Apparently, my trusted horse had run back to our camp at some point, which was what had made the twins decide to go after us. They had brought her and another horse with them, which I was very grateful for because I wouldn't have survived running back from the star elves' camp with a league of soldiers on our heels.

The ride back had been a quiet one. Mostly because I was too tired to speak, but also because I couldn't yet bring myself to explain what had happened. Thankfully, the twins were perceptive enough to understand that shit had gone to hell in some way and didn't push us to talk about it. I would explain it to them soon, but first, I needed to tell Elaran.

I half slid, half fell off Silver and landed hard on the grass but managed to stay on my feet. The sentries must have sent word back as soon as they spotted us because not only were there several stable hands ready to take our horses, there were also a large number of worried people waiting for us.

Elaran had his arms crossed and eyebrows drawn down in his usual grumpy pose but even I could see the anxiousness and relief that fluttered in his yellow eyes. Beside him stood Marcus, who wore his worried expression plain on his face, and Faye. The Queen of Tkeideru looked like she wasn't sure whether to yell at us or hug us. Man-bun and a couple of others from the Assassins' Guild were positioned a few strides away and watched their Master with assessing gazes as Shade slid off his horse next to me. I opened my mouth to say something but before I could, the pacing figure I'd seen from afar stalked forward and cut me off.

"You had your guild imprison me in my tent to stop me from riding out to bargain for your freedom." King Edward stabbed a finger at his brother's chest while anger mixed with profound relief danced in his black eyes. "If you ever do that to me again, I will have you executed. Is that clear?"

Despite everything that had happened and everything I still had to do, I laughed. It was a surprised and broken sound and yet still full of real mirth. The sound broke the tension that had settled over our small group and many of the others chuckled as well.

I threw Edward a grin while motioning between the two Silverthorn brothers. "That's exactly what I said too."

Shade shot me a mock glare but didn't have time to comment before his little brother yanked him forward by the shirt and drew him into a tight hug. Surprise flitted over the assassin's face but then he wrapped his arms around Edward and closed his eyes.

Clothes rustled as Haela sidled up to me and draped an arm over my shoulders. I looped my arm around her back and pulled her closer.

"Thank you," I said, my voice heavy with emotion. Shifting my gaze, I met Haemir's eyes too. "Both of you."

He nodded and gave me a smile while Haela turned to grin down at me.

"Of course," she said. "Interesting things always happen when you're around and I didn't want life to start getting dull again."

Chuckling, I gave her a shove with my hip. She just tipped her head back and laughed into the star-speckled sky. A few strides away, still locked in a tight embrace, Shade was speaking softly into Edward's ear. The young king nodded against his shoulder while tears gleamed in his eyes. Behind them, Faye had been studying the twins and now turned to Elaran with her arms crossed and an eyebrow arched.

"Did you let them go after Storm and Shade?" she asked. "Or did they disobey orders and sneak out on their own?"

Elaran was silent for a moment before replying. "I let them."

I raised my eyebrows at him from across the grass but he only cleared his throat in reply. Haela leaned down and whispered in a conspiratorial tone.

"He was really worried about you." A mischievous glint crept into her eyes. "And besides, when I wanna do something, very few people can stop me from doing it."

"Don't we know it," Haemir muttered.

Elaran still looked slightly nervous as he waited for Faye to pass judgement on his decision to send the twins after us. But then she just blew out a soft chuckle and nodded.

"Good." She clapped a hand on his shoulder. "If you hadn't, I would've." After a nod in my direction, she drifted off. "Fill me in later. They look like they need to see a doctor."

Alarm shot through me as I remembered Shade's wound. Ducking out from under Haela's arm, I took a step towards the embracing brothers.

"He's hurt," I said to Edward and nodded at Shade's side. "Took an arrow in the side."

"What?" King Edward jerked back and flicked worried eyes over his brother.

Shade blew out an exasperated breath. "It's not that bad."

"He's also cut up and bruised," I continued as if he hadn't commented. "Get him to a doctor and make sure he stays there until they've checked all his injuries."

"Bossy, are we?" Shade said with a pointed look at me, but he let Edward take him by the elbow and lead him away.

Throwing him a smirk, I shrugged as if to say that he should already know that by now. He only made it two steps before Elaran's arm shot out and grabbed him.

"Hey," Elaran said. After a brief second of hesitation, he pulled Shade into a strong embrace. "I'm glad you're okay, brother."

Shade clapped a hand on Elaran's back. "Me too."

When they broke apart again, it looked like Shade was about to say something that I didn't want him to say yet, so I interrupted before he could.

"Go get him to the doctor now," I said to Edward before sliding my gaze back to Shade. "I'll fill Elaran in on everything that happened."

"We should do that together."

"No. You need to get that wound treated. It's better if I do it." Holding his gaze, I added with a bit more force, "Trust me."

His dark eyebrows creased slightly. I knew that he understood which part of the tale I was referring to but I wasn't sure if he understood why I wanted to tell Elaran alone. My only hope was that he trusted me enough not to argue.

He did. After another couple of seconds of frowning, he nodded and let King Edward steer him back into camp. Man-bun locked eyes with me and gave me a slow nod before he and the other assassins fell in behind their Master.

"Well, we should go get some sleep then," Haela said to no one in particular and slung an arm over her brother's shoulders. "There's a war going on, you know."

After lifting her free hand in a mock salute, she wandered off with Haemir. Marcus appeared to take the hint as well because he approached me and spoke for the first time since we rode into camp.

"I know I said 'be a wildfire' but sometimes, I really wish you were more of a candle."

A huff of laughter escaped my lips in reply.

Drawing me into his muscled arms, he placed a quick kiss on the top of my head. "I'm glad you're safe." He had probably been able to read whatever was on my face from the moment I slid off my horse because then he released me and said, "Whenever you want to talk, I'm here for you."

With that, he withdrew and lumbered back towards his tent.

"Thank you," I whispered at his retreating back.

That only left me and Elaran. Because of what I had to tell him, I barely dared meet his eyes. Drawing a shallow breath, I finally mustered the courage to tear my gaze from the disappearing Storm Caster and shift it to the auburn-haired archer before me. He cleared his throat again and crossed his arms.

"So, you're not dead," he announced.

Despite the dread building in my chest, I chuckled. "It's good to see you too, Elaran."

Drawing his eyebrows down, he muttered something under his breath about troublesome underworlders and waved me forward. I fell in beside him as we made our way deeper into camp.

"I need to know everything that happened," he said. "Every detail might be important."

It took great effort to keep the trepidation from my voice as I replied. "Yeah."

My heart thumped in my chest the whole way towards the tent we used for our war councils. With every step closer to it, I formulated and discarded plans for how to break the news to him without crushing his heart completely. When he finally shouldered open the tent flap and I slipped in behind him, I still hadn't figured it out.

He strode straight to the large table in the middle and leaned down over it. Smoothening the yellowing paper with his hands, he pointed at a spot on the map.

"Their camp is still here, correct?"

I edged closer to him. "Yeah."

After staring at the detailed map of the landscape for another few seconds, he straightened and crossed his arms. "Alright, tell me everything. Start from the beginning."

So I did. I began with the easy parts. What their camp had looked like, my estimation of how many soldiers they had, and other technical details that might be important for the war.

Then I recounted what had happened when I tried to free Shade and the subsequent imprisonment, the almost-torture, and the pain ritual. Worry flared in his eyes at that part but he didn't interrupt. Maybe because I left out the part about what had actually happened to my feelings for Rain. He didn't need to know that. Not when I was about to crush his own heart.

After that, I also told him that we had discovered that even with captured Storm Casters, Queen Nimlithil wouldn't call Aldeor the White here. Elaran pressed his lips together in annoyance at that but only nodded. Dread curled in my stomach as I neared the end of my tale but I explained the rescue attempt and how it failed. And then I told him, clearly and without leaving anything out, what had happened to Illeasia and Hadraeth.

When I fell silent, he just stared at me uncomprehendingly for a few moments. Then he blinked, frowned, and let his arms drop down by his sides.

"What are you saying?" he asked carefully.

My eyes were soft as I held his gaze. "Queen Nimlithil forced Illeasia to complete the ritual. And she did."

"No." Elaran drew a hand through his auburn hair and began pacing the tent. "No, there had to be some kind of trick. She'd never do that to her daughter."

He continued stalking back and forth, shaking his head. I said nothing. The tent walls flapped slightly as a soft breeze rustled the fabric while Elaran's mind tried to come to terms with what I had just told him.

"Elaran," I said at last, my voice soft but firm. "I saw it myself. I saw it happen and I saw how she reacted after Queen Nimlithil killed Hadraeth. He was family to her and she should've been heartbroken, but she felt nothing."

Leather creaked as he continued pacing and shaking his head. Then, as if what I'd said finally caught up with him, he screeched to a halt and whipped around to face me.

"You were there when she did this to Illeasia." Not a question.

"Yes."

Dark clouds blew across his face. "And you did nothing to stop it." Also not a question.

"I tried." I held his gaze even as rage flickered behind his eyes. "I tried to stop it."

"Not hard enough." He let out a snarl. "If it had been Shade, you would've found a way to stop it."

I said nothing. Elaran raked both hands through his hair and began stalking back and forth once more. Spitting out a long breath, he shook his head again and again. Then he stopped and turned back to me.

"She's really... changed?" His voice broke on the final word. "She's like those empty people we saw in Sker?"

"Yes."

Complete and utter heartbreak shattered like glass in his eyes. He shot towards me. The devastation washed off his face, replaced by truly horrifying fury that burned like blue flames. Every survival instinct in me was screaming at me to run in the face of such devouring rage but I remained where I was as the furious elf advanced on me.

I did nothing, didn't so much as raise my arms to defend myself, as he grabbed fistfuls of my shirt and yanked me towards him.

"How could you let this happen?" he growled down at me. His face was so close to mine that I could feel his breath on my skin. "How could you let her do that to Illeasia?"

"I'm sorry," I whispered.

Letting go of my shirt, he shoved me backwards. Pain throbbed through my already battered body as my back slammed into one of the tent's support pillars. For a moment, I was reminded of when we first met. When he had stalked towards me across the grass of Tkeideru and provoked a fight because he wanted to beat me up. Back then, there had been such anger and hate on his face when he looked at me. I couldn't help being reminded of that as Elaran advanced on me again.

"Sorry?" He drove his hand into the wood above my head. "Sorry doesn't fix this! Sorry doesn't bring her back!"

His voice cracked and he slammed his hand into the support beam again and again. It vibrated against my back and made the whole tent shudder beneath the force of his muscles. I knew the ridiculous strength he possessed. Knew that if he decided to hit me instead of the wood above my head, then he would break bone.

All my instincts were screaming at me to get the hell out, or do anything other than stand there while an elven commander took his rage out on the closest thing at hand. But I didn't close my eyes or shrink away. I only remained standing there, looking at him with soft eyes.

He grabbed the collar of my shirt again and yanked me upwards. "I only asked you for one thing. To make sure Illeasia was safe." He choked on her name. "I never ask anyone for *anything*! And this was the one thing I wanted. The one time I asked someone for something. And you let her..." His voice cracked again. "You let them hurt her. Let them rip out her heart."

My cold black heart was shattering into a million broken shards. Because he was right. Elaran never asked anyone for anything. All he ever did was protect everyone else and do everything he could to help them and keep them safe.

This was the one time he had dared to be selfish. To ask someone for something.

And I had failed him.

"I know," I said.

With his fists still buried in my shirt, he pulled me from the support beam and then threw me towards the exit. I stumbled several steps and had to brace myself on the tent wall to avoid falling.

"Get out!" Elaran screamed. Rage and heart-wrenching pain swirled in his eyes as he stabbed his whole arm towards the tent flap. "I said, get out! I don't ever want to see your face again."

Taking my hand off the thick fabric that made up the walls, I nodded and averted my gaze. Without another word, I slipped out of the tent and into the night.

The sounds of fists striking wood followed me.

This was the reason why I had wanted to handle this on my own. Why I had deliberately sent Shade away so that he wouldn't be here when I told Elaran what had happened to Illeasia. I had known that he would react like this. I mean, who wouldn't? And I had done it for one simple reason. Because I could take it.

It was much better if Elaran gathered up all his rage and pain and sorrow and heartbreak and took it all out on me. My hardened heart carried so much already, so what was one more thing? Better I bear it alone. Elaran was going to need Shade to get through this, so it was better if I alone was the villain in this story. That way, he would at least have Shade to help him through this pain.

Wings flapped and birds cooed as I slumped down on a crate outside the tent that housed our messenger doves.

My eyes burned. I *could* take it. But that didn't mean that everything that had happened these last few hours hadn't fractured that cold dead thing in my chest.

Tipping my head back, I stared up at the glittering expanse of stars.

And then I cried.

Cried for lives lost and dreams broken.

Cried for Illeasia. For Hadraeth. And for Elaran.

For everything that had happened to Shade and for the terror that had almost paralyzed me when I didn't know if he was dead or alive and when they had threatened to torture him and when he had been shot and bleeding in that tent.

I cried for Rain and for the love I no longer felt for her. The one person who had cared about me when I was only a scrawny kid on the streets of Keutunan. The person who had been my first real family and who was now no more than a stranger. A face in the crowd.

Cried for the bone deep fear that Elaran might never forgive me for what I let happen to Illeasia. That I might have lost a crucial part of the family I had sacrificed Rain for.

For the vow to protect my friends that I had made and that I wasn't strong enough to keep.

When it mattered, I had not been enough.

So I watched the silver stars dusted over the dark blue heavens.

And I cried.

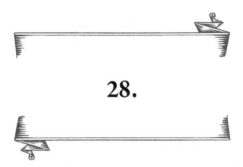

# 28.

I awoke to the sound of cannon fire. Jerking upright, I tried to remember where I was while also scanning for any threats. A double bed, piles of weapons, and black cloth walls stared back at me. Right. Our tent. I looked down at the figure sleeping next to me. Shade.

He had found me last night after the doctor was finished with him. Had taken one look at me, standing alone in the darkened camp, watching white wings flap into the night with dried tears still on my cheeks, and had led me back to our tent. I had given him a censored version of how my conversation with Elaran had gone down. Since Shade had already suspected that the elf would be devastated, angry, and heartbroken, I had only confirmed his suspicions. There was no need for him to know that Elaran had been angry with me, so I'd left that part out.

Exhaustion had caught up with both of us as soon as we set one foot inside the tent. After only barely managing to strip off our dirty and bloody clothes, we had fallen into a deep and dreamless sleep in each other's arms.

I shifted my gaze to the small clock on the table. It was early afternoon. The fighting had been going on since dawn and neither of us had been woken by it. Though, considering how little both Shade and I had actually slept in the past two days,

I supposed it wasn't inconceivable that our bodies had taken matters into their own hands and simply kept us unconscious until we at least resembled living human beings again.

Being careful not to disturb the sleeping assassin, I gently lifted the covers from my thighs and slid out. A hand shot forward and snaked around my wrist. I stifled a gasp of surprise and turned to glare at Shade.

"You could've just said *good morning*," I huffed.

His hair was mussed with sleep and there were slight imprints on his cheek from the sheets but he managed a smirk. "What would be the fun in that?"

"Bastard." I pulled against his grip around my wrist and when he didn't let go, I arched an eyebrow at him expectantly.

Pushing himself into a sitting position, he searched my face. "Are you okay?"

"Always am," I said, trying to muster my usual arrogant swagger that felt a bit too far away at the moment.

Shade's fingers didn't move from my arm. Rolling my eyes, I heaved a deep sigh before looking back at him again.

"I don't know," I finally admitted.

He released my wrist.

While climbing out of bed, I motioned at the bandaged wound on his side. "You?"

"I've been through worse."

I knew he had. We both had. So I just nodded and grabbed a set of clean clothes from my trunk. Shoving my legs into a pair of dark gray pants and then picking up a tightfitting black shirt, I got dressed with efficient moves. Metal clanged faintly as I flipped open the lid of another chest and began strapping on new blades. Behind me, steel hissed through the tent as Shade slid his swords into the scabbards across his back.

Warm fall winds smacked into my face as I stepped out of the tent with Shade close behind. I huffed and smoothened my braided hair back again. The boom of cannons kept echoing through the afternoon air.

"Master," a voice said from my right. Slim, the blond assassin with whom I'd had a somewhat rocky relationship in the beginning, had apparently been standing guard outside our tent and now fell in beside Shade.

"What's going on at the front?" Shade asked as we made our way towards the battlefield.

"Shit's gone to hell," Slim replied. When Shade cast him an odd look, he added, "Master."

"What do you mean?"

"The star elves have joined the battle."

"Fuck," I swore.

"Yeah," Slim went on. "The armies from Sker, Beccus, and Frustaz are still hammering our soldiers from Keutunan and Pernula but now they're backed up by elven archers too. The Storm Casters have their hands full blocking the trebuchets but they're trying to deal with the star elf archers too. It's not going so well though."

Shade raked his fingers through his hair as we rounded a cluster of brown tents. "How long?"

"Elaran says it will be a miracle if the lines don't break before nightfall."

My heart skipped a beat at the sound of his name but with the grave news being relayed, I didn't think anyone noticed. The sound of clashing steel and screams of the dying grew louder with every step as we left our camp behind and started the trek towards the ridge. I swallowed. Queen Nimlithil had at last sent in her own soldiers. We were now fighting four armies and we might not survive until nightfall. Shit.

"There's more," Slim said.

Mud and grass clung to our boots as we neared the back of our forces atop the hill. "What?"

The blond assassin lowered his voice. "Discontent is spreading through the ranks. A lot of the men from Keutunan and Pernula are pissed because they're the only ones dying while all the elves are just standing safely behind the lines."

"They're not standing safely behind the lines," Shade ground out. "They're archers who provide the rest of the army with invaluable ranged support. Without them, we'd already be dead."

"I know. But the other soldiers don't think like that. They only see their dead friends in the mud and the unharmed elves atop the ridge." Slim shrugged. "And they're pissed because they think it's unfair."

Spitting out a curse, Shade shook his head. "Any talk of desertion?"

Slim was silent for a moment. When the commanding eyes of his Guild Master slid to him, he cleared his throat. "Some."

"Damn fools." Lightning crackled behind his black eyes for a second but then he expelled a forceful sigh. "Alright, let's just focus on surviving the day and then we'll figure out a plan for the rest of it."

How had everything gone to hell so damn quickly? Just overnight, Elaran's heart had been shattered, the star elves had sent in their archers, our lines were breaking, and our soldiers were talking about deserting. How had it come to this?

The clashing of swords from the plains ahead and the booming of cannons from the coast reached deafening levels as the three of us weaved our way towards the battlefield. Steering well clear of Elaran, I yanked out my hunting knives and aimed for the swarm of black-clad assassins moving through enemy ranks like wraiths. Shade and Slim drew their weapons as well.

Panic and chaos hung in the air but so far, the lines held. I flicked my gaze over the men in black and red and the ones in dark blue and silver who fought desperately on the front lines while elves in white armor fired volley after volley of pale arrows at them. Whooshing came from atop the hill as Storm Casters sent blasts of wind to stem the onslaught. Screams of wounded and dying still cleaved the afternoon air.

We had to make sure the lines held. Gripping my knives tightly, I nodded at Shade and then darted down the hill, straight into the bloodbath. The lines had to hold.

THE LINES HELD. BARELY. But it hadn't been enough to stop the terror and fury festering within our ranks because everyone in camp knew that the lines would not hold another day. Tomorrow, only certain death awaited us. Hopelessness was spreading like a disease through camp, and soldiers from Keutunan and Pernula muttered and threw accusatory glances at the wood elves from Tkeideru. Dinner had long since come and gone and we were far into the evening when things at last came to a head.

"I've had enough of this!" Queen Faye snapped from somewhere behind a cluster of tents.

Shade and I exchanged a glance and hurried towards the sound. When we broke through the ring of tents, we found the Queen of Tkeideru and a group of soldiers from Pernula standing on a wide swath of empty grass. Elaran, with hands resting on his swords, was positioned between the humans and his queen.

"We left our home to come here to help defend *your* city!" Faye shouted at the men. "And you're blaming us because *not more of us are dead*?"

"All we're saying is that we're all down there dying on the battlefield while you stand there on the hill," one of the soldiers replied. "It doesn't feel right."

Murmurs of agreement went through the soldiers who had gathered by the tents along the rim of the open space. On the other side, King Edward and Lord Raymond appeared. The young king flicked his eyes around the area, confusion on his face, while Lord Raymond only watched the confrontation with a grim expression.

"We're not standing on the hill!" the silver-haired queen shot back at him. "Do you have any idea what role our archers have played in this war? If it weren't for us, *all of you* would already be dead."

"Tell that to all our brothers lying dead in the mud!"

"That's enough," Shade said in a voice dripping with command, and stalked forward. "The elves are not the enemy."

"Yes, they are! Those star elves are the ones behind all this. What's to say these elves aren't in on it too?"

While I followed Shade further into the circle of tents, I flicked my gaze around the gathered soldiers. Many of them were nodding in agreement. A group of dark-haired men from

Pernula puffed up their chests and took a couple of steps forward. Next to a bland-looking man, two blond soldiers from Keutunan shifted nervously on their feet as if they were worried that this would turn into a straight up fight right here in camp. On their other side, I saw four faces I recognized.

Faelar and Cileya had appeared from the throng and were marching towards Elaran with Ydras close behind. Marcus had followed them but stopped before the open swatch of grass. Concerned golden-brown eyes swept across the increasingly agitated mob.

"I said, that's enough," Shade growled.

"You know what?" Faye said, shaking her head. "I'm out. We're out." A harsh laugh ripped from her lips. "I should've learned my lesson long ago, when your ancestors slaughtered my people, not to get involved with humans."

"Faye," I began, pleadingly.

"No," she cut me off. "I didn't sign up for this. To get my people killed protecting ungrateful humans." Disdain flashed over her face as she whirled on the soldiers who had started the altercation. "You don't want us standing on the hill? Fine. You get your wish. We're leaving. Tonight."

Ydras came to a halt next to the wood elf queen. "So are we. For Cileya," he motioned at the redheaded mountain elf a few strides away, "I agreed to try but I'm not sacrificing my people for this either."

"Ydras!" Marcus called and took a half step forward.

The mountain elf elder gave an apologetic shrug. "Sorry, Marcus. But I've told you many times, it's always best to leave the outside world alone. That's how we survive." He shifted his gaze to Faye. "You're welcome in our mountains to wait this out until you can sail home."

"I'll take you up on that." Faye turned to Elaran. "Get everyone ready to leave. Right now." With a sneer on her face, the Queen of Tkeideru spat on the grass in front of the Pernulans and then shouldered past them. "Good luck surviving without us tomorrow."

"Faye!" I called and made to follow her but Elaran drew his swords and blocked my way, letting his queen disappear into the maze of tents. My voice turned soft as I addressed him instead. "Elaran, don't do this. Please. You're the commander of our armies. Without you, without the elves, we won't stand a chance."

Anger and pain filled his eyes as he stared back at me. "What do I care? Illeasia is already gone." With that, he stalked after his queen.

My mouth dropped open. But I had nothing to say so I only watched as he prowled back into the darkness.

A nervous ripple went through the gathered crowd. The two blond soldiers from Keutunan looked even more worried than before. One of them spoke softly to the other, but in the ringing silence that the elves had left in their wake, we all heard them perfectly.

"We barely survived today. Without archers, we're all gonna die tomorrow."

Another buzz of apprehension shot through the soldiers and more of them began repeating the same fear. I didn't exactly hold any authority with the armies of Keutunan and Pernula so I flicked my gaze to Shade. The High King opened his mouth but before he could produce any sound, another voice cut him off.

"No, we're not."

Leather creaked and weapons rustled as everyone turned to the man who had spoken. Lord Raymond. The senior member of the Keutunian Council of Lords stroked a hand over his moustache and drew himself up to his full height.

"We are not going to die tomorrow." His face was a hard mask. "Because we are leaving too."

"What?"

The disbelief on my face was mirrored by both Shade and King Edward.

"Excuse me?" the King of Keutunan said, turning to stare at his advisor with eyebrows that almost reached his hairline.

"You heard me. Our soldiers are leaving tonight as well. We are going back to Keutunan."

Edward's face darkened. "You do not have the authority to make that decision. *I* am the ruler of Keutunan."

"You are a child!" Lord Raymond flung an arm in Shade's direction. "You are a child who has been manipulated by his older brother. A brother who is an assassin and who murdered your own father."

King Edward looked like someone had slapped him. Not a lot of people knew that Edward had in fact also been a part of the assassination of his father because Shade had taken the blame for it in order to protect him, and the pain from that seemed to still linger.

"Be very careful how you speak to my brother," Shade warned in a voice as cold and deadly as poison.

"There you go again," Lord Raymond scoffed. "The assassin king resorts to threats. As expected." After smoothening his clothes, the noble lord gave the gathered crowd a nod filled with finality. "The Keutunian army is leaving tonight. Back to Pernula and then on board our ships from there." He turned to his king. "You can either join us or be left behind."

An oppressive silence fell over the area as he turned on his heel and strode away. Edward whipped his head between us and the retreating advisor.

"He'll come around," he said. "I'll talk to him. Just... I'll talk to him."

Without waiting for a reply, he rushed after Lord Raymond. The soldiers clad in the dark blue and silver of Keutunan exchanged glances. Then, as one, they withdrew.

"It's fine," I said to Shade, a note of desperation in my voice. "We still have the Pernulan army." Throwing out an arm, I motioned at Marcus, who had returned from wherever he had slunk off to for the past few minutes. "And the Storm Casters."

Meeting my gaze, Marcus shook his head. "They're leaving too. Almost all of them are leaving with the mountain elves."

"What?"

"And you do not have the Pernulan army," a commanding voice added from somewhere behind me.

Whirling around, I found Malor striding out of the shadows. He crossed his powerful arms over his chest and leveled disapproving eyes on Shade.

"I thought you'd be the one." He shook his head, making his long black ponytail swing over his back. "But you played this badly, boy. I have friends in the north. I'm taking the Pernulan army there so that we might have a chance to salvage this war."

Shade's voice was a midnight wind. "It's my army."

Malor swept his strange reddish-brown eyes over the Pernulan soldiers around us. "Then whoever wants to stay here and die with you can do so." He stabbed a muscled arm towards the part of camp where the elves were already packing up their things. "The elves are gone. The Keutunians are gone. Follow me to the north, or stay here and die. It's up to you."

Not bothering to wait for them to make up their minds, he stalked away. Worried murmurs drifted through the gathered soldiers.

"Don't even think about it," Shade warned.

"He's right." One of the Pernulans who had started the fight with the elves gave his king a shrug. "Without the others, this is gonna be a bloodbath. And this ain't the hill I'm dying on." He jerked his head to his companions. "Let's go."

That broke the spell and all the remaining soldiers around us left as well.

Shouts echoed through the night air as orders to leave were repeated until the whole area was filled with the sounds of a disbanding army.

I stared at the soldiers pulling down tents in practiced moves.

Metallic dinging rang across the dark grass as weapons and supplies were hastily gathered.

And just like that, our army was gone. The elves and most of the Storm Casters were heading west towards the mountains. The Keutunians were making for their ships and the Pernulans were rallying around Malor to go north.

When the sun rose tomorrow morning, this hill would be completely empty. There would be nothing to stop the star elves as they advanced on Pernula.

Shade's face was an unreadable mask as he watched the organized chaos unfurl around us.

Grass crunched to my right. I turned to find Marcus making his way towards us with the same blank expression on his face.

"What do we do now?" he asked.

I stared at the dark horizon. "Now we run."

# 29.

Candlelight danced over the smooth obsidian walls. I paced back and forth along a dark red carpet while waiting for Shade to get ready. What was taking him so long? Next to me, Marcus was studying the splendor of Blackspire with a slight frown on his face.

"Do you really think this will work?" he asked.

"It has to," I replied. "It's our only chance."

After it had become clear that our army was really breaking up and fleeing into the night, a few of us had raced for Zaina's ship on the coast. While the elves slipped away to the west, and the Pernulans and the Keutunians were marching north, Zaina had sailed me, Shade, Marcus, Edward, and a few others straight to Pernula. The star elves were coming for the city and we didn't have one second to spare if we were going to get everything ready.

"It's done," a man's voice rumbled from down the hall.

Stopping my pacing, I turned towards it. On the other side of the corridor, looking very out of place, were two warriors. I smiled as Yngvild and Vania closed the distance between us.

"All the gang leaders are gonna be there," Yngvild said.

"Good."

As soon as I stepped onto the docks of Pernula, I had sent word to the Black Emerald. There was a lot to be done and not a lot of time for it but I knew that if anyone could make it happen, it was Vania and Yngvild. When they came to a halt before me, Vania scrunched up her pale eyebrows and frowned down at me.

"You're not wearing that," she announced.

Confused, I glanced down at my body. I was wearing the kind of clothes I always wore. Burglar-friendly garments in black and gray, as well as my custom-made vest full of knife slots.

"What's wrong with this?" I asked.

"You always wear that," she said.

"Exactly."

"Exactly," Vania repeated as if that was supposed to make things clearer. Before I could question it, she lifted a long black pouch she had been carrying over her arm. "You're wearing this."

Narrowing my eyes at her, I muttered back, "Seeing as I'm your gang leader, I thought I gave the orders."

She only pointed at the closest door and arched her eyebrows expectantly.

Next to her, Yngvild let out a rumbling laugh. "You're better off just doing as she says. Trust me. I've been arguing with her for almost fifteen years now." The huge battle axe across his back shifted as he shrugged his broad shoulders. "Still haven't won a single argument."

A satisfied smirk played at the corner of Vania's stern lips. On my other side, Marcus only gave me a helpless shrug while trying to suppress a chuckle. I rolled my eyes.

"Fine." Throwing my arms up, I stalked towards the indicated door.

It led to a small office of some kind but it was deserted so I just stomped across the threshold and then leaned back against a desk with my arms crossed. Vania shut the door after her as she entered. Opening the large black pouch, she pulled out several garments.

"Here, put these on," she said.

Since I had already concluded that protesting was futile, I did as she asked. With every piece of clothing I lifted, my eyebrows rose further.

"Where did you even find these?" I asked.

"I had them made."

Suspicion crept into my voice while I finished changing into the garments she'd brought. "Why?"

Her blue eyes glittered as a slight smile spread over her lips. "Because you still need a push sometimes."

I chuckled and shook my head. Last time she thought I'd needed a push, she and Yngvild had ambushed me with a tavern full of underworlders who swore a blood oath to me and declared me their gang leader. Say what you will about Vania and her no-nonsense attitude, but she did have a certain flair for dramatics as well. When she wanted to.

She gave me a satisfied nod as I stuck the final blade back in its sheath. "*Now* you're ready."

After shooting back a half exasperated, half amused look, I followed her back into the obsidian hallway.

"Wow," Shade and Marcus blurted out in unison.

Heat crept into my cheeks as they stared at me with mouths gaping. I was wearing body armor made of what looked like black dragon scales. It fit my form perfectly and Vania had even had knife holsters made in the same spots as on my vest. The material was thick enough to protect better against attacks but still flexible enough to allow any kind of acrobatics I wanted to engage in. Sharp points stuck out from my shoulders and curved upwards slightly to complete the look and give it an even deadlier aura.

The Master Assassin dragged his gaze over my body with deliberate slowness while a smirk pulled at his lips. It made the ridiculous blush on my cheeks deepen. I wanted to throw something at him but before I had the chance, Edward interrupted.

"It will look even better now," he said to Shade.

I frowned at the young king before looking back at Shade. Blinking, I drew back slightly when I realized what he was wearing. A slick black suit that enhanced his toned body and ended with a stiff high collar that accentuated his sharp cheekbones. To top it all off was a spiky black crown of unforgiving obsidian. He looked like some dark king straight out of a story. And man, he looked good.

Edward opened the black box he'd been carrying and held it out to Shade. Before I could question what in Nemanan's name was going on, the assassin lifted the item from the box. I stared at it. It was *another* spiky black crown of unforgiving obsidian.

"Here," he said. "This one's for you."

Flicking my gaze between his smirking face and the gleaming crown, I shook my head. "You can't be serious."

"You're about to give people some pretty terrifying news, so it's important to project strength and unity," King Edward supplied.

A smirk blew across Shade's lips. "And I think the Queen of the Underworld needs a crown, don't you?"

Yngvild and Vania nodded their agreement. I glanced to Marcus for support that this was the most ridiculous thing I'd ever heard, but he was beaming at me with a wide grin on his face. Blowing out a sigh, I gave up on trying to convince them that this was absurd and instead stalked towards Shade. With careful movements, I took the dark crown from his outstretched hands. It was surprisingly heavy.

After glaring suspiciously at the spiky piece of oversized jewelry, I lifted it.

"Nemanan save me," I muttered and placed the crown on my head.

Shade raked his gaze over my body again, black eyes glittering. "You look glorious."

"Why is it that everyone suddenly felt the need to have clothes and crowns made for me?" I grumbled in reply.

Vania crossed her toned arms over her chest. "Because if we didn't, you would wear the same plain thief clothes every day for the rest of your life."

Chuckling, Shade hiked a thumb towards the blond warrior. "I like her."

Before I could spit out the retort that was brewing on my tongue, running footsteps echoed from down the hall. A slightly disheveled-looking young man skidded to a halt on the red carpet a few strides away from us and bowed at the waist.

"My king," he said. "We're ready."

Shade flashed me a smile. "Showtime."

THE LARGE SQUARE OUTSIDE Blackspire was packed with people. Standing in the bright open areas were ordinary citizens who had come when their king called them. In the shadows were the underworlders who had answered the call from their queen.

Sometimes, well most times, I still had trouble believing that the Queen of the Underworld was actually me, but I kept my spine straight and my chin high as Shade and I strode onto the raised platform side by side. With the imposing attire we wore, authority almost seemed to ripple off us like black waves. The two shady underworlders who somehow ruled this city.

"Citizens of Pernula," Shade called across the mass of people, who quieted instantaneously. "As many of you already know, a great host is heading for our city. Queen Nimlithil and her armies are marching on Pernula as we speak."

Fear rippled through the crowd. I studied their faces from atop the platform. Mothers pulled their children closer and husbands wrapped protective arms around their wives. The overcast sky painted the normally so colorful city in a bleak gray hue.

"Therefore," the High King of Pernula pressed on in an unwavering voice, "all civilians must evacuate the city immediately. You will return to your homes soon, so bring only what you deem necessary and only what you can carry."

Worried voices rose from every corner. People cried out about what to do with their shops, their sick and elderly, and the possession they couldn't carry. Cutting an arm through the air, Shade silenced them all.

"Panic is our enemy," he boomed across the nervous citizens. "Gather what you need quickly but calmly and then head for the side gate. There will be guards there to help you. Those who are able should begin making their way towards Hidden Oaks Cove. A temporary camp will be set up there where you will be safe while we deal with the situation in the city. The sick and elderly should head to the docks and seek out a woman named Zaina. She is the captain of the Mistcleaver and she's standing by with ships to ferry those who are unable to make the trip by land."

The panicked frenzy that had been spreading died down as people began talking amongst themselves, nodding, pointing, and making plans for the journey. Shade's assurance that they would only be there temporarily and would get to return home probably helped too. Even though we didn't actually know if it was true.

"Help your friends," Shade said. "Help your neighbors. But make sure that all civilians have evacuated the city as fast as possible. Do not panic. Do not fear. We will survive this."

The High King of Pernula took a step back. Surprise buzzed through the crowd as I stalked to the edge of the platform and raised my voice.

"Those orders were for the upperworlders," I called out in a strong voice. "These are for the shady types."

Dark chuckles rose from the shadowy parts of the area. I let a confidant smirk drift across my lips as I held out my hand and squeezed it into a fist.

"The Queen of the Underworld calls upon your blood oaths." My voice echoed off the obsidian palace behind me. "I told you that there would come a time when we would have to defend our city and our way of life against people who would seek to destroy us. That time is now!"

The civilians before me looked around the square with surprise and confusion on their faces. It didn't matter. I wasn't talking to them anyway.

"Get your crews ready," I continued. "And at sundown, all gang leaders will meet at the Black Emerald where we will plan the destruction of our enemies."

More dark laughter drifted from the shadows. Spreading my arms wide, I called up the darkness from my soul. My eyes went black as death, and tendrils of dark smoke snaked and whipped around my limbs as I flashed my intended audience an evil grin tinted with madness.

"Let's show the invaders what happens when you mess with underworlders."

The ordinary citizens of Pernula looked both frightened and hopeful as answering cheers rose from the thieves and murderers hidden among them.

"Everyone has their orders," Shade said, stepping up beside me. "Get to it."

Snapping out of their daze, the crowd lurched into action. Colorful awnings in yellow and green and red were pulled back into shops. Pots of flowers were moved aside to make room for carts, and the few guards who had remained in Pernula this whole time steered the flow of people in the right direction. I tried to keep the apprehension off my features as I pulled the darkness back into my soul and strode off the platform, because I had seen two faces I recognized.

"I didn't think jewelry was your thing." Liam grinned at me and nodded at the crown on my head as he and Norah approached. "Unless you're stealing it from others, I mean."

Huffing, I threw a glare at the smirking assassin next to me. "Yeah, well, *someone* apparently thought I was a little too plain for a queen without it."

"It was a good call," Norah said. "It makes you look even more powerful." A slight smile spread across her beautiful face as she studied the obsidian spikes on my head. "And kind of... terrifying."

Shade chuckled and winked at me as if to say, *I told you so.* I shot him another glare but before I could retort, Liam cut in and changed the subject.

"So it's really true, then? The star elves are coming to take the city?"

"Yeah." I narrowed my eyes at them. "And I want you on the road to Hidden Oaks Cove as fast as possible. Like, right now. I don't want you anywhere near the city when the fighting starts."

Liam looped an arm around Norah's back and rested his hand on her hip. "We'll start packing right away." He glanced down at the gorgeous teacher. "But we can't leave straight away because we're going to sail there with Zaina instead of going by land."

"Good. That way she can keep you safe."

"It's not that. It's just that..." He trailed off and cleared his throat as if he had accidentally said too much.

"It's just what?" I asked, suspicion lacing my every word.

"Nothing." Forcing a smile onto his face, he waved a hand in the air.

"You're a terrible liar. Especially for a thief."

Liam flicked his eyes around the area before turning back to me with a pleading look on his face. Not feeling particularly merciful, I just stared back at him with eyebrows raised expectantly.

"It's just..." His hand flapped around the air like some kind of disoriented butterfly. "Well..."

"I'm pregnant," Norah announced.

Shade and I both turned to gape at her. A soft blush crept across her cheeks at the attention but she straightened her white skirt and flashed us a smile.

"Yeah," Liam added somewhat superfluously with a smile that was both hopeful and slightly embarrassed.

Striding forward, I threw them both into a hug. "Congratulations! I'm so happy for you."

"Congratulations," Shade echoed over my shoulder.

After releasing the beaming couple, I retreated and leveled serious eyes on them in turn. "Now I definitely want you away from the city as soon as possible." I turned to Norah. "Have you told Zaina?"

She fluffed out her long black curls again after my hug had flattened them. "Not yet."

"Do that. Like, right now. She's still on board the Mistcleaver." I nodded in the direction of the docks. "Just pack some essentials and head down there straight away."

Liam's dark blue eyes glittered mischievously. "You're so bossy."

"Right?" Shade said.

I just cut them both a scorching scowl and flapped my arms at Liam and Norah to get a move on.

"Alright, alright, we're going," Liam said but strode towards me instead. Wrapping me in another warm hug, he spoke softly in my ear. "Good luck."

I smiled against his shoulder. "I don't believe in luck."

"Shut up," he said, his voice full of mirth. "Yes, you do."

Stepping back, I flashed him another grin. "Alright, yeah I do. I just thought it sounded cool."

"Uh-huh." Turning to Shade, he held out his hand. "Keep her safe."

The Master Assassin clasped it. "Always."

"Keep *me* safe?" I huffed and crossed my arms. "I'll be keeping *him* safe, thank you very much."

All three of my friends laughed at that. Shaking my head, I tried and failed to suppress a smile of my own. The previously packed square was almost empty now. Only Shade's assassins and some of his staff from Blackspire, along with Yngvild and Vania, lurked on the other side of the platform. I tore my gaze from the two blue-eyed warriors waiting for me and shifted it back to the happy couple before me.

Liam threw an arm around Norah's shoulders, and when both of them looked at me, a heavy weight settled in my stomach. It felt as though we were saying goodbye. Permanently. The plan we had concocted was insane and beyond risky so this might very well be the last time I ever saw these two extraordinary people. Or anyone, for that matter.

Shaking off the feeling, I forced a smile onto my lips and nodded towards Norah's pregnant belly. "We'll celebrate properly when all this is over, yeah?"

"I would like that," Norah said.

Liam managed a much more convincing smile than me. "We'll see you soon."

Shade and I nodded back, even though I wasn't sure either of us truly believed it. After one last look, the teacher and the hatmaker turned around and walked away. Worry gnawed at my bones as I watched them disappear across the square.

The armies of Tkeister, Sker, Beccus, and Frustaz would soon be upon us and before that happened, we had to get every single civilian out of the city and get all the underworlders ready for a fight. I swallowed. This had to work. By all the gods, this had to work.

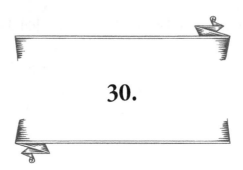

# 30.

The streets of Pernula were like the bones of a clean-picked carcass. Completely empty. With all the civilians successfully evacuated, and all the underworlders getting ready in the shadows, no one was left to traverse the wide roads bathed in bright afternoon light. I watched the abandoned potted plants swaying sadly in the breeze. Soon this colorful city would be painted in only one hue. Red.

While the obsidian walls of Blackspire rose before me, I tried once more to sort through the emotions swirling around inside me. My body had had time to rest and recover thanks to the time we gained by sailing here on Zaina's ship while the armies coming for us traveled by land, but my mind hadn't enjoyed the same reprieve.

Everything that had happened in the star elves' camp, and the aftermath that had followed it, had left me angry, sad, and worried. I was also terrified that this crazy plan of ours wouldn't work and that I would only get my friends killed and doom the whole Underworld to extinction. And then there was also the jumble of feelings about Rain that still didn't quite add up because parts of them were now missing. All in all, it formed a gigantic pile of shit that I had neither the time nor the courage to face right now. So I did what I always do. I hid the mess that was my heart and soul behind a cocky swagger.

Drawing a hunting knife, I slipped through the door and into the study where one of the clerks working in Blackspire had told me I could find their High King. Shade was standing with his back to me, palms braced on the table before him, poring over a large map of the city. I snuck forward. Surprise and anticipation coursed through me when he still didn't look up. Gliding up behind him, I whipped my knife up and placed it against his neck.

He started. Ever so slightly. The movement was there and gone again almost before it happened. But I had seen it.

An evil grin spread across my lips. "You're getting sloppy."

"Sloppy?" I could hear the smirk in his voice. "I *let you* do that."

"Whatever you need to tell yourself." Keeping the blade against his exposed skin, I flashed him another wicked smile even though I knew he couldn't see it from behind. "Now, admit that I won."

"You can never win against me unless I let you."

"Oh, please do keep going. Now, you'll have to admit that I won *and* say 'please remove the knife.'"

A dark laugh slipped from Shade's lips. "Revenge, huh? And you accuse me of holding grudges."

"Don't you know? I'm the queen of holding grudges." I pressed the blade a bit harder against his throat. "Now say it. Or do you want me to make you beg for it?"

He moved like a viper. Twisting, ducking, and striking in one fluid movement. And then he had me disarmed and leaned back over the table. With one hand gripping the collar of my leather armor and the other holding my knife against my own throat, he tilted me further backwards.

I had managed to shoot a stiletto blade into my palm, but short of actually stabbing him through the arm, I couldn't really do anything with it from this position. So instead, I just tightened my hold on the wrist that was forcing me off balance. The sturdy wooden tabletop dug into the back of my thighs as my weight shifted. If he released his grip on me now, I was going to topple back first onto the table.

"You thought you could pull something like that on me?" His midnight laugh drifted through the air. "Someone really ought to teach you some humility."

Despite the vulnerable position I was in, I shot him an arrogant grin from across the blade's sharpened edge. "Yeah, no one has ever succeeded in doing that. But you're welcome to try."

Pulling me back up a little, he leaned forward until his breath caressed my face. "Careful now. Or I might take you up on that."

The smile on my face was nothing short of villainous. Shade's eyes glittered in response and then steel clattered as he took my hunting knife from my throat and dropped it on the tabletop at the same moment as I retracted my stiletto blade. Placing his hands on the back of my thighs, he lifted me onto the table. I drew my fingers through his silky black hair before locking them behind his neck and pulling him towards me. Lightning crackled through me as his lips ravaged mine.

His hands slid to the small of my back while he stepped closer, nudging my legs wider and pushing me further back on the table with his hips. Paper crunched, followed by the distressed clinking of small metal figurines as they toppled over on the map behind me.

"The...battle...plans," I panted between kisses.

He grunted against my lips and waved a dismissive hand at the inconvenient sheet of paper I was currently crinkling. A soft tear sounded as a thrust of his hips sent me sliding more firmly onto the table.

With an exaggerated sigh against his lips, I dragged my remaining hunting knife from its sheath and placed the cold sharp edge against his throat. "We are not ruining our battleplans."

Both amusement and slight frustration danced in his eyes, but he stilled. Pushing forward, I forced him to take a step back from the table so that I could hop down and leave the poor map in peace. As soon as I had removed my knife and placed it on the table beside its twin, the Master Assassin advanced on me again. In order to spare our battleplans, I slid away from the table.

Shade ran his gaze up and down my body as he backed me across the room. "You've really taken a shine to those clothes, huh?"

Ever since Vania had given me that leather armor that looked like black dragon scales, I had started wearing it more often. Especially when I was expecting trouble. It provided better protection than my regular clothes but was just as easy to move in. And let's face it, it made me look really badass.

"What can I say?" I shrugged. "I like having them on."

A sly smile spread across Shade's lips. "I like them even better off."

My retreat came to an abrupt halt when my back hit the wall with a soft thud. Shade continued advancing on me. He only stopped when his toned body was so close that I was forced to press myself back against the cool obsidian in order to have any room to move at all.

Raising my hands, I trailed my fingers down the buttons on his crisp black shirt. "You know, I think I like this shirt better off too."

His warm laugh danced against my lips. "Do you now?"

Cocking his head to the right, he brushed his lips over my jaw while I unbuttoned his shirt. When it was open, I drew my hands up his abs and chest until I reached his toned shoulders and pushed the shirt off them. The black garment rustled as it fell to the floor.

A dark moan rumbled from his throat as his hands moved to return the favor. I intercepted him. Placing a palm against his warm chest, I pushed him back. Surprise flickered over his face but when he saw the evil smile on my lips, he only narrowed his eyes. With Shade an arm's length away, I reached for the fastenings on my leather armor. Locking eyes with him, I started stripping it off with deliberate slowness.

Shade took a step towards me, but when he moved, my fingers stopped working. I stared at him with that evil smile still on my lips. He let out a soft growl but retreated again. Holding his gaze, I started up the slow process again.

A dangerous hungry glint appeared in his eyes as he watched me. "My black-hearted thief, what are you doing to me?"

Cool air wrapped around my chest like silk as I finally shrugged out of the thick leather garment that had been protecting my torso. Shade bit his lip, and before I could even start on my pants, he grabbed the back of my thighs and hoisted me up. I wrapped my legs around his hips as he pushed me back against the wall. Dragging my fingers through his hair, I arched my back as his lips worked their way down my throat and towards my collarbones.

I let out a small gasp of surprise when the cold obsidian suddenly disappeared from behind me. Moving my hands further down, I locked them behind his neck as Shade carried me towards the divan further in. In a smooth motion, he laid me down on the soft cushions while bracing his knees on either side of me.

Leaning back on the sofa, I unlocked my fingers from behind his neck and began tracing the muscles of his chest. His skin was warm against mine as I continued downwards. Just as my fingertips reached the top of his abs, two strong hands encircled my wrists. Guiding my hands towards his knees, he pinned them there while still straddling me.

A sly smile spread across his face as he ran his eyes over my exposed chest. Still keeping my arms trapped by my sides, he reached up and braced one hand on the couch while placing the other high up on my jaw. He drew his hand downwards. A shiver coursed through my body as his fingers brushed that sensitive spot behind my ear. He stole the gasp from my lips.

While his mouth continued stealing my breath away, his fingers worked their way down my throat. After tracing them over my collarbones, he started down my side.

"Ah, my cold-hearted assassin," I breathed against his lips. "Now what are *you* doing to me?"

Wildfire roared through my veins as his fingers caressed my ribs. Pulling against his weight, I tried to free my hands but in the face of his strength, it was useless. I would only be able to touch him back if he allowed it.

Shade's lips sent searing bursts through me while his hand slipped lower. Lightning crackled over my skin at his touch. I arched my back as a shudder coursed through my body and a moan ripped from my lips.

A sharp knock sounded from the door, followed by hurried footsteps. "My king, there's–"

The royal messenger trailed off and blinked at the scene before him while his mouth flapped up and down like a stranded fish. Bloody murder glittered in Shade's eyes as he turned towards the surprised man with calculated slowness. The color leeched from the messenger's face. And then he bowed. Low.

"Please forgive me, my king. I didn't know that... I..."

"What is it?" Shade ground out.

When the messenger swallowed nervously and flicked his gaze to me, I was abruptly reminded that I was lying half naked on a divan with a Master Assassin on top of me. Embarrassment seared my cheeks and I wasn't sure whether I wanted to hide behind a pillow or throw a knife at the messenger's face.

Shade's expression darkened when he noticed the brief glance at me. "See to it that your eyes don't stray again."

All the blood drained from the messenger's face and he dropped his gaze immediately. "Of course, my king. Forgive me, my king." Still staring at the floor, he cleared his throat. "I was sent to tell you that King Edward awaits you on the balcony. He said it was urgent."

"Message received." Shade flicked his wrist. "Out."

Black and red robes fluttered through the air as the messenger bowed again and then practically ran out of the room.

I let out a self-conscious chuckle and rested my forehead against the arm Shade was still bracing on the couch next to my head. "Well, that was embarrassing."

Wood groaned as Shade climbed off me and got to his feet. With his eyes on the now closed door, he shook his head.

"I should have him fired," he muttered. "Or assassinated."

A dark laugh escaped my lips as I sat up and swung my feet over the edge of the sofa. "Or maybe we shouldn't be doing stuff like this in such a public place."

Shade reached down. Taking his calloused hand, I let him pull me to my feet. But when I made to slip away and retrieve my discarded clothes, his other hand shot out. With a firm grip on my chin, he tilted my head up to meet his gaze.

"I'm the High King and you're the Queen of the Underworld." His black eyes glittered as a sly smile spread across his lips. "I think we can do whatever the hell we want."

# 31.

Boots thudded on a soft red carpet. We had almost reached the door to the balcony when a tall man with bulging muscles rounded the corner on the other side of the hallway. Marcus blinked as he saw us but continued towards us at a brisk pace.

"I saw the ships." He flicked his golden-brown eyes between me and Shade. "This is it then?"

We stopped by the open door to the balcony to wait for him to catch up. Warm afternoon winds swirled in from outside, making the sheer drapes flutter and filling the room with Pernula's signature scent of spices.

"Yeah, it is," I replied.

Marcus gave us a grim nod before the three of us stepped out onto the balcony. The low-hanging sun painted the black obsidian around us in gold as we strode towards the lone figure by the railing. This far up, we could see across the whole sprawling city, all the way to the glittering sea beyond. A mass of ships flying the dark blue and silver of Keutunan lay waiting just off the docks.

King Edward heaved a deep sigh as we took up positions next to him. "They're leaving on the evening tide." He turned to look at his brother. "And I'm going with them."

Shade braced his hands on the balcony railing and nodded. "I suspected as much."

"I know that I'm young and that I'm not a military leader," Edward continued. "But they're *my* people. I need to go with them."

"I know." Shade straightened and clapped a hand on his little brother's shoulder while giving him a sad smile. "I wish I could just hide you away someplace safe to protect you until all this is over... but you're the King of Keutunan. Your people need you."

Edward nodded. Golden light played in his dark hair as he moved. For a moment, the two of them only watched each other in silence. Then, Shade drew Edward into a tight hug.

Marcus and I exchanged a glance and then turned to stare out at the unnaturally empty city while the two brothers spoke softly to each other. Only dust clouds swirled in the deserted streets where there had been droves of people milling about earlier. I had never seen a place this big and this empty before. It was unsettling. Maybe this was what it would look like thousands of years from now, when everyone was dead and only the bones of the world remained. I shook the morbid thought from my mind as King Edward raised his voice again.

"Stop looking at me like that," he said.

He and Shade had broken apart and the assassin was indeed watching him with a somber expression on his handsome face.

"Stop looking at me like this is the last time you will ever see me. This is not the end." Edward stabbed a finger in Shade's direction as if to emphasize the point. "We will see each other again soon."

"Of course." Shade forced the sadness from his face and gave him a confident smile instead. "See you soon."

Apparently satisfied with the change in attitude, King Edward gave him a firm nod before shifting his gaze to me and Marcus in turn and doing the same. Then, he simply strode away. I was immensely grateful for it because I wasn't sure I could handle a tear-jerking goodbye right now.

As soon as the young king had disappeared back into Blackspire, Shade turned to the muscled man next to me. "Marcus, I would like you and your Storm Casters to go with him."

"What?" Marcus frowned back at him. "With the fight that's coming here, you want me to leave?"

"Storm Caster powers aren't suited for this kind of fight. Close quarters in cramped alleys. It would knock down buildings and destroy more of the city than it would save. Edward will need you more than we will."

Marcus crossed his powerful arms. "I'm not just Ashaana. I'm a swordsman too."

"I know." Shade raked his fingers through his hair and looked towards the door. With his eyes still on the spot where his little brother had disappeared, he let out a long sigh. "It's just, if anything happened to him... I wouldn't be able to live with it." He shifted his gaze back to Marcus. "Please."

I blinked. Shade didn't often say *please*. In fact, I wondered how many times he had ever said *please* in his entire life. Probably less than a handful. Marcus seemed to realize it too because his expression softened, but he still looked reluctant to agree to leave.

"You sure you'd be alright without us?" he asked, turning to me.

"Yeah. Like he said, this is gonna be more guerilla fighting than open battle and we've got a whole host of bloodthirsty underworlders on our side." I shot him a confident grin. "We'll be fine."

Marcus held my gaze for a few more seconds but then turned to Shade and nodded. "Alright. I'll get the other Ashaana and we'll go with your brother."

The assassin held out his hand. "Thank you."

Nodding again, Marcus clasped it. After letting go, he turned to me and took a step forward until he was close enough to plant a quick kiss on the top of my head.

"Give them hell," he said as he drew back, a wide grin on his face.

I flashed a wicked smile back at him in response.

When his muscled form had disappeared through the door, I shifted my gaze to the city beyond and leaned down on the railing next to Shade. He was staring at the ships bobbing in the glittering sea.

"Thanks," he said. "For backing me up and getting him to go with Edward."

Shifting my weight, I leaned closer until my arm brushed against his. "The things we do for family, right?"

"Yeah."

We continued watching the golden rays dance across the rooftops of Pernula in comfortable silence. Soon, all that would be left in this city were underworlders. Murderers and warriors. Bomb makers and poisoners. Everyone with any skill in the noble art of killing. Not to mention Shade's Assassins' Guild. And me.

However, the Underworld might be big but far from everyone was a fighter. There were four armies descending on us. If our enemies sent in a majority of them all at once, and especially if they brought elven archers, then we would be dead before the end of the first day. But we were gambling that Queen Nimlithil wouldn't want to sacrifice her own star elves and that she wouldn't risk sending in most of her other forces in one fell swoop.

If she did as we had predicted, then we would live. If not, we'd die. I stared at the wide city stretching out all around me. Only time would tell if we were right.

# 32.

Dust clouds rose around the unit of soldiers marching towards Pernula. It was a mixed company of warriors from Beccus, Frustaz, and Sker. Bad call. Those men probably weren't used to fighting as a cohesive unit. It was also only a small portion of the army. Also a bad call. A malicious smile spread across my lips. It was exactly the size we had been hoping for.

The four armies had arrived outside of Pernula's gates yesterday. After setting up camp, they had waited until nightfall and then sent billowing white mist towards our walls. Apothecary Haber, who had come with us when we fled the battlefield on the plains, had raised his defending shield of green mist and blocked their attempts every time. When the sun rose above the horizon, we had thrown open the front gates. Queen Nimlithil no doubt expected a trap, which it indeed was, but had eventually sent the unit now stomping towards our city.

Slinking down from the city walls, I made my way back to where my gang was waiting. Yngvild already had his huge battle axe in his hands, the muscles on his tattooed arms bulging as he lifted it slightly at the sound of my approach. When he saw that it was me, he lowered it again.

"They're coming," I said as I came to a halt before them.

Vania's perceptive blue eyes found mine. "How long?"

"They'll be here in fifteen." I shifted my gaze to Yua, the slim dark-haired thief who had done well during my war with the Rat King. "Head over to Rowan's crew and tell them to get ready."

She nodded and slipped away.

We had divided the city into sections and each gang was responsible for their part. There were several roads to take after walking through the main gates. On every single one, there were underworlders waiting to ambush them.

With a wicked grin on my face, I signaled to my gang to get ready. We spread out.

Minutes dragged by while we hid in the shadows and inside the buildings. Then we heard it. The resounding boom as Kessinda and her Black Waves crew pushed the main gates shut behind the enemy unit that dared to come into our city. Silence fell. More time ticked by while the soldiers no doubt tried to figure out what to do.

At last, marching boots echoed between the buildings down the road. I shrank back into the shadows of a side alley. The sun was slanted in the sky, which made the tall structures of Pernula cast deep shadows on the ground and between the houses. Perfect for an ambush.

The enemy host stomped towards us. There were a lot fewer soldiers than I had seen from atop the wall, so they had probably decided to split up, but it was still a considerable force. The first ranks of armor-clad men passed by my hiding place. I watched the tense set of their jaws as they flicked nervous eyes around the area. Oh, they had no idea what hell awaited them.

When the last row had passed us, I nodded at the cluster of people waiting in a pocket of darkness across the street. Wordlessly, we moved forward. The others who were waiting behind me moved as well. I snuck on the balls of my feet until I was directly behind one of the soldiers in the last line. A brief glance confirmed that everyone else had done the same. I gave a quick nod.

And then we all slit the throat of the soldier before us. Hands across mouths prevented any dying gasps as I and all the other stealthy killers in my guild dragged the entire row of dead soldiers into the waiting houses. When the corpses had been handed over to non-fighting members of our gang, we slunk back out on the street.

Prowling forward, we began our hunt anew.

Warm blood slipped over my hands as I sliced my knife across the throat of yet another unaware soldier. Clamping a palm over his mouth, I dragged his dying body towards the nearest building.

We had already eliminated four rows when the soldiers at last noticed that there was a whole bunch of people missing behind them.

"Hey!" There was a sharp note of panic in the young man's voice as he called out to his friends while whipping his head from side to side. "Where are the others? There should be..." He seemed to be counting in his head. "Like four more lines behind us."

The whole squad ground to a halt. Fear bounced from face to face as they whirled around, looking in every direction, but still unable to locate their friends.

"Weapons out, eyes sharp," the leader commanded.

Steel sang as the soldiers drew their swords. When they were on high alert like this, it would no longer be possible to pick them off from behind. Leaning out through the window of the building where I had deposited my latest victim, I raised my hand and flashed a couple of signals.

And then all hell broke loose.

From every rooftop, gang members who were skilled with ranged weapons rained fire down on the street. The soldiers screamed as they scrambled to defend themselves from the death coming for them from above. Little did they know that it was only the beginning.

Doors banged open behind them and warriors from my gang welled out onto the dusty stones. Yanking two throwing knives from my shoulders, I shot out of the building as well.

Sharp thuds sounded and two soldiers went down, clawing at the blades sticking out of their throats. On the other side of the squad, Yngvild loosed a battle cry that shook the very walls around us, and swung his huge axe into the disorganized rows of enemies. Raw terror marred their faces as they beheld the enormous warrior coming for them but before they could run, Vania darted through their ranks like a snow leopard, slicing as she went.

The leader's shouts to re-form the lines were drowned out by the rising screams of dying men. And then the first soldier bolted. A breath passed as the rest of them stared at the young man fleeing up the street, farther into the city. Another volley of crossbow bolts whizzed through the air and struck breastplates with loud thuds.

Armor clanked and boots thudded as all the soldiers broke rank and ran for their lives in the same direction as the first one. Exactly where we wanted them. With help from our crossbow-wielders, we herded the panicked squad along the route we had picked out. And straight into Red Demon Rowan and her crew.

Their cries rose to deafening levels as the soldiers realized that they were now trapped between two lethal forces. Their leader was screaming at them to get back in line. I met Rowan's gaze from across the crowded street while the squad was forming a loose circle with their backs to one another and our two crews on either side. She flashed me a wicked smile. We attacked.

Darting forward, I flung two more throwing knives. They struck the closest pair of soldiers straight in the throat. Blood bubbled from their lips as they collapsed on the street, leaving a gap in the ring. Undiluted fear shone in their eyes as the soldiers hurried to step over their friends and close their ranks again before the first wave of underworlders broke against their defense.

Steel clashed and echoed down the street as our three forces collided. Drawing my hunting knives, I twisted and sliced. Screams of pain shattered through the air as I severed hamstrings and slashed arms. I jabbed my blade into one soldier's throat while he was busy trying to defend himself against the blond streak that was Vania. Yngvild bellowed another battle cry as he swung. A resounding crack split the air as his axe fractured armor and flung people away like broken seashells. I fought my way into their circle.

As soon as their lines broke and a hole appeared, warriors poured through it. With attackers both in front and behind, the fight turned even more frenzied. Blood sprayed across my face as I slit a man's throat from the side while he was busy trying to defend his other flank. And then the immediate area around me was quiet.

I used the second of grace to scan the street. A figure on the other side of the broken ring of soldiers caught my eye. Rowan. She darted and zigzagged through the mass of enemies like a woman possessed. Everywhere she went, men fell screaming to her sharp sword and before they had even hit the ground, she had already slain her next victim. Red hair flowed in the wind created by her own movements and caught the sunlight, making it look like a mane of fire streamed behind her. For a moment, I just gaped at her.

When the last of the screaming soldiers lay dead in a sea of corpses, I strode towards the redheaded gang leader. Stopping before her, I gave her an assessing stare. Her face was splattered by heavy red streaks and it looked like she had washed her hands in blood. I knew that I looked exactly the same.

Raising my eyebrows, I gave her a wicked grin. "And you keep telling me that *I'm* a violent one."

Green eyes glittered as her lips curled upwards. Her smile was a slash of white in her blood-painted face. "Why do you think people call me *Red Demon Rowan*?"

Despite the carnage around us, I tipped my head back and laughed. The sound bounced into the bright blue sky and mingled with the noise of screaming and clashing blades that rose from every part of the city as we slaughtered the invaders. It was music to my ears.

We had won the first battle. Now, we just needed to keep doing this with every enemy unit that was sent into our city. Tipping my head back down, I flashed Rowan another approving smile and held out my arm. She clasped it with a matching grin on her face.

Unless Queen Nimlithil sent in an overwhelmingly large force all at once, then we would win this. A small song of victory began in my heart. We might actually survive this.

# 33.

"We won't survive this."

Shade cast me a sidelong glance while we jogged along the city wall. "I know."

When night had fallen and not a single person from the unit they had sent into Pernula had returned, a human commander had ridden up to the gates. For the next hour, he had bellowed up at the walls that the next time soldiers approached the city, it would be their entire army. The message was clear. Surrender now, or come sunrise, face the full wrath of their armies. We wouldn't even survive it if they sent in half of their forces. If they sent in all of them, we were dead.

My heart thumped in my chest. "So what do we do?"

"We fight. Even more sneak attacks than before. No outright battles at all if we can avoid it. And hope that we can outlast them."

As we reached the eastern side of the city walls, we trailed to a halt. Drawing myself up on the edge, I sat down and gazed out at the dark blue sea. Bright moonlight reflected off the star-speckled waters. Leather creaked as Shade sat down beside me.

"Well, we did always know that we might die here," I said, picking up the thread of conversation from before. "And I suppose this is as good a place as any."

Waves lapped against the empty docks below. I studied the dark expanse before me. Somewhere out there, a little farther north, was the Lost Island. Keutunan and Tkeideru. It felt like a lifetime had passed since I was nothing more than a bad-tempered thief in the Thieves' Guild. Robbing people blind, eating breakfast at the Mad Archer with Liam, trying to get out of whatever trouble my smart mouth had landed me in that day. It felt like a completely different life. And in some ways, I suppose it was.

"Do you ever think about it?" I asked.

"Think about what?"

"What it was like before all this started. Before we met the elves and killed King Adrian and the Pernulans invaded and we sailed here and well... everything that has happened since."

Shade turned his head and peered down at me. "You mean back when I was ambushing you on the streets of Keutunan whenever I felt like it?"

I narrowed my eyes at him. "I ambushed you too."

"Did you?" The corners of his lips curled into a wicked smirk. "Do you remember that the second time I ambushed you, when I brought some of my guild with me, you got down on your knees and begged my forgiveness for being rude to me?"

Heat flared into my cheeks. I *had* done that. Back then, I was terrified of Shade. He was the infamous Master of the Assassins' Guild and I was just some random thief who had not treated him with the respect befitting a Guild Master. Let alone the Master of the death guild. So I'd been right to be afraid. It was still embarrassing, though.

"Bastard," I muttered.

His rippling laugh drifted across the dark blue waves.

"Well, I also pulled a knife on you inside..." I trailed off. Leaning forward on the cold stones, I squinted at the dark horizon. "Is that...? Are those... ships?"

Both of us climbed to our feet, as if that would make our night vision better. A few more minutes passed and then the contours became clear.

"Yes." Shade let out a breathless laugh. "Yes, they are."

WOOD GROANED AS A GROUP of people stalked down the pier. Shade and I stood side by side, watching them approach while waves crashed against the shore all around us. The party of eight stopped in a half circle before us.

"Shade," a very familiar voice said. His dark eyes slid to me. "The Oncoming Storm. It has been a long time."

I couldn't keep the smile off my face. "Guild Master Killian."

On the salt-stained docks of Pernula stood the entire Keutunian Underworld. My three Guild Masters from the Thieves' Guild studied me intently. Killian inclined his head slightly at the both of us before hooking his shoulder-length black hair behind his ear, while Eliot only watched me with a face of stone. Amusement glittered in Guild Master Caleb's observant brown eyes as he smiled at me.

Next to the three thieves stood two brothers: Mick and Donnie, the muscled leaders of the Bashers' Guild. And beside them, a woman with long red hair. Madame Margaux. The Mistress of the Pleasure Guild. On the other side of my old Guild Masters was a man with blond hair whom I had never seen before but I assumed must be the leader of the new Assassins' Guild, and a man with piercing blue eyes. Rime, the Beggars' Guild Master.

Hope fluttered in my chest. The Underworld had come.

"We got your letter," Caleb said to me, mirth still twinkling in his eyes.

"I didn't think you would come," I replied.

It was true. When I sent that letter to them, it had just been a fool's hope. After all, why would the underworlders of Keutunan sail all the way to Pernula to fight in a war? Underworlders didn't fight in someone else's war.

Killian crossed his arms. "We have no intention of letting this war spill onto our own streets. War is bad for business. Better it is fought and ended here."

Shade nodded at him, at them all. "We're very glad you're here. How many did you bring?"

Boots thudded on the planks farther out on the pier. A lot of boots. Sly smiles spread across the face of all eight Guild Masters but it was Eliot who answered in his grating voice.

"Everyone."

My heart swelled. Everyone. They had brought everyone. With the combined might of the Pernulan and Keutunian Underworlds, we might actually stand a chance of winning this.

"Thank you," I said softly.

All eight of them nodded back at me in acknowledgement. Shade gave my arm a quick squeeze before motioning towards the city.

"Come." A smile flashed over his mouth. "We have a lot of scheming to do before the night is over."

Rime answered with a smile as sharp as his eyes while striding forward. "Just like old times."

The other Guild Masters chuckled. "Just like old times."

While the leaders of the Keutunian Underworld followed Shade towards the city, I lingered on the pier, waiting for the horde of underworlders who were following them. Or more precisely, waiting for one particular underworlder.

Some of the people who strode past nodded at me in acknowledgement. Most of them were members of the Thieves' Guild who recognized me from when I was living with them too, but others I didn't recognize at all. Though, I had always had something of a reputation back in Keutunan. The Oncoming Storm was a name whispered with awe throughout the Underworld. So they probably knew *of me* rather than knew me. I nodded back at them.

Before long, a tall and muscled man with a shaved head appeared in the crowd. His gray eyes lit up as they beheld me and then he was elbowing his way towards me. I strode towards him and let him wrap me in a fierce hug.

"I've missed you, trouble," he said, a laugh rumbling through his chest.

"I've missed you too, Bones."

After an extra tight squeeze, the Thieves' Guild gatekeeper placed his hands on my shoulders and drew back to study me. A wide grin spread across his face as he took me in.

"I hear you've gotten into some trouble since I saw you last," he said.

*Some trouble* was the understatement of the decade. I grinned back at him. "Oh, you know, gotta keep it interesting."

Another rumbling laugh shook his broad chest. "Yeah, life at the guild is much less interesting when you're not there, for sure."

The procession of disembarking underworlders was thinning out so we started down the pier as well. Soft chatter and exclamations of surprise drifted into the night as the people around us got a better look at the humongous city before them. Even Bones was staring open-mouthed at the tall walls when we passed through the harbor gate.

"How's Liam, by the way?" Bones asked as we made our way through the darkened streets. "Last I heard, he'd found a girl here."

"Yeah, Norah." A smile spread across my lips. "He's good. He's got a job now. Selling hats."

"Liam sells hats?"

Chuckling, I nodded. "Kinda funny, right?"

Bones laughed too. "Yeah. But so, he's an upperworlder now?"

"Yeah."

"Huh." Bones drew a large hand over his shaved head while a considering look passed over his face. "It kind of makes sense, though. When you think about it. I always thought he was a bit too... nice, a bit too kind, for the Underworld."

"I know, right?"

He turned to peer down at me as we rounded the corner onto yet another moonlit street. Clusters of underworlders walked ahead of us. They all looked to be studying the city. Either for its beauty or surveying it for any potential advantages it could provide in the fight to come. Sincerity burned in Bones' gray eyes as he looked at me.

"But so, he's happy?" he asked.

"Yes, Liam is happy. Very happy, I'd say."

"And you?"

I shrugged. "I'm still alive."

Amusement danced over his face as he shot me a knowing look. "From what I've been told, you're a bit more than just alive. I hear you're the Queen of the Underworld over here."

Grinning up at him, I lifted my shoulders in another light shrug. "Maybe."

He laughed and clapped a hand on my shoulder. "I always knew you had it in you."

We had reached the large square that Shade and I had picked as the gathering point when we saw the ships on the horizon. The few messengers and clerks from Blackspire who had elected to stay in the city were there to help direct people to temporary places to sleep and get ready for the battle.

My eyes found the cluster of Guild Masters in the middle. Shade was with them, no doubt giving them information to pass on to their guilds. After that was settled, they would scheme. We would scheme. I glanced back at Bones.

"Go on, Queen of the Underworld." He grinned down at me. "Go be important."

I placed a hand on his muscled arm and gave it a quick squeeze. "When all this is over, we're gonna sit down, have an ale, and talk. For real."

"Yes, we are." His gray eyes glittered as he nodded towards Shade and the other Guild Masters. "And then you're going to tell me the story of how you and the legendary Master of the Assassins' Guild and lost prince of Keutunan became an item."

Heat flushed my cheeks. Glancing away briefly, I kicked at a loose stone with the toe of my boot. How had he known that? For Nemanan's sake, he had only just arrived here and he hadn't even seen me with Shade.

Bones laughed his rumbling laugh and squeezed my shoulder. "I could see it from a mile away, kid."

Clearing my throat, I shot him a mock glare. "Well, you always were a perceptive one."

He winked back in response. Shaking my head, I gave his arm a swat before starting towards the other leaders of the Underworld. After a few steps, I turned around to face him again while continuing to walk backwards.

"Alright, it's a promise. And drinks are on me." Grinning widely, I spread my arms. "Because I may or may not also own a tavern now."

At that, Bones tipped his head back and laughed so loudly that the sound bounced between the buildings and made other underworlders glance over in surprise. I raised a hand to my brow and gave him a salute before turning and trotting away.

When all this was over, we would sit down and have a whole bunch of drinks. There was so much I wanted to ask him, about my former guild, about himself, about Keutunan. And so much I wanted to tell him. Bones. I really had missed him. *Soon*, I promised myself. We would get to do all that soon. First, we just had an impossible war to win.

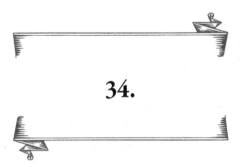

# 34.

"They're coming!"

The words echoed between the buildings as they were passed from one mouth to the next. My heart slammed against my ribs. This was it. Today was the day we would find out if our crazy plan to beat the star elves' overwhelming numbers actually worked. Or if it would cost us this war.

With my pulse smattering in my ears, I flicked my gaze around the area where I knew other underworlders lay in wait, even though I couldn't see them.

The arrival of the Keutunian Underworld had been a blessing on two fronts. Firstly because they bolstered our own numbers but secondly, and most importantly, because their presence here and their own scheming minds had birthed the most ingenious plan of all. One that utilized every single person in this city's rather vast Underworld. Now, all that remained was to see if it worked.

Stamping feet marched closer. I swallowed. They were almost here now. Just like last time, we had thrown open the main gate. That was a tactic to both draw them into our trap and also to avoid having them use the trebuchets on the city. They wanted to come in, and we wanted them to come in, so we let them. Hopefully, we hadn't bitten off more than we could chew.

Metal clanked as the soldiers closed in. I wondered how many there were. The scouts on the walls would of course have an accurate count already and had probably relayed it to Shade, but I was too far into the city to have easy access to that information right now. I rolled my shoulders as the noise of marching soldiers grew louder. Well, it mattered little how many there were, I supposed. They were all going to die anyway.

The first unit rounded the corner. Annoyance flashed over their faces and their pace slowed a little when they realized that the wide street they had been using turned into a narrow alley on this side. After some snapped orders from their leader, they clustered together to fit their ranks into the cramped space before continuing forward. I waited.

Quick hands shot out of windows and gaps between buildings. I watched with pride as the thieving hands found their marks and then withdrew without being noticed. When half of the force had passed by, I glided out of the shadows. My fingers traced over rough leather and found the clasp I was looking for in a matter of moments. Unhooking it, I lifted off my prize and melted back into the shadows. The soldiers marched on.

After silently placing it on the ground, I grabbed the nearest windowsill and started up the side of the building. An overcast sky painted the rooftops in a grayish light as I stalked the squad of Sker soldiers from above. They might be battle-hardened men who were confident in their victories of the field, but in here, they had no idea just how outmaneuvered they really were. But they were about to find out.

Shouts rose from the front of the column as they rounded another corner and marched straight into a wall of warriors.

"Battle formation!" the leader screamed.

Men in the gold and brown armor of Sker reached for their weapons as a horde of bashers barreled straight for them with bats, swords, and axes raised. I cackled as shock and panic rippled through the outer ranks like crashing waves. Their belts were empty. You see, that's what happens when you march through an alley filled with thieves who can steal your weapons right off your belts without being seen. Terribly inconvenient, really.

Blood sprayed into the air as the charging warriors collided with the unarmed outer ranks while the rest of the now thoroughly confused squad tried to reorganize itself. Taking a running start, I leaped off the low end of the roof and rolled to my feet in the middle of the fray.

The soldier closest to me went down in a screaming heap as I severed his hamstrings before he even knew I was there. I jabbed a hunting knife into his throat on the way down. A sword whizzed through the air behind me. Whirling around, I threw up my blades to block it even though I knew I might very well be too late.

Two resounding cracks echoed between the buildings. I blinked as blood splattered my face. None of it was mine. In front of me stood a Sker soldier with a surprised expression on his face. To be fair, in that situation, I would've been surprised too. Wet squelching noises rose as Yngvild pulled out the battle axe he had wedged in the man's ribcage at the same time as Bones had crushed the soldier's skull with a heavy bat. Yngvild and Bones exchanged a glance as the dead soldier crumpled to the ground.

"Nice hit," Bones said.

Yngvild looked from the caved-in remains of the man's skull and then back to Bones. "Yeah, you too."

Another wave of Sker soldiers rallied and charged towards us. I ducked under the first man's arm and drove my knife into his armpit. The impact made the sword in his hand clatter to the stones. Bones used the opportunity to whack him in the back of the head while Yngvild swung his axe into another soldier's back.

"I see you've already met," I said while parrying a sword from my other side.

A moment of silence followed as Bones and Yngvild dispatched their own opponents and then glanced at each other again.

"You know each other?" they said in unison as they flicked their gaze to me.

"Yeah." I whirled and slashed my blade across a Sker soldier's thigh. "This is Yngvild. He helps me run my crew here." Yanking a couple of throwing knives from my shoulder, I hurled them at another enemy charging at us. Dull thuds sounded as they struck home. "And this is Bones. He's a friend of mine from the Thieves' Guild."

Yngvild slammed the sharpened edge of his axe into another Sker soldier's side before taking a moment to study the bulging muscles of the bat-wielding man I had indicated. Incredulity filled his voice as he finally blurted out, "You're a *thief*?"

"I'm the Thieves' Guild gatekeeper." Bones lifted his broad shoulders in a shrug. "So I'm more of a bash-people's-heads-in kind of guy."

"Hey, me too!"

As if to prove the point, Bones smacked his heavy bat into the closest soldier's wrist, making him drop his weapon, while Yngvild rammed his axe into the man's unprotected chest. Body parts thudded against stone as he collapsed to the ground. And then everything was silent.

Having the outer ranks discover their weapons missing right as they were attacked had thrown the whole squad into disarray and had made it easy for the ambushing warriors to finish the job. After an encounter with both thieves and bashers, the soldiers of Sker hadn't stood a chance.

"You should come have a drink at the Black Emerald when all this is over," Yngvild said to Bones while wiping off his battle axe.

"I'd like that." Bones spun his bloodied bat and rested it over his shoulder before turning to grin in my direction. "You could fill me in on all the trouble this one has caused."

A wide smile spread across Yngvild's face. "And you about all the shit she pulled back in your city before she came here."

"Guys." I smacked my lips. "Standing right here."

Rumbling laughs shook their chests as they turned to me with matching grins on their faces. Rolling my eyes, I shook my head but couldn't stop the smile tugging at the corner of my lips. I had a feeling that Bones and Yngvild were going to like each other a lot.

"Hey," a sharp voice said from the shadows on my left.

Turning, I found a thin man dressed in rags peeking out from a small gap between the buildings. If I hadn't known what to look for, I would've thought that he was part of the house.

"Assassins are needed two streets east. Contact in five. Bashers five streets north. Contact in fifteen." And with that, the beggar was gone again.

I wiped my bloody knives on a dead soldier's pants before sticking them back in their holsters. "Break's over, I guess." After shooting the two muscled fighters a mock glare, I trotted away while calling over my shoulder, "If you're gonna gossip about me, at least make me sound epic."

Their deep laughs followed me as I slipped between the wooden houses and headed east. Between the tall buildings around me and with the thick clouds above casting everything in a foreboding gloom, it felt as though I was passing through a rip in the world. Like a secret passageway connecting different points in the universe. One full of dead bodies and blood and the other of clean empty streets. Streets that would soon also run red.

"Help! Someone, please help!" a woman's shrill voice cut through the air. "No, stop. I'm not one of the invaders. I was just trying to get away. Please!"

Armor clanked as a group of people hurried towards the sound. I picked up the pace and ran the final stretch between the wooden walls until I reached another street. This one wasn't empty. At the far end stood a beautiful woman, clutching her light blue dress with shaking hands. A squad of Beccus soldiers rounded the corner.

"There were Pernulans here," the leader said without preamble.

The woman nodded. I shrank back between the wooden walls as the man marched past my hiding spot and advanced on her.

Motioning for the other soldiers to stop, the leader fixed her with a hard stare. "We have no interest in killing civilians. Just tell us where they went."

Black shadows slunk out of the darkness behind the soldiers and glided towards them like wraiths. I drew a hunting knife on my way forward as well.

"They heard you coming and left," the woman said in a trembling voice.

"Where did they go?" the leader pressed.

Stopping directly behind my target, I waited for the rest to get into position as well.

The woman lifted her hand and pointed. "They went that way."

And then throats were slit. Surprised choking erupted as the Beccus soldiers had their breathing abruptly cut off while pistols and crossbow bolts were fired from the rooftops. I lowered the red knife in my hand and moved towards the next living enemy but he was already sagging to the stones with a wooden shaft sticking out of his chest. In a matter of seconds, the squad in black and yellow armor lay dead and dying on the streets of Pernula.

"You're a great actress," said a man I knew very well to the woman in the blue dress.

A sly smile spread across her lips as she flicked her long hair back behind her shoulder and rearranged her dress. "Acting is the first thing you learn in the Pleasure Guild."

Man-bun inclined his head in acknowledgement. I was just about to ask him if he'd seen Shade when a wrinkled woman with sharp eyes popped out of a pocket of darkness.

"This area is clear for now," she said, her voice coming out as a rasp. "But they'll need assassins seven streets west in about twenty minutes, bashers eight streets south in about the same time, and thieves ten streets north. They'll be making contact there in about fifteen minutes."

I met Man-bun's gaze from across the sea of corpses. He gave me a nod before motioning for the assassins around him to move out. After wiping my blade and sticking it back in its sheath, I climbed up the side of the nearest building and took off north across the rooftops. No rest for the wicked.

The day wore on in the same murderous fashion. Assassins slit throats from the shadows. Thieves stole enemy weapons right off the unsuspecting soldiers' bodies. Bashers cracked skulls and broke bones and severed limbs. Whores lured victims into traps like sirens. And beggars kept a flowing information network running through the whole city. It was a bloody masterpiece.

When Shade and I had formulated our battleplans, we had only been thinking like stealth killers because, well, we *are* stealth killers. So we had used the fighting members of the Pernulan Underworld but we hadn't utilized the non-fighters. When the leaders of the Keutunian Underworld showed up, that had all changed. They had known exactly how their own guild members could contribute to the fight and the same could be applied to the rest of the underworlders as well. So instead of fighting as gangs, we had split up the Pernulans according to skill.

The Pernulan Underworld far outnumbered the one from Keutunan but the Guild Masters were in charge because they knew how to get their sections organized. All the warrior types fought with the bashers and the stealth killers with the assassins. The thieves ganged up and stole everything they could get their hands on while the alluring women joined forces with the Pleasure Guild. Everyone without a specific skillset but who knew how to move through a crowd unseen worked with the

Beggars' Guild to relay information between the different factions. And I moved between different groups of thieves, assassins, and bashers because... well, I'm me.

Blood splattered my face as I slashed my knife across a Sker soldier's throat. Twisting down and around, I aimed for another one. Clashing steel vibrated above me as a sword stopped the blade that had been coming for my head. I returned the favor by ramming my knife into the throat of the man who had been about to skewer Shade.

"They only sent in about a third of their army," Shade said by way of greeting.

This was the first time I had seen him all day. With the thick cloud cover it was impossible to tell exactly what time it was but it had to be late afternoon.

"And Rime sent word from his faction that the whole city is almost cleared now," he continued.

"Good." I blocked a strike to my ribs with one hand while hurling a throwing knife with the other. "Did you send the messages?"

Metallic ringing bounced around the alley as Shade slammed his swords into his opponent's futile attempt at blocking. "All three went out at first light."

"Then let's start the final phase."

Blades slashed and the soldiers around us went down. In the brief pause we'd bought ourselves, Shade wiped his forehead with the back of his hand. It only served to smear more blood across his face.

"Go ahead. We'll mop this up." Blood dripped from the edge as he lifted one of his swords to point at the battling assassins and soldiers a few strides away.

"You're not coming?"

Shade spun his blades in his hands while advancing on our enemies again but before he joined the fight, he threw a smirk over his shoulder. "You're so much more dramatic than I am, so you'll do fine on your own."

I glared at his back as he disappeared into the battle again. Dramatic, huh? I'd show him dramatic.

Taking off at a run, I aimed for the large square close to the main gate that I had been working my way towards for the last hour or so. Two thirds of Queen Nimlithil's army still waited outside the gates and if we were to stand any chance of winning this, we had to pull off this final part perfectly. Climbing the wall of a building next to the square, I let out a soft chuckle. I guess it was a good thing that I could be a rather dramatic bastard when I wanted to.

Gunshots echoed between the buildings. On the stones below, the fear and panic that hung over the square were reaching terrifying levels. I grinned as I strode past the underworlders on the roof and made for the edge.

Soldiers in brown and gold, black and yellow, and light blue and white crowded the area in front of me. Every time there had been survivors after one of our guerilla attacks, we had herded them here. Once they had reached this place, we had kept them trapped here with the help of pistols. People from this continent weren't used to handling firearms thanks to Queen Nimlithil banning them long ago, but the citizens of Keutunan were well used to them. Standing atop the roofs of the buildings that boxed in the square, they shot anyone trying to leave. Those who didn't want to die huddled in the middle.

As the day wore on, more and more soldiers made it here. The ones who strayed too close to one of the exits died in a hail of bullets. Every time that happened, their panic grew. As I watched them from the edge of the roof, I could almost taste the sour tang of fear on my tongue.

Reaching deep into my soul, I pulled out the darkness and threw my power wide. Screams of terror rose as black clouds shot out across the area. Lightning crackled through the dark mist and deafening thunderclaps split the air. I let it go on for another few seconds before pulling the storm back and wrapping it around me instead. Eyes black as death in a blood-smeared face met the soldiers as they turned to stare up at me.

"You should never have come here," I boomed across the crowd.

I shoved a cover of black clouds over them again. Lightning danced through the darkness. Men screamed. Then I pulled it back. And the soldiers screamed again because among them now lay men with their throats slit. Under the cover of darkness, assassins had killed some of the soldiers. I flashed them a smile tinted with rage and insanity.

"This is a city filled with demons and wraiths," I bellowed. "You should never have come here."

The frightened soldiers whipped their heads between me, their dead companions, the unseen assassins who were responsible for the deed, and the people leveling guns at them from the rooftops. Soon, the fear would turn into hysteria.

"But we will give you one chance. Only one." I stabbed an arm towards the street that led straight to the main gate. "Run. Run and tell the rest of your army that this is the gate to hell. Do that, and we might let you live."

Tendrils of black smoke whipped around me like lethal snakes and lightning crackled over my skin. The crowd below me flicked nervous eyes between me and the escape route I had pointed out as if they weren't sure whether they could trust me not to have them shot if they moved towards it. Smart.

"W-what are you?" a soldier from Sker called in a trembling voice.

A malicious grin slashed across my face as I raised my arms and called up a wall of black smoke shot through with lightning. "We're the Underworld."

Boots scuffed as the soldiers closest to my side of the square backed away. I lifted one hand to point at the street leading to the main gate while I raised the other towards the sky. Squeezing it into a fist, I jerked it down.

"Run."

Lightning zapped the stones. And the soldiers ran. Gunshots echoed through the air as the underworlders atop the roof made sure that all the fleeing enemies used the road we wanted. The one that led out of the city.

Staying on the rooftops, I followed the fleeing herd of soldiers as they sprinted towards the open gate ahead and elbowed one another out of the way in their hurry to escape. Below me, the streets ran red with blood.

As planned, our horses were already saddled and waiting in the stables next to the gate. I dropped down from the roof and crossed the area on foot while the last of the panicked soldiers disappeared into the landscape outside.

"You're kind of scary, you know that?" Bones said as he fell into step beside to me.

"That's what I said!" Yngvild added as he too joined me.

I flashed them a wicked grin as we reached the edge of the horse pen. Shade stalked towards me from the other direction while signaling for our horses to be brought forward. His assassins were already in the saddle.

"That went well."

Turning, I found Vania and Rowan striding towards us as well. They were both covered in blood like a second skin. A short distance to the right were four more people I recognized. My three former Guild Masters, as well as Rime, were making their way to us.

"Yeah," I said, answering Vania's comment. "Now we just have to make sure that the rest of the plan actually works."

Horses neighed as Silver and Shade's black and white stallion were brought forward. The Master Assassin turned to the small group that had gathered around us.

"You can handle the rest?" he asked.

Red Demon Rowan shot him a confident grin. "We'll hold the city. Go make sure they never come back."

"We will stay a while as well and help secure the city," Guild Master Killian said.

Rime backed him up with a nod that confirmed the Beggars' Guild, and probably the other guilds as well, would do the same. Shade nodded back at them in acknowledgement.

Killian's black eyes found Shade's. "It was a pleasure to scheme with you once more, Shade."

The Master Assassin flashed them a smile. "And you."

Sticking a boot in the stirrup, he climbed into the saddle. I turned to do the same but stopped when my former Guild Master spoke up again.

"The Oncoming Storm." A slight smile, something that I had almost never seen on his face, drifted over Killian's lips. "You have become a fine leader. Know that you will always have a home in the Thieves' Guild, should you want it."

"Thank you," I said, and truly meant it.

All three of my former Guild Masters nodded back at me.

Shifting my gaze to Rowan, I let a villainous grin snake over my lips. "Hold down the fort. We're going hunting."

White teeth flashed in her blood-soaked face in reply. "You really are a violent one."

I chuckled and turned to Vania, Yngvild, and Bones. "And then we're gonna have that drink."

"Yes, we are," Vania said.

"And I'll get to hear all about the schemes you've pulled before you met us," Yngvild filled in.

Bones' gray eyes twinkled as he smiled back at me. "I'll see you soon, trouble."

"I'll see you soon," I replied, an equally warm smile on my face.

Then I swung myself onto Silver's back and dug my heels into her sides. Hooves against stone filled the area as Shade and I rode out the gate with his Assassins' Guild behind us. A swarm of black death to hunt down an army that far outnumbered us.

Atop the city wall, Apothecary Haber shot a thick plume of dark smoke into the air.

We had survived the battle for Pernula. Now we just had to survive the war.

# 35.

Frantic soldiers crashed into their own forces, screaming about demons and gates to hell. The two thirds of the army that still remained on the plains stirred restlessly as the survivors of the battle for Pernula shoved their way through the ranks and ran. Shade and I pulled our horses to a halt right outside the main gate as we watched the chaos unfold further out.

Queen Nimlithil was nowhere to be seen. She was most likely waiting somewhere at the rear of the army, safely surrounded by her star elf archers. Just as we had hoped. Convincing the human soldiers to run would be far easier if there weren't any stoic star elves there to pacify them. I glanced at Shade. Now we just had to make sure the humans actually turned and ran. And so far, we were not enough.

Confusion rippled through their ranks as the survivors elbowed past, and they cast uncertain looks at their commanders but they stood their ground. *Come on.* We needed to do this now. If we waited, the moment would be lost. *Come on.*

Ferocious battle cries split the air behind us.

Countless boots smattered against the ground as a whole host of soldiers rounded the city walls and barreled straight towards us from behind.

A wide smile spread across my lips.

*Yes.*

Shade shot me a satisfied smirk. And then we were off.

Dust swirled around us as Shade and I galloped towards our enemies with the Assassins' Guild behind us and another army on our heels. The men on the front ranks jerked back and retreated a couple of steps at the sight of the force plowing towards them. Battle cries echoed off Pernula's tall stone walls and soared into the thick gray clouds above. Boots slapped against the ground. Armor clanked.

From atop Silver, I could see further into the human armies before us. The survivors were still shoving their way through and the sound of an attacking force made them even more frantic. Since the ranks further in couldn't see what was happening across the grass, they had no idea what was coming for them. All they knew was their fleeing friends screaming about demons and wraiths.

Restlessness rippled through the three armies. And then a section in the middle turned and ran. Ran with their panicked friends who had just survived hell and who bellowed that hell was now coming for them again. Once that first group turned and ran, another followed suit. And then another. And another. Until it created a chain reaction and the armies of Frustaz, Beccus, and Sker broke ranks and scrambled to get away.

I screamed into the sky as Shade and I galloped at the front of the charging army and drove our enemies back. Drawing on my powers, I sent a wave of black clouds billowing around me and lightning shooting through the dark smoke until I truly looked like death itself riding a pale gray horse over the plains.

Deafening noise filled the whole area around us. Fleeing soldiers in front, advancing warriors behind, thundering hooves all around. And screaming. Battle cries, shrieks of terror, and useless orders bellowed at panicking men.

The assassins and I slowed our gallop so that we wouldn't make contact. Not yet. Chasing our prey, we kept just out of range the entire time that the soldiers ran over the grasslands.

Then the fleeing armies stopped. Abruptly. Soldiers were hauled by their armor back into position and ranks were closed. The human armies had at last reached the spot where the star elves had been hiding, which had no doubt forced them to stop running. Weapons were raised as the humans spread out in an enormous circle, forming a vast sea around the cluster of white and silver in the middle.

Dusk was close now. The grayish light filtering through the thick clouds grew fainter with each passing minute. We didn't have a lot of time left. But it would have to be enough. I drew a deep breath. Even with the army at our backs, we were far outnumbered. And now that our enemies had stopped running, it was time to fight. Time. Yes, we were indeed almost out of time.

Orders were snapped from the ranks before us. And then the collective armies of Sker, Frustaz, and Beccus gathered their wits and advanced on us.

I gripped the reins tighter in my hands.

Furious soldiers, embarrassed by their fleeing and their fear, charged towards us with rage crackling on their faces.

My heart slammed against my ribs.

Swords were raised. Armor clanked. Revenge danced on their faces.

This was it.

Screams rose.

But it was not from us. And it was not from their front lines. It was from their flanks.

From the sea, a horde of men dressed in armor of dark blue and silver charged the unprotected flank. Flags bearing entwined silver-colored thorns on a dark blue background snapped in the breeze.

On our enemies' western flank, a swarm of arrows sped through the air and descended on them with lethal precision. Figures in green and brown, as well as gray, were barely visible as they moved through the vegetation.

From behind me, rows upon rows of soldiers in black and red welled forward like a tidal wave and hurtled across the flattened grass.

The armies of Pernula, of Keutunan, and of Tkeideru had come.

Gunshots echoed across the landscape as the soldiers of Keutunan fired into the eastern flank. From the west, wood elves and mountain elves loosed arrow after arrow into the lines of enemy soldiers, while the men from Pernula crashed into their forces from the north. Shade and I exchanged a look, matching smirks on our faces.

"Good thing we had a spy in our camp," Shade said.

I chuckled. Indeed it was.

In the evening after our final battle on the plains, we had decided on a plan. We all knew that our lines wouldn't hold another day and that it was a miracle we had even survived that day, so we had to do something else if we were to stand a chance of survival. Which was why we had come up with this crazy scheme.

Dissent was already growing so we just used what was already there. With the help of some of Shade's most trusted soldiers, we orchestrated the whole show we put on in the middle of camp. Since Elaran was such a terrible liar, we'd had Queen Faye do most of the talking as she pretended to take the elves and disappear into the White Mountains with the mountain elves, leaving the humans to their fate.

After that, we had Lord Raymond play his part. Drawing on the fact that King Edward was young, and the messy history with Shade, we could construct a convincing ruse for why the senior member of the Council of Lords could seize the Keutunian army and sail back to their island.

Malor hadn't been at all difficult to get on board. I think he rather liked putting Shade in his place and pretending to take control of the Pernulan army. After all, he was the Senior Advisor of Pernula and greatly respected by the soldiers.

And we had done all of this for one man. A bland-looking man who had watched it all from beside two blond soldiers from Keutunan. The spy.

Ever since we were ambushed in the Stone Maze, we had known that we had a spy in our camp. While Shade and I had been Queen Nimlithil's prisoners, the Assassins' Guild had managed to root out the spy. When we finally knew who he was, it was easy to put on a show just for him. And we did.

He reported that our army was broken up and our allies were leaving. Which was true. To a point. While we sailed back to Pernula, the elves headed west. But not to hide in the mountains. No, they were circling around Queen Nimlithil's army.

King Edward and Lord Raymond had done the same. As soon as they left Pernula, they sailed out and then back down the coast in order to hit our enemies from the east.

Malor had taken the Pernulan army north in order to protect the civilians we sent on the road to Hidden Oaks Cove.

Queen Nimlithil had attacked Pernula, thinking that there was no army left to defend it, only to find that we had pulled a fourth army out of the shadows. The Underworld. The trap was set and our enemies walked right into it to be slaughtered.

And then when Shade had sent out those three messenger doves this morning, the other three parts of our still united army had moved into position. The plume of black smoke Haber sent up had been the trigger. And then we had tightened the noose around our enemies' necks.

Man, it really was a brilliant plan.

Steel clashed, arrows whizzed, and pistols boomed. Dread was spreading through the ranks before us as the soldiers of Sker, Beccus, and Frustaz scrambled to reorganize themselves and beat back the attack that pounded them from three different directions. And then it sounded. A horn blaring retreat. We couldn't let them, because we had to kill Nimlithil while we had the chance.

Shade snapped orders to the soldiers around us. To the east and west, our other allies no doubt received the same instructions. Our army seemed to suck in a collective breath. And then we pushed.

The very ground seemed to shake as our ranks of soldiers took a heavy step forward, shoving the enemies back. Metal clanged. Raising their swords, the Pernulans heaved forward again. Out on the plains, the elves did the same. A volley of arrows. A step. Another volley. Another step.

We had been running low on bullets even before we got here so the Keutunians drew their swords and advanced across the grass as well.

A small song of victory rose in my heart. If we could just force them back enough to get a clear shot at Queen Nimlithil, then we could win this.

Bows twanged as the elves fired another volley. Storm Casters from both the east and west sent a blast of wind slamming into the already retreating ranks.

Just a little more.

The air shook. Silver tossed her head and paced to the side as it sounded again. A great booming noise. I whipped my head around. Everywhere, horses were becoming increasingly skittish. Tossing their heads, snorting, and stomping their hooves. That same boom split the air again.

"Dismount!" Shade snapped.

We all slid down from our horses just as another boom echoed across the trampled plains. It was coming closer. The rhythmic booming reached deafening levels. I swallowed. If this was...

The source of the noise became visible on the horizon. My knees almost buckled. It *was*.

A ferocious roar loud enough to shatter glass tore through the air and rolled across the landscape. Our horses bolted back towards Pernula. I stared unblinking at the monstrosity flying towards us.

The white dragon was here.

Bathed in the gray light of an overcast sky, Aldeor the White spread his gigantic wings and banked east. I couldn't think past the blood pounding in my ears as he aimed straight for the Keutunian army and opened his jaws.

Fire cascaded out of his mouth.

A heartbreaking scream shattered out of Shade as the column of fire shot straight towards Edward and his army. But I could do nothing as death sped towards them.

Orange flames scattered into the sky as they slammed into an invisible shield above the army.

Shade pressed a hand over his mouth. Mine was gaping wide open as I watched the dragon fire be redirected into the white clouds above. Then the final piece clicked into place. Storm Casters. We had sent Marcus and a bunch of Ashaana with Edward. They must have slammed up a barrier of wind to block the dragon fire.

Aldeor the White roared in frustration but he was already speeding towards the west. The very grass beneath my feet trembled at the sound of the angry dragon, but I couldn't hear anything over the sound of my own thumping heart as the white dragon flew towards my other friends.

Figures of green, brown, and gray clustered together on the grass. I tried to spot Elaran, the twins, Faye, and my other friends but I was too far away to see who was who.

Fire shot through the sky again. I sucked in a desperate breath as it barreled straight for the elves.

Flames of orange and red were shoved backwards even farther than last time until they almost hit the dragon who had unleashed them.

I pushed out a shuddering sigh of profound relief. Cileya and most of the Storm Casters had gone with the elves when we split up. My head was pounding with the relief that had chased the bone-deep terror away.

The white dragon banked again.

My heart stopped beating.

He was coming straight towards us.

While the dragon had kept our flanks busy, our enemies had managed to retreat further. But our army was still here. The Pernulan soldiers clustered around the group of assassins and all of them seemed to be looking at me. Because I was Ashaana.

There was only one problem. I was only one person.

The other parts of our army had a group of Storm Casters who could direct a coordinated blast of wind to push the fire back. I whipped my head across the enormous army around me. There was no chance in hell I alone would be able to protect everyone.

Beating wings boomed through the air as Aldeor drew closer.

Not taking my eyes off him, I pulled out the darkness. Shade was saying something but I couldn't hear him over the dread ringing in my ears. I swallowed against my parched throat. We were going to get wiped out.

The white dragon opened his jaws.

I lifted my arms.

Flames leaped out of his mouth and shot straight at us. Gathering every smidgen of strength I had, I shoved my hands towards it. Wind blasted from me but it wouldn't be enough. I already knew it wouldn't be enough.

Earsplitting screaming reverberated through the air. I wasn't sure who it was. It might have been me. But someone was screaming like a banshee.

The fiery death slammed into an air shield above.

And every ember of the spearing flames scattered and shot backwards towards the gray clouds. I stared at the orange and yellow flying into the quickly darkening sky. There was no way I had pulled that off.

Around me, people were gaping. And someone was still screaming like a banshee.

Aldeor the White roared in fury but steered back towards the cluster of white and silver in the middle of the army. His wings boomed through the air as he circled the camp. The message was clear. Retreat and let Queen Nimlithil's army pull back as well or he would unleash hell on us again.

Across the grass, the wood elves and mountain elves were already backing away and moving towards us instead. On the other side, the Keutunians did the same.

Apparently satisfied with our actions, Aldeor the White circled one last time and then folded his wings as he dove and landed in the middle of Queen Nimlithil's camp.

Without the booming of his wings, the silence was so loud that my ears were ringing. Or maybe it was because of my terror. Or that banshee howl. I frowned. That had grown quiet as well.

"What happened?" Shade asked. His voice was unusually flat, as if he too was in shock.

"I don't know," I whispered back.

The world around me seemed to be tilting slightly. I wasn't sure if it was because I had used up so much power so quickly, or because of the horror of almost dying, or because of the shock that we had actually survived. Or maybe all of it combined.

"I don't like people who hurt people just because they think they can decide how people should live," a voice said behind me.

Whirling around, I found a small girl with shoulder-length black hair and dark eyes trotting up on a horse.

I blinked at her. "Milla?"

Milla, the girl I had rescued from the Trader in Sker a year ago, gave me a strange smile from atop her brown mare. "Hi, Storm."

We had both lived in the Ashaana camp in the White Mountains for months earlier this year but I hadn't spent that much time with her. From the moment I met her, I had found her very odd. She was now thirteen years old but she sometimes spoke and acted like she was eight years old. But at the same time, when I looked into her eyes, the person who stared back was someone who had seen far too much for someone who was only thirteen. Whatever had happened to her before she ended up at the Pink Lily Pleasure House in Sker had made its mark on her.

I waved a hand towards the air above us. "You did this?"

She glanced up at the sky above as if she could see the remnants of the wind shield. "Yes."

"How?"

Milla tilted her head back down and studied us with curious eyes. "Morgora says that I'm the strongest Storm Caster she has ever seen." A strange smile drifted over her lips. "Maybe that's why I have to scream so much when I release my powers."

Closing the distance between us, I reached up and placed a hand on her leg. "Thank you."

She patted the horse underneath her but looked at me. "You're welcome." Grabbing the reins again, she made to ride off towards the approaching elves and Ashaana. "Marcus and the others tried to keep me away from the fight. They said I was too young." She glanced down at me before urging her horse on. "But I also have the right to fight for the people I love."

A surprised laugh ripped from my throat as I watched the small girl trot away across the grass. Well, she was right. And by Nemanan, I was glad she was.

Raking my fingers through my hair, I tipped my head back and heaved a sigh so deep I thought it would never end. That had been far too damn close.

"On the plus side, we're still alive," Shade said as he wrapped an arm around my back. That usual smug certainty was back in his voice again.

I tilted my head back down and leaned into his strong body. "True. But our plan also went to hell and now we're gonna have to fight our way through a sea of soldiers to get to Queen Nimlithil, while also battling a dragon."

Shade sighed. "There is that."

"There is that."

Drawing strength from one another, we watched as the rest of our army made their way towards the Pernulans setting up camp behind us.

Man, it had been such a good plan. And it had almost worked. Almost.

If we had just managed to kill Nimlithil before Aldeor showed up then we would've stood a real chance at winning this war.

Now, with a host of men that still outnumbered us and an angry dragon guarding the queen, our chances were plummeting fast again. Heaving another deep sigh, I shook my head. How were we supposed to survive this now?

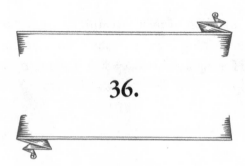

# 36.

Fabric rustled as the tent flap was thrown open. I looked up from where I sat on the bed, expecting to find Shade striding through the tent that had been assembled for us on the plains as soon as our armies had rejoined, but it was someone else entirely who appeared inside the dark walls. Elaran.

We hadn't said more than a few words to each other since he took out all his anger and devastation about Illeasia on me and threw me out of the tent, telling me he never wanted to see my face again. Dread coiled in my stomach but I couldn't bring myself to move. So I just sat there on the mattress and watched him as he let the dark fabric fall shut behind him.

His yellow eyes met mine and for a moment, he hesitated. Then he stalked forward. Sitting while he prowled towards me made me feel vulnerable but I made no move to stand. I had already decided that if he wanted to scream at me or beat me up, then I would let him, so there was no point in getting into any kind of defensive stance.

I braced myself as he closed the final distance between us.

Elaran, still holding my gaze, sank to his knees before me where I sat on the bed. A soft gasp of genuine surprise made it past my lips. I had never seen him look so vulnerable. Lifting his hand, he hesitated. But when I made no move to pull back, he took my hand in his and rested them both against my thigh. He still didn't break eye contact.

"I'm sorry," he said. "What I did to you was unforgivable."

"It's okay," I breathed.

"No, it's not. I am ashamed of how I behaved after you told me what happened to Illeasia." His voice broke slightly on her name. "My world shattered when you told me what had happened, but that is no excuse for what I did to you."

"You needed someone to blame. Someone to be angry at."

A sad smile blew across his face. "And that right there is what made my shame even worse when I finally figured it out. You *let me* hurt you so that I wouldn't hurt so much."

Tears brimming in my eyes, I smiled back at him. "Isn't that what friends are for?"

"No." He shook his head. "I am truly sorry for what I said and did to you that night. Can you ever forgive me?"

I reached out and placed my free hand against his cheek. "You have nothing to be sorry for. There is nothing you could do that would make me hate you." A mischievous smile tugged at my lips as I let my hand drop again. "Except maybe to lecture me on starting fires or on making things blow up or on being a useless city dweller who stomps through the woods like a pregnant moose."

Elaran chuckled. "Well, you're still the most disagreeable person I've ever met." Holding my gaze, he squeezed my hand. "But you're family to me."

Choking back a sob, I pushed to my feet and pulled Elaran up with me before wrapping my arms around him. "You're family to me too, you grumpy elf."

He stiffened in surprise at the unexpected hug but then leaned into it and squeezed me tightly. His auburn hair slid over his shoulder and fell like a curtain around my face, bringing with it his signature scent that I could only describe as a warm afternoon in the forest. I couldn't stop the tear sliding down my cheek as relief washed over me. Elaran didn't hate me. He didn't blame me for what happened to Illeasia. But what made another tear run down my cheek was that he had called me family. Family.

For a moment, we just stood there, holding each other and being relieved that neither of us were angry with the other. Then, fabric rustled again.

"You're hugging? By Ghabhalnaz, I'm going to remind you of this moment until the end of time."

Elaran and I jumped back and turned to glare at the smirking assassin who had just sauntered into the tent.

"Shut up," we muttered in unison.

Shade flashed us a wicked smile as he strode towards us. "What? If you—"

We all whirled towards the entrance again as a fourth person stalked inside. Malor crossed his arms over his broad chest.

"Good, all three of you are here." He jerked his head towards the tent flap. "Come with me. It is time."

"Time for what?" I asked.

But the muscled advisor was already striding back out. His black ponytail swung across his back as he shouldered open the dark fabric and ducked out of the tent. I rolled my eyes as his black and red attire disappeared into the night.

"Well, shall we?" I waved a hand towards the entrance.

Shade and Elaran seemed about as exasperated as I was by Malor's mysterious mumbo jumbo but they nodded and stalked after him. I sighed as I followed them. It seemed as though there would be more surprises before this night was over.

DARKNESS HUNG HEAVY over the deserted grasslands. At least the heavy cloud cover had been blown away by strong fall winds earlier in the evening, which allowed a bright moon to illuminate the area. I was incredibly thankful for that because I would never have been able to make the long journey out into this empty piece of land without getting hurt or lost if there hadn't been moonlight and stars to light the way.

"Don't you look impatient?" a smug voice grumbled.

Turning towards it, I found Morgora stomping across the darkened grass. Shade and I exchanged a glance, as did Elaran and Faye, while Morgora came to a halt in front of Malor.

"Hello, old fart," Morgora said, a twinkle in her steel gray eyes.

"Hello, old bat." A smile tugged at Malor's lips. "I hear you were worried about me. Sent these younglings to rescue me."

"Bah." Morgora crossed her arms and burrowed into her gray shirt neck and scarves. "Worried? Why would I worry about you?"

His strange reddish eyes glittered in the starlight. "It's good to see you."

"Of course it is." She huffed and shot a glare in his direction. "Well, it's good to see you too."

A brisk night wind tore across the plains and ripped at my clothes. I flicked my gaze between the two odd people before us who seemed to watch each other with both grumpiness and longing mingling in their eyes. When there was a moment of silence, I was about to finally ask how in the hell these two weirdos knew each other but before I could, Faye cut me off.

"Elaran," she said, a sharp note in her voice.

"Yeah," he replied. His voice also held a tone of shock. "I can feel it too."

"How is that even possible?"

"I don't know."

Before I could demand to know what this new threat was, grass crunched somewhere to our right. Shade, Elaran, Faye, and I all whipped towards it. A short figure strolled out of the shadows and into the patch of moonlight we were standing in. My mouth dropped open.

"You?" I blurted out.

"Hello, city girl." The old man with the weather-wrinkled face that I had met in the forest outside Keutunan a couple of times smiled as he fixed his gaze on me. Thousands of years' worth of wisdom still seemed to swirl in his light green eyes. "The storm has come. I am glad to see that you are on the right side."

I blinked at him in confusion before my memories finally caught up with me. Every time I'd met him, he had told me that there was a storm coming and that I should make sure to be on the right side. Apparently, this had been it.

"Wait, you know each other?" Faye broke in and motioned between the two of us.

Snapped out of my surprise, I frowned at her. "*You* know each other?"

"Well, yeah–"

"Let's skip the questions until afterwards," Morgora cut us off. Completely ignoring the elven queen, she turned towards the short man. "Athla, it's been a while."

So, his name was Athla. I had asked him about his name but he had never told me.

"I'm glad you stayed," Athla replied.

"Well, after that bloody speech you gave, we didn't have much of a choice, did we?" She adjusted her arms over her chest again. "I've regretted it more than once, I'll have you know."

Before they could get into any lengthy debates on whatever it was that they were talking about, Malor held up a hand and silenced them. Then, he turned to us.

"We have much to tell you and a lot of it will come as a shock, so it's best if we just get to it." He tipped his hand towards the flat expanse of grass on our left while shifting his gaze to Morgora and Malor. "Shall we?"

They nodded and stalked out into the grassland. I met Faye's gaze.

"Do you have any idea what's going on here?" I asked.

She shook her head. As I glanced to Shade and Elaran, they shook their heads as well. Giving up on trying to piece together the utterly insane mystery that surrounded the three individuals currently striding away from us, I just shook my head as well and watched them until they were three dark specks in the moonlight.

They spread out so that there was some distance between them and then they just stood there for a moment. I furrowed my brows. *Okay. Now what?*

Three huge dragons exploded to life in the dark grass.

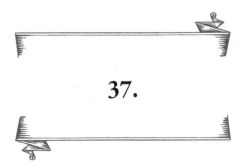

## 37.

Terror shot up my spine. I stumbled back across the grass while gasps of shock ripped from my friends as well.

Three dragons stared back at us.

My heart slammed in my chest and I worked my mouth up and down but no sound made it out. The three dragons advanced on us.

Elaran snapped out of his shock and stepped in front of his queen while Shade threw out an arm as if to shove me behind him. I placed a hand on it but gently moved it aside as the dragons drew closer.

When they moved into the patch of moonlight again, I could make out the color of their armored skin. The one on the far left was gray, the color of steel, while the middle one was of a reddish hue. The dragon on the right was green. The same color as...

I blinked. Twice. And then my mind finally caught up with reality.

Morgora, Malor, and Athla were dragons.

As if sensing that the two humans and two elves before them had finally grasped what was going on, the dragons shrank back into their human skin again. Morgora readjusted the gray scarves around her neck while Malor brushed specks of dust off his sleeveless tunic. Athla just strolled back to us in his rumpled clothes. All three of them had wide grins on their faces.

"I haven't done that in ages," Morgora said and stretched her powerful body.

"Me neither," Malor said.

They all came to a halt a few strides away from us. Silver stars glittered in their eyes. Eyes that were of the same color as their dragon form.

"You're dragons," Shade stated, somewhat superfluously.

Malor chuckled. "Yes, boy, we're dragons."

I massaged my forehead. "But Queen Nimlithil said that the dragons were all gone. When magic disappeared, the dragons did too. That's what she said. And no one has seen any dragons since..." I trailed off as a lightning bolt struck. Whipping my head towards Athla, I stared at him wide-eyed. "Oh by all the gods, you were the green dragon at the waterfall."

Athla smiled at me. "Yes."

"Stop." Shade held up a hand. He seemed to be trying very hard to keep from pacing. "Start from the beginning."

Wind ruffled our hair as another night breeze drifted across the dark plains. Morgora and Athla both looked to Malor. The tall man nodded before turning back to us.

"There will be time to explain everything, but it is not tonight." He motioned towards the star elves' camp far in the distance. "When Nimlithil and Aldeor set their plans in motion and sucked magic from the world, most of the dragons left. We can use magic ourselves but we can't share it with others."

"But we have magic," Elaran interrupted.

"And so do the Storm Casters," I added.

"Yes." Malor motioned towards the green-eyed man next to him. "Part of that was a gamble by Athla."

Athla cleared his throat and flashed an apologetic smile in Elaran and Faye's direction. "I thought that I could give you magic after the spell to shield the island was in place but it didn't work the way I expected. Normally, using magic only drains a person's energy. But in order to share it with you while the spell is in effect, magic demanded a steeper price."

"Life," Faye finished.

"Yes. I could only share my magic with you if the cost for it was part of your life." He shrugged. "Every time I've visited you, if you remember, I've tried to get you to use magic as little as possible. I never meant for you to pay with your life for using magic."

Elaran's mouth dropped open a little and his face went slack as if he just realized something. "That's why our magic only worked on the island, isn't it? When we're here on the continent we've never been able to feel our magic. Until right now when you walked out of the shadows."

"Yes. Another unfortunate side effect of the magic draining spell. I have to be close by for your magic to work."

Faye looked like she had already figured that part out but Elaran drew his hand through his hair and blew out a breath while shaking his head. Confusion crept into my mind. I turned to Athla.

"But then why does my magic work?" I asked. "I can use it everywhere and it only requires energy, not life. It's the same for all the Storm Casters."

"That's because of me," Morgora muttered.

I turned to her in surprise.

"Ashaana powers come from me and they're hereditary," she simply stated as if that was explanation enough.

"I don't understand," I said.

She huffed and smacked her lips as if explaining these things were slightly annoying when there was a war going on. "Athla gave powers to people who had none. That's why the rules were different. He shouldn't have been able to share his magic while Nimlithil's spell drained magic from the world so in order to do that, the magic demanded a steeper cost. My powers were already in your bloodlines because I had shared them with your ancestors long before the spell was in place, so the rules follow the normal rules of magic."

My head was spinning. Pressing the heel of my hands against my temples, I tried to make sense of all of this and also figure out which question to ask next. However, before I could, Shade spoke up.

"Why us?" he asked.

The three dragons in human skin looked back at him in silence as if they knew what he was asking but were reluctant to answer.

"You have been hiding as humans for... centuries?" Shade arched an eyebrow. "And now you've brought people out here into a remote part of the plains and shared your closely guarded secret. But you only brought the four of us. Why?"

"Because you're the leaders of the people fighting against Nimlithil," Malor said.

The assassin narrowed his eyes. "What about Edward? He's the King of Keutunan. And then there's Marcus and Ydras."

Athla shifted uncomfortably on his feet but it was Morgora who answered.

"Marcus would never agree to let you do what we're about to ask you to do."

Malor slid his gaze to Shade. "And neither would Edward."

All four of us narrowed our eyes at the dragons.

"And what is that?" Shade asked.

"Ride into a battle that will most likely get you killed," Malor said. He held Shade's gaze. "We each had to pick one person for this. And I chose you."

Athla glanced at Faye. "You are here because I respect you and I wanted you to know the truth. And because I knew you would do what was right." His light green eyes moved to Elaran. "And you are here because you are the one I chose."

Morgora huffed and flicked her hand in the air while leveling eyes of steel on me. "Yes, well, and I picked you."

My mouth was suddenly very dry. "Picked for what, exactly?"

"This battle is going to end, one way or another, tomorrow," Malor said. His reddish eyes were full of determination. "Aldeor has finally come out of hiding which means that the time has come at last to make our move. At first light, the three of us and the three of you are going to fly into the heart of their camp and kill Nimlithil and Aldeor."

Alarm bells blared inside my skull. "When you say fly, you mean...?"

"Fly with us, yes," Malor said. "We can only take one rider each, at least if they're to have any chance of staying on until we land, which is why we could only choose one person."

"And we chose you," Morgora grumbled and flapped her arms. "There. Enough chitchat. Now get back to camp and get some sleep. Sharpen your knives. Whatever you need to do. Because tomorrow, you will be in the fight of your life."

And with that, she stalked away across the grass. Malor chuckled and shook his head at her retreating back but when he turned back to us, his reddish eyes were soft.

"She's right," he said. "I know you have a lot of questions but there will be time for that afterwards, if we survive. Right now, you need to prepare for battle." He jerked his head at Athla. "Come on."

While the two of them strode after Morgora, I tried to get my head to stop spinning but all I could hear was Malor's choice of words. *Have any chance of staying on until we land. If we survive.*

Faye sucked in a deep breath. "Wow. Did not see that coming."

A laugh ripped from my lips. It was a panicked and desperate sound. The others laughed as well, their sounds unnervingly similar to my own. Shade draped an arm over my shoulders as the four of us started back towards camp.

The flickering light from campfires that soon appeared in the distance seemed far too normal to be real. Everything that had happened tonight was completely insane. The strange man who had spoken in riddles when I met him in the woods outside Keutunan was a dragon. The Senior Advisor I had helped escape from Sker when the star elves conquered the city was a dragon. The woman who had trained me for seven months to be a Storm Caster was a dragon. It was absolutely insane.

Regardless of all that madness, however, the dragons had been right. If we were indeed heading into the final battle against Nimlithil and Aldeor tomorrow then I had a lot to do before the night was over if we were to stand any chance at winning. Blowing out a sigh, I shook my head at the star-speckled sky above.

When the sun crested the horizon, the craziest thing that had happened this century would take place. Something so ridiculously absurd that the gods were surely laughing at us.

I, a thief from the Underworld, would ride a dragon into battle.

Nemanan save us all.

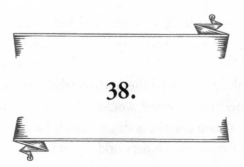

# 38.

I was a thief. A cat burglar. I was not afraid of heights. No, the
thought that someone who frequently ran across rooftops
could fear high altitudes was entirely preposterous. And yet I
clung to the spikes on Morgora's neck and pressed myself into
her gray scales as if it was the only thing keeping me in the land
of the living. Which it was.

Far below, the grasslands passed by with alarming speed as
we closed in on the army camped ahead. I tried to focus on the
first light of dawn reaching its pale tendrils over the vast sea to
the east instead of the fast-moving ground below. When I'm on
a ship, I get seasick. Apparently, I had the same problem when
riding a dragon. But Morgora had informed me in no uncertain
terms that she would roast me alive and eat me if I threw up on
her, so I swallowed the bile rising in my throat and focused on
my other senses.

Cold morning winds stung my cheeks and ripped through
my hair and clothes. The air tasted different up here. Crisp and
clear. Kind of like breathing in chilly mist. Still gripping the
jagged spike before me, I shifted my gaze to my companions.
Atop the large red dragon in the middle was a figure dressed
all in black. Twin swords gleamed in the early morning light
as Shade rolled his shoulders. On his other side, Elaran sat

gracefully on top of the smaller green dragon, a curtain of auburn hair fluttering behind him like gleaming fire.

Another feeling shoved out the fear of falling off, the nausea from the motion sickness, and the apprehension at the coming battle. Wicked satisfaction. A grin spread across my face as the booming of great leathery wings filled the air all around me and cries of alarm went up from the camp we were descending on. Death on wings had come for our enemies.

At the sight of the dragons speeding towards them, the soldiers of Sker, Beccus and, Frustaz scrambled out of their tents and ran for their weapons but their attention was soon occupied elsewhere. Under the cover of night, the forces of Keutunan, Tkeideru, and Pernula had prepared for a surprise attack from the east, west, and north. I had argued that we should just fly into Queen Nimlithil's camp and attack at night, but the more military savvy people in our group had reasoned that we would need the rest of our army to keep their army busy so we could focus on killing their queen. Seeing the chaos that was spreading as our forces launched their attack led me to conclude that my friends had been right.

Deafening roars split the heavens as Morgora, Malor, and Athla screamed their challenge at Aldeor the White. Arrows fired from human bows hurtled towards us. I tightened my grip on Morgora. She bellowed again and opened her jaws. Orange flames shot from her mouth. On the ground, soldiers screamed and bolted as Malor and Athla spit raging fire down on them as well.

Scorched earth was all that remained in the ruts that their dragon fire had created. After that, no other arrows were fired from the humans. Instead, they ran from the center of camp and focused on battling the enemies swarming them from the outside. Good. Malor had explained that they would need all their strength to fight Aldeor so they couldn't waste it on the human armies. Thankfully, it appeared as though this display of force had been enough to get the message across.

The elven archers, on the other hand, were a different story. I blinked against the tears that the cold wind ripped from me as we neared the cluster of white and silver in the middle of camp. The star elves would keep firing at us until Queen Nimlithil ordered them to stop. We couldn't let them. The dragons had to kill Aldeor and Shade, Elaran, and I had to kill Nimlithil. We couldn't have star elves shooting at us while we did that so we had formulated a ridiculously risky plan. Or gamble, more like it.

I swallowed as Morgora dove straight towards camp. Now, it was time to find out if our plan was going to work. If not, I would be dead in forty seconds or so. My heart slammed against my ribs as the ground grew larger. That is, if the landing didn't kill me first.

A screeching bellow echoed into the chilly air. Aldeor the White answered the challenge that had been issued and leaped from his position at the center of camp. Gigantic white wings glittered in the pale morning light as he flapped hard. He was far larger than any of the three dragons on our side and the blasts of wind that his huge wingspan produced sent tents and elves flying across the grass in a wide circle. Only the queen's majestic tent and a few others that were directly below him were spared the torrent. Just as we had hoped.

White canvas and silver hair fluttered in the wind as elves were tossed away when the great dragon hurried to get airborne.

My stomach lurched as Morgora banked and swerved around him. Malor and Athla did the same on his other side.

Green grass and flattened tents grew larger. I thought my heart was going to leap out of my chest. *Almost now. Almost.*

When we were so close that Morgora's wings almost slapped the ground, she tilted. My every instinct was screaming at me to hold on tighter but I did as Morgora had instructed and simply let go. Air whooshed in my ears as I slid off her hard scales and free-fell the final bit to the ground. I let my instincts kick back in.

Anyone who spends their days running across rooftops learns how to land pretty fast, so I used everything I knew to smoothen the landing enough not to break anything. The impact still sent a jolt through my entire body but I managed to roll to my feet without shattering any bones.

Across the grass, Shade and Elaran were climbing to their feet as well. The three of us exchanged a nod. And then we ran.

Drawing a deep breath, I sprinted across the trampled grass towards Nimlithil's pavilion. A wall of star elves had re-formed around it. All of them had bows drawn and pointed at us. If the second part of our plan didn't work, then I was about to die in a hail of arrows in a few seconds.

Blasts of wind slammed into the landscape. I stumbled and almost tripped over a crumpled tent as the force of it struck the area around me. It smacked into the ground again. And again.

The star elves facing us rocked to the side as well but remained on their feet. They loosed their arrows. I had to resist the sudden strong urge to squeeze my eyes shut.

Nothing hit me.

White shafts scattered like sticks in the wind as Athla flew in a tight circle over the camp, slamming air down on the ground with his powerful wings. Hope fluttered in my chest. It worked. With him altering the currents, it was impossible to shoot accurately. The star elves seemed to realize that as well because they drew gleaming swords instead and sank into a defensive position.

The world shook. I was thrown off balance as a blast of air coincided with another force of nature above. Rolling to my feet, I cast a glance at the sky. Malor and Morgora had finally slammed right into Aldeor. His gleaming white body dwarfed theirs but they clawed and snapped their jaws while their wings boomed across the landscape.

Shade and Elaran had closed the distance between us and now fell in behind me, keeping one hand on my leather armor. I drew a shuddering breath. It was time for part three of our plan and this one was all on me. Reaching into the wildfire rage burning in my soul, I yanked out the darkness. Black clouds exploded around us. Elaran and Shade tightened their grip on my leather armor but kept running. I shoved my arms forward.

Hurricane winds crashed into the ranks of waiting star elves, and under the cover of artificial darkness they didn't even see it coming. Shouts reverberated through the air and mixed with the roaring dragons above as soldiers were flung away by my powers, creating a gap in their lines. Since I was able to see through the darkness, I grabbed a hold of Shade and Elaran's hands and sprinted towards it. They matched my speed, trusting that I would guide them.

Armor clanked and orders were bellowed as the star elves struggled to their feet but with the blinding smoke that still blanketed the area, they couldn't attack us. We shot through their broken ranks and darted inside the flat expanse of grass they had been protecting. As soon as we were safely inside, I pulled the darkness back. Shouts rose. We were inside their protective circle, barreling for their queen's tent but we were once again visible. Blood pounded in my ears. *Come on.*

Fire roared behind us.

*Yes!*

Shrieks of alarm echoed over the ruined camp as the star elf soldiers were forced back by the torrent of fire that Athla sent towards the ground. The smell of burning grass filled the air.

In the silence that followed, the star elves once again screamed orders to run after us. Flames erupted again.

I almost cried in relief. It had worked.

After we broke through the main part of Queen Nimlithil's force, Athla's job would be keeping them back and keeping their arrows away from Malor and Morgora while we battled whatever portion of her soldiers was still left in here to protect their queen. Breathing fire in a steady ring between the soldiers and us while sending bursts of wind at them was a great way of doing that.

That wicked part of me wished we could've just torched the whole star elf camp, and killed Nimlithil that way, but I knew that had never been an option. Princess Illeasia was here too.

My eyes flicked across the ruined camp as I ran. Flames of orange and yellow leaped into the bright sky further out, and between them, soldiers in white and silver armor could be seen trying to find a way through it. Inside the ring of fire, ripped fabric and bits of broken wood lay scattered across the flattened grass. Civilian star elves huddled together behind the shattered remains of their tents. Fear shone in their eyes as they flicked them between the three dragons fighting in the air above and the fire surrounding them. Servants, cooks, and other tradespeople who just wanted to survive the slaughter. They didn't deserve to die in a fiery inferno.

Captain Hadraeth's face drifted past in my mind. He hadn't deserved to die either. And there had to be more soldiers like him. Soldiers who followed orders but didn't believe in this war or in Queen Nimlithil.

It would have been so much easier if we could've just had Athla burn the whole camp to cinders but doing that would make us as bad as Nimlithil. Even I, who didn't really have much of a conscience, agreed with that.

Steel sang before us but the sound was drowned out by the clashing dragons above. I had to resist the urge to watch Malor and Morgora battle Aldeor when a deafening roar split the air. Whatever was happening up there was nothing I could affect. The squad of star elf soldiers who rushed out to protect Queen Nimlithil's tent, on the other hand, was what I should be focusing on.

Waves of hot air rolled over us as Athla sent more flames shooting to the ground behind us. Terror flashed over the soldiers' faces as they took in the sight they had stepped out to find but they quickly composed themselves and nocked arrows in their large white bows. This far in, they weren't affected by Athla's disruptive torrents of wind.

Next to me, Shade and Elaran drew their swords. Every breath felt as though I was inhaling shards of glass but the headlong sprint would soon end. Sucking in air, I raised my arms and slammed them forward just as the star elves prepared to fire.

A gust of air barreled for them and knocked them back into the white pavilion before their arrows left their bows. Loosing a battle cry, I yanked out my hunting knives and leaped across the grass.

My shoulder slammed into the breastplate of a soldier struggling to his feet and knocked him back to the ground again. He went down in a flailing of limbs with me on top of him. Before his back had even connected fully with the ground, I rammed my left-hand knife into his throat. Rolling off him, I swiped with my other blade. It produced a sharp sound as it carved a rut in the armor of the closest elf but it failed to pierce it.

Steel flashed before my eyes. I threw up my other knife to stop the sword coming for me but I already knew that I wouldn't make it.

Metallic ringing filled the air as Elaran slammed his sword down and absorbed the impact. I blinked once in surprise. Sparks flew from his sword as Elaran shoved back his opponent's weapon. Shooting to my feet, I used the opening to jab my knife into the star elf's neck. Elaran and I exchanged a nod before turning back to the fray again.

Pain crackled through my side. My new armor deflected blows better than my usual clothes but getting hit in the ribs with a sword hilt still hurt. The elf who had delivered the blow looked back at me in surprise when I gasped because he hadn't been aiming for me. He had been trying to block Shade's swords and had accidentally slammed into me as I turned around. The moment of inattention cost the elf his life as the assassin drew a sword across his neck.

Reaching up, I yanked four throwing knives from my shoulders and hurled them towards Shade. He didn't even flinch as the blades flew past over his shoulders and buried themselves in the two elves who had been sneaking up behind him. Their heads snapped back with sickening cracks and they toppled backwards with knives sticking out of their foreheads. I flashed Shade a smirk but didn't have time to see his response because steel whizzed through the air behind me.

My instincts screamed at me to duck, so I did. A sword flashed past in the air where my head had been only moments before. Twisting with the motion, I aimed for my opponent's chest. The hunting knife skidded across his breastplate, leaving a deep rut but not drawing blood. I straightened but before I could strike again, an armored elbow slammed into my cheek.

Black stars danced before my eyes and in panic, I threw out my powers. Thick clouds blanketed the immediate area around me and made it impossible for my attacker to see me. I only hoped it didn't affect Shade and Elaran as well. When my vision came back into focus, I slashed my blade across my opponent's throat before yanking the darkness back. There was no point in fighting with it out if that meant I was putting Shade and Elaran in danger.

"Enough!" a voice of command cut through the fighting.

At the sound of it, the star elf soldiers backed away. I gave my head a quick shake to clear it and flicked my gaze towards my two friends. There was blood on both of them but they didn't look injured. Satisfied with my assessment, I turned to the source of the commanding voice.

Queen Nimlithil stalked forward in a decorated silver gown and a sparkling headdress that looked so incredibly out of place on a battlefield that I almost laughed. Almost. Because next to her was another elf. Illeasia.

I glanced at Elaran. His face slackened as he took in the empty expression in her pale violet eyes.

The queen and the princess stopped a short distance from us while the remaining soldiers closed ranks around them, making it impossible for me to get a knife through.

Queen Nimlithil raised her chin and leveled a hard stare at Elaran. "Stand down."

"What?" I spit out.

She didn't even bother looking at me. Still keeping her eyes on Elaran, she flicked a hand between me and Shade. "Make the two of them stand down and back off. Right now."

Elaran bared his teeth at her. "Or what?"

"Or Illeasia gets hurt."

Shock hit me like a basher's bat to the face. I jerked back and whipped my head between the queen and her daughter. As if on command, Illeasia lifted a small silver knife and placed it against the delicate skin on her arm.

"You're bluffing," I said. "You won't hurt your own daughter."

"My daughter knows that sacrifices are sometimes necessary in war." She pressed her lips together as she looked at Elaran. "Now, surrender. Make the two of them surrender and then have your armies surrender as well. You are the commander, after all. Do it now. Or Illeasia will start cutting herself."

Dread washed over me. Elaran's worst nightmare had come true. He was going to have to choose between Illeasia and his people. Us. My heart thumped in my chest. And I had no idea what he was going to choose.

# 39.

Roaring dragons clashed above us and crackling flames seared the ground on all sides. Far away, steel clanked and gunshots echoed as the war on the flanks continued as well. Fire reflected off the white gems in Queen Nimlithil's jewelry as she flicked her elegant hand again.

"I will not tell you again. Surrender or I will have Illeasia start cutting herself."

The silence stretched on. Dread coiled in my stomach because I wasn't sure I wanted to hear Elaran's answer.

"Go ahead."

It took all my considerable self-control not to whip my head towards him and gape. Instead, I turned with calculated casualness. Elaran had drawn his eyebrows down and regarded the queen and the princess with a disinterested look on his face.

"I beg your pardon?" Queen Nimlithil said.

"I said, go ahead." He shrugged. "I don't care what you do with her now. She's already ruined so if you want to start cutting her up too, then go ahead. I don't want her anymore so I couldn't give less of a fuck."

His face was a mask of cool indifference with hints of disgust lacing it. Queen Nimlithil blinked at him in surprise. Then, suspicion crept into her eyes and she motioned for Illeasia to begin.

Elaran's yellow eyes slid to Illeasia but the expression on his face didn't shift as the princess pressed the knife against her skin. Nimlithil studied the wood elf and then looked at me and then Shade in turn, seeking proof of what was going on here. We just gave her a shrug while a bland expression drifted over our faces, as if we'd known this all along. Right as Illeasia was about to split the skin on her arm, her mother spoke up again.

"Stop." When she shifted her attention back to Elaran, her eyes were flashing with displeasure. "I never saw you for the shallow person you truly are. You never cared for my daughter at all, did you?"

A cruel smile curled Elaran's lips as he scoffed. "No."

Incredulity washed through my whole body. I knew, I mean *I knew*, that he was lying but even I couldn't tell that he was lying.

Queen Nimlithil flashed her teeth in a sneer before flicking her hand at Illeasia, telling her to step back. The princess lowered the knife and retreated while Nimlithil motioned at her soldiers again.

"Take them."

I hurled two throwing knives at her. Metal dinged as they were batted away by the soldiers' swords. I had already known that getting a knife through was impossible right now but that wasn't why I'd thrown them. They had been a distraction.

Tendrils of black smoke whipped around me and lightning crackled over my dark armor as I darted forward. I kept it close to me so that it wouldn't affect Elaran and Shade, but would still provide me with an advantage. Queen Nimlithil was right there. If we could just force our way through then it would be over.

A wave of fire from Athla lit up the white breastplates before me. Steel sang as I leaped through the air. With black smoke rolling off me, I crashed into the ranks of star elves in their glittering white armor. We collided like a storm of light and darkness in a cataclysmic battle for survival.

I twirled through the chaos and lost myself in the dance of death set to the eerie music of dying screams, roaring dragons, and crackling fire. Athla loosed a thundering bellow in warning.

"Storm!" Elaran called.

Parrying the sword before me, I rammed my hunting knife into one soldier's neck while flicking a glance towards Elaran. "What?"

He slashed clean through a star elf's armor and then pointed with his blood-dripping sword. I ducked out of a strike to my head and squinted in the indicated direction while blocking another blow.

A horde of elves in pale armor had made it past the flames and were barreling towards us. Redirecting a thrust, I let a sword slide down my blade while I flung a throwing knife into my opponent's face.

"Cover me!" I yelled back at Elaran.

In a matter of moments, Elaran and Shade were slaughtering their way towards me. I did my best to defend myself while also backing away. We didn't have time for this. Trusting that my friends would have my back, I simply turned and ran.

No one stabbed me so I figured that Elaran and Shade protected me. I skidded to a halt behind them on the grass and drew my arms back wide. *Shit*. There were so many of them. This was going to require everything I had. I slammed my arms forward.

I had poured everything I had into that blast so when it struck the charging star elves, it flung their whole line back. Silver hair fluttered in the air as the elves spun up and down repeatedly before disappearing back behind the wall of flames again.

Exhaustion washed over me. I fought the urge to sink to my knees and instead turned back around. My powers were completely drained but they hadn't been that much use in this fight anyway. With Shade and Elaran here, and Illeasia next to Nimlithil, I couldn't just go all out and blast everything to smithereens. But still. I wish I could have.

For a moment, hopelessness shot through my body. There were still so many soldiers between us and Queen Nimlithil. Blood coated all three of us and I wasn't sure if Shade and Elaran were injured. In the sky above, the dragons still clashed like forces of nature. How were we supposed to make it through this?

Shaking my head, I shoved back the bleak thoughts that threatened to overwhelm me and dashed back towards my friends.

Blood sprayed into the air. I drew my blade across the back of a soldier's knee right as Elaran swiped at his neck. Continuing with the movement, I stabbed at another's chest. Pain vibrated through my wrist as the flat of a blade slammed down on it. I lost my grip on my hunting knife. Shooting a stiletto blade into my palm, I whirled around and drove it into the closest body I could find. A muffled grunt escaped as the thin blade pierced armor. I yanked it out.

It didn't move. Alarm blared through me as I was forced to release it and jump back in order to avoid being split in two.

Shade redirected the sword while I scrambled backwards and pulled out another throwing knife.

Two soldiers charged Elaran. I hurled the blade at the one on the left, who went down in a heap of limbs, while Elaran engaged the other.

An earsplitting scream echoed across the world and blood rained from the sky. Heavy drops landed on my brow and ran down my cheek but I didn't dare take my eyes off the fight ahead to check who the wounded dragon above was.

Athla tightened his circles around us and beat his wings furiously while pouring an all-consuming inferno on the ground in order to keep the other star elves back. I parried another thrust but a second sword sliced through the leather armor on my arm. Blood welled up through the cut in the black fabric.

I threw out my other arm blindly to gain time to recover. A few strides away, Shade sucked in a sharp breath. Red bloomed from a wound across his ribs. Panic pounded in my head as three more soldiers descended on him. Yanking out my remaining throwing knives, I hurled them at the attackers but I didn't have time to see if they struck home because an enemy sword took my other hunting knife from my hand.

My last stiletto blade was barely in my palm before I had to block another strike from behind. Twisting around, I stabbed at the ambusher but a blow landed at the back of my knees before I could.

Heavy drops of dragon blood fell from the sky as I crashed down on the grass. A white boot kicked the stiletto from my hand but I managed to roll away before something more lethal hit me. I ripped out the knives strapped to my thigh as I shot to my feet. Armored fists smacked into my back.

Air exploded from my lungs as I stumbled forward but I stayed on my feet. Whirling around, I found a wall of star elves closing in. My chest was heaving. I cast a glance behind me and found Shade and Elaran backing towards me as well.

With our backs to each other, we faced down the advancing ring of star elves. Behind them, Queen Nimlithil was gliding towards us. Rage crackled through me. Loosing a battle cry, I sprang forward.

Steel ground against steel as my knives met the soldiers' long swords but they didn't budge. I shoved forward but against their weights, it was useless. Pain shot through my leg. I let out a sharp cry as a blade sliced across my thigh but the sound was abruptly cut off as an armored fist backhanded me across the cheek.

My knives flew from my grip as I slammed into the ground. Pushing myself up on my elbows, I tried to scramble away but my head snapped back again as a boot connected with my jaw. I crashed back first into the grass again.

The blue sky swam above me but my survival instinct screamed at me to move so I rolled over on my stomach. A brief glance behind informed me that Elaran and Shade were being overwhelmed as well. I yanked the knife from my boot and struggled onto my knees.

Cold steel bit into my throat. With the black spots still dancing over my eyes and the pain pounding through my body, it took another second to realize that a sword rested at the base of it. My throat was raw but I sucked in a shuddering breath and lifted my boot knife.

The sword dug further into my throat. Blood tricked down my skin. I let my hand drop back by my side right as Queen

Nimlithil stepped up beside the soldier holding a blade to my neck.

Thuds echoed as Shade and Elaran were forced to their knees beside me as well. Freezing dread sank into my stomach. They had been disarmed and blood leaked from cuts all over their bodies while bruises were already forming on their faces. Star elves in white armor closed in all around us.

Queen Nimlithil's pale violet eyes were like chips of ice as she looked down on us.

The three of us tried to move. To fight. To do anything. But hands clamped on our shoulders and arms and blades at our throats rendered any kind of resistance impossible.

In the bright sky above, Malor and Morgora fought for their lives against Aldeor while Athla kept the archers on the ground at bay. Deafening roars echoed across the plains and booming wings made the very ground shudder. Further out, our friends were still fighting. Haela and Haemir. Faye. Marcus. Edward. Everyone in our three armies fighting to buy us this chance to kill Queen Nimlithil. And we had failed.

Unarmed, surrounded, and on our knees, we stared up at the elf who had torn our lives apart in her mad struggle for a world free of pain. The elf who was going to pass judgement on us right here on the plains.

After all I had been through and everything I had done. After all the deaths and broken hearts. After the miraculous escapes and timely arrival of our allies. After all my scheming. After all I had done to make sure we won, it was going to end right here.

Bitter disappointment spread through my body like poison and mingled with the crippling fear for my friends.

Steel clashed and gunshots boomed.

Fire roared in the grass.

Dragons clashed.

Queen Nimlithil gave us a cold smile as blood fell from the sky and painted her silver dress red.

We had gambled.

And we had lost.

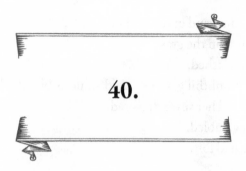

# 40.

The rows of soldiers in white and silver armor shifted as more star elves arrived. Violet eyes stared down at us from behind decorated helmets. Still gripping my boot knife, I calculated whether I could throw it accurately and have it hit Nimlithil's throat before I was skewered. As if in reply, the cold edge of steel at the base of my throat pushed further in. The answer to my calculations was a resounding no. More soldiers pushed up behind Queen Nimlithil as she gave us a pitying smile. I narrowed my eyes at them.

"How can you even serve her?" I bellowed across the gathered star elves. "She killed Hadraeth! The Captain of the Guard. *Your* captain. She shoved a sword through his throat while he lay on the ground!"

The star elves only looked back at me with faces of stone.

"She killed one of your own," I continued. "How can you still follow her orders after that? How?"

"We obey our queen," one of them said simply.

"Your queen?" I scoffed and slid my eyes to Nimlithil. "You forced your daughter to complete the ritual by threatening to kill Hadraeth if she didn't. She did it to save his life and then you killed him anyway." Shaking my head, I spit out a curse. "I might be a liar and a murderer and a godsdamn demon in human flesh but I am nothing compared to you. How could you do that to your daughter? And to Hadraeth?"

As if on cue, Princess Illeasia appeared at the edge of the circle of soldiers. Her eyes were devoid of all emotion as she watched Elaran kneeling on the ground with a sword to his throat.

"My daughter is much happier now that she has cast off the yoke of pain," Queen Nimlithil sniffed. "And as for Hadreath, he was a traitor and he deserved to die. I am glad I killed him."

The rows of soldiers shifted again to make room for more star elves but none of them came to our aid. Sagging back on my heels, I tipped my head up and heaved a deep sigh. Red and gray wings split the air and claws ripped as Malor and Morgora fought Aldeor far above us. Athla continued circling, spewing fire, and blocking attempts to loose arrows. But none of them could help us right now. Faye and the twins, along with the rest of our army, were too far away as well. We were on our own.

"Did you really think you stood a chance?" Nimlithil asked.

A humorless laugh ripped from my lips as I tipped my head back down and met her gaze. "No, we didn't stand a chance in hell."

Queen Nimlithil motioned at the battles still raging on all fronts and her voice took on a smug note. "What are you going to do now? You have used everyone you know. You even managed to persuade the mountain elves to come down from their mountain for the first time in centuries."

I grinned up at her defiantly. "Impressive, I know."

And that wasn't even the half of it. I had called on every single friend and ally I had, and even the ones I hadn't contacted myself had shown up to help me. The people of Pernula,

Keutunan, the elves of Tkeideru. Apothecary Haber. Marcus and the Ashaana. Milla. Maesia. Zaina and her pirates. Yngvild, Vania, Rowan, and the Pernulan Underworld. Ydras and the mountain elves. Bones, my old Guild Masters, and the entire Keutunian Underworld. Morgora, Malor, and Athla. Literally every single person in this whole world who could even remotely be considered my friend had already arrived and saved my ass. I had no more friends to call on.

"But now you have no allies left to use," Queen Nimlithil continued as if she had read the thoughts in my eyes. "You have played all your cards. And you have no friends and allies left to save you."

"I know," I said. "I suspected that it would turn out like this. That there was no chance in hell that me and my friends would win this."

The ring of star elves shifted again as I twirled the knife in my hand.

Steel sang into the morning air.

Queen Nimlithil blinked and sucked in a gasp of surprise. Only a wet gurgling sounded. Still twirling the knife that had never left my hand, I let an evil smile spread across my bloodstained face.

"I knew that there was no chance in hell that me and my friends would win this," I repeated as I studied the sword sticking out of Queen Nimlithil's throat. "Which is why I reached out to an enemy."

The tip of the sword was pulled back through her neck from where it had been shoved in from behind. It produced a wet sliding sound on the way out.

Utter shock pulsed through the gathered crowd like waves as Queen Nimlithil struggled to breathe while blood ran down the front of her silver gown from the gaping hole in her throat. Gems clinked faintly as she collapsed on the ground to reveal a star elf in gleaming white armor standing behind her with a bloody sword still raised. Raising the other hand, the elf pushed off the decorated helmet and let it fall to the ground.

Gasps rippled through the crowd and the soldiers around us jerked back as they all turned to gape at their queen's assassin.

Lady Nelyssae stared down at her dying queen with not a shred of remorse on her beautiful face. "You killed Hadraeth. *You* deserved to die."

The soldiers around us didn't stop us as Shade, Elaran, and I struggled to our feet. They were too busy staring uncomprehendingly at the noble lady disguised as a soldier who had just rammed a sword through their queen's throat to avenge the murder of the captain she had loved.

Lady Nelyssae met my gaze and gave me a forceful nod in acknowledgement.

I nodded back.

It had been a fool's hope. The night Shade and I had gotten back from Queen Nimlithil's camp, I had sent a magical messenger dove to Lady Nelyssae back in the City of Glass. I knew she had loved Hadraeth so I had explained what the queen had done to him and that if she wanted revenge, I might be able to create an opportunity for her if she traveled here. After the dragons had told us that we were flying into the final battle against Nimlithil, I had sent another dove, telling Nelyssae to get ready. Getting Queen Nimlithil to confess while the lady waited in the crowd had been my final hope. I hadn't been sure that she would actually go through with it, though. But she had.

Strained gasps came from Queen Nimlithil as her body spasmed. Only a few seconds had passed since the sword had appeared in her throat but the soldiers had been frozen ever since. That sound, however, seemed to snap them out of it.

"Traitor!" someone shouted from the edge of the ring.

*No!* I saw the disaster about to happen and did the stupidest thing I had done in an entire lifetime of idiotic decisions. I leaped forward and shoved Lady Nelyssae aside.

I heard the impact more than I felt it.

My body jerked back and I stared down at my stomach. A long white shaft was sticking out of it. I opened my mouth to speak but something wet got caught in my throat and I ended up coughing blood onto my chest instead. And then I toppled backwards.

Pale violet eyes stared at me from only a breath away. It took me a moment to realize that it was Queen Nimlithil lying on the grass beside me. Her body spasmed. Blood trickled down her graceful neck. Chaos was spreading around me but I just rested my cheek against the blood-slick grass and watched the light dim in those hateful violet eyes. It might have been a fraction of a second later, or a hundred years, but at last, every shred of life left her face. Her body stilled. And her eyes glassed over. Queen Nimlithil of Tkeister, queen of the star elves, protector of Tkeiwed, Wegh, Frustaz, and Beccus, and savior of Weraldi, was dead. The queen was dead. Long live the queen.

"Hey!"

A hand appeared under my cheek and tilted my head back up. The bright blue sky above was filled with battling dragons and I was vaguely aware of elves in white armor fighting each other around me but then a face I knew very well appeared in my vision. Shade.

My mind was growing muddled. I drew a shuddering breath to speak but was cut off by an earth-cleaving roar. Everyone around me whipped their heads up but I was already staring at the sky. A huge white dragon tore free from the gray and red ones around it and dove straight towards us with terrifying speed.

Screaming echoed across the trampled grass as star elves fled before the heartbroken dragon who shot towards his now dead friend. A friend who lay right beside me. While gleaming white armor disappeared from the corner of my eyes, the figure in black stayed firmly put.

Aldeor the White raced towards us. Behind him, Malor and Morgora shot through the sky to catch up. Heavy drops of blood splattered on the ground like rain. Rain. A thought tried to push its way to the front of my mind but all I could see was the white death diving towards us.

The very air shook as a deafening roar split the heavens and something green slammed into the white dragon. Aldeor was shoved to the side just as something red and something gray crashed into him as well.

Gentle fingers were tracing something on my stomach but I couldn't tear my gaze from the four battling dragons above. A large red jaw clamped around a white neck. Unearthly screaming followed it. And then it was abruptly cut off as the red dragon tore out Aldeor the White's throat.

White wings flapped uselessly as the pale gleaming bulk spiraled downwards. My mind was growing fuzzy. Or at least I think so, because I had a sudden urge to smile. I had never seen a dragon die before but I was pretty sure I should be sad about it. So why did the sight of Aldeor the White falling through the morning air fill me with relief?

The earth beneath me shook as he crashed down on the grass beyond the white tents. I blinked and raised my head to see better.

A pulse strong enough to knock down tents flattened me to the ground again. Maybe it was my delirious mind but the air felt different now. More flavorful. More sparkly.

Yes, I was definitely delusional.

But why? I glanced down my black dragon scale armor. A white arrow protruded from my gut. *Oh. That.*

"Hey!" Shade snapped again and slapped my cheek lightly. "Stop that. Don't close your eyes."

I hadn't even realized that my eyes had been fluttering. Focusing on his face above me, I tried to piece together what was going on but it was hard to think past the numbing pain that spread through my stomach. Reality crashed over me like an ocean wave.

Oh. Right. I had jumped in front of an arrow meant for Lady Nelyssae. And now I was dying.

Someone was yelling orders around me and racing feet hurried back and forth but I couldn't bring myself to care.

"How ironic." I laughed but it only ended up making me cough blood onto the grass. "In some ways, this all started when Rain died. And she died just like this. From a gut wound after trying to save someone she didn't really care about." Another coughing fit racked my body. "And now I'm gonna die like that too. Kinda fitting, isn't it?"

"You're not going to die," Shade growled at me.

Reaching up, I tried to put my hand against his cheek but I only managed to smear blood on it before my arm dropped back on the ground. "We would've had a good life."

Tears welled up in his eyes as he squeezed my hand hard. "We *are going to have* a good life. Do you hear me? You just need to hang on a little while longer."

I let my head fall back against the grass and heaved a deep sigh. Blood bubbles popped on my lips instead. It was growing increasingly difficult to breath and a darkness that wasn't mine pressed in from the corners of my vision. My whole body throbbed. Who knew that dying was so damn painful?

Shade slapped my cheek again. My eyes snapped open but I was having a hard time focusing on anything. He had told me that I just needed to hold on a little more but I had dealt enough death blows myself to know when things were beyond repair. Even if we could somehow find a doctor all the way out here, in the middle of our enemies' camp, my chances of survival were practically none.

But I couldn't bring myself to be bitter about it. We had killed Queen Nimlithil and Aldeor the White. That, in turn, had shattered the spell which would mean that all the armies fighting our friends would find themselves without a real reason to keep fighting. I smiled into the growing darkness. And Princess Illeasia would become herself again. She would become the new Queen of Tkeister and she and Elaran would get their happily ever after.

Liam and Norah and their unborn child were safe. Haela and Haemir could go on adventures and Faye could return to her home. Bones and the Thieves' Guild wouldn't be facing an invasion. Yngvild, Vania, Rowan, and the Pernulan Underworld could go on living their life of freedom. King Edward could rule Keutunan in peace. And Shade was alive.

It was too bad that I wouldn't be there to see any of it. But knowing that everyone I loved was now safe made me not feel so sad about dying. If I could buy their safety and happiness with my life then that was a price I was more than willing to pay.

Shade's handsome face hovered before my eyes. I smiled up at him even as I coughed more blood onto my neck. It was worth it. *He* was worth it.

Darkness pressed in closer.

I had had a remarkable life. And in the end, I *had* been enough to keep everyone I loved safe. And that was enough for me.

I drew a shuddering breath.

And closed my eyes.

# 41.

Fireworks sparkled inside me.

And pain stung my face. And people screamed. A lot. Well, if this was hell then it was to be expected, I supposed. Forcing my eyes open, I got ready to face the God of Death in his realm.

Yellow eyes glared down at me.

Blinking, I squinted up at them. The God of Death looked a lot like Elaran.

"Hey!" a commanding voice snapped from my other side. "I said, no closing your eyes. And when I give orders, I expect people to obey them."

My head pounded but I angled it slightly and found a Master Assassin staring at me. My cheek throbbed in pain under his palm.

Fireworks continued sparkling inside me and with every passing second, lucidity returned to my senses. I was not dead. I was lying on the bloodstained grass in the middle of the star elves' camp. Shade was slapping me and ordering me around and Elaran was...? I squinted at the hands hovering over my stomach.

I jerked up. "Stop! What are you doing?"

Strong hands on my shoulders shoved me back in the grass but before Shade could lecture me, Elaran spoke up.

"I'm healing you, what does it look like? Now lie still. Troublesome underworlder," he added under his breath.

"But you can't! It will cost years of your life."

Shade still held me firmly in place on the grass. "Queen Nimlithil and Aldeor are dead."

"I know."

He just looked at me expectantly as if I was missing something obvious. Realization hit me like a shovel to the back of the head.

"Magic," I breathed.

"Yes," Shade replied. "The spell shattered, and without it, magic returned. Normal rules now apply to Elaran's magic. It only drains energy. Not life."

"Huh." I slumped back on the grass but I couldn't stop the crazy laugh bubbling from my throat. It grew until my whole body was shaking.

"Stop moving," Elaran grumbled.

I had to focus on something else, or the sheer absurdity of what was going on would consume me whole and turn me into a lunatic, so I slid my gaze to Elaran. "You lied before."

He was silent for a moment, no doubt concentrating on keeping me alive, or maybe just trying to figure out what I was talking about, but he eventually replied. "Vilya told me that if it came down to a choice between Illeasia and you, there would be a third way. But I had absolutely no idea what that bloody third way was supposed to be." He glanced at me. "So I thought, what would Storm do?"

Surprise flitted through me like startled butterflies. Then I chuckled. "Lie."

"Yes."

Grass crunched to my right as white boots trampled past and fabric flapped somewhere further out as well. All the clashing of steel and firing of pistols had gone silent. I returned my gaze to Elaran.

"I've been trying to teach you how to lie properly for months now," I said. "I had no idea that you were actually paying attention."

A slight smile tugged at his lips. "Yes, well, I figured that if you could learn how to ride a horse and make a fire, then I could learn how to lie convincingly."

Closing my eyes, I laughed loudly into the bright morning sky.

"Hey!" Shade slapped me again. "No closing your eyes."

"And no moving," Elaran added.

I rolled my eyes but they were both grinning at me, so I just did as they wanted without further complaint.

After what felt like a very long time, Elaran heaved a deep sigh and sat back on his heels. "There. Good as new." Drawing his eyebrows down, he crossed his arms and glared at me. "Don't go jumping in front of any arrows ever again."

Pushing myself into a sitting position, I flashed him a wicked grin. "You know I can't promise that."

While he grumbled about troublesome underworlders again, I reached out and squeezed his hand.

"Thank you," I said, holding his gaze.

He nodded a bit self-consciously while rising to his feet. A surprised gasp tore from my lips as Shade hauled me up as well. Glaring at him, I swatted at his hands until he let me go. I could stand on my own, thank you very much.

Elaran glanced at a silver-haired elf issuing orders a short distance away. Even despite the terrible events that had transpired, life once again rolled off Princess Illeasia like waves of sunlight.

"I should..." Elaran began.

"Go." I smiled at him. "We'll catch up later."

After nodding at us, he strode across the grass and joined the person he loved most in this entire world. Joy swirled in my cold black heart.

A hand on my jaw forced my face back to the assassin next to me. "Don't ever do that to me again."

A fiendish grin spread across my mouth. "Or what?"

Shade just pulled me into a kiss so desperate that surprise shot through me. By Nemanan, he must have been really worried about me.

More blood smeared into my hair as he drew his fingers through my ruined braid. I returned the favor.

For a moment we just stood there, two souls mingling, while relief that we were both alive crackled like lightning around us.

Then a pointed cough interrupted the moment.

"You didn't die," Morgora announced. "Good."

Malor shot her an amused look before turning to us. "What she means to say is, well done. We couldn't have done this without you."

The clothes that Morgora, Malor, and Athla wore were covered in rips and slashes. However, where I expected gaping wounds to be, only scars peeked out. All three dragons smiled at us, though Morgora looked more like she was grimacing, and then turned to leave.

"Wait," I blurted out. "Why?"

Malor rested his hands behind his back as he turned around to peer at me. "Why what?"

"Why us? Why pick us for this battle? And when you say that you couldn't have done this without us, what does that even mean?"

"You were the best people for the job," Morgora muttered. "Satisfied?"

"No." I threw my arms out. The movement made me sway slightly but Shade placed a hand on my shoulder to steady me. "I'm a thief! I'm not a savior who rides dragons into battle. It's absurd. I'm a bad person who does bad things."

Athla's green eyes twinkled. "Yes, but bad is not always evil because good can also be evil and darkness can bring light.'"

I narrowed my eyes at him. "Why do I feel like I've heard that somewhere before?"

"Because I told you that in the forest outside Keutunan years ago."

The memory snapped in place. He had indeed told me that in the forest outside Keutunan years ago when Liam and I were heading out to visit Tkeideru. Suspicion crept into my mind.

"You knew this would happen?" I said.

Metal clanked as a group of star elves hoisted the ruined remains of a camp kitchen and carried it across the grass. Morgora pushed her steel gray hair back as a gust of wind snatched some strands loose, but none of the dragons replied. Eventually, Malor cleared his throat.

"Athla has the gift of foresight," he said as if that explained everything.

I didn't like where this was going.

"So you knew this would happen?" I pressed again.

"No." The smile on Athla's face was apologetic but sincere. "The thing about time is that nothing is ever certain. It all depends on the choices people make."

Leather creaked as Shade shifted beside me but none of us spoke. We only waited for the green dragon to go on. At last, Athla let out a small sigh.

"I knew that a Storm Caster from Keutunan would end up being important, but I didn't know how."

"I've been important?"

"Well, you alone have not been important."

"Ouch," I huffed.

Athla chuckled. "What I meant to say was that your life has been entangled with important people, which is what also made you important. The pieces were already there but they needed someone to nudge them in the right direction."

"I have long tried to convince the rulers of this continent to band together to mount a unified force that would draw Aldeor out of hiding so that we could kill him," Malor broke in. "But there has been too much ill will, too much rivalry, too much politics, for me to get them to work together. But now several nations and people joined together to fight back against Nimlithil."

"And what in Nemanan's name does that have to do with me?"

Athla gave me a secretive smile. "If you hadn't been the murderous little thief you are, you would never have been blackmailed into going to Tkeideru. And if you hadn't done that then you would never have helped Keutunan and Tkeideru form an alliance that later saved them from an invasion by the Pernulans."

"And if you hadn't decided to go to Pernula and help Shade become General, then he would never have ruled the city," Malor added. Shade huffed in annoyance but the muscled advisor only grinned at him. "It's true, boy. It was her contacts in the Pernulan Underworld that gave you your first title."

A smirk slashed across my face as I looked up at Shade. He blew out an exasperated sigh and shook his head but didn't argue the point.

"And without Shade ruling Pernula, we would never have won this war," Malor continued.

Now it was the assassin's turn to smirk down at me. I jabbed an elbow in his ribs.

"Then you rode out and got yourself, as well as Elaran and Shade, captured by Queen Nimlithil and taken to the City of Glass," Athla said. "If you hadn't done that, then Elaran and Illeasia would never have met and formed a strong bond between the star elves and the wood elves."

"And if you hadn't chosen to keep your Ashaana powers then you would never have gone to the White Mountains and you and Marcus would never have met and Faelar and Cileya would never have met and all of these people would never have come together and created enough of a threat to get Aldeor to come out and shit would have been worse," Morgora muttered and flapped her arms. "You get the bloody point. Are we done yet? I'm hungry and tired and too damn old to be standing around answering questions."

Malor and Athla chuckled but I only stared at the three of them. A strong wind carried the scent of burned grass to my lungs. Blinking, I tried to make sense of everything these dragons were telling me.

"Yeah, I get the point, but what are you actually saying?" I shook my head in disbelief. "I'm some kind of chosen hero, or what?"

A pleasant laugh drifted from Athla's lips and that glimmer of amusement was back in his light green eyes. "No, that is the most interesting part."

I threw my arms out. "Then who am I?"

"No one. Your parents were ordinary workers who died when a sickness swept through Worker's End." Mirth played over his weather-wrinkled face. "You really are just a random thief from the Underworld."

Silence rang like bells in my head. I really was just a thief from the Underworld. I knew that was supposed to make me feel disappointed, but the truth was that relief washed through me upon hearing that.

Shade draped an arm over my shoulder and flashed me a smirk. "Hey, we can't all be long lost royalty."

"Shut up," I muttered and elbowed him in the ribs again but I couldn't stop the smile tugging on my lips.

"I took you in for a while," Athla continued. "Since I've known for a long time that a Storm Caster would somehow be important in ending this and bringing magic and dragons back, I have tried to force other people onto that path."

I raised my eyebrows.

"Yes," he said. "There have been a lot of other Storm Casters before you and I've tried to force this destiny on them all. It didn't work that well." A thoughtful expression drifted over his face. "I didn't consider how important free will was. Anyway, when I saw you on the streets and felt your latent powers, I took you in for a while with the intention of making you take this path too. But then..." He smiled. "Well, it hadn't worked yet so I figured I could try something different. So I let you back out on the streets." A wistful smile tugged at his lips as he shrugged. "Everything you did after that was your choice."

"I'd say it worked out rather well," Malor supplied with a satisfied nod.

My head was spinning. Athla had taken me in to raise me after my parents died. And then he had just put me back out on the streets again. Should I be angry about that? I tried to find that flicker of rage at being left to grow up alone on the streets of Keutunan but I couldn't find it. If he hadn't done that, I wouldn't have become the person I was today. And I liked the person I was today.

But more than that, what I had done hadn't been some predetermined destiny. No. Everything I had ever done had been my own doing. My own choices, my own mistakes, my own hard work and scheming and bloody fighting. I had accomplished it all. That, more than anything, filled me with a sparkling wave of satisfaction. When Athla had put me back on the streets, he had given me the freedom to live my life in the way I wanted to. I'd had complete freedom. And I had used it to carve out *my own* destiny.

"Yes, yes, and Malor and I were the only dragons who stayed because of Athla and his damn speech about the future when someone could come and start a chain of events that would break the spell and bring dragons and magic back." Morgora shook her arms in the air, making her shredded gray shirtsleeves flap and fall down to her elbows. "Very dramatic. Are we done now?"

"I–" Athla began.

"If you say 'I told you so' I'm going to transform back into a dragon and eat you," Morgora snapped.

Even I chuckled at that.

Athla just smiled at the grumpy old woman. "I was only going to say, I think we can save the comprehensive history of dragons for another time."

"Good." And with that, she stalked across the grass.

Malor shook his head at her retreating back but before the two of them could leave as well, Shade spoke up.

"So, dragons will be coming back to Weraldi?" he asked.

Athla and Malor exchanged a look. "Yes, we believe so."

Shade chuckled. "Pernula is going to become an interesting place to rule."

"This *world* is going to become an interesting place," Malor corrected. His reddish eyes glittered in the morning sun as he looked at the assassin and the thief before him. "But you will figure it out. You always do."

After nodding at us, both of them strode after the stomping Morgora who was already halfway across camp.

I glanced up at Shade, who still had his arm draped over my shoulders. A lopsided smile decorated his lips.

All around us, star elves were working to rebuild their camp while the armies of Frustaz, Beccus, and Sker looked to be retreating across the plains. Brisk winds snatched at my hair and despite the smell of ashes, gunpowder, and blood that laced the air, I drew in a deep breath.

A short while ago, I had almost died. But now here I was. Alive. And so were the people I loved. My cold dead heart was still cracked after everything I had been through and it would take time to process all the emotions. To grieve. For Rain. For

Hadraeth. And to sort through the jumble of mismatched feelings in my chest that the failed spell had left behind.

It would take time, but Malor was right. I would figure it out. I always did.

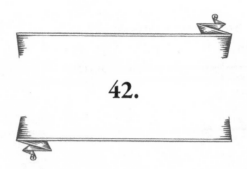

# 42.

"I still can't believe you not only met a dragon without me – again! But you also rode a dragon into battle without me!"

Shifting on my feet, I chuckled at the distraught look on Haela's face. "Next time I'm riding a dragon into battle, I'll make sure to bring you."

"You'd better." She grinned at me.

Waves crashed onto the shore far below. I swept my gaze across the crowded area. It was beautiful. Tables and chairs decorated in white and silver and violet and green and brown and yellow occupied the grasslands below the hill. All of it was illuminated by glittering white light that floated like magical orbs in the night. The sky was a vast expanse of dark blue covered in the silver dust of countless stars. Atop the hill where we stood were two pillars of white light shining like gems by the edge. And below, the crashing sea.

A murmur of anticipation hung over the area but it wasn't quite time yet, so I drifted over to the group where Liam, Norah, Zaina, and Marcus stood while Haemir pulled Haela away to wherever Faye was waiting with the other wood elves. From across the grass, Lady Nelyssae gave me a nod in acknowledgement. A small smile drifted over my lips as I returned the gesture before she disappeared into the crowd while I moved towards my friends.

Shade intercepted me halfway across the grass.

"Where were you?" I asked as he fell in beside me.

"Making sure that Elaran had everything he needed."

"And did he?"

He flashed me a smile. "Wait and see."

I huffed and considered stabbing him with the knife hidden in my fine black garments but decided against it. When we reached the group of humans, Liam beamed at me.

"This is going to be amazing, isn't it?" he said.

"Yeah, it really is," I replied.

Norah fluffed out her white skirts before resting a hand on her pregnant belly. "I've never been to... well, anything like this before."

"Me neither," Marcus said. Moonlight played in his golden-brown eyes as he grinned. "My father is probably turning in his grave right now. The son of the great Marcellus attending–"

"Marcellus?" Zaina interrupted. Her dark eyebrows creased. "You're the son of Marcellus and Juliana?"

Marcus drew back and blinked in surprise at the pirate. "Yeah, how did you know my mother's name?"

"I'm... well, *we*," she gestured at her sister, "are the daughters of Hamed."

If he had looked surprised before, now he was gaping at her. Then, sudden realization snapped in place across his features. "Oh by Werz, that explains it! I thought you looked familiar the first time I saw you." He tipped a hand in Norah's direction. "Norah's face is softer but you... you look just like him."

"Guys, what's going on?" I interjected, looking from one astonished face to the next.

His crisp shirt rustled as Marcus turned to me. "You remember I told you that my mother fell in love with and was going to run away with a smuggler before Marcellus killed them?"

"Yeah?"

Zaina raised her hand and waved it a little in the air. "That was my father. Well, our father."

Now it was my turn to gape at them. Zaina slapped Marcus' broad chest with the back of her hand while a warm grin stretched across her face.

"I guess the family just got bigger," she said.

"Welcome to the family," Norah said and then turned to peer down at her belly. "Did you hear that? You're going to have an uncle too."

Joyful laughter drifted into the star-speckled heavens as Marcus embraced his new sisters. A warm and fuzzy feeling spread through my soul. To think that out of such terrible tragedy, could come such amazing love.

A hush fell over the gathered crowd.

King Edward snuck up to us and whispered, "It's time."

Shade and I flashed the others a smile before following him and moving closer to the two glittering pillars at the edge of the bluff. Before long, two figures strode across the grass. They approached from opposite sides and then met in the middle, where the white pillars had been sunk into the ground. Happiness fluttered in my chest as I looked at them.

Princess Illeasia was wearing a deep purple gown with glittering white gems that flowed around her and made it look like she was wearing a slice of the night sky. In front of her stood Elaran in beautifully tailored garments of a deep green color. Small details embroidered on it brought out the yellow in his eyes. His auburn hair fell down his back and a crown of green leaves decorated his brow.

But the one thing they both wore that made me almost weep with happiness was smiles so radiant they could have lit up the night together.

Shade looped his arm around my back as we watched the two joyful elves clasp each other's hands.

"I promise to love you for all the long years of my life," Elaran said to Illeasia. "To protect you and laugh with you and share this life with you. As Nature is my witness."

Illeasia smiled back at him. "I promise to love you for all the long years of my life. To protect you and laugh with you and share this life with you. As the Stars are my witness."

Light glittered in their eyes as they took a step closer and kissed. A cheer rose. The love that sparkled between Elaran and Illeasia at that moment was such as the world had rarely seen before and would rarely see again. I smiled with all my heart as they turned towards us and raised their joined hands into the sky.

"Let's get this party started!" Faye called from the other side of the hill.

Laughter rang out as the words were echoed from every pair of lips. I pulled Shade with me as we descended the hill and made for the tables overlain with food and drink. Music in the cheerful tunes of the wood elves filled the area. I laughed again as Illeasia dragged Elaran to the middle of the grass and swung him around in a dance that neither of them knew the steps to.

Elaran stepped on her dress and stumbled into her which made Illeasia throw her head back and laugh with unrestrained joy. A wide smile spread across Elaran's face as he twirled her around and danced completely off rhythm with the music.

In that moment, my heart was so full that I thought it was going to burst.

Happiness really did suit him.

"Well now we're talking, people!" Haela's laughter bounced off the colorful decorations. "I knew you actually knew how to party."

Haemir grinned at her. "Told you."

"Oh shush." With a wide smile on her face, Haela grabbed her brother and a surprised Faye by the hand and pulled them both towards the dancing couple.

I smiled at the flabbergasted expression on Keya's face as Faye yanked the soft-spoken elf with them too as all of them joined the dance, leaping and twirling. Mirth twinkled in his golden-brown eyes as Marcus joined them as well. After a moment of hesitation, Faelar and Cileya did the same. When Norah saw that even the most taciturn and serious of elves had joined the festivities, she promptly marched Liam onto the grass. Rippling laughter drifted between the glittering lights and mingled with the tunes of cheerful music as elves and humans filled the grassy dancefloor with life.

"Let's go, Shade." Edward stopped in front of us, hands on his hips, and jerked his chin towards the dancing people.

Shade flicked his eyes between his little brother and the uncoordinated debauchery unfolding before him. "I don't–"

"Yes, you do." A wide smile spread across his face. "Let's show them that the Silverthorn brothers know how to party too."

Before Shade could protest, Edward yanked him by the arm onto the bubbling dancefloor. The Master Assassin looked at me beseechingly but I just flashed him an evil grin and lifted my shoulders in amused shrug. While shooting a mock glare at me in response, Shade allowed his little brother to pull them both into the dance.

Even from across the sea of twirling revelers, I could see Zaina's eyes sparkle mischievously as she set her sights on a dark-haired woman who had been hiding in the crowd. Lady Smythe laughed self-consciously as the smuggler pulled her into her arms but then she grabbed the front of Zaina's shirt and yanked her into a forceful kiss. From atop a chair nearby, her son watched with a grin on his face as his mother made out with a pirate in the middle of an elven wedding.

The smile on my face widened.

Happiness suited them all.

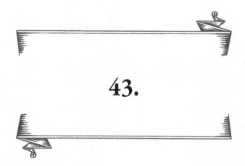

# 43.

Lying bundled in blankets on the grass, I watched the sun rise bright and clear over the horizon. Next to me, Shade lay sleeping on his side with his arm draped over my chest. We were both still in the clothes we had worn at the wedding. As was everyone else. The previously so crisp garments were now rumpled after hours of partying and then sleeping on blankets and pillows in the grass right there below the hill by the sea.

The festivities had lasted well into the morning and it was only a few hours ago that everyone had succumbed to the pull of sleep and lain down in the soft grass. Even Elaran and Illeasia.

Turning my head, I watched the assassin beside me. His black hair was tousled and his face soft with sleep. It had been a night like none other. I couldn't even remember a time when I was this happy. Lifting my hand, I traced gentle fingers over Shade's cheekbones and down to his lips.

"Admiring my pretty face, are we?" Shade smirked as his eyes fluttered open.

Staring into his glittering black eyes, I arched an eyebrow at him. "Humility isn't your strong suit, is it?"

He grinned. "Neither is it yours."

Before I could retort, he stole the words from my lips with a mischievous kiss. I drew my fingers through his hair, which at least helped smooth it a little. He drew back slightly and pushed a loose strand of hair back behind my ear before resting his hand on my cheek.

"I don't tell you this enough but..." Stroking his thumb over my cheekbone, Shade held my gaze intently. "I love you, my black-hearted thief."

A shuddering breath escaped my lips and I closed my eyes for a heartbeat while his words filled my soul. Opening them again, I let all of that show in my eyes as I looked back at the man who held my scarred heart in the palm of his hand.

"And I love you, my cold-hearted assassin."

His eyes sparkled as he smiled at me and drew me closer. For a long while, we just lay there in each other's arms, bundled in colorful blankets in the soft grass, and listened as a new world dawned.

Birds chirped their morning greetings in the trees while the rest of the guests woke as well.

"It is time."

I blinked and pulled back from Shade's embrace because I recognized that voice. Pushing myself up on an elbow, I squinted at the surprise visitor.

Vilya stood in the middle of the grass filled with tables and sleeping wedding attendants. She was wearing the same dress I'd last seen her in. The one that looked to be made of actual vines and flowers. Her long blond hair, decorated with leaves and colorful flowers, flowed down her back as she turned and spread her arms. That impossibly beautiful face was set in a smile that held both joy and sadness.

"It is time," she said again, her voice ringing clearly across the grass. "Wood elves of Tkeideru, follow me."

After sweeping yellow eyes across the clearing that were far too old to belong to someone who looked so young, she turned and strode away.

Surprised silence followed her. I watched as she slowly walked away from the coast and in the direction of the plains farther inland. The others seemed to be doing the same. Then, the spell broke.

"Well, you heard the mysterious elf with a dress made of vines," Haela called out as she jumped to her feet. Swinging a hand in the direction Vilya moved, she let out a loud laugh. "Wood elves of Tkeideru, forget your hangovers, we have a mystery to solve!"

Scattered chuckles rose from the other elves as they struggled to their feet. Some of them pressed hands to their heads to no doubt stop the throbbing from all the alcohol consumed but most of them just brushed grass off their clothes and got ready to leave.

Shade and I exchanged a glance.

"Should we...?" he began.

"Yeah, I'm not missing this."

Rolling to our feet, we both gave our bodies a good stretch before following the wood elves to whatever mystery was about to unfold.

DEAD EARTH STRETCHED out around us where we stood on the plains just north of Tkeister. Turning in a slow circle, I tried to figure out why Vilya had brought us out here. Elaran and

Illeasia were standing next to Faye and they appeared to be doing the same.

"This used to be Tkeideru," Vilya declared in a voice that carried across the land.

Sadness flashed over the wood elves' faces as they studied the barren land that had been their ancestors' home before Queen Nimlithil's grandmother had destroyed it in a fit of rage.

"The trees were burned down," Vilya continued. "But the soul of the forest was preserved by a brave young wood elf who gave up her own life to give her descendants a chance to rebuild her home. Her name was Vilya."

I blinked at her in surprise while a ripple went through the gathered wood elves. The breathtaking elf spoke again.

"I am no one. And everyone. I am a relic from a time long gone. Waiting for the time to come again." She spread her arms towards the dead lands around her. "I am the soul of the old Tkeideru. And the time has now come for the forest to rise again."

Another shocked murmur went through the gathered crowd as Vilya began melting into the ground. Her dress of vines and flowers soaked into the gray dirt and filled it with vibrant colors. When she was halfway down into the land, she turned a smile towards the wood elves around her. It was heart-wrenching in its beauty.

"Trust your hearts. Trust your souls. And raise the trees."

And then she disappeared into the ground. Shock at what I was witnessing still clanged through me when Shade took me by the arm and moved us farther back while Faye ordered the others to form a wide circle around the colorful spot. Illeasia planted a kiss on Elaran's cheek and then slipped towards us as the ranger moved into the ring.

"I don't know any more about this than you do," Queen Faye called out. "So we'll just do as she said. Trust our hearts and our souls and raise the trees."

The very air seemed to vibrate with magic as Faye, Elaran, the twins, and all the other wood elves who had come here for the wedding, closed their eyes and raised their arms.

A gasp ripped from my lips.

Green buds popped up from the dirt around us. They spread in a wide circle until the entire area around us as far as we could see was covered in a blanket of green. And then they shot up.

Shade staggered backwards and pulled me with him as majestic trees shot out of the ground. Leaf-covered branches sprouted out of the wide trunks and bushes jumped up behind the rising trees. A carpet of thick green grass grew under our feet. Flowers of every color bloomed in the greenery and gleamed like jewels in the morning light. Where Vilya had disappeared, a great tree with an open pavilion at the bottom, exactly the same as the Heart of the City in Tkeideru, now stood.

"Wow," Illeasia said.

Haela turned towards us and waved her hand at the mind-bending magic that we had just witnessed bring an entire forest back to life. "What do you think?"

I flashed her a grin. "Well, it's brown at the bottom and green at the top."

Laughter echoed through the woods. I laughed with them.

Soon this place would be filled with life again. A home for the wood elves on the continent who had lived like nomads in other cities for far too long.

Faye strode across the lush green grass until she stood directly before Elaran. With a conspiratorial smile on her face, she held his gaze while motioning at the forest around her.

"The new Tkeideru will need a leader," she said in a voice that carried far into the trees. "I vote for you."

Elaran drew back and blinked at his queen while the other wood elves echoed her words.

"These lands lie right next to Tkeister." Faye motioned for Illeasia to approach. "You could rule them together."

"You want me to...?" Elaran stammered while Illeasia sidled up to him and looped her arm through his. Mirth sparkled on her face.

Queen Faye nodded at the both of them. "I can think of no one better."

To my surprise, the powerful voice that rose into the air next belonged to Faelar. "To the King and Queen of Tkeister and New Tkeideru!"

Elaran turned to his long-time friend and brother-in-arms with a look of surprise and love on his face. Faelar sent him a wide smile in reply.

"To the King and Queen of Tkeister and New Tkeideru!" we all echoed before the flustered ranger could protest.

Leaves rustled as a morning breeze swept through the thick canopy above. All around me, the smiling faces of wood elves shone like bright suns. Elaran drew his hand through his auburn hair as he stared in wonder at the forest around him.

From the coast, a dark smudge sped across the bright blue sky. Birds. Their cheerful chirping soon filled the forest. I watched with happiness in my heart as life returned to the once dead land. Life. It really was such an extraordinary thing.

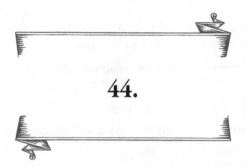

# 44.

Obsidian walls gleamed red in the light of the setting sun. Standing on the balcony high up in Blackspire, Shade and I watched the last light of day paint Pernula in hues of gold and orange.

"Master," a voice said from behind.

Shade and I both turned to find Man-bun standing in the doorway. He still wore the traditional black clothes of the Assassins' Guild. As did the rest of them. Shade might be High King of Pernula but he would also always be the Master of the Assassins' Guild.

"Yes?" Shade said.

"King Edward sent word. He and Queen Faye and the rest of them just reached the Lost Island. Their journey back went smoothly."

With a satisfied expression on his face, Shade nodded. "Thanks, Reaper."

My mouth dropped open.

"Your name is Reaper?" I blurted out before I could stop it.

Man-bun looked back at me, uncertainty creasing his brows. "Well, yes. It's actually Heart Reaper, to be precise, but it's a bit of a mouthful so most people usually just call me Reaper."

Shade tilted his head to the right and frowned down at me. "You didn't know?"

"No." I let out a soft chuckle. "Reaper. Gods, if you only knew what I've been calling you in my head all these years."

As soon as the words had left my mouth, I regretted them. The two assassins exchanged a look.

"What have you been calling me?"

Scratching my neck, I cleared my throat. "Man-bun."

Dead silence descended on the balcony. I wanted to give myself a high five. In the face. With a chair. This was not going to end well.

The quiet stretched on for another second and then a roaring laugh bounced between the obsidian walls as Man-bun tipped his head back and laughed with unrestrained amusement. It was such a surprisingly happy sound from someone who was usually so serious. When Shade's rippling laugh joined Man-bun's roaring, I couldn't stop the corners of my mouth from curving upwards as well.

"Just wait until the rest of the guild hears about this." Man-bun chuckled and shook his head before turning to Shade and dipping his chin. "Master." Once Shade had nodded back, he turned to me. "Storm."

"Reaper," I replied, barely hiding the smile in my voice.

He flashed me another amused grin before disappearing back into Blackspire. Leather creaked as Shade and I turned back to the golden city before us.

"All these years and you never knew his name?" he said.

I lifted my shoulders in an embarrassed shrug. "No. I never caught it there at the beginning and once we'd known each other for a while, it became a bit too awkward to ask."

Shade chuckled in reply. Throwing him a glare, I huffed and shook my head. Damn assassin.

For a while, we just stood there atop the balcony and watched the sun set over the sprawling city before us. Standing so close that our arms brushed against one another, we lent strength and comfort and companionship to each other.

"Queen Nimlithil has been defeated," Shade said at last. "The threat of invasion is gone and no one has to live in fear of being forced to give up their ability to feel. Magic is back and the dragons are returning. All our enemies have been vanquished and everyone we love is safe." He swept an arm over the railing to encompass the gleaming city below. "I'm the High King of Pernula and you're the Queen of the Underworld." Turning, the Master Assassin who loved me beyond reason looked at me with glittering black eyes. "What do we do now?"

"Now?"

Air scented with spices on a warm summer day filled my lungs as I drew a deep breath and took in the view.

White sails snapped in the breeze to the east where ships lay anchored in the harbor. The shimmering sea was streaked with pink and gold. On the streets below, ordinary citizens milled about between the colorful awnings and potted flowers. Vines rustled as an evening wind drifted across open terraces. And deep in the shadows, the underworlders were getting ready for a night's work.

I smiled at the city before us.

Our city.

"Now, we get ready for another adventure."

# Acknowledgements

I don't like saying goodbye. Ever since I was a kid, I have always hated it. And this time is no different. One would think that I would be used to it by now. After all, I have lived in three different countries and multiple different cities, I have traveled far and wide, and everywhere I have met lots of extraordinary people, and I have had to say goodbye to all of them. But it never does get any easier, does it? The most ridiculous part of it all is of course that the people I'm saying goodbye to this time aren't even real. They're characters in a book. But they feel real to me. I have lived inside these characters' heads as much as they have lived inside mine. They are a part of me. So yes, no matter how ridiculous it might be, I am now sitting here with tears in my eyes writing this.

Storm's adventure is over. And that makes me really sad to think about. But here's the thing. I might not be writing any more books about Storm, Shade, Elaran, and all the other characters I've spent years with, but that doesn't mean they're gone. Their life goes on. Only off page. Storm will continue getting into trouble in the Underworld, Shade will continue ordering people around, Elaran will continue stalking through the forest, the twins will continue making mischief. They will all continue living, even though I'm not writing about their new adventures. And that thought actually makes me really happy. So, thank you for joining me and Storm on this journey – and here's to new adventures!

As always, I would like to start by saying a huge thank you to my family. Mom, Dad, Mark, thank you for the enthusiasm, love, and encouragement. I truly don't know what I would do without you. Thank you for reading all the books in this series and for all the support you have given me throughout.

Lasse, Ann, Karolina, Axel, Martina, thank you for taking such an interest in my books and for being so kind and enthusiastic. It really brightens my day.

Another group of people I would like to once again express my gratitude to is my wonderful team of beta readers: Deshaun Hershel, Jennifer Nicholls, Luna Lucia Lawson, and Orsika Péter. Thank you for staying with me during all these books. To know that I have always been able to rely on you to read each new book and provide feedback means the world.

To Catherine Bowser and Catherine Myers, thank you for being there from the very beginning. Thank you for supporting me and encouraging me when I needed it the most. If it hadn't been for you, I would most likely never have continued writing this series after the first book.

To Faye Ostryzniuk, Laura Bartlett, and Madi Watson, thank you so much for being so amazingly kind, enthusiastic, and supportive. Talking with you always makes my day. And thank you for all the extraordinary things you have created. I sometimes still can't believe how lucky I am to have met you.

To Tyler Ryan, thank you for taking a chance on my book. Never had I imagined that something like that would happen to me, and I could never have guessed all the amazing things it would lead to. So, thank you so much for taking that chance on me. It has brought me a lot of happiness.

To Mandie Sagen, thank you for all that you have done for me. Everything from sharing your thoughts and feelings about the characters to telling others to read the series to sending me screenshots of any lingering typos – it all means so much to me. Thank you for being such a kind soul.

To Lotte Hoes, thank you for being so kind and so passionate about the things you love. And thank you for everything you have created. Your enthusiasm truly means the world.

To Francesca Ryde, thank you for your continuous support and for all the kind and wonderful messages you send. Hearing your thoughts on the new book or sneak peek always brightens my day.

To Danielle Novotny, Ebony Cashin, Eileen Curley Hammond, Jennifer Soucy, Laura Maybrooke, Max Drew, and Medina Berisha, thank you for everything you have done to support me. Your kindness and enthusiasm have made all the difference.

To my amazing copy editor and proofreader Julia Gibbs, thank you for all the hard work you always put into making my books shine. Your language expertise and attention to detail is fantastic and makes me feel confident that I'm publishing the very best version of my books.

To Dane Low, my extraordinary cover designer, thank you for creating all of these gorgeous covers for me. You have knocked it out of the park every time.

I am also very fortunate to have friends both close by and from all around the world. My friends, thank you for everything you've shared with me. Thank you for the laughs, the tears, the deep discussions, and the unforgettable memories. My life is a lot richer with you in it.

Before I go back to writing my next series, I would like to once again say thank you to you, the reader. Thank you for supporting me through this entire series. It's because of people like you that I write.

As always, if you have any questions or comments about the book, I would love to hear from you.

You can find all the different ways of contacting me on my website, www.marionblackwood.com. There you can also sign up for my newsletter to receive updates about coming books. Lastly, if you liked this book and want to help me out so that I can continue writing, please consider leaving a review. It really does help tremendously. I hope you enjoyed Storm's adventure and that I will see you on the next adventure to come!

Printed in the USA
CPSIA information can be obtained
at www.ICGtesting.com
LVHW041318090923
757485LV00011B/19

9 789198 638776